Authors featured in
The COYOTE ROAD

Kim Antieau

Christopher Barzak

Steve Berman

Jedediah Berry

Holly Black

Richard Bowes

Michael Cadnum

Charles de Lint

Carolyn Dunn

Carol Emshwiller

Jeffrey Ford

Theodora Goss

Nina Kiriki Hoffman

Kij Johnson

Ellen Klages

Ellen Kushner

Kelly Link

Patricia A. McKillip

Pat Murphy

Delia Sherman

Will Shetterly

Midori Snyder

Caroline Stevermer

Katherine Vaz

Elizabeth E. Wein

Jane Yolen

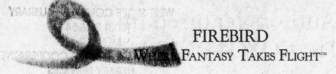

FIREBIRD
Where Fantasy Takes Flight™

A Stir of Bones	Nina Kiriki Hoffman
The Blue Girl	Charles de Lint
Changeling	Delia Sherman
The Changeling Sea	Patricia A. McKillip
Dingo	Charles de Lint
The Dreaming Place	Charles de Lint
The Faery Reel: Tales from the Twilight Realm	Ellen Datlow and Terri Windling, eds.
Firebirds: An Anthology of Original Fantasy and Science Fiction	Sharyn November, ed.
Firebirds Rising: An Anthology of Original Science Fiction and Fantasy	Sharyn November, ed.
Firebirds Soaring: An Anthology of Original Speculative Fiction	Sharyn November, ed.
The Game	Diana Wynne Jones
The Green Man: Tales from the Mythic Forest	Ellen Datlow and Terri Windling, eds.
Hannah's Garden	Midori Snyder
Little (Grrl) Lost	Charles de Lint
Mister Boots	Carol Emshwiller
The Riddle of the Wren	Charles de Lint
Spirits That Walk in Shadow	Nina Kiriki Hoffman
The Sunbird	Elizabeth E. Wein
The Tough Guide to Fantasyland	Diana Wynne Jones
Waifs and Strays	Charles de Lint

The
COYOTE
ROAD
Trickster Tales

⊷⊶⊷

Edited by
ELLEN DATLOW & TERRI WINDLING
Introduction by TERRI WINDLING
Decorations by CHARLES VESS

FIREBIRD
AN IMPRINT OF PENGUIN GROUP (USA) INC.

FIREBIRD

Published by the Penguin Group

Penguin Group (USA) Inc., 345 Hudson Street, New York, New York 10014, U.S.A.

Penguin Group (Canada), 90 Eglinton Avenue East, Suite 700, Toronto, Ontario, Canada M4P 2Y3
(a division of Pearson Penguin Canada Inc.)

Penguin Books Ltd, 80 Strand, London WC2R 0RL, England

Penguin Ireland, 25 St Stephen's Green, Dublin 2, Ireland (a division of Penguin Books Ltd)

Penguin Group (Australia), 250 Camberwell Road, Camberwell, Victoria 3124, Australia
(a division of Pearson Australia Group Pty Ltd)

Penguin Books India Pvt Ltd, 11 Community Centre, Panchsheel Park, New Delhi - 110 017, India

Penguin Group (NZ), 67 Apollo Drive, Rosedale, North Shore 0632, New Zealand
(a division of Pearson New Zealand Ltd)

Penguin Books (South Africa) (Pty) Ltd, 24 Sturdee Avenue,
Rosebank, Johannesburg 2196, South Africa

Registered Offices: Penguin Books Ltd, 80 Strand, London WC2R 0RL, England

First published in the United States of America by Viking,
a member of Penguin Group (USA) Inc., 2007
Published by Firebird, an imprint of Penguin Group (USA) Inc., 2009

1 3 5 7 9 10 8 6 4 2

Preface copyright © Ellen Datlow and Terri Windling, 2007
Introduction copyright © Terri Windling, 2007
Decorations copyright © Charles Vess, 2007
Copyright notices for individual contributors appear on the last page of this book.
All rights reserved.

LIBRARY OF CONGRESS CATALOGING-IN-PUBLICATION DATA IS AVAILABLE

ISBN 978-0-14-241300-5

Printed in the United States of America

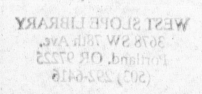

This book is dedicated with a chorus of coyote song
to Sharyn November, who supports our forays into
myth so wonderfully and so well.

—E.D. & T.W.

CONTENTS

PREFACE *by Ellen Datlow and Terri Windling* 1

INTRODUCTION *by Terri Windling* 5

ONE ODD SHOE *by Pat Murphy* 27

COYOTE WOMAN *by Carolyn Dunn* 49

WAGERS OF GOLD MOUNTAIN *by Steve Berman* 54

THE LISTENERS *by Nina Kiriki Hoffman* 82

REALER THAN YOU *by Christopher Barzak* 108

THE FIDDLER OF BAYOU TECHE *by Delia Sherman* . . 131

A TALE FOR THE SHORT DAYS *by Richard Bowes* . . 157

FRIDAY NIGHT AT ST. CECILIA'S *by Ellen Klages* . . 180

THE FORTUNE-TELLER *by Patricia A. McKillip* 204

HOW RAVEN MADE HIS BRIDE *by Theodora Goss* . . 215

CROW ROADS *by Charles de Lint* 219

THE CHAMBER MUSIC OF ANIMALS
by Katherine Vaz 245

UNCLE BOB VISITS *by Caroline Stevermer* 267

UNCLE TOMPA *by Midori Snyder* 280

CAT OF THE WORLD *by Michael Cadnum* 284

HONORED GUEST *by Ellen Kushner* 293

ALWAYS THE SAME STORY *by Elizabeth E. Wein* 317

THE SEÑORITA AND THE CACTUS THORN
by Kim Antieau 336

BLACK ROCK BLUES *by Will Shetterly* 348

THE CONSTABLE OF ABAL *by Kelly Link* 374

A REVERSAL OF FORTUNE *by Holly Black* 418

GOD CLOWN *by Carol Emshwiller* 437

THE OTHER LABYRINTH *by Jedediah Berry* 450

THE DREAMING WIND *by Jeffrey Ford* 465

KWAKU ANANSI WALKS THE WORLD'S WEB
by Jane Yolen 486

THE EVOLUTION OF TRICKSTER STORIES AMONG
THE DOGS OF NORTH PARK AFTER THE CHANGE
by Kij Johnson 489

Further Reading 519

About the Editors 524

About the Illustrator 526

The
COYOTE
ROAD

Trickster Tales

PREFACE

Ellen Datlow and Terri Windling

Welcome to the third volume in our "mythic fiction" anthology series, featuring new stories inspired by the ancient themes of mythology. In *The Green Man*, we explored the folklore of the forest; in *The Faery Reel*, we looked at faeries and other nature spirits from around the globe. Now we turn our attention to Trickster: an unpredictable and irrepressible figure found in stories all around the world. A liar, a thief, a clown, a troublesome meddler, and a sacred world creator, Trickster is a paradoxical creature who is wily and clever, yet also very foolish; he is both a cultural hero and a destructive influence, usually at one and the same time. Mythic tales about Trickster are often funny, but don't mistake him for a harmless buffoon. Trickster can be dark and deadly to encounter. At the very least he'll deceive or rob you blind; and even the gentlest brush with Trickster is likely to turn your life upside down. Trickster is a boundary crosser, a violator of rules, an agent of change and transformation. Alan Garner, the great British fantasy writer and folklorist, calls Trickster "the advocate of uncertainty. . . .

He draws a boundary for chaos, so that we can make sense of the rest. He is the shadow that shapes the light."

The key to spotting a mythic Trickster (as opposed to a lesser con man or fool) is to remember the double aspect of his nature: he is *both* good and bad, *both* wise and witless, *both* sacred and profane. In some tales, for example, Trickster is credited with giving humans fire, language, hunting skills, lovemaking, and the creative arts . . . but in others he's the one who brings us hunger, disease, painful childbirth, and death. Trickster appears in many different guises in world mythology, sometimes playing a central, starring role in a culture's most sacred stories and sometimes prowling the edges, darting into the tales just long enough to shake things up. Sometimes he takes the form of a god, such as Hermes in Greek mythology or Legba in African lore. Sometimes he appears in animal shape, as in the Coyote, Raven, and Rabbit stories of various Native American tribes. Sometimes he's a meddlesome faery, such as Puck or Robin Goodfellow in English folklore and the shape-shifting phookas of Ireland. Sometimes he's a larger-than-life human being, such as Jack in Appalachian folktales or Till Eulenspiegel in Germany. Trickster is male in most myths and legends, but a few female Tricksters can also be found—such as the charming, seductive, and deadly *kitsune* (fox maidens) of Korea and Japan.

Clowns, comedians, carnies, con men, and the masked actors of the commedia dell'arte (the folk theater of Italy) are all descendants of Trickster to a greater or lesser degree, using their wits to confound and astound, playing fast and loose with society's rules. Whole holidays are dedicated to Trickster's spirit of anarchy, mirth, and misrule, such as midwinter Carnival festivals, the Jewish Purim, and the Christian Feast of Fools.

Though as an archetype Trickster is as old as the hills, he's a thoroughly contemporary figure, too, still very much a part of our culture today. Captain Jack Sparrow from *The Pirates of the Caribbean*, Bart from *The Simpsons*, and J. R. "Bob" Dobbs from the Church of the SubGenius are just a few of the many Tricksters who turn the status quo topsy-turvy in modern life. Of all modern Tricksters, however, the infamous Bugs Bunny is surely the best known and best loved. Bugs fits the archetype perfectly: he's a sly, anarchic, troublemaking clown, a hero and delinquent at one and the same time. He violates the usual social rules (he steals, he cheats, he dresses in drag, he bonks people over the head with hammers), and yet it's Bugs we root for and not his human nemesis, the plodding Elmer Fudd.

Fantasy author Ellen Kushner writes, "I have to confess, I didn't really like Bugs Bunny cartoons when I was little—they were irrational, violent, and made me uncomfortable—but I sure did watch them all the time. And that's something to re-member. Whether you're a twenty-first-century person watch-ing Trickster on the family altar in your living room, staring into the communal campfire of the movie theater, or hearing traditional stories in a sweat lodge or under the stars, one thing you have to remember is: Trickster is not your friend! Trickster's acts may benefit people, or damage them—Trick-ster doesn't really care, as long as the trick is a good one."

When we decided on Trickster as the theme for this anthol-ogy, we knew we were in for a bumpy ride—for it's always risky to draw Trickster's attention! Nonetheless we forged ahead, asking a number of our favorite writers to give us their take on Trickster tales—and they came through for us handsomely indeed, despite all the tricks that the Lord of Misrule could throw at them. Some of the stories they sent to us were based on specific Trickster figures from world mythology, while others were infused with the Trickster spirit of rule breaking and boundary crossing, of lives and worlds turned upside down, of wickedness disguised as virtue and salvation embedded within acts of destruction. In this book you'll find tales set in the past, in the present, and in the timeless lands of worlds that never were. They are tales of conniving gods, wily mortals, clever animals, shysters and deceivers of all sorts; stories that show what happens when you break the rules and raise a finger to the fates, for good or for ill.

To be on "the coyote road" in Native American legends means to be headed to a wild, unpredictable, and transformative destiny . . . to follow the path of Trickster, which is neither a safe nor comfortable place to be. Walk warily. He may rob you of the things you love most, or gift you with the things you most need. Or both. But one thing's certain. He's going to shake you up. And probably have a good laugh about it, too.

INTRODUCTION

Terri Windling

Now listen, I'm going to tell you a story. This was back when all the animals were people, before the Human People came. Creator called all them Animal People together and said, "There's going to be a change. New people comin', and you old people got to have new names. You come 'round tomorrow morning, and you can pick your own new names, first ones first until they're gone." And then he goes home to bed.

Well that Coyote, he goes back to Mole, his wife, and he's all frettin' now, he's scratchin' and he's thinking hard, and Mole, she's lookin' nervous 'cause there's always trouble close behind when Coyote starts to think. "Mole," he says, "build up that fire, I'm going to stay awake all night. I'm going to be the first in line tomorrow at Creator's door. I'm going to get a strong new name. A better name. A power name. Maybe I'll be Bear," he says. "Or maybe I'll be Salmon. Or maybe I'll be Eagle, and then they'll treat me with respect." So Coyote, he sits down beside that fire and tries to stay awake, but just a little while later he's fast asleep and snoring. Mole lets him sleep. She's thinking if Coyote gets *a better name then maybe he'll just up and leave, that mangy, sneaky thing.*

Mole waits until the sun is high, and then she wakes her husband up. Coyote runs right over to Creator, but he's much too late. All the power names are gone. All the little names are gone. The only name that's left now is Coyote—which nobody wants. Coyote sits down by Creator's fire, quiet now, and sad. It makes Creator start to feel real bad to see him sit like that. He says, "Coyote, my old friend, it's good you have the name you have. That's why I made you sleep so late. I've got important work for you. The Human People are comin' and you've got to go and help them out. They won't know anything, those ones, not how to hunt, or fish, or dress, or sing, or dance, or anything. It's your job now to show them how to do it all and do it right."

Coyote, he jumps up and he's all smilin' now, with all them teeth. "So I'll be the Big Chief of these new people!" Coyote says.

Creator laughs. "Yeah, somethin' like that. But you're still Old Coyote, you know. You're still a fool; that's what you are. But I'll make things easier for you. From now on you'll have these special powers: to change your shape, to hear anything talk except the water, and if you die you can come back to life. Now go and do your work."

Coyote left that teepee very happy. He went to find them Human People and to do his work. He went to make things right, and that's when all the humans' troubles began. . . .

It is winter now as I sit in the Sonoran Desert of Arizona, contemplating Coyote and his sack full of Trickster tales. In a number of Native American cultures, it is considered inappropriate, even dangerous, to tell tales about Coyote at any other time of year; it is disrespectful to Coyote and unlucky to attract his attention by telling his stories out of season. Wild coyotes, cousin to the Trickster of legend, often appear in the dry streambed just beyond my office window. They are beautiful creatures, untamable, sensibly wary of humankind. It is not at all unusual to see coyotes here in the desert outskirts of Tucson, but there seem to be more and more of them lately—drawn here by my interest in their stories, the traditionalists would say. It is one thing to read Coyote tales as I first did years ago in New York City, far from the creature's natural haunts; quite another thing to read them here, where coyotes roam the yard at night, making an eerie noise that sounds remarkably like laughter.

It is in the desert that I've begun to truly understand how myths are drawn from the bones of each land's geography—and how very different oral stories become when they are committed to the printed page, divorced from the land that birthed them. Too often printed versions of Coyote tales read (to urban and suburban readers) like simple children's fables: this is why the beaver's tail is flat, this is why the sky is filled with stars. In the oral tradition, Coyote stories are marked by their combination of outrageous (sometimes X-rated) humor with elements of great profundity; they are stories in which the sacred and profane are tied ineluctably together. "They are funny stories," a Navajo friend tells me, "but they are also sacred and serious. Trickster reminds us not to be too simplistically dualistic in our thinking; that good can come out of bad and vice versa; and that right and wrong are not always poles apart."

Although Coyote may be the best known mythic Trickster in North America, other popular Tricksters can be found in myths and legends all around the world, from the woodlands of northern Canada to the rain forests of the Amazon, from the Faery glens of the British Isles to the haunted shrines of the Orient. Tricksters are contradictory creatures: they are liars, knaves, rascals, fools, clowns, con men, lechers, and thieves— but they are also cultural heroes whose tricks can do great good as well as great harm, and whose stories serve to uphold the very traditions mocked by their antics. As folklorist Christopher Vecsey notes, regarding Trickster in West Africa: "By breaking patterns of culture the Trickster helps define those patterns. By acting irresponsibly, he helps define responsibility."[1] It is Trickster's role to shake things up, to ignore established conventions, and to transgress traditional boundaries, thereby initiating acts of change and transformation, for good or for ill.

Trickster can be an agent of creation or destruction, a cunning hero or a predatory villain; most often he is an ambivalent figure, shifting back and forth from one mode to the other. He is often portrayed as a creature at the mercy of overweening vanity and prodigious appetites (for food, for sex, for social power and recognition), perpetually undermined by these things and yet also perpetually undaunted by failure. As Robert D. Pelton comments in *The Trickster in West Africa*, Tricksters are "beings of the beginning, working in some complex relationship with the High God; transformers, helping to bring the present human world into being; performers of heroic acts on behalf of men, yet in their original form, and in some later forms, foolish, obscene, laughable, yet indomitable."[2]

The word *Trickster* first appeared in the *Oxford English Dictionary* in the eighteenth century, where it was defined as "one who cheats or deceives." The term was adopted by scholars of literature and folklore from the nineteenth century onward, used to designate a wide range of rascals, from the "wise fools" in Shakespeare's plays to the prankster phookas of Irish legends. In the early years of folklore studies, scholars collecting stories in Africa, Asia, and the Americas often toned down the bawdy, scatological humor recounted in traditional Trickster stories, or they omitted these tales from study altogether, considering them too rude, crude, or frivolous for publication. Likewise, some indigenous storytellers refrained from telling Trickster tales to folklorists and anthropologists—either to spare the scholars embarrassment or because the foreigners failed to comprehend the serious intent behind such earthy stories. "It was hard," a Navajo storyteller explained to me, "for the *belagana* [white man] to understand how funny stories could also be sacred stories. Coyote shows what will happen if you fail to live in harmony and to take care of your relatives. Coyote is always hungry, he's always lazy, he's always chasing after someone else's wife. He doesn't think about anybody but himself. He does everything wrong, he messes everything up. It's funny, but it's a warning too."

Three influential books in the twentieth century helped to establish and define Trickster as a specific kind of mythic archetype (although scholars to this day still argue about the parameters of the definition): Norman O. Brown's *Hermes the Thief: The Evolution of a Myth* (1947), Paul Radin's *The Trickster: A Study in American Indian Mythology* (1956), and E. E. Evans-Pritchard's *The Zande Trickster* (1967). With these works, and publications inspired by them, folklorists began to understand just how widespread the Trickster archetype was, and to gain a better appreciation of the cultural importance of Trickster stories. Robert D. Pelton recalls that when he first heard the Trickster described during an introductory course to the history of religions at the University of Chicago, he was fascinated. "To be sure, I knew of medieval fools, Hasidic rabbis, Zen masters, and the intensity of contemporary religious communities; they all suggested that comedy was an essential aspect of seriously lived religion. Among those engaged in the sacred, laughter kept breaking out. Yet until I met the Trickster, I had not realized that many so-called primitive peoples delighted in celebrating this disruptive power instead of squelching it or using it to launch some dull theory about institutional stress, comic absurdity, or the psychological value of playing around. Moreover, while these people were discovering laughter at the heart of the sacred, they, like so many Flannery O'Connor prophets and profiteers, were insisting that this discovery of laughter revealed the true being of daily life."[3]

Some Trickster tales are shockingly sexual and scatological, reveling in the very things least welcome in polite society: dirt, feces, flatulence, vomit, prodigious appetites, and outsized body organs, along with the kind of slapstick violence epitomized by *The Three Stooges*. Karl Keréyni, in his classic essay on the archetype, calls Trickster "the personification of the life of the body."[4] Trickster gleefully punctures all pretensions of gentility, all attempts to live in the mind and not the flesh; he is a creature of the body, of impulse and desire; he contains all the flaws of humankind writ large . . . as well as our boundless optimism, picking himself up after each disaster, irrepressible as ever. Psychologist Carl Jung viewed Trickster as an expression of the shadow side of a culture, the embodiment of all that is repressed and disowned—the greedy, needy rascal that lives somewhere inside every one of us. In recognition of the Trickster within, we delight in his outrageous escapades . . .

and then, being ethical creatures, too, we also savor Trickster's comeuppance when his tricks have failed, his ego has been deflated, and chaos has been restored to order.

Fantasy writer Midori Snyder notes, "We enjoy Trickster's boundless energy, his refusal to observe the normal taboos, his gigantic appetites, because they reflect our own appetites in their most unvarnished, unsocialized state. Look at Uncle Tompa, the Tibetan Trickster, who poses as a woman in order to seduce a wealthy man into marriage. As the wedding gifts are packed on Uncle Tompa's horse, and the crowd assembles to wish the 'bride' farewell, Uncle Tompa raises his skirts and reveals his true anatomy, much to the merriment of the crowd and the utter shame of the bridegroom. There's more to Trickster than meets the eye, however—we can't just write him off as a prankster and a fool. In the Winnebago Trickster cycle, Trickster spends most of the epic engaged in bawdy, gluttonous activities, creating disaster wherever he goes—yet in the closing episodes of the epic, he also travels through the land as a culture creator, carving out a place for humans to live in the world of nature. Among the Khoisan of South Africa, Mantis does the same, creating, organizing, shaping the world which man will inhabit. Even Prometheus in European myth is both Trickster (when he steals fire from the gods) and culture hero (when he lifts the darkness for mankind)."[5]

It is interesting, even puzzling, to note that the vast majority of Trickster figures are male, even though trickery and duplicity are hardly limited to one gender. There *are* a few female Tricksters—such as the seductive, deceptive fox maidens (*kitsune*) of Korea and Japan, wisecracking Baubo in Greek Eleusinian myth, clever Aunt Nancy in African-American tales, and a female Coyote in some stories told by the Hopi and Tewa

Indian tribes. Such wily women are rare, however, and seldom do they enjoy the cultural status of their masculine counterparts. (The majority of Hopi and Tewa stories, for example, feature the usual male Coyote.) In "Trickster and Gender," Lewis Hyde posits three reasons why male Tricksters are the norm: "First, these Tricksters may belong to patriarchal mythologies, ones in which the prime actors, even the oppositional actors are male. Second, there may be a problem with the standard itself; there may be female Trickster figures who have simply been ignored. Finally, it may be that the Trickster stories articulate some distinction between men and women, so that even in a matriarchal setting this figure would be male."[6]

Trickster is a consummate shape-shifter, turning up in many different forms in myths and legends around the world. Sometimes he's a god, an animal, a mischievous faery or other supernatural creature. Sometimes he's a human simpleton, a Zen master, a Muslim mullah, or the devil waiting at the crossroads. But "not just any rogue or antihero can properly be termed a Trickster," notes literary scholar Helen Lock. "The true Trickster's trickery calls into question fundamental assumptions about the way the world is organized, and reveals the possibility of transforming them (even if often for ignoble ends)."[7]

The Greek god Hermes, known to the Romans as Mercury, is one of the classic Tricksters of Western myth. Hermes is the god of messengers, of merchants, and of financial transactions—but he's also, in his dark aspect, the god of liars, gamblers, and thieves. The illegitimate son of Zeus by a nymph named Maia, Hermes was not born to divinity but had to win his place among the Immortals, using charm, cleverness, and duplicity to achieve this aim. His very first act, as a babe in arms, was to steal the sacred cattle of Apollo, covering up the deed with clever tricks and a packet of lies. The adult Hermes is portrayed as wily, lusty, and unpredictable, with a soft spot for pranksters, fraudsters, and con artists of all stripes. Hermes is also the god of thresholds, of open doorways, and of travelers on the road. He is the psychopomp who guides the dead from the lands of the living to the Underworld, and is one of the few capable of moving safely between these realms. He is, in Lewis Hyde's evocative phrase, "the lord of in-between"—the god who guides or thwarts men as they pass from place to place or from one state of being to another.[8]

Loki in Norse mythology is another classic Trickster figure: full of clever pranks that both undermine and benefit the gods of Asgard. Loki's parentage is in dispute, for in some accounts he is the child of giants and in others he is nephew to Odin himself. He is an irrepressible liar, schemer, thief, and lover of practical jokes; he is also a shape-shifter, with the rare ability to switch genders. In the early Norse tales, Loki is portrayed as an exuberantly amoral character, virtues and faults all mixed together. His actions are alternately helpful and harmful as his various schemes bring trouble upon the gods or, conversely, bail them out of trouble. In later tales, however (under the influence of Christianity), he becomes an almost Satanic figure. His last trick is an evil one, for it causes the death of Baldr, Odin's son. The gods imprison Loki in a cave; and there he's destined to remain until the battle of Ragnarök, when he'll emerge to lead an army of the wicked against Asgard.

Eshu-Elegba, the Trickster god of the Yoruba people of West Africa, is one of the four warrior deities known collectively as the orisha. He is the god of the threshold and of the roads, as well as the god of communication, charged with the task of carrying human prayers to the other orisha. He is a complex, multidimensional Trickster with a central role in Yoruban cosmology, a mediator between the human realm and the sacred, numinous world. Eshu can be benevolent or malign—and is usually both these things at once, delighting in playing tricks on human beings and the other gods. He is related to Legba, the wily, unpredictable Trickster of the Fon people of West Africa, who is also associated with thresholds, gateways, roads, and travelers. Legba is "the opener of the way" in voodoo ceremonies; he is the facilitator of communication between the human and spirit worlds, between men and women, between different generations, and between the living and the dead. Depicted as an old, old man in tattered clothes, Legba can be both kind and cruel and is never to be entirely trusted.

Maui, the great Polynesian Trickster, is at home in both New Zealand and Hawaii, where he's known as both a world creator and a meddlesome troublemaker. Half divine and half mortal, Maui is the abandoned son of a goddess, rejected by his mother because of his human patrimony. Small and ugly, but possessed of physical strength and crafty intelligence, Maui survives, thrives, and demands his place among the other gods. In the tales of Maui's preposterous exploits he is credited with creating the land from the sea, lifting up the sky above it, forcing the sun to move more slowly, and bringing fire to humankind. Yet all of these good things come about, in the proper slantwise Trickster fashion, as the result of Maui's avid pursuit of his own desires. He eventually causes such trouble for the gods that they conspire to destroy the half-mortal upstart, and Maui is killed while trying to gain immortality for human beings. As he dies, his blood makes shrimp turn red and forms the colors of the rainbow.

A large number of Trickster figures come in the form of animals and birds, sometimes interacting with human beings and sometimes only with other animals. Coyote, who is both man and animal, falls into this category. His tales are told by indigenous cultures from the Arctic down to Mexico—particularly by tribal peoples of the American Southwest and Western Plains. (The female version of Coyote is found in New Mexico and Arizona.) As folklorists Richard Erdoes and Alfonso Ortiz note, Coyote "combines in his nature the sacredness and sinfulness, grand gestures and pettiness, strength and weakness, joy and misery, heroism and cowardice that form the human character. . . . As a culture hero, Old Man Coyote makes the earth, animals, and humans. He is the Indian Prometheus, bringing fire and daylight to the people. He positions the sun, moon, and stars in their proper places. He teaches humans how to live. As Trickster, he is greedy, gluttonous, and thieving."[9] Many of Coyote's exploits end in failure, often culminating in his death. Yet like the irrepressible Wile E. Coyote in the old Road Runner cartoons, he's always on his feet again in time for the next tale, as cocky as ever.

Hare is the primary Trickster figure of other Native American tribes, particularly among the Algonquin-speaking peoples of the central and eastern woodland tribes. The Great Hare known as Nanabozho (or Manabozho, or Nanabush) is a powerful, complex character. In some tales, he's a cultural hero—the creator of the earth and of humankind, the bringer of light and fire, the founder of various arts and crafts, and teacher of sacred rituals. In other tales he's a clown, a thief, a lecher, and a cunning predator—an ambivalent, amoral creature who dances on the line between right and wrong.

We also find Trickster rabbits and hares in stories ranging from Asia and Africa to the hedgerows of Great Britain. In the *Panchatantra* tales of India, for instance, Hare's cleverness and cunning is tested by the wiles of the elephant and lion, while in Tibetan tales, Hare must outwit the ruses of the predatory tiger. In Nigeria, Benin, and Senegal there are stories of a cunning, deceitful hare who is equal parts rascal, lecher, buffoon, and cultural hero. African hare stories traveled to North America on the slavers' ships, where they mixed with Native American tales (such as rabbit stories of the Cherokee), evolving into the famous "Br'er Rabbit" tales of African-American lore, and into the "Compair Lapin" stories told by French Creoles in Louisiana. In the British Isles, the hare is a wily Trickster associated with faeries, witches, and the goddess of spring. He is a shape-shifter and messenger between the realms of the gods, the dead, and the faeries under the hill.

Anansi the Spider is a Trickster whose tales are known in many parts of Africa, the West Indies, and far beyond. His tales are generally humorous ones, with Anansi in the role of antihero: he breaks the rules, violates taboos, makes mockery of sacred things; he gets what he wants by plotting, scheming, lying, and cheating. Anansi is famously lazy, greedy, pompous, vain, and ignorant—but he's also very, very clever, usually outwitting everyone around him. Another Trickster spider can be found in tales of the Lakota and Dakota (Sioux) tribes of the American Midwest. Iktomi is a small but powerful creature, devious and mischievous, and like most Native American Tricksters, he is both comical and sacred. It was Iktomi who created time, space, and language and gave all the animals their names, but he's also a thief, a glutton, a lecher, and "the grandfather of lies." Like Coyote, Iktomi is a shape-shifter who can appear in the form of a handsome young man; his "love medicine" is powerful and has caused the downfall of many young girls. In this respect, Iktomi resembles Kokopelli, another Trickster figure found in the American Southwest. Kokopelli is a hunchbacked flute player who wanders the canyons, carrying a magical sack; he's famous for playing tricks on those he meets and seducing young women.

Raven is the central Trickster figure for many tribes on the North Pacific Coast—a creature born, according to some old tales, from primordial darkness. Raven is revered as a world creator, feared as a source of chaos and strife, and laughed at as a clown and fool; his tales can be dreamlike and phantasmagorical, tinged with sorcery. Fox, Mink, Blue Jay, and Crow are some of the other Trickster characters in the tales of the many tribal groups of North America, in addition to Tricksters who are supernatural beings rather than animals, such as the Blackfoot's Old Man Napi, the Hopi's Skeleton Man, the Northern Cheyenne's Veeho, and the Métis's Whiskey Jack.

Other animal Tricksters around the world include the famous Monkey King of China. He's a magician, a shape-shifter, an incorrigible prankster, and an inveterate creator of chaos, exasperating even the Buddha, who kept him trapped under a mountain after one of his pranks. Lord Hanuman, the monkey god of India, is sometimes considered a Trickster because of his animal shape and mischievous spirit, yet he doesn't exhibit the amorality usually associated with the Trickster archetype; he is a brave and noble character, a hero, and a devotee of Lord Rama.

Fox is a Trickster often found in Japanese, Korean, and Chinese tales. Fox Tricksters are expert shape-shifters and are generally dangerous to encounter. They can be male or female, young or old, beautiful or frightening in appearance. In Chinese legends, fox Tricksters attain their magical powers in one of two ways: by long years of arduous study (after which they are rewarded with the power to become human); or by posing as a human man or woman, seducing a member of the opposite sex, then stealing his or her life force. Fox maidens (*kitsune*) take on human guise to marry unsuspecting mortal men, using elaborate tricks, lies, and illusion to conceal the truth. Such tales usually end in tragedy, with the wife's or husband's death—but in some stories the passage between the mortal and magic realms is successfully negotiated, in which case the marriage prospers and produces half-mortal children. Fox also appears as a rather nasty Trickster in the European folk tradition, where he's known as Renard, Renardine, or Mr. Fox. Appearing in the form of a man with fox-red hair, he's a handsome and smooth-talking knave who tricks girls into marrying him, and then murders them and eats them. In *The Tales of Renard the Fox*, a European epic of the Middle Ages, the fox is a satirical Trickster figure: a greedy, wily rascal who dupes peasants and the nobility alike.

A similar figure is Puss-in-Boots, one of the best-loved Tricksters in fairy tales: a vain and silly creature, yet clever enough to win a castle and a princess for his master. When we turn our sights to the faeries themselves, as portrayed in European faery lore, we find there's more than a touch of the Trickster archetype in their makeup. Faeries come in many guises, but a number of them can fairly be described as mischievous, crafty, canny, clever, amoral, and unpredictable, fond of tricks, illusions, deceptions, and outwitting mortals. Puck is a faery of this type; he is charming and highly duplicitous, best known for his troublemaking role in Shakespeare's

A Midsummer Night's Dream. Puck, who also goes by the name Robin Goodfellow, is related to Welsh faeries known as the Pwca, as well as to faeries called Pukje in Norway, Puke in Sweden, and Pukis in Lithuania—all impulsive, volatile creatures whose tricks can be both delightful and cruel.

There are also a number of human Tricksters found in tales around the world: "wise fools" and "clever simpletons" who make their way through life with a combination of wit, naivety, and luck. The "Jack" tales of Great Britain and the Appalachian Mountains of North America feature a well-known hero of this type, as do the stories of Till Eulenspiegel told in Germany and among the Pennsylvania Dutch. Such tales often feature a peasant hero who uses his craftiness to triumph over men and women of the higher classes. The high are brought low, the low are raised high, the social conventions are turned upside down. The little guy wins—not because he's virtuous, but because he's clever and sneaky.

Trickster appears in religious folktales too, turning up in humorous stories of riddle-loving Christian saints, clever Hasidic rabbis, and wily Muslim mullahs. The "Crazy Wisdom" stories of Tibet are the comical teaching tales of Zen Buddhist lamas who believe that laughter, foolishness, and contrariness can lead to wisdom. "Tibet harbored the extraordinary gnostic tradition originating from the enlightened yogic adepts and 'Divine madmen' of ancient India," explains Lama Surya Das. "These inspired upholders of 'Crazy Wisdom' were holy fools who disdained speculative metaphysics and institutionalized religious forms. . . . They expressed the unconditional freedom of enlightenment through divinely inspired foolishness . . . vastly preferring to celebrate the inherent freedom and sacredness of authentic being, rather than clinging to external religious forms and moral systems. Through their playful eccentricity, these rambunctious spiritual Tricksters served to free others from delusion, social inhibitions, specious morality, complacence—in short, all variety of mind-forged manacles."[10]

A number of Native American spiritual traditions have a role for clowns and other contrary characters within their most sacred rituals. It is the task of the clowns to be unruly, disruptive, and outrageous, and it is said that some ceremonies have not properly begun until somebody laughs. All clowns, both spiritual and secular, are descended from the Trickster archetype—as are comedians, jesters, medieval court fools, the masked actors of the commedia dell'arte, and the anarchic puppets in Punch and Judy shows. All such figures make use of outlandish behavior to cross over social boundaries and to mock and satirize the status quo, sometimes making quite serious statements in the guise of foolery and humor.

There are holidays that belong to Trickster, allowing his spirit of disruption and transgression to flourish, if only for a few days each year. In the Middle Ages, the Christian Feast of Fools, with its roots in the Roman Saturnalia, included outlandish revels in which all the usual social conventions were reversed: men dressed as women and peasants as priests; they danced and played dice in church, then paraded through the streets singing obscene songs—letting off steam one day a year in order to be good during all the rest. Carnival festivities in Catholic countries were intended to serve a similar purpose before the hard, lean days of Lent. Carnival, too, had its roots in older pagan midwinter rituals in which laughter and satire were given a social outlet and a sacred context. Journalist

Alan Weisman described Carnival in a small village in Spain in 1993:

This is when, for a few moments each year, the people reign. Power is concentrated in the masks thundering by, borne by the sons of the village itself, lashing the crowd ever harder. Priest and politician alike must hide or be pummeled with insult and ridicule; the world is turned upside-down and shaken until the established order cracks loose. Anything is possible, everything is allowed: Humans transform themselves into animals; males become females; peons strut like kings. Social station is scorned, decorum is debunked, blasphemy goes unblamed. In neighboring villages, normally sober citizens drench each other with buckets of water; in Laza, they sling rags soaked in mud until everyone is reduced to muck. Bags appear containing ashes, flour, and—most prized of all— fertilizer crawling with red and black ants. A frenzy erupts; the air fills with stinging, fragrant grime, coating everyone with the earth's sheer essence. Men and women throw each other to the ground and roll in the street. With any luck, the heavens will be shocked and the new season jarred awake. Then, once again, day can steal hours back from the night, vegetation will arouse from hibernation, spring will heave aside winter, and what was dead can live again.[11]

Trickster is still alive and well in the twenty-first century, for he's infinitely adaptable, appearing as a stand-up comedian, a shock-jock DJ, a Hopi clown embarrassing the tourists, a cartoon rabbit munching on a carrot, a coyote sneaking through the underbrush. Contemporary storytellers have put their own twist on traditional Trickster myths, using the old stories as springboards for creating new Trickster tales for our time. You'll find Trickster plying his trade in such clever novels as Charles de Lint's *Someplace to Be Flying*, Neil Gaiman's *Anansi Boys*, Maxine Hong Kingston's *Tripmaster Monkey*, Margaret Mahy's *The Tricksters*, Lloyd Alexander's *The Remarkable Journey of Prince Jen*, Christopher Moore's *Coyote Blue*, Louis Owen's *Bone Game*, Midori Snyder's *Hannah's Garden*, Stephanie Spinner's *Quiver*, Ellen Steiber's *A Rumor of Gems*, Gerald Vizenor's *Chancers*, and many others. (For a longer list of contemporary Trickster fiction, see "Further Reading" at the back of this book.)

Though female Tricksters have long been overshadowed by their masculine counterparts, they too are now turning up in increasing numbers in fiction and other forms of storytelling—from television comedies to music videos to children's picture books. This indicates to me that there's nothing essentially male about the archetype; liars and fools come in both sexes, as do culture makers and destroyers. It's simply that Trickster becomes more relevant to the lives of women and girls in societies where they have gained a measure of independence and personal freedom. Trickster, after all, is the mythic embodiment of the ultimate Free Spirit, unwilling to be bound by society's conventions, traditions, and expectations. Trickster shows the creative potential in such freedom, as well as its potential for disaster. We can all learn from that, men and women alike, and we all have a bit of Trickster in us.

"Every group has its edge," notes Lewis Hyde, "its sense of in and out, and Trickster is always there, at the gates of the city and the gates of life, making sure there is commerce. He also attends the internal boundaries by which groups articulate their social life. We constantly distinguish—between right and wrong, sacred and profane, clean and dirty, male and female, young and old, living and dead—and in every case trickster will cross the line and confuse the distinction. Trickster is the creative idiot, therefore, the wise fool, the grey-haired baby, the cross-dresser, the speaker of sacred profanities. . . . Trickster is the mythic embodiment of ambiguity and ambivalence, doubleness and duplicity, contradiction and paradox."[12]

Whether male or female, animal or human, thief or hero, villain or clown, Trickster's role is to break out of every box we try to put him in. As soon as we think we know just what he is, she's shape-shifted into something else, tossing us a grin, handing us a fast line, setting us up for another trick. The writers in this book have explored some of the many forms that the Trickster archetype can take (inventing a few new ones as well), and my hat is off to each of them for the wonderful stories they've come up with. But don't stop there if you want to meet Trickster—go read some of the fabulous Trickster myths that have been handed down through the centuries. And if you ever have the chance, walk out into the Arizona desert some night when the moon is high and full. You'll hear the coyotes laughing . . . and Trickster will be right behind you.

Sit down, have some coffee, pay attention now. Here's one more about Coyote. He's walkin' there by that lake yonder, that lake over there by my uncle's place. And Coyote, he's tired, he's hungry, his bag is heavy, and he sees some geese. So he sets this big heavy bag down on the ground.

"Coyote, Coyote," say them geese, "what's in that big old heavy bag?"

"It's songs," he says.

"Coyote," says them geese, "how come you have so many songs?"

He puffs up his chest and he smiles with all them teeth, and then Coyote says, "I have strong visions, and that's how come I have so many songs."

"Well okay then, let's have us a big dance."

But Old Man Coyote shakes his head. "These are powerful songs. You can't mess around with these songs. If you want to dance, you're going to have to dance just like I tell you to dance."

"Well okay," them geese agree.

They pound down the grass by the edge of that lake and make a big place for dancing. Coyote takes out his dancing sticks. "Now you got to close your eyes," he says. "These songs are powerful medicine songs. If you open your eyes you might get hurt real bad."

So the geese all close their eyes and Coyote sings and the geese commence to dance.

"Keep your eyes closed!" Coyote says, and he hits one of them geese with his sticks. "Wait, stop!" says Coyote. "This here geese opened his eyes and now he's dead! You'd better all keep your eyes closed."

And then them geese, they start to dance again.

Coyote snatches another one and commences to strangle him. That geese is squawking, and Coyote says, "That's right, my friends, sing loud as you can!"

But one old geese, he opens one eye just a peep, and now he sees what's goin' on. "Run away, brothers!" he cries, and off they go—but not before Old Man Coyote fills his belly real good.

"That was sure some good trick," said Coyote, and he went along his way.

ENDNOTES

1. "The Exception Who Proves the Rules: Ananse the Akan Trickster" by Christopher Vecsey, published in *Mythical Trickster Figures*, edited by Hynes and Doty (University of Alabama Press, 1997).

2. *The Trickster in West Africa: A Study of Mythic Irony and Sacred Delight* by Robert D. Pelton (University of California Press, 1980).

3. "West African Tricksters: Web of Purpose, Dance of Delight" by Robert D. Pelton , published in *Mythical Trickster Figures*, edited by Hynes and Doty (University of Alabama Press, 1997).

4. "The Trickster in Relation to Greek Mythology" by Karl Kerényi, published in *The Trickster*, edited by Paul Radin (Bell Publishing, 1956).

5. *Trickster Makes This World: Mischief, Myth, and Art* by Lewis Hyde (Farrar, Straus & Giroux, 1998).

6. *Trickster Makes This World: Mischief, Myth, and Art* by Lewis Hyde (Farrar, Straus, & Giroux, 1998).

7. "Transformations of the Trickster" by Helen Lock, published online in *The Southern Cross Review*, 2002, http://www.southerncrossreview.org/18/trickster.htm.

8. *Trickster Makes This World: Mischief, Myth, and Art.*

9. *American Indian Trickster Tales*, by Alfonso Ortiz and Richard Erdoes (Viking, 1998).

10. "Crazy Wisdom and Tibetan Teaching Tales Told by Lamas" by Lama Surya Das, http://web.archive.org/web/20011025185750/http://www.netcontrol.net/themata-new/255002/

11. "The Sacred and Profane of Spanish Carnaval" by Alan Weisman, published in the *Los Angeles Times Magazine*, April 11, 1993. The article can be found online at: http://www.endicott-studio.com/rdrm/rrcarnaval.html.

12. From *Trickster Makes This World: Mischief, Myth, and Art.*

ONE ODD SHOE

Pat Murphy

You've probably seen those shoes by the side of the road. Just a shoe, lying in the dust just off the roadway. Not two shoes together. One odd shoe.

Sometimes it's a kid's shoe. You can figure out how those got there—kids messing around on a long car trip, a brother teasing his sister by holding a stolen shoe out the window. "Hey, I'm going to drop it. I'm going to . . . oops."

But what about the women's high-heeled pump, the dusty wingtip, the hiking boot? What brings those shoes to the side of the road?

I'm going to tell you about some of them. I'm going to tell you about a young man who should have known better, but didn't. His name was Mark.

My name's Dezba, but everyone calls me Dez. I'm a member of the Navajo Nation. My mother belonged to the Many Goats Clan, my father to the Coyote Spring People. I'm the daughter of a storyteller, and my mother is the daughter of a storyteller.

I was born on the reservation, and we didn't have a TV

when I was growing up. Instead of watching cartoons on Saturday mornings, I helped my mother tend the sheep and milk the goats and gather eggs from the chickens. I helped my grandmother collect the plants she used to dye wool that she wove into rugs to sell in the reservation store. In the evenings, I listened to my grandmother and my mother tell stories. They told stories about their lives, about our neighbors, about the tribe, about the creation of the world and Holy People like Changing Woman and Coyote.

After I graduated from high school, I left the rez to go to the university in Flagstaff. During the summer, between semesters in college, I worked as a cook at an archaeology summer camp that a bunch of professors put together. The professors set up camp just outside the western border of the reservation and brought in fifty or so students—some of them seniors in high school, some of them in college. For two months, the professors taught the students about archaeology and anthropology, and the students helped the archaeologists excavate an old pueblo where Indians had traded with each other something like a thousand years ago.

I set up the camp kitchen. I set up the dining hall—a bunch of picnic tables with a tarp rigged over them to provide shade. I trucked in the food and the mail, and I kept everyone fed. It wasn't hard work. Between meals, I spent a lot of time just hanging out and listening and watching. You can learn a lot that way.

So let me tell you about Mark. He was a good-looking guy and he knew it. A freshman in college, tall and muscular. He had an easy grin and he wasn't afraid to use it. Particularly when there were cute women around.

I kind of figure that Mark's mother had always told him

he was wonderful. He believed her—which was good, because you should believe your mother. Up to a point, anyway. At a certain point, you must put what your mother says aside and think for yourself. She says you can't possibly break that new colt that bucked off both your brothers—and you try it anyway. She says you can do no wrong and you . . . well, let's just say you know better.

I think that Mark believed his mother completely when she told him how absolutely perfect he was. I guess that's not necessarily bad—in my freshman psychology class the professor talked about low self-esteem. People who have that could use a bit more self-confidence. But Mark did not have a problem with low self-esteem. Truth be told, he was full of himself.

In the first couple of weeks of the summer, Mark cozied up to Nascha, a high school senior from Shiprock. Nascha had grown up on the rez, but I hadn't met her before she came to the dig. Her family was from Shiprock and mine was from Flagstaff, about a hundred miles away. But she'd seen me ride in the rodeo at the Navajo Nation Fair at Window Rock, and I'd seen her dance in powwow at the same fair. She was very serious about her studies and was planning to attend Diné College in Shiprock.

Every night, the students sat at the picnic tables and listened to one of the professors talk. And every night Mark sat by Nascha and whispered in her ear and held her hand and generally romanced her. Late at night, as I slept in my tent by the kitchen, I heard them at the picnic tables, talking and laughing.

That would have been very sweet—young love and all that—except for one thing. Just about every day, Mark got a letter in the mail from a girl back home. Ginny Alexander was the name on the return address. Ginny wrote in purple ink and always put a big red heart by Mark's name on the address.

And that would have been fine, too—it was Mark's trouble and no business of mine—if Nascha had been a bit more experienced in the ways of the world. But she was a sweet girl who had always lived at home. When I told her about the letters from Ginny Alexander, she said that Mark told her he had broken up with Ginny, but the girl wouldn't stop writing him. Nascha believed that Mark was her soul mate and that they would be together forever.

So Mark had a girl back home and a girl in camp—and then, two weeks into the summer, Tanya arrived. A college freshman from Los Angeles, Tanya was tall and slender, with short curly blond hair. She arrived late one afternoon. Mark happened to be in the dining room when she drove up in a battered old Volvo and wandered over in search of a professor.

Mark's eyes lit up when he saw her, and he smiled that easy smile and watched her like a hungry dog eyes a steak. He offered to show her around the dig.

So that's the start of it: a cocky young man, a couple of women, and an archaeological dig. Maybe you're wondering when I'm going to tell you about those shoes. Don't worry—I'll get to them eventually. But not just yet.

Like I said, every evening, the professors would talk to the students about archaeology and anthropology, about Native American stories and customs. Sometimes they got it right and sometimes they got it wrong, but mostly it was okay.

The night after Tanya arrived, one of the professors told the students a story about Coyote. That's Coyote with a capital *C*, the trickster god who gets into everybody's business. It was Coyote who brought fire to the First People—but it was also Coyote who brought death into the world. Coyote is a troublemaker from way back. When I took physics last quarter, the professor talked about entropy, the tendency for everything to get messed up. Coyote is a force for entropy. But Coyote is also a force for good (though whose good is always open to question).

The professor knew some true things about Coyote. He told the students about what he called a Navajo folk belief: if a coyote crosses your path, you'd best turn back. That's true enough, but I wouldn't call it a folk belief. I'd call it just plain common sense.

The professor talked about Coyote's role in the Navajo world: Coyote tests boundaries and breaks rules. Coyote lives in two worlds, hunting in the wild and sneaking into the village to steal food. When the gods gather, good sits on the south side of the hogan, evil sits on the north side, and Coyote sits in the middle near the door, ready to join up with either side, depending on what's convenient.

Then the professor told the old story about how Coyote taught the deer to run away from people, so that the people wouldn't kill and eat all the deer. The professor didn't do a great job of telling the story—my mother does it better. But the professor was really just telling the story to talk about how important Coyote was to keeping the world in balance.

While the professor was talking, I watched the students. Mark sat by Tanya and Nascha sat alone. She had arrived at the lecture late and Mark hadn't saved her a place like he usually did. I could tell by the look on Mark's face that he was not thinking about Coyote. I figured he was wondering how he could get into Tanya's pants.

~ ~ ~

The next day was Saturday, a day off from digging. Nascha was going to Shiprock to see her family. Her uncle came by to pick her up early in the morning. I got up and made her breakfast before she left.

We sat at the picnic table and had fry bread and coffee. She told me that Mark had gone off on a long walk with Tanya the night before. Nascha was sad and confused. I didn't say much—there didn't seem to be any point. Then her uncle rolled up in his pickup and Nascha went off for the weekend.

Mark came by later, with Tanya at his side, to get breakfast. He was grinning—happy and hungry. When he came back for seconds on scrambled eggs, I was careful to give him the burned bits from the bottom of the pan.

He sat at a picnic table with Tanya and a few other students. Cindy, another high school student from Shiprock, was there. Jack, one of the graduate students, was talking about a party that evening. "Every Saturday night, folks from digs all over the area get together at Coyote Hot Springs," he was saying. "One of the guys from Black Mesa dig told me about it last weekend. You can soak in hot water and find out what the students at other digs are up to."

"How far is it to the hot springs?" Tanya asked.

"About forty miles," Jack said. "All dirt road, though. He drew me a map."

"I can drive my Jeep," Mark said, looking at Tanya. He had a red Jeep. Nascha had said that his parents had given it to him when he graduated from high school. "I can give you a ride."

"Great," Tanya said, but she was still looking at Jack. "I wonder why it's called Coyote Hot Springs."

Mark grinned. "Maybe because it's a good place to look for trouble," he said. "A good place for folks who know how to break the rules, like Coyote." It was clear that he counted himself among them.

I wasn't around for this next part. But that's okay. My grandmother tells the story of how Coyote brought the people fire, and she wasn't around for that. So I'll tell you how I think it was, and that will be good enough.

Tanya rode with Mark. Cindy and a couple of other students rode with Jack in his old Volkswagen van.

I think maybe a coyote crossed the dirt road in front of Mark's Jeep. I'm not sure about that—but if it did happen, Mark just kept going. He flirted with Tanya along the way—I won't bother to tell you about all that. It was the usual sweet-talking courtship sort of thing, with Mark listening to Tanya as if she was the most interesting person in the world and telling her about how wonderful she was—how pretty, how smart.

The sun was low in the sky when they reached a tumble of boulders at the base of a low hill. An assortment of dusty cars and trucks was parked nearby. When Mark turned off his ignition, he could hear tinny music. The sound ended and an announcer said, "You're listening to KAFF, today's best country music, broadcasting from Flagstaff."

Mark followed Jack and the others on a trail that snaked around the boulders to a pool of water about twelve feet across. The water steamed and the air had a faint stink of sulfur. Country music—a woman singing about a man who done her wrong—came from a boom box; half a dozen people in swimsuits lounged in the hot water or on the boulders around the pool.

"Hey, Jack," one of the men called from the water. "Good

to see you, man. Welcome to Coyote Hot Springs Spa and Archaeological Resort."

"How's the water?" Tanya asked.

"Just warm enough," the man said. "If you want hotter, head uphill. You'll find small pools here and there. The higher you go, the closer you get to the source—and the warmer the water. But I think this pool is just right. There's some beer in a cooler by the boom box. Help yourself."

Jack was already kicking off his shoes. Mark smiled as Tanya pulled off her T-shirt, stripping down to her swimsuit. He figured he'd get a beer and then join her. He found the cooler and was opening a beer when he noticed a good-looking woman, standing off by herself.

She was tall—almost as tall as Mark. Long black hair, tied back in a braid. She wore cutoff jeans, a T-shirt, and Navajo moccasins, the kind that wrap around the ankle and button on the side. The moccasins were made of red-brown buckskin held closed with a silver button. She had long legs and an evil grin. Mark liked that. Her grin widened when she saw him coming toward her, and he liked that even more.

"Oh, you don't want to talk to me," she said. "I'm not your kind."

"What do you know about my kind?" Mark said, returning her grin. He liked a challenge. The thrill of the chase made the capture all the sweeter. He wondered what dig she was from.

Her grin widened even more. "You'd be surprised at what I know," she said. "I know too much about you."

"That's good," he said, boldly putting his arm around her shoulders. "That'll save us some time."

"Hey, Mark!" a woman's voice called. As Mark turned to

look toward the sound, the tall woman ducked under his arm.

It was Cindy. "Hey, Mark," she said. "Could I talk to you for a minute?"

"Uh, sure. I guess." He glanced after the tall woman and saw her head up the trail toward the other pools.

Cindy told him that she wanted to talk to him about Nascha. She knew how close he and Nascha were. And she knew he'd want to know how upset Nascha was with the attention he was paying to Tanya. Cindy told him about it in detail. At great length. She was quite sincere and well meaning.

"I just thought I'd better tell you," Cindy said.

Mark nodded, trying to think of what he could say.

Cindy patted his arm. "I'm sure it's just a misunderstanding," she said.

"Sure," he managed.

"Let's head back and go for a swim," she said.

He shook his head. "I think I'll check out the other pools," he said, and he went up the hill, in pursuit of the tall woman.

The path wound its way through sandstone boulders that had been shaped by the desert wind into grotesque forms. Twisted pillars of stone reached up to the darkening sky. Windworn holes in the stone looked like eyes watching him as he passed by.

The sound of the boom box drifted up to him—another woman singing about some man who'd done her wrong. The sunset light was turning the clouds in the western sky a lovely shade of pink.

Around a turn of the path, he found a small pool, not much bigger than a bathtub. He considered stripping down and soaking in the steaming water. But he thought about the tall woman in cutoffs, and he kept climbing in the fading light, past pillars of stone that watched him with vacant eyes.

A light breeze blew, sending a dust devil swirling past him. He followed the path around a large boulder that looked a little bit like the head of a howling dog, its snout pointed toward the sky.

Just around the bend, beneath the strangely shaped boulder, was a pile of clothes. And just past the clothes was a pool of steaming water. And in the pool of steaming water was the woman. Her eyes were closed. She was relaxing.

Mark took one more step, so that he was standing between the woman and her clothes. Then he said, "How's the water?"

The woman opened her eyes and stared at him. "The water's fine," she said.

"You must be from Black Mesa," he said. "I'm from the Sunset Crater dig."

She narrowed her eyes and stared at him. "I told you once: you really don't want to talk to me."

"That's where you're wrong," he said. "You're exactly who I want to talk to. I'd like to talk to you for a while. And then I'd like to get to know you a little better."

"Not very likely." As she spoke, she stood up. She wasn't wearing a swimsuit.

Mark should have known better. I know that, and you know that, but he didn't know that. He didn't move. He blocked the path to her clothes. She stood in front of him, one hand on her hip. She made no move to cover her body with her hands. When he stared at her, she stared right back.

"You really don't have a clue, do you?" she said.

Mark didn't move. He had planned to flirt a little, and then back off, but she was starting to piss him off. She sure wasn't acting the way women usually acted with him. She was too bold, too bossy. It was great to see her naked, but she wore her nakedness like a challenge. As if she were saying—*Here it is and you can't have it.*

"Not only do I have a clue, I have your clothes," he said.

"Yeah. So hand me my shirt, will you?" she asked.

Mark wasn't evil—just clueless. He knew he couldn't just keep her clothes. So he tried to flirt, in a ham-handed sort of way. "I'll give you your shirt if you'll answer a question. Are you with the Black Mesa dig?"

"No."

He asked questions and she got her clothing, one item at a time. He learned that she was not with the Luepp dig, nor the North Williams dig. He learned that she didn't have a boyfriend. He was down to her last shoe when he decided to up the ante.

"One shoe left," he said. "I'll give it to you if you give me a kiss."

"A kiss?" she said. She was fully dressed now except for one shoe. She stood beside the pool. She had one hand on her hip. "How old-fashioned."

"No, not an old-fashioned kiss. A proper modern kiss." He grinned at her, trying for an air of bravado.

She shook her head. "Not just now," she said.

Then, without another word, she turned and walked away. Two steps took her into the darkness.

"Hey!" Mark said. "Wait a second. I have your shoe."

But that was all he had. The woman was gone, leaving him holding a single moccasin.

Mark searched for the woman, hopefully at first, then with increasing disappointment and confusion. He didn't know what to do. The woman was gone and he had her shoe.

Finally, he headed back to the big pool, taking the moccasin with him. No doubt she'd show up at the big pool down below. Then he'd give her back her shoe. Hey, he wouldn't even ask for a kiss. Sure, she was good-looking, but she had an attitude he didn't like. He would just give her back her shoe and be done with it.

He put the moccasin in the back of his Jeep and joined the folks in the pool. Students from half a dozen digs had joined the group. Tanya was flirting with a guy from the Black Mesa dig, and Mark couldn't get her attention. Mark asked around among people from the other digs about the woman he had met, but no one seemed to know her. She never showed up and claimed her shoe. He drove back to the dig alone, having struck out with the women from other digs. It wasn't a good evening. He didn't know what to do with the moccasin, so he set it on the dashboard of his Jeep.

The next morning I was getting some canned food from a box in my truck and saw the moccasin on the dashboard of Mark's Jeep. It was a Navajo moccasin—a nicely made one. Hand stitched from fine buckskin. The sort of moccasin a woman would be proud to wear to a powwow.

Mark arrived at breakfast late. When I was dishing him up some scrambled eggs, I asked him, "Where'd that moccasin in your Jeep come from?"

Mark muttered something about meeting a woman at Coyote Hot Springs.

"You want to give that shoe back," I told him.

"What are you talking about?"

"It's a bad luck shoe. You better give it back."

"A bad luck shoe? Is that some kind of Indian thing?"

I thought of it more as a commonsense kind of thing. "It's wrong to keep it," I said.

He shook his head. "Whatever," he said, and walked away.

I wasn't around for this next part either. But here's what Mark said happened, more or less.

Mark slept in a small tent at the edge of the meadow on the far side of the dining area. The weather on Sunday night was warm and clear and he left the tent unzipped. He folded the trousers and T-shirt he would wear the next day and set them beside his sleeping bag. He put his boots beside his clothes.

A word about those boots. Other students had shown up at the dig wearing old running shoes or hiking boots. Not Mark. He had a lovely pair of Red Wings—stylish, six-inch, lace-up boots of sand-colored leather that was soft as a baby's bottom. Nice boots. Probably set Mark's parents back a couple of hundred bucks.

Anyway, that night, Mark stuffed his clean socks in his left boot and put his flashlight in his right boot, so that he could find it if he needed it in the middle of the night. He set his boots in the bottom of the tent, where they'd be protected from the morning dew. He crawled into his sleeping bag and looked up at the stars. He heard a coyote howling in the distance. And he fell asleep.

He woke to the sound of tearing fabric. Half asleep, he peered toward the bottom of the tent, where the sound was coming from. The moon had risen, and he could see the dark shadow of an animal at the end of the tent. It had its head inside his tent. As he watched, it started to pull its head out of the tent. It had one of his boots in its mouth.

"Hey!" Mark shouted, grabbing for the boot. The animal growled and pulled its head out of the hole in the tent, taking Mark's boot with it. By the time Mark wiggled out of his sleeping bag, the animal was halfway across the meadow. A coyote, running off with a boot in its mouth. Before Mark could even begin chasing it, the animal was gone.

Mark stood in the meadow in his underwear, staring after the coyote. This had to be a dream, he thought. Coyotes don't steal shoes. So he crawled back into his sleeping bag and went back to sleep.

But in the morning, he found that his right boot was gone.

The left boot was still there, looking a little forlorn without its mate. His clean socks were still there, tucked inside the left boot. His flashlight was there, too—lying on the floor of the tent beside the left boot. But his right boot was nowhere to be seen.

He pulled on his clothes and went to the dining area barefoot, carrying his left boot and his socks. He told everyone what happened. People seemed to think it was pretty funny. Even Nascha, who had returned from Shiprock on Sunday night, was less than sympathetic. "I guess you'll have to go barefoot," she said. She was having breakfast with Tanya and Cindy. The women had been talking.

Mark stood there for a minute, holding his left boot and looking forlorn. I had warned him to give back that bad luck shoe. Too late now.

Mark couldn't work on the dig without shoes. So he decided to drive into Flagstaff to buy a pair of sneakers.

"Good luck," I told him as he left the dining hall. He gave me a funny look. I knew that he didn't think he needed luck to drive to the shopping mall and buy a new pair of shoes. But you already know that he didn't know much.

I wasn't around for this next part. Mark didn't tell me about it, either. In fact, I've pretty much made it up entirely. But I'm pretty sure about the way it went. I know how things go, when those things involve Coyote Hot Springs.

So Mark headed out the long dirt road to the highway. He was a couple of miles from the dig when he spotted a boot lying in the dust by the side of the road. He pulled over, thinking it might be his—the coyote might have carried his boot for a while before dropping it. But the boot by the road was a battered black cowboy boot in size 8, rather than the size 10 that Mark wore. Still, it was a boot, and a right boot, too. It seemed somehow promising. He wasn't the only one who had lost a boot around here.

He was at the turnoff that led to Coyote Hot Springs. Looking down the dirt road to the hot springs, he saw another boot. Maybe it was the mate of this cowboy boot. Or maybe it was his lost boot. He drove down the road to see.

The shoe by the side of the dirt road was a black wingtip. He stopped and considered it. Right foot, size 10. Not his boot.

Mark peered down the side road. In the distance, he could see something lying beside a clump of sagebrush. He continued down the road. People always do. That's just the way these stories go.

Beside the sagebrush there was another shoe—a beige huarache. Mark didn't bother to check the size. He just kept driving, following the road to Coyote Hot Springs. Every mile or so, there was another shoe. A hiking boot beside a cholla plant, a patent leather pump lying in a patch of dried grass. Mark followed the trail of shoes.

The dirt area where the cars had been parked the night before was empty. Mark parked and started to step out of the Jeep. But the minute his bare foot touched the hot sand, he stopped. Way too hot to go barefoot.

After a moment's hesitation, he slipped his remaining boot on his left foot. He took the Navajo moccasin from the dashboard of the Jeep and slipped that on his right foot. Surprisingly, it fit.

He considered that bad luck shoe, trying to figure out what to do with it. Finally, he decided that he'd take it back up to the small pool where he had found the woman bathing. Maybe he thought about how I told him he should give it back. Maybe not.

Coyote Hot Springs was deserted. Hot air rising from the large pool made the rocks on the other side of the water seem to shimmer and move.

It was hot, climbing the hill to the small pool. He felt goofy wearing two different shoes—but no goofier than he had felt when chasing a coyote in his undershorts. When he reached the pool, he sat down to rest in the shade of the boulder shaped like a howling coyote.

The hot water in the pool steamed like a hot bath. It had been goofy to come here, he decided. But since he was here, he might as well soak his tired muscles before heading off to town.

He took off his mismatched shoes and his clothes and he set them on the ground in the shade of the boulder. Then he eased himself into the hot water.

The pool was just the right size for him. It was shaped more or less like a bathtub, with a gentle slope at one end that made a perfect backrest. He leaned back and relaxed, closing his eyes. The hot water felt great. He'd go to town and buy some new shoes, he thought. Then he thought about how he would sweet-talk Nascha and Tanya when he got back to camp. It would all work out fine.

A sound woke him from his daydreams and he opened his eyes. The Navajo moccasin, which he'd left by his pile of clothes, was gone. So was his boot.

He sat up straight in the pool. Then he heard the sound that had awakened him again—a sharp bark.

He looked up the hill and saw a coyote watching him intently. The animal was lying on her stomach in the shade. Her fur was reddish brown with a dark streak down the center. Between her front paws was his boot.

"Hey," he said in an aggrieved tone. "That's mine."

The coyote tipped her head to one side and let her tongue loll out, grinning at him.

He stared at the coyote. "You can't take my boot."

The coyote's grin widened. She licked her lips with her long red tongue and grinned some more. As she kept on staring at him, he became very aware that he was naked.

"That's really rude," he said. "Why don't you just leave me alone?"

The coyote clamped her jaws around the boot and stood up.

"No, wait," he said. "Don't take my boot!"

The coyote sat down and set the boot down between her front paws.

"Come on," he said. "Give my shoe back."

She yawned, licked her lips again, and grinned, her tongue lolling from the corner of her mouth.

The coyote stared as he got out of the pool, dripping wet and naked. He turned his back as he pulled on his shorts, but he knew she was still watching him. He pulled on his shirt and turned to face her.

The coyote was standing now, the boot at her feet. He wondered if he could chase her off and grab his boot. Before he could move, the coyote sprang at him, crossing the distance between them in three bounds, leaping up and striking at his shoulders with her paws. He stumbled backward, tripping, falling onto his butt. The coyote's muzzle was inches from his face. He could see her teeth—long, sharp, and yellow. He could smell her breath—the worst doggy breath you could imagine, stinking of carrion.

Then she gave him a big kiss. That long, wet, carrion-stinking tongue swept across his face and dipped into his mouth to touch his own tongue.

He jerked his head backward, spitting and gagging, as the coyote sprang away. She bounded away up the hill. Her long tongue lolled from her mouth, as if she were laughing. And she disappeared from sight among the boulders.

He rinsed out his mouth with water from the pool—once, twice, three times. He thought about all the diseases you might catch from being French-kissed by a coyote. Why would an animal behave like that?

Maybe he remembered then: "Just give me a kiss," he had said to the woman. "I'll give you your shoe back." Maybe he realized that the coyote had done to him what he had tried to do to the woman.

Probably not. And even if he did, he probably didn't think that the situations were the same at all. But whatever he thought about it, at least he had his boot back. One boot, anyway.

He headed down the hill, wearing one boot. It wasn't easy. He would touch the ground with his bare foot just long enough to take a step—then balance on his booted foot, giving his bare foot a chance to cool off. It took a long time, but eventually, he made it back to the truck.

In the dirt by the truck, he found his other boot—slightly chewed and smelling of coyote, but otherwise intact. He put it on and drove back to camp. He didn't see any shoes by the road on the way back. He tried not to think about what had happened. He had his boot back, and that was all that mattered.

That evening, he sat beside Nascha at dinner and tried to sweet-talk her. "I don't want you to be mad at me," he told her. He put on his best sincere expression.

She gave him a dubious look.

"I'd do anything—" He was going to say he'd do anything to make things right between them, but at that moment his right boot gave his foot a tremendous pinch. It felt like his foot was caught in the jaws of a hungry coyote. "Ow!" he said, grabbing his foot.

Coyote has her ways, you see.

"What's the matter?" Nascha said.

"My boot," Mark said. He rubbed his foot gingerly as the pressure let up.

"What were you saying?"

"I want to make—" He was going to say he wanted to make her happy, but his boot clamped down on his foot, and he couldn't get the words out.

It wasn't a good summer for Mark. Every time he tried to sweet-talk a woman, his boot would chomp down on his foot and he had to stop.

And you know, it wasn't just that boot. He went to town the next weekend and bought a pair of sneakers, and the same thing happened with his right sneaker. The minute he started to lie, that shoe bit his foot like a hungry coyote.

So he never did get into Tanya's pants. He never made up with Nascha. In fact, he didn't have any luck with any of the women for the rest of that summer.

I don't know what became of Mark. Maybe he learned to tell the truth. Probably not. Maybe he confined his romancing to the beach, where he could lie with impunity, wiggling his toes in the sand. But most women would wonder about a guy who never put his shoes on.

Like that anthropologist said, it's Coyote's job to set the world right. Of course, you may not agree with the way that Coyote sets things right, but that's not Coyote's problem. It's yours.

So what about those shoes by the side of the road? Well, now you know that you'd best leave those alone. Someone, somewhere, is up to no good, and Coyote has decided to set the world right. So drive on by. Leave those markers for someone who needs them. I hope it's not you.

PAT MURPHY's writing has won numerous awards, including the Nebula Award, the World Fantasy Award, and the Seiun Award, the latter for the best science fiction novel translated into Japanese. Her work ranges from scientifically accurate science fiction to psychological fantasy to magic realism. When she's not writing fiction, Pat specializes in having interesting jobs: she wrote books about science for the Exploratorium, San Francisco's museum of science, art, and human perception; she was marketing director at The Crucible, a non-profit school dedicated to teaching industrial arts and fire arts (from blacksmithing to fire eating). Currently, she edits books for Klutz, a publishing enterprise that began in 1977 with *Juggling for the Complete Klutz* and today creates hands-on how-to books for kids. Pat's latest novel is *The Wild Girls*. Her Web site is www.brazenhussies.net/murphy. Her favorite color is ultraviolet.

～

AUTHOR'S NOTE

People often ask writers where they get their ideas. What these questioners really want to know is: Where do stories come from? The answer is simple—and completely useless to those who ask.

Stories come from the totality of the writer's experience—from all the things the writer has done and seen and heard. "One Odd Shoe" came from a road trip to Bishop, California—a long drive through the desert and the mountains, with plenty of time for thinking on the way. It came from a summer I had spent on an archaeological dig near Flagstaff, Arizona, sifting the dirt in a ruined pueblo for bits of broken pot and pieces of worked stone. It came from seeing shoes by the side of the road. It came from knowing young men (and young women) who should have known better. It came from a love of tricksters, from hearing coyotes in the desert night, from the wind-etched sandstone pillars in Goblin Valley, Utah, which I visited long ago. All the bits and pieces came together and made a story. Simple as that.

COYOTE WOMAN

Carolyn Dunn

From the deep hills
and dark wet
earth,
a bay moon of time
and after-rain, she moves glistening
past wild alata
jimson smoke, cedar
and sage.
He has called her
one last time
and it is in her blood
to answer.
Woman,
he calls,
will you ever
heed me?

Laughing,
baring her eyeteeth,

she moves through
the burning sky
cloaking the black earth
with fur.
Tell me a story,
she whispers,
a sound only
he can hear,
a sound above the crying
of last night's
feast.

A story,
he says,
about a dog of a woman
who won't answer
the call
of the one who
tamed her first
by voice,
then by touch,
then by song.

A story,
she whispers,
of land
and longing
and winds
that terraced over mountains,
across plains,
bringing madness

from the land
of our birth.
These are our worlds,
formless,
yet from within
the story of my heart,
the part of me
you could not take
away.

I'm dying,
he said
and there will be nothing
left but willows,
palm bark,
and voices
in the trees.
What will you sing
when my bones
in the ground
turn to dust?

A cry to the moon,
she answered,
the wind
a breath from
a fire's touch
upon your skin.
I'll sing a song
of death,
a toll for you

who trapped my voice
with your pale touch.
My voice is my own
and no wax,
no sealing string,
no empty hole
can keep it from moving
on the wind
across simmering
black canyons,
pine, and
chaparral.
And my voice
will never leave
this land,
lighting fires
and fountains,
from here
to your
soul.

CAROLYN DUNN, poet, playwright, musician, and mom is the author of three books of poetry and the coauthor (with Ari Berk) of *Coyote Speaks*. Her fiction and poetry have appeared in numerous anthologies; she also coedited two anthologies of contemporary American Indian literature.

A playwright and performer, she is a member of the Mankillers, an all-woman Northern-style drum group, and is affiliated with Native Voices at the Autry, a national native theater company based in Los Angeles.

To find out more about her work, please visit her Web site at www.carolyndunn.com.

～

AUTHOR'S NOTE

Most Indian stories about Coyote show him as a male trickster figure; but he can also appear as a she, and oftentimes in my life, she's hanging around. This poem is about Coyote Woman, who takes in strays wherever she goes. I like to think of her, walking along the cliffs of Southern California, on a warm desert night, picking up lost and lonely pups and giving them a home to call their own.

WAGERS OF GOLD MOUNTAIN

Steve Berman

A spinning coin danced across the polished wooden desk-
top. Two pairs of green eyes—one a shade of the brightest jade, the other cloudy like tarnished copper—stared at one
another.

"Come now, m'dear, you do owe me another attempt to
court favor." The man drew deeply on a cigar, which leaked
smoke worthy of the finest incense.

The woman caught the coin, tapping the edge with a lacquered nail. "The stakes?"

"Perhaps love?"

"Always love," she said with a bored sigh. "Whatever happened to the old days, when all you cared for was wealth?"

"That was before I saw you in all your varied forms, before
you taught me some new tricks."

"So by your own country's adage, you must be a new dog,
Buren."

The man showed a wolfish grin and barked a laugh. "All
native-born are, m'dear. We all are."

"Not love. You're never satisfied with the outcome anyway." She spun the coin once more between them, its face shifting between a gold dollar and a bronze coin with a square hole in the middle. "I know what you truly want." She allowed the sleeve of her silk robe to slide up, exposing the creamy skin of her forearm.

"Now that remains to be seen." He cocked his head, as if hearing a sound, but the room had grown quiet except for the slight chime of the coin's travels. "The youth approaching promises to be fair game." He blew out a puff of smoke. "Life and death?"

The woman raised the corners of her lips, which had taken the color of spilt blood. "Agreed."

Outside a small Union Hill storefront, Ji Yuan glanced at the gilded letters on the window, ones utterly foreign to him even after months of living in San Francisco. He wished he could muster the courage to stop one of the Americans passing by and ask if this was indeed the correct shop; his countrymen working beside him at the shirt factory would whisper of a place where one could *koutou* to evil spirits for favors. Yuan had thought they told those stories to refresh the spirit from the long hours with needle and thread, but now he had no choice but to hope a measure of truth lay behind such talk.

He did not seek the spirits for himself. Though at times his empty stomach would writhe and he often struggled to keep his eyes clear when the hunger made the world spin, he worried only for his brother.

Late every night, on the walk back from work, Yuan would chant under his breath to Amita Buddha, hoping that he would not find the body of his brother lying in the street outside the dilapidated building where they shared a tiny room with so many others. None inside would suffer a corpse in their midst, and they would have carried him out, unceremoniously dumping the body like offal.

For weeks now his brother would barely move from the pallet, his damp body suffering from fevers. Yuan kept none of the money he earned for himself. Whatever remained after paying the landlord went to food and medicine for his brother. Yuan had to first chew the food for Chen, and he felt ashamed when he would weaken and swallow some rice, or even worse, a morsel of pork. He subsisted on tea and ignored how his clothing had begun to hang loosely.

He pulled on the thick brass door handle and walked inside. Two desks faced the windows: the left, gaunt and bamboo; the right, heavy wood. Stretched across the floorboards, an animal skin between them divided the room in half. He glanced at the strange heads at each end of the long hide, resembling something close to that of a donkey but with far more hair. He knelt down and regarded the blunt teeth.

"Curious?" The smell of jasmine heralded the voice. Yuan looked up to see a beautiful Manchu woman seated behind the bamboo desk. He had not heard her enter. He quickly averted his eyes from her jade gaze out of proper respect and modesty. From her dress and countenance she clearly ranked higher than him. Her dark hair was tied in a bun wrapped with fragrant flowers.

"I have not seen its like," he said in Cantonese, with a bow.

A different voice answered in English. "Certainly not." A snort followed the statement. Yuan turned to the right to see a white man standing next to the other desk. He looked like so many other Americans: fat with prosperity, red beard oily, hair slicked, dressed in layers of scratchy wool.

"That's a pushmi-pullyu," he said, stabbing down toward the hide with one hand. "Damn rare. Might have been the last one." He raised a cigar to his thick lips.

Yuan had learned only a bit of the odd American language, yet he understood the man as well as if he had spoken Cantonese. He quickly figured that fact—so unlikely, if not impossible—to be proof that the very spirits he had been warned about stood before him.

A bit scared, yet on guard to keep his back straight to show no fear, Yuan bowed again, to each in turn, keeping his head down.

"None of that," muttered the man. "You'll never get ahead in California keeping your eyes on the dirt." After a long pull on his cigar, he chuckled. "Unless, of course, you're looking for gold."

"Buren, do not taunt him. He is desperate." He glimpsed the stately woman rising from her chair. Her perfume became for a moment cloying, almost too much to bear, and Yuan shuddered when he felt the sudden scratch at the back of his neck. He blinked and the sensation abruptly stopped.

"That is why he is here before us. Is that not so, Yuan?"

The youth did not remember telling her his name but nodded humbly. He felt more than uneasy before the pair. Fear had begun to sour his empty stomach. These could only be spirits and not flesh. Still, he had no choice but to remain there—he actually fell to his knees and scraped his forehead on the soft hide of the pushmi-pullyu; his brother would surely die without help, and a poor coolie had nowhere else to turn.

Buren nudged Yuan with his boot. "Get up. If I wanted to look at a pigtail I'd be visiting the sty."

Yuan hesitated a moment, face flushed with shame at the man's ignorant remark at his plaited *bianzi*, the hair honoring his father, which had grown long after seventeen years.

"Better." With a chubby hand, Buren began flipping a coin in the air. "So you want a better life for your brother?" Again he snorted. "Why not ask for a little good fortune for the both of you?"

"I would not dare—"

"No, your kind never do." Buren turned to his comrade. "Hang-ne, I think he's our cully."

The woman nodded slightly. "We are willing to offer fortune in return for recovering something lost."

"A hatchet," Buren added.

"One locked away. We want it brought back to us before sundown."

"A hatchet?" Yuan failed to keep the surprise from his voice. Why would such a strange pair be so eager for the return of something so common? Surely they had the wealth to buy a hundred hatchets.

"Here," Buren said as he threw the coin. It landed in Yuan's open palm as something different. A metal key.

"Is there nothing else you would have me do?" The thought that his brother's life depended on recovering something so trite seemed like an insult. Or was Amita Buddha testing him?

"I thought your kind to be quiet and diligent." Buren bent down and lit a fresh cigar from an oil lamp that Yuan had not noticed on the man's desk. Yuan caught a whiff of the smoke, which oddly, smelled like his favorite fish soup. His mouth watered and he swallowed hard to keep focused.

Hang-ne reached out with cupped hands and caught a measure of smoke drifting off Buren's cigar. She molded it with her nimble fingers until the wisps took shape. She then blew across her palms, and a gray swallow ruffled its feathers.

"Follow this through the city."

The bird took flight immediately, circling the room.

Yuan bowed a final time and left, watching the swallow escape when he opened the door.

He took care to trail the bird through the winding streets. The squat buildings of brick and iron he passed looked like foreboding giants compared to the welcome conditions of Chinatown—though cramped, the neighborhood teemed with a festive life, evident in its aromatic chophouses, raucous gambling parlors, and red-and-gold-painted storefronts.

Yuan kept wondering why the pair would want a hatchet. The youth normally distracted himself from the drudgery of work or the pangs of hunger with chants to Amita Buddha. Even after so many months away from Guangzhou, he remembered the little prayers the monks had taught him. His mother had wanted the saffron-robed men to accept him into their midst. "You are too clever to be a farmer, Yuan," she always told him. "Chen inherited my back, while your mind is sharp like your uncle's." Because he was too poor to afford the books to study for civil service exams, the monastery seemed the best fate for Yuan.

That is, until Chen heard of the fortunes of Gold Mountain. Yuan's brother began daydreaming in the fields about the wealth of California and ignoring his chores. A few men of the village had already left. But if Mother had not died from a long fever, Chen would never have decided to leave China. Yuan dared not risk losing his only kin, and their ancestors' spirits demanded Chen's safety; monks could neither marry nor father children. So Yuan left the monastery before he had shaved his head or taken robes. He swallowed the disappointment. No longer had he the comfort of having a plotted future; instead, uncertainty filled the long voyage aboard a steamship. Family came before all other things, even the promise of the Pure Land, that unearthly realm where Amita Buddha would teach him the path to Enlightenment.

The swallow finally settled on a cornice of a thickset stone building with wide steps. But neither of the pair had mentioned that so many white men would be coming and going through its door. He opened his hand and regarded the key, now warm with his touch. It occurred to him that neither Hang-ne nor Buren had locked the hatchet away. So then who would keep something from powerful spirits, and why?

He watched the site from across the street for a while. Not a single Han or Tang had entered. Yuan knew well enough that certain places in San Francisco were only for the whites. Perhaps forcing him to cross the threshold was a test of courage.

He recalled the words of his mother. *Fire draws the eye first, smoke last.* Better to be subtle than bold.

He waited until one prosperous American began walking toward the door and then quickly moved behind him, close enough so that to onlookers he would appear as the man's faithful servant. Few would question a menial following his master.

Inside, he found many uniformed men. Yuan had never had any dealings with a policeman, even the ones that patrolled Chinatown. He shied away from everyone and took to walking slowly, pressed up against the wall.

One officer noticed him and motioned for him to come over to where the man stood. Yuan hesitated, unsure if he should comply or feign ignorance. He finally shuffled closer. The man spoke some English at him, little of which Yuan understood. The youth began nodding and mumbling "Yes" over and over; he had observed other countrymen dissuade the attention of whites with such a tactic. But the officer grabbed him by the arm and began pulling him toward the front doors. Yuan expected to be thrown out. At the last moment though, someone nearby called out to the man who held him. The officer looked torn between pushing Yuan out the door and dealing with the other man, but whatever duty called him won. He shoved Yuan forward and then left with his fellows.

As soon as the officer turned away, Yuan hid around a corner. As he calmed himself with some silent chanting, he tapped the key to his chin rhythmically. He glanced down the hall facing him. At the nearest door, he tried the lock. The key turned effortlessly. Yuan smiled. Perhaps Amita Buddha showed favor on his selfless cause. Cautiously, he opened the door enough so his gaunt form could slip through.

The room he found himself in opened to another hall, this one holding rows of cages. Against the far wall another officer rested on a chair tipped back.

Sitting on a dingy mat on the floor of the first cage was a fellow countryman.

The guard opened his eyes. "What you doin' here?"

"Here for brother," Yuan replied in more broken English than he normally dared. As he hid the key up his sleeve, he lifted an arm toward the man in the cell. Amita Buddha would forgive him, as he had not truly uttered a falsehood.

"If that's your brother, you've a sad family." The man laughed harshly.

Curious, Yuan slowly walked over to the cell, wary of the guard, who watched and seemed almost amused.

The man inside looked as old as Yuan's father. But he could never recall seeing the elder Ji as battered. Blood stained an ear, and the left eye was so swollen it had clamped shut. His clothes were tattered but had once been respectable—not like the rags Yuan wore.

He called out to the man, who might have been dozing or meditating.

A single eye opened. "Has the Tong arranged my release?"

"The Tong?" Yuan knew little of the Tongs—secretive societies involved in crimes—and what he did, interested him about as much as embracing a snake.

"If you do not know, then you are not from them," the man said with a groan.

"Perhaps they have sent someone as you say."

"No. I am paying for my foolishness. They have abandoned me, their best hatchet man, to rot in jail."

When he heard the man's words, Yuan felt as if he had been struck by a fist and he clutched hold of the cool iron bars, which caused the man in uniform to yell and rise from his seat. Yuan backed away and meekly apologized again and again. He left the jail feeling that he was the fool.

As he started back on the path toward Chinatown, he inwardly cursed the pair for tricking him—not only with the truth behind their "hatchet" but for wanting him to release an obvious criminal, a dangerous man, which would have been horrible for his karma.

Unless the man was innocent. He stopped to consider this,

but the very idea that the pair would have so misled him to perform a noble act seemed unsound.

"Returning empty-handed?"

Yuan looked around. In the doorway of a white medicine shop stood Hang-ne. He knew he should ignore her, that nothing good could come from listening to her, as her words would no doubt be sweet but lies. Still, the youth could not resist his tongue.

"I should have known better than bargain with evil spirits. I remember now the saying. 'Great souls have wills, feeble souls have wishes.'"

She casually waved her hand in the air, as if the remark were an annoying fly. "Please, show me a man without wishes, and I will know he's in the ground. Consider that some things are best left unspoken. How can one tell the truth unless discovered for oneself?"

"So you would have me become a criminal for freeing one."

"I would have you save your brother for releasing one." Her face took on an almost maternal countenance. "I can see Chen," she said, her jade gaze no longer on him or the surrounding crowd but raised to the sky. "Poor boy. Limbs too feeble to rise, breath shallow like a dying carp's. He would wallow on the soiled mat had he the strength. He waits for you. Though his dreams are raw, aching for release, he knows your presence makes life bearable." She looked at him and her eyes seemed to possess an unnatural glow. "How long will you sanction his suffering?"

Hang-ne held up a horn bowl. "Inside here is *lingzhi*. Heavenly fodder that will heal all your brother's ills, return him to the best of health. Save his life, earn him more years than his late Majesty, the Emperor Qianlong." She lifted the lid and brought it close to his face.

He peeked inside. The herb looked so simple, unassuming, like some root anyone might dig up for the pot. Perhaps, he wondered, all magic needed deception.

"All you have to do is fulfill our request and return Chaap the Hatchet to us. Alive. His breath ensures your brother will breathe tomorrow."

"And if I choose to walk away from all this?"

"Then I shall curse your brother. He will not live to see the rains come." She motioned as if to dump the bowl's contents, but at the last moment switched it to her other hand.

He could not let his brother die. He had not crossed the sea, not taken up with white barbarians, only to lose the last of his family. "Then I have no choice."

Hang-ne nodded. "Such a clever child." She stepped back into the crowd of passersby and he quickly lost sight of her.

He turned back toward the jail but had only walked a block before his steps faltered. The most wonderful smells held him. He snorted the air greedily. Drool fell from his slack jaw, his belly moaned and rolled like a wounded animal.

"I remember the first time that I heard this land called Gold Mountain." Buren's voice carried through the masses of people passing by. "What a wondrous name. I knew then that any wager with a coolie would be most entertaining."

The crowd on the street parted and seemed to stand in a daze. Buren sat at the head of a long table covered in expensive linen. Gilded platters covered every inch of the tabletop. Yuan saw a roasted pig with an apple stuffed in its mouth, calf tongue, cooked birds, some with feathers still clinging to the glazed flesh. Bowls of soups and stews, dishes of sweetmeats and candied treats. Much of the food he had never seen before, yet he could well imagine the sumptuous tastes as his nose caught and devoured the essence of each and every dish.

Buren tied a napkin around his neck. "Well step closer." He lifted up a tankard of beer and blew the foam from the top. "Come now, Ji, I won't bite." He laughed. "Not when I have all this." So saying, the spirit tore a leg free from a duck. A flap of succulent skin, oozing grease, dangled from the meat.

Yuan took a few hesitant steps, more fearful of breaking down, becoming a ravenous beast, losing his mind and eating and eating without end, than scared of Buren.

"I know back there you went yellow—" Buren stopped, and suddenly guffawed so deeply, saliva sprayed over the table. He did this for quite a while as Yuan ground his teeth together in frustration. The youth's hands clenched and unclenched and he had begun to wonder if the spirit would notice just a small morsel missing, when the man's laughter died down to a few chuckles and Buren could speak again.

"Yes, yellow. But my esteemed associate told you what would happen if you did not bring the Hatchet back." As he said it, he cracked the leg bone and sucked at the marrow.

Yuan nodded.

"Good, good. But Hang-ne did not tell you everything. You see, this is more than an amusement to us. There are stakes."

"And what is the wager?"

Buren belched loudly. No one else on the street seemed to pay attention. "The little woman is more than an associate, Ji. She's a rival, too. An enchanting rival." He threw the bone over his shoulder. "Someday you'll understand."

Yuan swallowed the insult. "So what you are saying is—"

"Go ahead and bring the Hatchet back to the shop, but I want him brought back dead."

Yuan stepped back; the shock at such a grim request, so casually made while Buren sipped soup from a bowl, drove away thoughts of the tasty food. "Kill him?"

Buren nodded. His beard gleamed wet. "Your reward will be far greater than anything Hang-ne can offer. I rule this California, have so ever since the settlers needed to barter souls for firewood and water. I'm offering great prosperity for you and your descendants. They will never want for food, always have coins in their pocket . . . California will always treat them well, I swear."

Another promise. Yuan wondered if he could trust either spirit. "And if I refuse?"

Buren shrugged and lifted up a tureen lid. "Hunger and poverty will be the only things served at your table, your children's table, your grandchildren's table. Do not tell me you are so cruel?"

"But dead?"

"He's a thug. What do you care if he lives or dies?" Buren sunk his teeth into a handful of meat and bloody juice ran down his wrist.

Yuan opened his mouth to say something when a horse's whinny broke the air. He turned around and barely dodged the hooves as a rider passed by. When he looked back Buren and his feast had vanished.

His mouth tasted bitter and sour. The thought of having to . . . no, he refused to consider it. Any children he had would suffer the shame that their father was a murderer. Buren did not understand filial piety, the devotion family demanded and the honor in accepting such duty. What allegiances, what loyalties did an American spirit possess? Yuan thought none.

He had to free Chaap. That he knew. But he would not do disservice to his ancestors, nor risk never entering the Pure Land. His brother, once healed by the herb, would see to it that he did not suffer so badly.

When he saw the jail he wished he had never desired the wealth and fortune that Gold Mountain promised. It had been all a lie, one piled atop another. He should never have believed the letters, the stories about life in the New World.

As Yuan climbed the jailhouse's steps, he saw an officer, perhaps the same one who accosted him before, call out to him. The youth hesitated, unsure what to do. Then something flew down into the face of the man. The swallow Hang-ne had conjured. A grateful Yuan used the distraction to reach the door and slip inside.

He found the guard asleep, a bottle of liquor half-hidden under the desk. The hatchet man glanced up but, seeing it was Yuan again, curled back on the mat. Only when the youth called out his name did he rise.

"Tell me your crime."

"Why? Do you seek to torment me? Who are you?"

"Tell me and I shall set you free." He held up the strange key, confident that it would unlock any door that led to the Hatchet.

Chaap walked over to the cell door. "I have been in Gold Mountain for many years. With the help of the Tong, I wanted for little. Coin, food, respect, all due me. One thing I lacked. A woman who would become my wife, keep my home, bear me sons. The Americans do not want us to marry, you know. That is why there are so few Chinese women here. So I heard of a magical pair that would grant wishes . . ."

Yuan felt the key's teeth bite his hand as he inadvertently squeezed. Why should he be so surprised? He should expect nothing and everything from those two spirits. They played their games, waged their little war, with anyone desperate enough, foolish enough, to enlist their help.

"Are you all right, my friend?" Chaap reached out and grasped Yuan by the shoulder. For a moment, the youth worried that the man's grip would tighten and force him to open the door. But once he had recovered, the hand left him.

"Yes, I am fine," he lied. He felt light-headed. He wished he had stolen some food from Buren's table, and then felt ashamed.

"Well, I went to them, and they agreed to aid me. They found me a wonderful woman, who they made fall in love with me at once. She lives on Waverly Place. But before I could go to her, they needed a favor in return."

"What did they ask you?"

"They told me to take my hatchet, which had only known service for the Tong, and chop at the wheels of a carriage. A small price, wrecking the property of a white man, I thought, for a dutiful wife."

"Yet not so small after all."

Chaap shook his head. "Not when it is the mayor's carriage, not when it crashes. Not when people come forward seeing you there."

Yuan stepped back. He had hoped that he would hear Chaap's story and discover him innocent, but that had been a childish hope. The man was guilty. Across the sea, a man taking an ax to a county magistrate's property would find himself beheaded. Chaap should be punished rather than be rewarded with freedom. Even a white man did not deserve to go unavenged.

As he unlocked the door, Yuan could feel a sense of heaviness about his limbs, as if the weight of the deed dragged him further from the blessing of the Pure Land.

"So tell me how you came to have that key?"

The youth leaned against the cage door. "The pair gave it to me."

"The pair? So they seek to make amends for the mischief done to me."

Seeing a smile on the battered face made Yuan feel worse, and he remained silent. Why deceive him? "We should go back to them."

"Indeed, I will, but first I would claim my wife."

"No—"

"Thank you, my friend, for being the hand that rescued me. I hope one day to repay your help."

Chaap ran for the door. When Yuan moved to stop him, the world seemed to tilt, to slip out from underneath him. He found himself on the floor, blinking and nursing a bump on the back of his head. The Hatchet was gone.

Yuan looked at the coin on the floor by the cage. What had once been a key was no more. He did not trust its magic and so left it in front of the policeman who still snored off his drink.

Back in Chinatown, Yuan found Chaap sitting on the dirt in front of a building with a cheerfully painted balcony. The man had his head down, as if defeated or once more awaiting an executioner. He expected Chaap to run when he went up to him, but he barely moved.

"I am a fool," the hatchet man muttered. "Bring me back to jail. I deserve my fate."

"What has happened here?"

"Peer into the window and you will see her."

Chaap refused to say anything more, so Yuan slowly piled some old crates and debris that would allow him something nearly steady to stand upon. He worried that he might faint once more and topple off, but he had to know the truth, at least the truth about something.

The window looked into a small writing room. He could just make out a dark-haired woman sitting in a corner chair, reading a book. Piles of papers, loose rolled scrolls, and stacks of more books surrounded her. Yuan had never seen so many kept words in all his life.

The wooden box he stood upon creaked and he glanced down to see a board split beneath his feet. When he turned back to the window, a horrible face inches from his own startled him. He cried out, confronted with wild black eyes, a muzzle, and horns like some cross between dog and dragon. The beast barked, and Yuan lost his balance, toppling off the pile. If not for Chaap quickly catching him, the youth would have struck the street.

"You saw her?" The hatchet man helped Yuan to his feet.

Yuan looked back at the window and shuddered. "Yes, yes."

"I cannot marry her."

"Of course not."

"My family, my friends, they would all laugh at me."

"Laugh? They would begin your funeral."

"'Poor Chaap,' they would say." The man sat back on the ground.

"A wife like that . . ."

Chaap nodded. "All those words in her head."

"Words? What about the horns?"

The hatchet man turned to Yuan. "What are you talking about?"

"She is a monster."

Chaap shrugged. "Worse than that. She is learned. Probably far more than the men taking exams back home. What man wants a learned wife? Who will cook and clean? Not her. She would be full of ideas and strange notions."

Yuan listened, feeling lost. Had Chaap not seen the same woman, the one with the terrible face? Or had he been the mistaken one?

"All that I did was for nothing. A curse upon those two!" The man rubbed his arm. "Pity they took away my hatchet."

The words reached in and crushed Yuan's heart. How would he ever be able to convince a betrayed Chaap to return to the pair's shop now? Through force? Even battered, the man outweighed Yuan by countless *jin* and could easily overpower him. He had failed. Failed the lying spirits, his sick brother, brought dishonor to his ancestors, as their ghosts would suffer without descendants who would pay tribute to their memory.

He nearly collapsed on the ground next to Chaap, and realized that any passersby might mistake the two for father and son, both distraught over some hardship. But Yuan knew that neither of them were likely to have family after that day.

If only he had been as wise as his mother had believed him to be. He closed his eyes and tried to think, to ignore the groans coming from the man next to him or his stomach beneath. He calmed himself, chanting *"a-mi-ta-bha"* softly again and again.

A proverb which one of the monks was fond of came to

mind. *Distant water won't quench your immediate thirst.* Yuan knew this referred to working with what little he had rather than chasing after things. Perhaps there might be some way to convince the girl to come along. A smile from her might be enough to sway Chaap.

"Please wait here," he said to the hatchet man, and entered the building.

Yuan hoped the door he knocked on was the right one. A stout middle-aged man opened it after the second rap. By his simple dark clothes, Yuan guessed him to be a servant.

Yuan bowed slightly. "I am in desperate need to speak with your mistress."

The servant looked him up and down and scowled slightly. "I can take any message to her." He did not step aside.

"This involves her betrothed."

The man's brow furrowed. "I have heard nothing from my queen, Hang-ne, of this." He began to close the door in Yuan's face.

"Wait."

The servant paused. "Be warned, mortal child, I can smell a lie." He bared sharp yellow teeth. At the sight, Yuan nearly forgot what he intended to say next.

"They sent me. I have the Hatchet down below." He prayed that there was more truth than falsehood in his words to satisfy whatever thing the servant was.

What had once been an ordinary face transformed into the awful head that had peered at him from the window. The muzzle sniffed the air a moment. Yuan gasped.

"Enter," growled the servant, his face slowly returning to that of a man.

He led Yuan through small, cramped rooms filled with precious statues, paintings, and maps.

With a strong arm he pushed the youth down to sit on a hard bench. "A moment and you may see her."

Yuan judged the girl who came out to be as old as Chen, perhaps even as old as himself. Swathed in layers of costly silks and gold bands, her slight frame looked more burdened by the wealth than exalted. Her ivory-painted face held an expression of sadness.

"You have news of Geng Chaap?"

He bowed very low before answering, "I do."

She nodded her willingness to hear.

Yuan breathed in deeply and hoped that he had heard enough gilded tongues that day to lacquer his own. "The most honorable and favored Chaap waits down below for his beloved." Standing in a far doorway, he glimpsed the servant. "He wishes to present you to the great spirits, Hang-ne and Buren," he quickly added.

She brought a hand up to cover her mouth.

"Are you nervous? Have no fear. Geng Chaap has gathered much attention to himself these past few days. Even the Americans know him, and their men in uniform have guarded his life." His words seemed to cause her more distress and he watched as a single tear formed in the corner of her eye.

He went on both knees. "Please, let me know what I have done to sadden you so."

"I have not met Geng Chaap but I have met Hang-ne. It was she that took me from my home and brought me here."

Yuan waited patiently, sure she would tell more.

"My father is a minister in Gansu. He has no son and

humored my childhood wish to study." She lightly touched a nearby scroll. "Now he must mourn me as dead and consider himself punished."

"But why?"

"One night a woman whom I had never met before came to our household. She handed me a message, one that read I was to be married to a stranger. By the time I had finished reading, I found myself elsewhere. Here."

Stolen away, Yuan thought, all because Chaap hungered for a wife. He suddenly felt shame that he had attempted to trick her. He had acted no better than the spirits had.

"Hang-ne conjured a foo dog to keep me from escaping." She turned in the direction of the servant, who bowed at her. "He watches over me until the wedding."

"Forgive me." He brought his head low to the floorboards.

"For what?"

"For speaking falsely. I clothed my words so they would sound true. We have all been misled by spirits and I would not deceive you further. The one they have promised you to . . . I do not know him well, but I know his duty. He is a hatchet man, a thug, for a Tong."

He expected her to cry out in horror, perhaps even run, but she merely nodded sadly. "Mencius once said, 'We survive on adversity and perish in ease and comfort.' I can do no less."

Her acceptance of fate made his heart ache. If only there was some way to save them both. His thoughts began to gnaw at the idea.

"Unless . . ." Yuan said, rising to his feet. "I am no sage. You know the minds of many great men and may laugh at what I offer—"

"Your name."

"What?"

"I would know your name first before you say more."

He blushed. "Ji Yuan."

She nearly smiled. He suddenly yearned to see her do so and foolish thoughts of songs and tricks that might accomplish that came to mind.

"You were saying?"

"Chaap has no love for a wife wiser than him. You have no desire to marry him." He bit his lip, unsure of how much he should tell her. Part of him wanted to reveal everything, but for the sake of his brother's life he dared not. "There may be a way to convey all this to the spirits beyond such mischief." Yuan grabbed a nearby writing brush and a loose sheet of rice paper. "If you were to write him a letter, one that said his deeds have broken your heart, that he is now dead to you . . . trust me, things would be set right."

She regarded him in silence for what seemed like hours before taking the brush from his hand. "I have seen some wondrous things these past few days." She went over to a table, sweeping clean the top with her arm. "Can I not believe you are able to work miracles, too?" She bent down and poured a few drops of water onto the grinding stone, then pressed the ink stick. Moments later, she began to write.

The servant walked him to the door. Before the girl had handed over the folded note, she leaned in close. "Li Ming," she whispered with another near-smile. Her name, Yuan realized. He chanted it several times as he came down the steps.

Chaap remained outside, half-asleep. Yuan nudged the man with his foot. Before he told the hatchet man why they needed to return to the spirits' shop, he prayed once more to Amita Buddha that He might show just a little kindness to a fool's mission.

As the setting sun tinted the western sky shades of crimson, Yuan and the hatchet man found the shades drawn on the shop's windows. The youth worried he might be too late, but the door opened at his touch.

The pair waited for him. Buren sat behind his desk with his feet propped up on the top. Hang-ne leaned against hers. Both held slender glasses filled with an amber drink. A bucket of ice with a bottle inside rested on the strange hide between them.

Chaap seemed smaller and remained close to the door.

"Our Hatchet returns and apparently I win," Hang-ne said before taking a long sip.

"I'm always amazed that a brother could inspire such devotion." Buren put down his glass.

"Didn't you sell yours?"

He shrugged and sighed. "So, Ji, enjoy your brother's company, as it will be the sole comfort to you and your sons."

Yuan told himself to be calm, strong, that his plan would work. "I am afraid you are wrong."

"Oh?" Buren raised bushy eyebrows. "Unless you have brought us a ghost . . ."

Yuan handed the letter to Hang-ne. She glanced at it, then looked up with a measure of distrust before reading on.

"What's it say?" Buren asked.

She crumpled the note, her fingernails looking longer, sharper, like talons. "Unfair," she spat.

"I thought some things were best left unspoken," Yuan said, unable to resist smiling.

She held out the letter to Buren, who unfolded it. He started laughing. "Brilliant, Ji, far better than a ghost."

He had not expected the compliment. Wary that the pair might worm their way out of the deal, he voiced his claim. "So bringing back your hatchet man both alive and dead means I've earned both your gifts."

"I don't remember the last time someone swindled me. Or you, Hang-ne."

"No one would dare." Hang-ne seemed taller, broader than before.

"A woman scorned." Buren drained his glass and reached for the bottle.

"Scorned? Cheated!" She pointed a claw at Yuan. Her eyes burst into emerald flames. "I preyed upon fools for thousands of years. Your ancestors still plowed the dirt with their bare hands when I walked down from the Himalayas to the Middle Kingdom."

Chaap began whimpering and fell to his knees, begging for mercy. Yuan took a step back.

"I shall start with your limbs, slowly working my way to your chest, plucking out a rib at a time." Her fingers twitched with anticipation.

But as Hang-ne lunged forward, the champagne bottle intervened, jabbing her in the stomach. She doubled over, clutching her middle.

"Sorry, m'dear."

"Buren," she gasped.

The American spirit dropped the bottle and turned to

Yuan. "Clever, Ji. You knew I'd save you in the end."

Yuan nodded. On the inside, though, he trembled. "You swore that my children would be prosperous. There'd be no risk of her hurting me then." But up until the moment Buren acted, Yuan had not been utterly sure the spirit would intervene.

"At least allow a little maiming." Her eyes had returned to their normal lustrous jade green.

"No." Buren stepped between them. "Nothing that might impair his future. Even I have rules."

And honor, Yuan thought. Perhaps Gold Mountain held the promises his brother dreamt of after all.

Hang-ne straightened her dress and hair with normal fingers. "Have a care, Ji Yuan. I would not want to see you again."

She opened an unseen drawer in her desk and lifted out the bowl. He cautiously took it from her. He dared not check the contents.

Buren clapped his hands, and the sound echoed, transforming into thick laughter and the clink of spilt coins. Suddenly gilded dishes covered his desk. Yuan did not hesitate this time to grab the food, clutching a roasted hen that would more than feed his brother and him. He stuffed warm rolls into his shirt.

"What of Chaap?" he asked.

"Oh, perhaps another wife would be better," Buren remarked.

"Isn't Hsen the rat catcher recently a widow?" Hang-ne offered.

The hatchet man cried out and opened the doors, fleeing into the streets.

～　～　～

Yuan ran as fast as he dared through the darkening streets of San Francisco. When he arrived at the dilapidated building in Chinatown where he lived, a crowd stood outside, blocking his view of the door. Suddenly, he thought that he might be too late. After all he had gone through, it had not been enough. He pushed his way through the mass of people, spilling some food as he went but keeping a white-fingered grasp on the bowl with the miraculous herb.

In the center sat the strangest dog Yuan had ever seen, thick haunched and short-haired except for a curling mane around its head. It faced the building, ignoring the stares and whispers of the men, women, and children surrounding it. But when Yuan approached, it turned and the panting muzzle and black eyes were all too familiar. The foo dog barked, as if greeting him. The crowd turned to Yuan with interest.

Uncomfortable being watched by everyone, and eager to see his brother, Yuan guessed that the beast had been sent by Li Ming and not the two spirits.

The youth leaned down until inches away from the foo dog's muzzle. He glimpsed the hint of sharp teeth. "Tell your mistress I would be more than honored to meet her again, but after I tend to my brother, Chen."

The dog nodded and barked again. The crowd split to make room as it ran off.

After climbing the rickety steps and emerging into a dark hall, Yuan returned to his cramped room. Rows of sallow faces along the walls looked up at him. The smells of food brought murmurs and hungry looks.

Chen had not moved since early this morning. He tried to rise and greet his brother but failed to leave the dirty mat he lay on. Yuan lifted the lid on the bowl and took out the *lingzhi*, feeding it slowly to Chen. With every bite his brother's jaws seemed stronger, more determined.

A little girl came over to where Yuan sat and tugged at his sleeve before asking for a roll. He handed it over and she rushed back to her family, sharing it among them.

He felt another pull on his shirt and expected it to be someone else, but when he turned he saw Chen, sitting upright, perhaps for the first time in days, his eyes clear as he hoarsely asked for more.

Yuan laughed, the sound seeming so foreign amid such a dismal setting. Yet those around him smiled, too. "Of course, brother. There is more. From now on, I think there will always be more."

STEVE BERMAN sold his first short story when he was seventeen. Since then, his work has appeared in several anthologies, including *The Faery Reel* and *Japanese Dreams*. His debut novel, *Vintage, A Ghost Story*, was a finalist for the Andre Norton Award. He recently edited an anthology of young adult fantasy stories, *Magic in the Mirrorstone*. Steve lives in southern New Jersey with a most demanding familiar.

～

AUTHOR'S NOTE

I am indebted to the real Mr. Ji for "Wagers of Gold Mountain"—Xiao-ben Ji, my professor of Asian Studies. Through five classes he held me enthralled with lessons on Chinese custom and history. I knew I had to write a story to thank him for all his teachings. Because the story is set in mid-nineteenth-century San Francisco, I felt the need to include not only a Chinese trickster, Hang-ne, but also a decidedly American one in the figure of Buren. Both originated in a blend of legend and imagination; there is in Tibetan mythology a demon named Hang-ne, and Buren is a magical version of P. T. Barnum.

THE LISTENERS

~

Nina Kiriki Hoffman

It was hot in the women's quarters under the roof, even though the sun had gone down an hour ago. No breeze came through the small, high window to stir the air and give a breath of night. The flames of the oil lamps were steady as weighted threads. The air smelled of dust, sweat, and olives. The mistress, her eight-year-old daughter Panthea, three other female slaves, and Nysa sat spinning thick thread for winter cloth on this summer evening.

They had the door of the main room open, listening to the men in the men's room below. The men had finished their meal at dusk, and afterward a hetaera named Kalonike played melodies for them on a double flute. She was a pleasure woman famous for her musical ability; only the wealthiest could afford to hire her. The master was entertaining someone important tonight.

Nysa, at fourteen the youngest slave in the household, loved the melodies; she tried to hold them in her mind. Her mistress wouldn't allow her to get out her flute and try them tonight, not while the women were all listening for news, not while the men might hear. Nysa teased brown wool into thread between her fingers as her drop spindle whirled between her knees. Some women's work could be done in silence, the better to listen to the world below.

The music ended. Coins clinked against the mosaic floor of the men's room, and the soft voice of the famous hetaera murmured thanks and good night. One of the male slaves escorted her across the courtyard and let her out through the gateway.

Now the men were talking, but they were only one or two bowls drunk, not loud enough for the women to hear the conversation.

"Nysa," the mistress said, "go find out what the men are saying."

Nysa twisted her thread in a loop so it wouldn't unravel, then set her drop spindle on the floor, stood, and stretched. She slipped out the door and crept along the upper balcony, which looked out over the central courtyard. Lamplight spilled from the open door of the men's room across the way, lying like dusty gold over the family altar, where the household made a daily offering to Zeus and their patron gods. Shadows and laughter came from the room. Nysa huddled against the railing of the balcony perpendicular to the men's room, hugging her knees and peeking through the slats for a glimpse of the forbidden. The men reclined on couches around the walls of the room, with small tables in front of them. Multiple-wicked lamps on the tables warmed plates of food. Two of the male slaves walked from table to table, offering watered wine and a platter of olives to the diners.

"Doesn't it trouble you to treat people like animals?" asked one of the men. He had a barbarian accent she couldn't identify.

"What are you talking about? Hey, Megakles, bring that wine pitcher over here," the master said.

"These slaves," said the barbarian.

Kyprios came out of the room, an empty platter in his hands. He crossed to the kitchen with it. He was the handsomest of the male slaves in the household, but he knew his own beauty too well. He used it to get things from free men and citizens. Sometimes he came away from men's nights with gifts or coin. He never shared.

"We don't treat slaves like animals," said the master. "I don't let donkeys into my house. I don't let lions work in my kitchen. I don't let hounds weave my wool or press my olives or tread my grapes. We treat them like slaves. They are far more worthwhile than animals."

"In my country, we do not keep slaves."

"Your country must be poor, then. Megakles, pour more wine for our untutored guest. Have you ever tasted such a lovely flavor? We grow the best grapes in the region."

"Drakon," said Aristides to the master, "I noticed your youngest female slave in the market yesterday, attending Megakles while he shopped. Will you breed her soon?"

"Nysa? I don't know. Perhaps. She's fourteen; old enough, surely. She has a sharp eye—spots cheats at the market faster than anyone else in the household, has a swift hand at weaving, and she's musical—"

"And attractive," said Aristides. He was the master's closest friend. Nysa hid in the women's quarters if she could whenever he visited. She liked neither his hands nor his eyes on her. "If she were a free woman, I might write poetry to her. Since she's not, may I pay you to use her?"

The master laughed, and murmured something too low for

her to hear. Then he said, "She has the makings of a useful and productive slave. I don't know that I want to spoil her with childbirth yet."

"I could make it worth your while," said Aristides. "For your love of me, won't you grant me this boon?"

Nysa's hands clenched into fists.

"Do you want your child to nest in the womb of a slave?" asked someone else. "Let it be born a slave? Put it in your wife's womb, where it belongs."

Yes, Nysa thought. Do that.

"My wife has given me three fine sons," said Aristides. "What I want now is pleasure, and that girl has the look I like, almost a boy in her slimness, and her face is radiant with youth, and unblemished."

"You speak like a man in love," said the master. His voice had softened. Aristides could coax him into or out of anything.

Fear lodged in Nysa's liver.

"Hsst!"

She glanced up. Eudokia, the senior female slave, beckoned to her from the doorway of the women's quarters. Nysa rose and crept to her. They went over the threshold and shut the door gently behind them.

"What are they discussing?" asked the mistress in a low voice.

"Nothing of merit. No politics, no business," Nysa murmured.

"No philosophy?"

Nysa smiled. They were all entertained by philosophy, but the mistress had a hunger for it. Whenever Nysa returned from the market, the mistress commanded her presence and made her repeat whatever strange theories the men in the stoa had been talking about that day. Some free men could spend all day talking to each other in the shade between the columns of the stoa; they didn't have to hurry from one vendor to the next to supply the household with fresh fish or figs or goat's cheese. "No philosophy," Nysa said. "They're only speaking of women not their wives. There's some barbarian there who doesn't know our customs."

"Drakon said he invited a wood trader to his symposion tonight. Someone from the north, almost over the edge of the world. Did my husband speak of a woman not his wife?" The mistress's tone sharpened on the last question.

"No. It was Aristides only."

"Aristides." The word was cold even in the hot night air of the women's quarters. Nysa had not known that the mistress, too, disliked her husband's closest friend.

Shouts of laughter rang out in the courtyard. Eudokia eased the door open to let in light and air and sound again, and the women quieted. The jests were louder and cruder as the men dipped more deeply into the wine.

Nysa took up her spindle. With every wool ball she spun into thread, she prayed to Hermes, god of merchants, thieves, and travelers. Help me, she prayed. Oh, swift-footed Hermes, guide and guardian, who leads the souls of the dead to their final home, lead me out of the life I have now. Help me steal myself.

In the house where Nysa was born, before her first mistress sold her away from her mother, she had a sister, Kore, who was ten years older than Nysa. Kore danced at men's gatherings in the evenings. When Nysa watched Kore practice dancing, her heart rose up, and a taste crossed her tongue that was sweet and sour at once: Kore was too close to perfect. She was more than a slave. She was beauty walking.

One of the guests of the house saw Kore and wanted her.

Nysa was only five or six. She didn't know what negotiations took place. She only knew that later, her sister was too sick to dance, and then she grew big with child, and that child killed her. Mother didn't want her to see, but Nysa had to say farewell to her sister; she would not be kept out of the room where her sister's body lay. She saw all the blood.

The baby was alive, but the master didn't want it. He had no wet nurses in the house at the time and didn't want the bother of hiring one, so he took the baby out to the hillside where people left unwanted children to die.

That night Nysa couldn't sleep. She heard her sister's screams every time she closed her eyes. Finally she got up and crept to the altar in the courtyard. She nicked her finger with a paring knife and let the blood fall among the ashes of the daily fire. She prayed to Artemis that she would remain a childless virgin the rest of her life.

She prayed, but she didn't believe the goddess listened. No one listened to the prayers of slaves.

Before the sun was driven up over the eastern hills the next morning, Eudokia and Nysa took water jugs to the public fountain. Nysa liked the lion spout, but Eudokia favored the donkey spout. The lion spout ran slower, which gave Nysa more time to visit with other slaves and resident foreigners who were out on the same errand.

Lyris was a friend Nysa had made in her first household, the oldest slave Nysa had ever met, and still going out after water, though she had lost height and hair and teeth, and her hands were gnarled and twisted with age. She was there that morning, ahead of Nysa in line for the lion spout. When Lyris saw Nysa, she stepped out of line and joined Nysa at the end.

"Nysa, how are you?" Lyris asked as the women ahead of them gossiped about a man who had bought more sheep than he could pay for, and another whose wife paid her slave to sneak a man into her house when the husband was at the market, how the sounds of her lovemaking with the stranger were wilder than those she made with her husband.

"She cries aloud like a seagull," said one woman to the other.

"I am well," Nysa told Lyris. "My mistress is kind. The food is good, and there's enough of it."

"This is always your answer, but today your eyes say something else," Lyris said. They moved forward. The night-chilled earth was cold against the soles of Nysa's feet. Smoke rose from hidden courtyards in the centers of pale, red-tile-roofed houses all around them, into the lightening sky as households started their days with fire at the altars. The gods would be rich in smoke.

"I always hoped to have a skill," Nysa murmured.

Lyris nodded, her veiled head only shoulder height to Nysa.

"I play the flute. Not as well as Kalonike the Hetaera, but I know I can learn. I could entertain; I could play for festivals."

"Yes," said Lyris, and nudged her forward.

Nysa glanced toward the other line, where Eudokia stood, her empty jug sideways on her head as she spoke to her friend from next door.

"The mistress lets me sit with her and spin while she teaches

Panthea to read and write, so I have learned that as well. I could be a scribe or a messenger."

"We are running out of time for your point," Lyris said. There were only two women ahead of them in line now.

"I have never wanted to be a prostitute, but I fear the master will make me into one," Nysa whispered quickly.

"There are worse things," said Lyris.

Nysa stared into Lyris's eyes.

"A beating is worse. Being beaten for no reason is worse still. Being owned by someone who enjoys giving pain is a bad thing. Being a prostitute is not pleasant, especially at first, but the work is often over quickly, and sometimes you are given coin or favors in addition to whatever the man will pay your master."

Nysa's mouth opened, but no words came out. At Nysa's old household, Lyris was the best spinner and the best weaver. She could put patterns into the hems of cloth without having to consult a diagram. Nysa had imagined Lyris had always spun and wove.

Lyris gave her a merry smile. "Though you might not credit it, I was young once, and pretty."

"I am afraid," Nysa said. "I can't forget my sister."

Lyris set her jug on the ledge below the lion fountain; the spout sent water into it. "As to that, if you miss your courses, tell me, and I'll help you get rid of the child before it can harm you. I know all the herbs and doses."

"I don't want this fate."

"If it's fate, there's no escape." They stood silent while water gurgled into Lyris's pitcher, and then Lyris reached into a small purse hanging from her belt and took something out. "Perhaps it isn't fate yet," she said, holding out her hand.

Nysa reached out, and Lyris dropped something in her palm. Nysa closed her hand around it and hid her hand under her cloak, hoping no one had noticed.

She filled her pitcher and said farewell to Lyris.

As Nysa and Eudokia walked back to the house, Eudokia asked what Lyris had given Nysa, but she had hidden it already. "I don't know," she said. "I dropped it." Into her wallet.

"Why do you like that old woman, anyway?" Eudokia said. "She's like a crow, full of bad tidings."

"She's from my former household," Nysa said.

"Ah," said Eudokia.

Eudokia headed into the household to pour her water into one of the big hydria, water jugs they would draw from all day. Nysa stopped before the herm, guardian at the gate into the household's courtyard. In this form, the guardian had only a bearded face, which wore a benign smile, and his genitals; the rest of the god was a squared pillar. Nysa laid a corner of honey cake at the base of the herm, bowed her head, and passed inside.

Before she joined Eudokia in the kitchen, Nysa stopped against the wall, below the balcony where the mistress couldn't see her from the women's quarters upstairs, and took the thing Lyris had given her out of her wallet. It was a small, dark pressed brick of something about the size of her thumb. Nysa sniffed it; it didn't smell like anything to eat, but it had a strong fragrance that made her dizzy. Incense, she decided: a tribute to which god or goddess? Perhaps it was her choice. She tucked the incense in her wallet and took her pitcher into the kitchen to empty it, then went back to the public fountain for more.

∽   ∽   ∽

"Mistress, do the gods ever answer your prayers?" Nysa asked the mistress later that afternoon, when it was so hot all the women rested in the women's quarters, and some slept. Nysa had a pallet on the floor near the mistress's couch. The other slaves were actually asleep, she thought; no one had said anything for a while. They had let down the shade to cover the window so hot sunlight would not come in, and no lamps nor candles burned.

Nysa would have to get up soon and go down to the kitchen to grind grain for tomorrow's bread, but just now she rested.

"I have a fine son," the mistress said. Diomed, her boy, ten years old, was off at school all day, and spent his evenings with his father. One of the slaves in the household, a tall, bearded man named Telestes, was Diomed's paidogogus, his attendant; Telestes followed the boy to school and made sure he paid attention to his teachers. Telestes was an educated man, a captive of war who had been crippled in the fighting and sold rather than slaughtered. Sometimes Telestes tutored Diomed.

"I have a fine son, so that was one prayer answered," the mistress said. "I prayed for a second son, and that prayer was answered with a dead child."

Someone in the afternoon darkness groaned—whether from a dream or a memory, Nysa did not know.

The mistress had been recovering from the loss of her second child when Nysa came to the house. The mistress was a wild woman in those days, once she stopped being so sick she could not rise from her bed. Even after the fever left her, madness haunted her. She named the child, though it had not lived an hour, let alone the ten days a child should live before it received a name. She cut her hair in mourning, made herself a slave to her sorrow. It was all the four female slaves could do to keep her in her rooms, and Eudokia feared her wailing would be heard on the street, so she sealed all the windows up with sheepskin with the fur still on. They could scarcely breathe. Finally Eudokia, with the master's permission, fed the mistress poppy syrup to make her sleep.

The slaves found rest then, and after a course of given sleep and many dreams, the mistress found sanity. Eudokia had reminded her that Diomed, the son she already had, was too young to understand anything, and was distressed while his mother was mad. He was sheltered in a different room by the second senior female slave. The mistress regained her senses a little at a time. After a season she could embrace Diomed again; and then the master planted his seed in her, and she grew big with child a third time.

After three seasons of nightmares and nights full of apprehensive whispers and cries, the mistress gave birth to Panthea, who was a healthy child. Care for her daughter brought the mistress back from the precipice. Nysa felt as though she met her mistress for the first time.

Now in the afternoon darkness, Nysa had awakened the woman of nightmares and screams with her foolish question.

The mistress's tone turned meditative. "I was your age, fourteen, when I was to be wed, and then I prayed many times to Hera for a handsome husband. I never saw Drakon before we wed. The night of our wedding procession, he looked fine in the torchlight, an athlete with the face of Adonis. The next morning when I saw him by daylight, I still found his appearance pleasing, though what we had done in the marriage bed in darkness frightened and hurt me. Still, my prayers were answered. What the man was under the beautiful surface, well, Drakon is not so bad as others. My sister's husband, for instance."

Nysa had gone with the mistress to her sister's household. Of all the women the mistress visited, her sister was the one whose company she sought least. The household was small, with only two slaves. There was a stink of slops about the house that made it unpleasant, and flies lived there. The women's quarters were cramped and dark. The mistress's sister never burned more than one lamp. She sat far from it, huddling in the shadows, letting her guests enjoy the gleam of light.

While the mistress and her sister spoke, Nysa heard winces in the sister's whispering voice, small gasps, as if movement pained her. These were the sounds of someone who had been beaten. The slaves of the household also bore marks of beating and mistreatment. The cook's arm had been broken and healed badly. The guest cakes served the mistress were thin and without honey, and all the stories the sisters told each other were sad.

After one visit as they walked away from the house, the mistress had said, "She used to be my favorite sister, the one who danced, the one who laughed."

"All in all," the mistress said now, "I feel the gods have listened to me and treated me well. Not all my prayers have been answered, but the important ones were. Thanks to all gods and goddesses listening."

"Thanks for your answers, mistress," Nysa murmured.

Aristides came the next night for supper; he brought a younger man with him, Pelagios, a companion he often brought. The boy had been beardless before, but now dark hair grew along his jaw and below his nose.

Watching from the balcony above, Nysa saw Pelagios lay a hand on Aristides's shoulder, saw the way Aristides flinched it off.

The three men ate with only the slave Kyprios attending, and Pelagios left early. The conversation was too soft for Nysa to catch, though, with the mistress's permission, she spent the evening on the balcony above the men's room. Aristides stayed until the half moon set, and staggered as he left.

Nysa ground grain on a flat stone the next morning in the kitchen. Kyprios stopped beside her and spoke in a low voice. "They've negotiated your price. Aristides will have you tomorrow night."

Nysa clutched the grinding stone as though it were the only solid thing she knew. "Thank you," she whispered. Kyprios almost never spoke to the other slaves. As the master's favorite, he had a greater degree of freedom, and sometimes went off on errands that kept him out overnight. He had his own money, too. She wondered why he spoke to her. "Did he purchase me outright, or is it just the use of me he bought?"

"One night," said Kyprios. He wandered over to where the cook was taking fresh hot flatbreads from the pottery oven. Cook slapped his hand away from one, but he snatched another before she could stop him, and then he was out the door, laughing, juggling the bread from hand to hand.

Nysa poured the ground grain into a sieve and sifted the flour through the cloth into a pot, straining out the bran. She made all her motions without thought, she had done the job so many times before. Her mind fluttered.

Tomorrow he would take her, that toad, with his pinching

fingers and damp hands. If it were fate, there was nothing she could do about it but submit. Every day things like this happened, and the world went on just the same.

She set aside the pot of flour, put the husks into a basket, and poured new grain onto the flat stone. If it were fate—but what if it weren't? The little lump of incense Lyris had given her lay inside her wallet, against her hip. Tonight she would burn it after the household went to sleep.

The master went to someone else's symposion that night, leaving the mistress more freedom for music and play. Nysa played the double flute, trying to recapture the tunes Kalonike had played for the men. She had lost some of the phrases, and when the others tired of her stumbling attempts and asked for hymns and story songs, she played the ones they all knew. The mistress, feeling daring, asked Megakles to bring the game board upstairs. She had him set it on the balcony and invited him to teach the women how the pieces moved. He was scandalized but finally gave in to her teasing and chiding. Though he had seen the game played many times, he had never before played it himself, so everyone learned together how the pieces moved; the mistress proved quite clever in capturing her opponent's men.

Nysa watched and laughed with everyone else in the relaxed atmosphere that night. It took a long time for the mistress to tire and send everyone to their sleep, but the time finally came. Nysa lay down between the others and waited until she heard the slowed breath of sleepers all around her before she rose, put on her clothes, and stole outside and down the stairs.

The cook slept in the kitchen; her snores made Nysa feel safe in her silence. Nysa took a small pot from the pottery shelf and fished a still-glowing ember out of the oven into it, borrowed one of the small knives, dipped up a cup of watered wine, and ventured outside the household.

So late at night, all the households along the street were shut up and most of the torches snuffed; no sounds of singing or laughing came, even from the neighbors across the way, who usually had torches flickering in the courtyard later than anyone else, and whose slaves slept later in the morning, too. A few streets away some men called to each other in the slurred voices of those who had drunk too much, and farther away a night patrolman accosted someone for something, his tone strident.

Nysa knelt before the household herm. He was a dark pillar against the whitewashed wall beside the entrance, his face shadowed in the night. A small dog barked somewhere in the city.

"Lord Hermes, guardian and guide, slayer of the many-eyed Argos who was set to guard a girl in a cow's form, you who rescue those who are trapped, you who lead the dead into another life, patron of thieves and merchants, you who guard the roads and boundaries, I make offering to you." She held the cup of wine aloft, then poured its contents at the base of the herm. "I offer you incense." She took the block Lyris had given her out of her wallet and set it beside the ember in the small pot, then blew on it to encourage the fire. The scent that rose was strong and strange, an attack of flowers and dark woods and the musks of some animals. She hoped Hermes would like it; she wasn't sure she did. The smoke was dense; Nysa felt dizzy. She cut across her palm with the knife and leaned through the smoke to hold her hand at the base of the herm. "I have no unblemished animal to offer you; all

I can give you is part of myself. I offer you my blood," she whispered, shaking drops from her palm into the soil.

As she hunched before the herm, she felt ridiculous. The night was cool, the moon gone, stars shimmering in a rippling sky, and here she was, bare feet on the ground not far from where someone had dumped slops that morning, squatting before a statue when she should be asleep. She sneezed from the smoke, but it tickled inside her head. If the gods listened to the prayers of slaves, wouldn't all slaves be free? She swayed. The smoke was making her sick.

"What is it you want, little one?" asked a light male voice, salt as sea breeze.

Had she been discovered? Was it someone who would recognize her, report her disobedient actions to the master? Nysa tried to rise, but tottered instead and fell back. She glanced everywhere, but there was no movement in the street.

"Little one?"

A shadow above her, someone leaning forward, a dark silhouette against the dancing stars.

"Lord?" she whispered.

"Thank you for the gifts," he said. "What do you pray for?"

Was this the god? She leaned forward onto her knees and pressed her forehead to the ground between his feet, afraid to speak.

Breeze brushed through her short hair, cool, the breath of a cave. "Tell me," whispered the one above her.

"I want a new road," she told the dust. "Please, Glorious One, show me a path the leads another direction. I don't want to walk the one I'm on."

"If I set your feet on a new path, will you follow wherever it leads?"

Cold swept down her spine, prickled the hairs on her arms and neck. Someone said once never to trouble the gods, because they would offer trouble back.

Aristides had set a price for her, and he was a loathsome man. A path that led her away from him had to be better.

"I will."

"You will welcome change?"

"I will," she whispered to the dirt.

"Look up."

She leaned back and lifted her head, stared up at his silhouette. He lifted his wand, the one embraced by snakes, and struck her on the forehead with it. The force of his blow knocked her back into the road. Her forehead burned, and snakes squirmed inside her skull.

When next she opened her eyes, the sky was light with morning, and Eudokia, a handled cup dangling from her hand, squatted beside Nysa at the foot of the herm. Nysa's face, neck, and hair were wet and cold. Kyprios and Megakles stood above her. She turned her head. The small firepot had overturned, spilling its contents: Lyris's incense had burned to feathers of gray ash; Nysa's blood and the libation of watered wine she had given the god had been swallowed by the thirsty earth. She wondered if her encounter in the darkness was only a dream.

"Are you all right?" Eudokia asked.

Heat closed Nysa's throat. A shadow flickered across her vision; something shifted in her thoughts. She opened her mouth. "The sky berates the roof, jealous of its solid span."

"What?" asked Megakles.

"Seek the road's center," she said, and sat up. She scooted backward toward the center of the road.

"Nysa, have you gone mad?" asked Eudokia.

A red tile slid off the roof and crashed to the roadway, fragments flying. A chip struck Kyprios in the cheek. Blood welled up.

Eudokia gasped. Megakles stepped back and stared up at the roof. Kyprios pressed fingers to his wounded cheek and knelt beside Nysa, his pale eyes kindling. "You knew it," he said. "You knew that would happen. What is the mark on your forehead?"

She touched her temple, felt raised skin under her fingertips, swollen and warm. She felt along the edges of the mark, wondering what it looked like. She opened her mouth to say, "The god gave it to me," but her vision darkened again, and what came out instead was: "A space inside a blow where time stretches and pleats."

"She's lost her senses," Eudokia said. "Let's take her inside. Maybe more water will bring her back to herself."

Kyprios helped Nysa to her feet, put his arm around her, and led her through the gate into the courtyard.

The master stood beside the household altar, feeding kindling to the morning fire and muttering a hymn. He paused when they entered, then scattered grain in the flames and raised his hands to heaven with a last cry. The morning invocation was complete. He came to them. "What's this? What's this? What's happened?"

"We found her senseless in the street, master," said Kyprios. "Neither speech nor a slap could wake her. Eudokia had to pour water on her."

"Well, missy, what have you been up to, out of doors before dawn? What's that smut on your face?"

"What was omitted will be supplied reversed," Nysa said.

"What?" The master's face flushed with anger.

"Master, she has lost her mind," Eudokia said.

"Perhaps a beating will restore it to her," said the master. "Five lashes. See to it, Megakles."

"What was omitted will be supplied reversed, and what is given will be returned manyfold." The words spilled out of Nysa against her will.

"Ten lashes," said the master. "Mind you mark her neatly, and leave her looks intact; I've a use for her tonight."

"Master," said Kyprios.

Rage made the master shake, formed his hands into fists. "What is it?" he said in a quiet, menacing voice.

"Forgive me for speaking," Kyprios said. "We found Nysa at the base of the herm. I think perhaps she is godstruck."

"What do you mean?"

"She spoke a prophecy, and it came true."

"Oh?" The master turned his angry gaze to her. "Prophesy for me now. Will a beating cure what ails you?"

"Neglect were wiser and would yield a better crop." Inside her head, Nysa struggled. Better she were silent than saying things like this to the master. None of the words that came out of her mouth were her own, and she couldn't stop herself from speaking. "Sow blows and reap catastrophe."

"Megakles," said the master. "Fetch the lash."

Megakles, his feet dragging, took three steps toward the storage room where the lash hung.

"Husband," said the mistress from the shadowed balcony above.

"Wife?" His word was like a blow.

"You've forgotten the wine offering."

"What?" He looked at the altar, where the fire still burned, parching the grain he had given to the gods. He glanced beside him, where the jug of the libation should have stood beside the basket with the ritual grain in it. "Kyprios!" he yelled.

"Sorry, master," said Kyprios. "I was going to bring the jug to you when Eudokia summoned me outside."

"Get the jug now, and five lashes to you for ruining the morning offering and offending the god."

Kyprios bowed his head and ran to the kitchen, leaving Nysa swaying behind him. She edged over so she could lean on a wall.

The master began the morning hymn over. Kyprios, rushing back from the kitchen with the wine, stumbled on his return, and at the very moment the master should have offered the libation, the wine rose up out of the jug and rained down over altar, fire, and master. The master purpled with rage but didn't interrupt himself. By the time he finished the hymn, his voice had lowered to normal, and his color was clear. The new wine stains on his chiton spotted him like a leopard. He lowered his arms after the final shout. His face was at rest again.

Nysa had relaxed as she listened to the morning ritual. None of her words had been her own. They must have come from somewhere else. From the god. This was the new path he put her on? She had said she would follow where it led. What if it led to the lash, and on, right to Aristides's couch, where her other path had been leading? The god had answered her prayer. Fate had shifted, as she had asked. She would go where she was fated.

Everyone stood silent in the courtyard. The master glanced at them, Megakles halfway to the storage room that held the lash, stopped by his respect for the morning prayer, Eudokia a hunched figure at the gate, Nysa, who straightened away from the wall, Kyprios, who had fallen to his knees when he tripped, then stayed there, head bowed. Somehow the jug was still intact.

The master roared with laughter. "Forget the lash," he said. "'What was omitted . . .' Ha! The gods' wings have brushed the dust here today. Give me another prophecy, Nysa. What am I to do with you?"

"Cut out the tongue, and give it to the gods," she said. She clapped her hands over her mouth. No, she thought, no; is this the answer to my prayer? I lose my tongue? Now I shall learn to suffer without being able to speak another prayer. Why did you say that, whoever gives me words?

The master sighed. "And what I give will be returned many-fold? I wonder in what form? I hope the gods will be generous in return for my sacrifice of a good slave. Pack whatever things you'll need for Apollo's temple, Nysa. If you're going to tell the future, he's the god for you."

The mistress helped her pack her other robe in a basket, added her spindle, double flute, and a cup with handles, and gave her a small perfume pot painted with an image of one of the wind gods. The mistress's favorite scent was inside, a spicy scent too strong for a slave to use. "I shall miss you, Nysa," whispered the mistress.

And I you, Nysa thought, but the words wouldn't come. She touched her throat. She would have said the mistress had been kind to her and she appreciated it, but she had no words.

The mistress took Nysa's hand and pressed it to her belly. "Can you tell me if I'll give my husband another son?"

Nysa's hand grew hot, and so did her throat. Darkness

veiled her vision. "Two sons grow together, and will kill their mother," she whispered, then gasped and snatched her hand away. She rubbed her eyes, trying to erase the vision of her mistress's future.

The mistress stood silent. She handed the basket to Nysa without a word, and turned her back.

Nysa went down to the gate with her shoulders bowed, her gaze on the ground. Strangers' questions would be easier. At least, she hoped they would.

At Apollo Delphinios's temple, the master spoke to three priests. "A god struck her. She speaks in prophecies now. She said I was to give her to the gods."

"A slave?" said the youngest priest. "A child? Our oracles are older woman, beyond the age of childbearing, the distinguished wives of citizens. Are you sure?"

"What can I do but honor the request of the god?" said the master.

"Are you certain she isn't playing a trick on you?"

The master cocked his head and studied Nysa, who tightened her grip on the basket of her belongings and dropped her gaze to the bright mosaic on the temple floor. She had never visited this temple before. Apollo, god of healing, music, plague, justice, and foretelling; the god who punished the guilty, god of light. Nysa had spent most of her life in the dark of the women's quarters. She could not remember praying to Apollo for anything. Hermes was the one who had answered her prayer. Why was she here, in Apollo's temple?

"She foretold two things that came true. Nysa, is this where you belong?" the master asked.

Shadows cloaked her vision; she felt her mouth work. Words spilled out. "The unwelcome gift turns from a stone to a knife in the sheath."

"I don't understand that," the master said. "But now I don't have to. I leave her to you." The master touched her shoulder. "May the fates be kind to you." He bowed to the priests and left.

"Speak your future," said the oldest priest.

"I walk my words," Nysa's mouth said.

They asked her other questions, but no more answers came out of her until the youngest said, "Can you grind grain? Can you bake bread? Can you mend clothing?"

She nodded, smiling, even though her mouth said, "Fire does not rain, and water does not burn."

"Fire has no hands, but you do," said the oldest priest. "We'll find your right work."

The youngest priest led her next door to the residence where the sibyls lived when they weren't prophesying. Three very old women shared an upstairs room there, guarded by a Persian slave. There were downstairs rooms for the priests to use if they were busy at the temple and didn't care to go to their homes at night. Two domestic slaves tended to the household's needs. The priest introduced Nysa to the cook and the maid. "This is Nysa, late a slave in a larger household, and now a gift to the temple," he said. "She will live here."

The slaves greeted her and smiled until her silence stretched too long. "Is something wrong with you?" asked Melantha, the cook.

A shadow flickered before Nysa's eyes. "A river of grain runs down into darkness."

The cook looked to the priest. "Master?"

"She may be godstruck, or simple, or both," said the priest. "I leave her to you." He left.

"Fine," muttered the cook. She led Nysa to a slab table and gave her a grinding stone. Then she opened a large lidded jar and reached in with a pottery scoop, pulled it out. "Strange," she said, staring at the half-empty scoop before spilling grain onto the slab in front of Nysa. She peered down into the jar, lifted it. A trickle of grain ran out the bottom, some sliding down into a mouse hole under the wall. "Of all the—"

Nysa lowered her gaze and ground the grain.

By day's end, Melantha had decided that Nysa should sleep with the sibyls, rather than in the room next to the kitchen that Melantha shared with the maid. She and Tessa, the maid, introduced Nysa to the three old sibyls and put a pallet on the floor of their room for her.

Questions crowded through Nysa's head, but they wouldn't come out of her mouth. Weary, she lay on the floor and pulled her spare robe over her.

She woke in darkness in a room that felt too large and smelled of incense. People breathed around her, but these were not the sounds of Eudokia, who breathed with a sigh and a flutter as she slept, or the other slaves, or the mistress or her daughter.

Someone brushed her forehead with a warm hand. The mark there throbbed. "Hey," he said. "How do you like it here?"

She struggled for a second before she recognized the voice of the god. "I don't know." She touched her throat: for the first time since he had struck her, she spoke her own mind. "Why am I in Apollo's temple?"

"He has a place for women who speak the future; my priests wouldn't know what to do with you. Besides, I like to give him fine presents. It makes him gentle toward me. But remember: even though you're in my brother's temple, you can still make offerings to me."

"Thank you," she said, and almost laughed. Then she remembered where she had been headed that night, and how now she was somewhere else. "Thank you." The new road lay before her, leading to an unknown country, away from all the destinations she had always been afraid of, away from everything she had ever known.

Over the past twenty-some years, NINA KIRIKI HOFFMAN has sold adult and YA novels, juvenile and media tie-in books, short story collections, and more than 250 short stories. Her works have been finalists for the Nebula, World Fantasy, Mythopoeic, Sturgeon, Philip K. Dick, and Endeavour awards. Her first novel, *The Thread That Binds the Bones*, won a Stoker Award.

Nina's young adult novel *Spirits That Walk in Shadow* was published by Viking in 2006. Her short science fiction novel *Catalyst* was published by Tachyon in 2006.

Nina does production work for *The Magazine of Fantasy & Science Fiction* and teaches short story writing through her local community college. She also works with teen writers. She lives in Eugene, Oregon, with several cats, a mannequin, and many strange toys.

～
AUTHOR'S NOTE

Tricksters scare me; they represent chaos, an upending of the world. Sometimes this is a necessary thing—your life may be in a bad rut, and a trickster can jounce you out of that and into something new.

Though tricksters scare me, Hermes has always been one of my favorite gods, so I was happy when Ellen and Terri said I could write about him. In guidelines for this anthology, they said they preferred to avoid first-person stories set in the present day, so I decided to write something deeply historic for a change. I researched ancient Greece, since that was Hermes's natural milieu. Women lived very restricted lives there; slaves had more freedom, in some ways. I'm interested in the lives of women and slaves; "The Listeners" gave me a chance to explore them.

REALER THAN YOU

Christopher Barzak

What you think you know about the world isn't true. Nothing is real; it's all made up, and because of this you're forced to live in a world of illusion. That's the end of this story, the point I'm going to make. I'm telling you up front because I don't want you thinking this story has a comfortable ending. It won't make sense out of sadness. It won't redeem humanity in even a small sort of way. Now you know the price of the ticket, you can decide if you want to see behind the curtain.

Still there? Well, then. You must be that sort of person. Willing to be disturbed, or wanting to watch someone else being disturbed by life's many conflicts. There's nothing wrong with that, though, no matter what anyone says. All it means is you aren't afraid to look at difficult things in the world.

My name is Elijah Fulton. This happened in Japan at the beginning of the twenty-first century, when I was sixteen and my parents forced me to leave America. It happened in Ami, a suburb an hour away from Tokyo, on a trail in a bamboo forest.

I was running that day, as usual, because running or biking were the only ways I could get anywhere. You had to be eighteen to drive in Japan, so when we moved here, all the years I'd waited to acquire mobility had been taken away, my adolescence set back to zero. Without a car, I was stuck in our tiny house with my thirteen-year-old sister and my mom as she learned how to cook Japanese food with Mrs. Fujita, the wife of my dad's boss. So I ran to get away from everything. From my parents, my little sister. From Ami. If I could have, I would have run away from Japan altogether. But it's an island unfortunately, so I was stuck.

When I first started running, I didn't know where the roads led or even in which direction, so to be safe I circled the apartment complex next to our house. Every day I'd run a little farther. By the end of my first week I made it to the end of our road, and a few days later I crossed over to a road that ran over a hill, into a forest of bamboo and pine trees. It twisted through the woods for a long time, like a dream uninterrupted, until one day I came to a place where it split in two directions. One way curved out of the forest, opening onto a cabbage farm. The other way deteriorated into a dirt trail that wound farther into the forest.

Since I was trying to get away from the world, I took the second trail. There, under the gray-green bamboo shadows, locusts sawed strange melodies. I listened to the thud of my feet as I ran, and the rise and fall of my breathing. These sounds were a comfort. They made me feel like I could take refuge in my body while I was stuck living in a country I had no desire to live in.

As I ran, a dragonfly big as my hand flitted back and forth

around me, circling but never leaving. It was bigger than any dragonfly I'd ever seen. It made me think of fairies. From its size, I could understand why people once believed in them. But people will believe in almost anything, really. Sometimes you don't even have to try hard to convince them.

I must have been in a mood that day (as if I wasn't in one ever since we set foot on Japanese soil) because at some point I looked down to find that the trail had ended. When I looked up, I saw I was in a clearing, and at the back of the clearing, pressed into the shade, stood a tiny house.

The house had little stairs leading up to a door with a rusty lock hanging on it, and coins and braids of colored string lay scattered across the steps. As I looked closer, turning my head one way, then the other, I started to think that at any moment someone very small would unlock that door, swing it open, and step out. Maybe it was the dragonfly and all those thoughts of fairies. Maybe it was my mood that day in general. But no one opened the door to ask what I was doing there. Instead a rustling came from behind the house, and when I looked up, startled, I saw a red dog stepping out of the trees.

The dog was small with wide pricked ears, a pointed nose, and eyes green as jade. I decided it looked more like a fox. Not a real fox, but one that stepped out of a storybook. It had a rich coat of red fur and bib-shaped white down covering its throat. Lifting its nose to sniff the air, it cocked its head, inspecting me like I'd inspected the house.

While it circled I stood still, afraid it might attack me. I mean, it was some sort of canine and I was on its territory, so I expected it wouldn't be happy. It must have decided I was okay, though, because it eventually hung its head, uninterested, and walked away. I let out a breath but clenched up again a moment later. The dog was leaving, but it was taking the path I needed to leave by.

I decided to walk behind it. It was getting dark out, and I didn't want to be lost in a bamboo forest at night. I couldn't help but wonder what other creatures might come out to meet me if I still stood in that clearing when the moon rose.

As I followed it, the dog kept moving, only stopping to look over its shoulder occasionally, its black nose gently nudging the air in front of it. Whenever it did that, a little pang went off inside my chest, and I'd suddenly want to pet it, to wrap my arms around its neck and hold it like I used to hold my girlfriend back in the States before we broke up because I was leaving. The fox felt that familiar.

And that's when something weird happened. That's when I got the idea that our meeting wasn't an accident. As we left the forest I thought, It's leading me. It's taking me home again, isn't it?

Except it didn't lead home. Not all the way home, that is. When we reached the path to the intersection where I needed to cross over, it stopped, looked at me once more with those green eyes, then dashed into the woods. I stood and watched it slip through the poles of bamboo for a while. And afterward, after I couldn't see its flashes of red between the poles any longer, I ran the rest of the way home.

The name "Ami" has no meaning, but I think it has a secret one. In the *Dictionary of Secret Meanings*, "Ami" means "the most boring town in the world." With its Catholic-school-uniformed boys and girls walking the sidewalks, with its 1950s-looking housewives wearing aprons as they zoom down the street on mopeds, living there was about as exciting as *Leave It to Beaver* reruns.

It wasn't just the apron-wearing housewives on mopeds or Catholic-school-uniformed Japanese students wandering the streets that made life unreal there. Those all contributed, but it was more than that. It was the strange symbols on billboards instead of the Roman alphabet, it was the radio announcers spewing streams of incomprehensible chatter, it was the TV shows that made no sense, it was the way my family took everything in stride. It was all of those things together that made my equilibrium shaky.

My dad's boss, Mr. Fujita, got my dad acclimated to the area quickly, so I don't think he ever felt that vertigo. And Mrs. Fujita and my mom were dead set on becoming best friends. So both my parents had interpreters helping to make everything easier. With Mr. Fujita, my dad bought a car. With Mrs. Fujita, my mom learned which stores had the best groceries, which restaurants the best sushi.

My dad works for an electronics company but says I'm not allowed to mention its name. You can probably imagine which one, though. It's a big name brand in America and rhymes with *phony*. And that's the word I want to talk about for a while actually. *Phony*. Because that's what I thought about most of the people I met those first few weeks. They were phonies. Fakes. Or as my English teacher back home would have said in a very Shakespearean way, what I was dealing with was "a culture of charlatans." Everyone seemed to always be bowing and saying they were sorry and how they should have been the one to thank you for giving them the opportunity to present you with a gift, which to me seemed like the biggest guilt trip ever.

I wanted the bluntness of America. I wanted someone to lean on a car horn and shout out the window, "What the hell's the holdup?" I wanted someone to say they hated me. Stuff like that. Stuff that helped you know where you stood with a person. But the Japanese are all about subtlety. If they're mad, they just keep smiling, saying please and thank you. If you want to know what they think, you could forget it.

When I got back from my run that day, my sister Liz was watching a TV show with a host who was fond of saying "Hontooo?" to an audience that laughed whenever he said it. Liz laughed too, as if she understood the humor. Actually, she did understand the humor. It was me who didn't get it. Liz was only thirteen, but she'd spent the last three months before we moved studying Japanese, learning two of its three alphabets. When Mr. Fujita picked us up at the airport, she'd been able to greet him in Japanese. I liked my sister a lot, but she was too precocious really. Sometimes I felt like she was the one who should be getting ready to graduate and go to college.

When she realized I was in the room, she looked up, still giggling, and said, "*Konichiwa*, Elijah. *Genki desu ka?*"

"Okay," I said, sighing. "I guess." Usually I refused to respond to her if she spoke Japanese, but I didn't have the energy that day to refuse her. Liz looked at me suspiciously because of this, and her laughter faded.

"Are you okay?" she said again. "I mean, really?"

"Yeah," I said. "It's nothing."

I went back to my room and fell on my futon, thinking hard. The air was thick with moisture, and my small fan didn't do much but stir it. We had air-conditioning, but after our first week here we'd stopped using it. Some Japanese friends from Phony International had come over and freaked out when they saw it running. "This air is expensive!" they'd gasped, and my mom had listened, like she does to anything a Japanese person suggests to her. "When in Rome," she was always saying. But I'd always say, "We're not in Rome. We're in Ami."

I breathed in that wet air now and thought. Something big had occurred, but I didn't know how to explain it. I already knew I wanted to go back to the clearing. To that little house. To see that red fox dog. To feel the calm it gave me. It was the first time I'd felt that in months, and after having it for those few minutes, I wanted it like I was already addicted.

The next day I decided to tell Liz about it after we got home from school. Our parents had put us in a school for kids of English speakers. Mostly it was Australian kids who went there, but it was cool to be able to speak English, even though there were some differences between my English and the Aussies'. Like what the hell's a jumper? Why say "arse" and "bloke"? Anyway, when I told Liz about the house in the forest, she said, "It's a shrine you saw, Elijah. They put them in different places. Probably the one you saw was private. Like a family put it there, or maybe even just one person."

"It looked old," I said. "You know, in disrepair."

"Probably it's abandoned," said Liz. "Maybe the person who made it died."

"A shrine," I said, furrowing my brow. A minute later I said, "So what's it for?"

"For gods to live in," said Liz. She was eating up my interest. She leaned forward on her stool in the kitchen and said, "That's why there were things on the steps. They were offerings."

"Really?" I said. "That's sort of cool."

"Yeah," said Liz, "and what you saw is a small one. We should find out where the big shrines are nearby and visit. Those are huge and lots of people visit them."

"Maybe," I said, not committing. I liked my shrine without all the people. It felt like it was just for me and whoever had built it. And for the red fox. For the red fox, definitely. I don't think I would have had that feeling if I went to a shrine where a lot of people visit. And even though I was behaving myself in general, I didn't want to give anyone the impression I was settling in. That would have felt too much like I was losing something.

I went back to the shrine a few more times, but I never saw the red fox. I liked that the fox wasn't there—it made our encounter feel more special—but at the same time I was disappointed. I wanted to feel that eddy of wonder again. I wanted to know what it meant. So when I went back and the fox wasn't there, I became anxious like I'd been before I found the shrine, and a sort of longing began to grow inside me. Sometimes I could feel it, like a solid thing pressing, swelling in my chest. At those times, when the weight of wanting was heavy, I imagined a shrine being built inside me—a shrine like the one in the forest—and then I'd feel a little better.

I tried to get rid of all these feelings by hanging out with someone from the English school. I asked this kid Colin, who was from Sydney, if he wanted to hang out. So we went to a game center and talked about all the wack games they have at game centers like the one we were in. Pachinko in particular puzzled us. Pachinko parlors were everywhere—they flashed their neon billboards on every corner—but neither of us could figure out pachinko's purpose. It was sort of a mix between pinball and a slot machine. Colin said, "You must have to be Japanese to understand it."

"It's probably a joke on the *gaijin*," I said. "The Japanese in these pachinko parlors are really actors paid to look like they know what they're doing, but really they have cameras on us and we're being laughed at by a studio audience and fifty million Japanese viewers sitting at home while *gaijin* white boys from America and Australia speculate about pachinko's purposes."

"Like a Philip K. Dick novel," said Colin, laughing. "The author who wrote that story about the guy whose life was really a TV show."

"Oh yeah," I said. "I think I saw the movie version. Actually, Philip K. Dick could have been Japanese. He seemed to know a lot about how the world is never what it looks like. That's pretty much Japan through and through."

"What do you mean?" asked Colin.

"You know how everyone here says one thing and means another, how no one ever says what they really feel, how they're always complimenting you for speaking good Japanese. I mean, seriously, I accidentally said 'chicken *kudasai*' to this waitress once, and she practically melted all over me."

"I dunno," said Colin. "I think it's like that everywhere maybe."

"Have you ever been to America?" I asked. Colin shook his head. "You'll be in for a big surprise if you ever go," I told him. "People there say whatever they think."

"Really?"

I nodded. "Yeah," I said. "It's great."

"Sounds dangerous," said Colin.

"What do you mean?"

"I mean there are a lot of things I think about that wouldn't be good if I said them. Sometimes it's better to choose your battles and only say things that are important."

I nodded and told Colin maybe he was right, but I was really thinking he'd been brainwashed, and right then my effort to reach out and touch someone went down the drain. Colin was cool, don't get me wrong, but I wanted someone to understand me. I didn't want to argue about my feelings. Here I'd been thinking just because someone spoke English, we'd understand each other. But I guess there are languages within languages, and those can be foreign too, even when you think you're understood and understanding.

After that sublime day of disconnection, I decided the best solution to my restlessness would be to go somewhere that had more to offer than Ami. I decided on Tokyo. My dad made the hour commute every day without any problems. If Tokyo couldn't distract me from my longings, I figured nothing could.

I told my parents I'd be with Colin at a game center, which would hold off their questions. The nearest train station was in Ushiku, twenty minutes away, so I had my mom drop me at a nearby game center and told her Colin's mom would pick us up. After she drove off, I ran across the street to the station. Then it was an hour of nodding my head in time with other passengers, swaying to the lilt of the train as it pulled us farther away from the suburbs. As the train moved, I wondered about whether or not I'd find something to fill the space inside me. It was a terrible thing, wanting something, not knowing what it even was I wanted.

Before I knew it we had arrived, and as I stepped down to the station platform, I was immersed in a sea of dark eyes and fluorescent lighting. There was no stopping the downward rush of passengers. They picked me up and carried me away on their current. I kept bumping into shoulders, backs, and arms, saying *I'm sorry, I'm sorry, I'm sorry*. Someone spun me around in a circle as he ran past, and when I came to a stop I faced a stairwell up to the city.

When I made it to the top, the underground suddenly felt comfortable. It was late afternoon and the district was busy. Teenagers wearing leather pants and Catholic schoolgirl skirts and those leg warmers dancers wear and Victorian corsets breezed by me. Groups of girls wearing animal suits—tigers and chipmunks and skunks—stood in a huddle on a corner, laughing and shouting things at passersby through a bullhorn. They stared as I passed by, as if I were the weird-looking one. They had white paint streaked on their faces to look like whiskers. The boys were skinny like girls, wore their hair like girls, giggled like girls. Everyone seemed to be smoking. Arcing into the blue sky were the spikes of skyscrapers. TV shows played on the sides of buildings. I felt dizzy and almost fell down, but managed to back up against a wall before I toppled.

Tokyo was an origami city folded over and over until something was made of virtually nothing. Streets doubled back on each other, disappeared without warning, and later, after I got myself together, as I stepped into shopping centers, I found buildings hidden within buildings.

In Sunshine City, this mall that has something like seventy floors of stores inside it, I went into what I thought was a game room, called Namjatown. But the farther in I went, the farther in Namjatown went, too. It transformed from modern mall into ancient Tokyo alleyways, offering rides and games where the prizes were eels, and you could meet strange characters that looked like Hello Kitty, only more nefarious.

In the Toyota building, an entire wall had been made to look like a waterfall cascading down the face of a cliff. Vines and flowers grew, or looked like they were growing, along the edges of the rocks. Escalators led from one building to another, and soon I wasn't even in the Toyota building but somewhere else altogether, where an advertisement for watches was being filmed. *"Sumimasen! Kono heya ni haite wa ikemasen,"* someone shouted, and the next thing I knew I was being hurried off the set and back into the street.

Then it was night and neon outlined the city in pink, green, blue, and yellow. The streets were more full than they had been in the afternoon. Monks in robes strolled past me. Retail workers stood on street corners, hawking the wares of their respective stores. Groups of men wearing blue robes that covered them only to their butts danced in the street while holding shrines aloft on their shoulders. Drums beat out strange rhythms, though no matter where I looked, I saw no drummers.

By nine o'clock, I was beginning to think I should be leaving, but no matter what entrance to the train station I ran down, I couldn't remember the name of the line home. I tried asking people, but no one spoke English, or no one who was able would take the time to help. I ran into a white woman with blond hair and almost hugged her. But when I said, "I'm sorry, can you help me find the train to Ushiku?" she opened her mouth and said something very not like English.

I shouted, *"Sumimasen!"* to no one in particular, out of sheer desperation, but I didn't have any words to help me ask for directions.

Directions, directions. The bane of my life. I slouched down on a bench in the station and thought about how I knew exactly where I was going, back in the States. About how unfair it was that my dad had made us all come with him. Then I revised that thought. He hadn't made us come. Everyone wanted to, except me. Majority rules, even though sometimes majorities are wrongheaded. I kept thinking how the only good thing that had happened since we arrived was I'd found that shrine, and I'd seen that red fox. But even the red fox had disappeared on me.

Near midnight I got up to make one more stab at finding my train, and only a few minutes passed before I saw the strangest-looking Japanese girl I'd ever laid eyes on.

She stood on the platform, waiting for a train. She wore one of those animal outfits I'd seen a group of girls wearing earlier. This one was a fox costume, red with a round, white stomach. She had the hood down, so I saw her face clearly. And that, actually, was the strangest thing about her: not her costume or the fact that she held her purse in one hand and her bushy tail in the other, but that she was Japanese and her eyes were green.

I blinked, thinking of my red fox back in Ami. I cocked my head to the side like I did that day at the shrine. I must have stared for a while, too, because when I finally shook off my daze, I found her staring back with a smile. When she saw me snap back to reality, she put her hand to her mouth and giggled.

I was in love in one fast moment. Well, sort of. It was something like love, but conflicted. How do you fall in love with someone wearing a fox costume and not be worried for your sanity? Whatever the feeling was, it spun me. I found myself involuntarily raising my hand, like I was going to ask a teacher a question, and by the time I realized what I was doing, the girl was already walking toward me.

"You are lost," she said. "May I help you?"

"You speak English," I said.

She nodded. "I speak a little. Lots of people here do."

"No one I've asked."

"Then you ask the wrong people. Where are you going?"

"Ami," I said, and she raised her eyebrows.

"*Honto ni?*" she said, like she was that talk show host Liz found so funny. "*Ami machi ni sunde imasu,*" she said, pointing at her nose when she spoke. "Sorry," she said, registering my confusion. "You surprise me. I live in Ami too. You follow."

"I can come with you?" I asked.

"Yes," she said. "Come. I show you the way."

The ironic thing is, I'd been wandering around the line I needed. It's just that none of the signs in the station listed Ushiku as a destination. I didn't care, though. I was just happy to be finally getting home. The train was packed, but we managed to get seats instead of having to stand and hold on to the overhead straps. And when we settled in, I turned to her and said, "I'm Elijah."

"My name is Midori," she said. "*Hajimemashite.*"

"*Hajimemashite,*" I said back. Although I'd heard that greeting a gazillion times by then, although Liz had elbowed me several times over the first month to remember it, now I was glad I could tell her I was glad to meet her. Not just because she was helping me, but because I knew her secret. She wore a red fox outfit and her eyes were green. Not very clever, really. I knew from the second I laid eyes on her that this was my red fox from the shrine in the forest. She'd followed me to make sure I got home safely.

She took a mirror out of her purse and checked to make sure her makeup was still okay. Three lines of white face paint on each of her cheeks for whiskers, two upside-down Vs above her eyebrows for ears. Her makeup was fine, of course. She was just trying to make everything look real for me. I wanted to tell her she didn't have to pretend. I knew who she was and it was okay because I wouldn't tell anyone. I leaned my elbows on my knees and looked up at her as the train pulled us away from the city. When she clicked her mirror shut and found me staring, she said, "You are very interesting."

"I'm not interesting," I said. "But you are."

"What do you mean?" she asked, which annoyed me. I was hoping she'd take the hint and know that behind my words I was saying I knew her. I thought that was very Japanese of me. But of course she was being Japanese, too, and wouldn't say if she understood me.

So I said, "Your eyes are green. Japanese people don't have green eyes. That's very interesting, I'd say."

"These!" she said, pointing to her eyes and laughing. "These are contacts. Not real," she said. "Sorry."

"Not real?" I said. "Really?"

She popped one out, and there it was, a brown eye next to a green one. Another illusion. She wasn't my fox woman after all. I felt stupid then. I told myself to stop indulging in fantasies. After all, this was Japan, and I had to remember that nothing was real here.

"These are very expensive," she said. I said they sold them

back in America too. "I like having green eyes," she said. "I feel different when I wear them."

"Different how?"

"Like I am someone else," she said.

"Like you're a fox?" I chuckled.

"You don't like my costume?" she said, pouting.

"No, no," I said. "It's cute. Really."

"*Kawaii!*" she said. "Yes, very cute. I like it. My friends call me Kitsune when I wear it."

"What's Kitsune?"

"Foxwoman."

"Oh," I said. "That's how I thought of you when I first saw you. Foxwoman."

"See?" she said. "It fits me better than who I am when I'm not Kitsune."

"Who are you when you're not Kitsune?"

"Just Midori," she said. "Daughter of a cabbage farmer. Waiting, wanting, waiting. My father won't let me move out unless I get married. My mother died when I was little, so I don't have her to help me talk to him."

I was surprised by how frank she was, but instead of drawing her out more, I was stupid and asked, "If your dad's like that, how did you get to Tokyo?"

She put a finger to her white lips and said, "Shh, it's secret."

But you're telling me, I thought.

Then I said, "A cabbage farmer?" thinking it wasn't possible. But I told her where I lived, and we both laughed because that was her father's farm where my running trail went if you didn't take the path to the shrine in the forest. We were practically neighbors. She said we could take a taxi together from Ushiku, since we lived nearby, and that's what we did.

She called a taxi, and when we came to the place where her father's farm and the road to my house intersected, she paid the driver and we stood in the middle of the road until the taillights of the taxi disappeared in the darkness.

"You are safe going home now?" she asked.

I nodded. "Thanks for your help," I said.

"It is my pleasure," she said. "I am glad you give me the chance to welcome you to my country. I hope you will be happy here. I am. Now."

She bowed then, and I bowed with her. "*Oyasumi!*" I said, remembering what Liz told me every night before going to bed.

As she walked up the road to her father's house, she waved at me with her tail. "*Oyasumi nasai!*" she called back, and I ran in the other direction, feeling like a nutcase.

It was nearly two in the morning when I got in, and my mom and dad were waiting for me. "Where have you been?" they wanted to know. "You weren't at the game center when we came to pick you up. And we called Colin. He said he never went to any game center with you."

Lousy Aussie, I thought. Doesn't he know you're supposed to cover for each other?

I was too tired to lie, so I told the truth. And actually, though they were mad at me for lying, they didn't give me too hard a time. "I just wanted to do something fun," I told them. "It's not that hard to use a train system." They couldn't argue with that one. And by the time we went to bed, we'd settled on letting me take the train into Tokyo once a month if I wanted. Just no more lying about where I was going.

"If something happened to you—" said my mother. Then she stopped and looked like she might cry. "If something happened to you," she continued, "we wouldn't even know where to find you."

Americans have their own kind of guilt trips, unfortunately.

The next morning I got up to go running. I thought I'd stop by the cabbage farm and ask for Midori. I mean, we seemed to get along, and I decided maybe it would be good to have a friend who could tell me what people were saying, maybe even teach me a little Japanese. Or who knows? I couldn't tell how old she was. Friends would be cool, I thought, but maybe we could develop something. She couldn't be that much older, could she?

I was thinking these things as I rounded the bend and came up her father's drive. When I knocked on the door, a little old man answered and I said, "Is Midori home?" but he only furrowed his brows and crossed his arms in an **X** shape.

He said a lot of words I didn't understand, very angrily, then shouted, "No Midori!" and closed the door on my face.

I didn't know what to make of that exchange, so I turned around and ran back through the woods. Instead of going home, though, I took the path to the shrine in the forest.

It was still there with its coins and trinkets, the wood damp from a light rain earlier that morning. I shoved my hand in the pocket of my shorts and pulled out a hundred-yen coin. I knelt down and placed it on the steps that led up to the door and said, "Thank you very much" in Japanese, *"Arigato gozaimasu."* When I stood up again, a flash of something red behind the shrine caught my attention.

I leaned to look around the corner, hoping to find my red fox there, but it wasn't. Instead I found a pool of red and white cloth on the packed dirt. I went over and picked it up, pinched it between my fingers, and as it unfolded I saw it was Midori's costume. I looked around the clearing, but she was nowhere. I pictured her out of her costume, her naked body running through the bamboo thickets. I pictured her crouched behind a bush, staring with her green eyes while I stood a few feet away, holding her skin. Then it wasn't her but the red fox with its real pelt of fur and its real green eyes staring out at me. That was her real skin, I thought.

When I got home I called Mr. Fujita to ask if he could help me talk to the old man at the cabbage farm. He wanted to know why, so I told him I'd met a girl who lived there. When Mr. Fujita and I went there, the little old man answered the door again, and the two of them had a long conversation. It ended with the little old man bowing, closing the door on us.

As we drove home, I asked Mr. Fujita what they had talked about and he said, "He is very distressed by your question. He had a daughter once, yes. Her name was Midori, yes. But she killed herself many years ago."

"She did what?" I said. "Why?"

"He did not say," said Mr. Fujita. "We do not speak of such things, E-rye-jah. Please understand."

The next day I ran to the shrine again, wanting more answers. But when I got there, the fox costume had disappeared, too. I stood there for a while, unsure of what had happened, and when it finally hit me I felt so stupid.

It *was* her, I thought. I'd just allowed myself to be fooled when I found out the green eyes were contacts. I'd been too foolish to believe what I knew was the truth. I whispered, "I knew it was you," into the clearing, but nothing came back but a slight breeze. Not her. Not her voice. She'd made herself invisible to me.

～ ～ ～

I've never told anyone, but I have a picture of myself in my head that I sometimes think about. In this picture, I have no features, just a round face with curly brown hair and vague curves where the ears come out. It's not a picture, I guess, but an antipicture. Whenever I think of my mom or dad or Liz, their faces form without hesitation. My mom's sweep of black hair, Liz's sharp little nose, my dad's big earlobes, which Mr. Fujita's wife calls Buddha ears. "Buddha ears good luck," she once told him. They're so big he can balance a grain of rice on the lobes. But me? I can never really see what I look like.

I was thinking about this for a while after meeting Midori, about how she said she felt more herself as Kitsune than she ever did as Midori. I think I understood something about her then. Maybe I even understood why she killed herself. I think what happened was that she shed one pelt for a skin that felt more comfortable.

I won't say that everything changed for me after I met her. I still feel lonely, and more than ever I'm aware that I don't know myself as much as I should. I'm looking into that. It was the real reason why I didn't want to move here in the beginning. I knew if I took away the props of my America, I wouldn't know who I was any longer. I told Liz this a few weeks ago, and she said not to worry. "It's okay to change who you are," she said. "That's natural." I think she's the smartest kid on the block, and I'm jealous of her, but I'm glad she's my sister and not someone else's.

As for Kitsune, I keep thinking about her. I keep wishing I could ask her why she switched her skin in such a terrible, permanent way. I keep thinking how she said, "I hope you will be happy here. I am. Now." I keep wondering how she can be happy, no regrets, after leaving her old skin for her father to find.

I'm still not happy, but I'm calmer. Next year I'm going home to start college, and I suppose I'll be someone different then, too. I'll have to get used to it, this shedding of one skin for another. But like Liz says, it's sometimes necessary.

I have to apologize for something. I said at the beginning of this story that I wouldn't try to make sense out of sadness. That was a lie, though. A trick to catch those of you who, like me, would rather dwell on the failures of this world. The truth is, I do think there's a little sense to all the sadness. I think of Kitsune shedding her skin and know that there are ways of being in this world other than the one I didn't want to give up. I'm not going to take my life to change it like she did, but in her tragedy I've found a way to deal with things a little. Even the illusions of Japan don't seem like illusions any longer. Or else the rest of the world feels just as made up. And that's a sort of freedom really.

Nothing is more real than the masks we make to show one another who we are. Whether it's an animal girl or a business-man, whether it's a goth boy with many piercings or a Japa-nese housewife wearing an apron as she rides down the street on her moped, these are our masks. The best I can do is to love them.

CHRISTOPHER BARZAK grew up in rural Ohio and lived in Japan for two years, teaching English near Tokyo. His stories have appeared in *The Year's Best Fantasy and Horror, Salon Fantastique, Trampoline, Realms of Fantasy, Twenty Epics,* and other magazines and anthologies. Recently Chris returned from Japan and is now teaching English at Youngstown State University in Youngstown, Ohio. His first novel, *One for Sorrow*, won the 2008 Crawford Fantasy Award. His second novel, *The Love We Share Without Knowing*, has recently been published.

Visit his Web site at christopherbarzak.wordpress.com.

～

AUTHOR'S NOTE

When I first moved to Japan to teach English at Edosaki Junior High School, I didn't know much Japanese beyond being able to say hello and asking how someone was doing. It was difficult at times to feel comfortable in a place where I was cut off from my own language and dependent on the kindness of people I could rarely understand. Within a month, though, I began to learn more Japanese, and as I became better at communicating, I felt more at home.

Many of the oddities in this story are things I and my American friends have encountered during our stays in Japan. Technological advancements we haven't seen in America yet, strange characters roaming the streets, and a different set of manners and level of politeness are just a few of the things we had to adjust to. Living abroad, one of the first things you realize is that your language and culture aren't the center of the world, even if they're the center of yours. This is a difficult but ultimately freeing realization, and I highly recommend it.

It was those initial moments of frustration caused by not being able to exchange my feelings and ideas with others, along with the initial shock of being introduced to a culture that is an odd mix of the Far East, 1950s America, and *The Matrix*, that inspired "Realer Than You."

THE FIDDLER OF BAYOU TECHE

Delia Sherman

Come here, *cher*, and I tell you a story.

One time there's a girl lives out in the swamp. Her skin and hair are white like the feathers of a white egret and her eyes are pink like a possum's nose. When she is a baby, the loup-garous find her floating on the bayou in an old pirogue and take her to Tante Eulalie.

Tante Eulalie does not howl and grow hair on her body when the moon is full like the loup-garous. But she hides in the swamp same as they do, and they are all friends together. She takes *piquons* out of the loup-garous' feet and bullets out of their hairy shoulders, and doses their rheumatism and their mange. In return, the loup-garous build her a cabin out of cypress and palmetto leaves and bring her rice and indigo dye from town. On moonlit nights, she plays her fiddle at the loup-garous' ball. The loup-garous love Tante Eulalie, but the girl loves her most of all.

Yes, the girl is me. Who else around here has white skin and hair and pink eyes, eh? Hush now, and listen.

Tante Eulalie was like my mother. She named me Cadence and told me stories—all the stories I tell you, *cher*. When we sit spinning or weaving, she tell me about when she was a young girl, living with her pap and her good maman and her six brothers and three sisters near the little town of Pierreville. She tell me about her cousin Belda Guidry, the prettiest girl in the parish.

Now, when Belda is fifteen, there are twenty young men all crazy to marry her. She can't make up her mind, her, so her old pap make a test for the young men, to see which will make the best son-in-law. He make them plow the swamp and sow it with dried chilies and bring them to harvest. And when they done that, they have to catch the oldest, meanest 'gator in Bayou Teche and make a gumbo out of him.

I thought Tante Eulalie was making it all up out of her head, but she swore it was true. It was Ganelon Fuselier who won Belda, and Tante Eulalie was godmother to their second child, Denise.

Ganie cheated, of course. Nobody can pass a test like that without cheating some. Seemed to me like cheating was a way of life in Pierreville. The wonder was how the folks that were getting cheated never learned to be less trustful. I thought if I ever went to Pierreville, and Ganie Fuselier or Old Savoie tell me the sky is blue, I'd go outside and check. And if Murderes Petitpas came knocking at my door, I'd slip out the back.

Tante Eulalie's best stories were about Murderes Petitpas, when he was a young man, always up to mischief. Young 'Dres, she say, was like the grasshopper because he'd always rather fiddle than work, though 'Dres was too smart to get caught out in the cold.

How smart was he? Well, I tell you the story of Young 'Dres and the Fiddle, and you can judge for yourself.

Once there's this old man, see, called Old Boudreaux. He has a fiddle, and this fiddle is the sweetest fiddle anybody ever hear. His old pap make it himself, back in eighteen-something, and when Old Boudreaux play it, the dead get up and dance. Now, Young 'Dres thinks it's a shame that the best fiddler in St. Mary's parish—that is, Young 'Dres himself—shouldn't have the best fiddle—that is, Old Boudreaux's pap's fiddle. So Young 'Dres goes to Old Boudreaux and he says, "Old Boudreaux, I'm afraid for your soul."

Old Boudreaux says, "What you talking about, boy?"

Young 'Dres says, "Last night when you were playing 'Jolie Blonde,' I see a little red devil creep out of the f-holes and commence to dancing on your fingerboard. The faster he dance, the faster you play, and he laugh like mad and wave his forked tail so I was scared half to death."

"Go to bed, 'Dres Petitpas," says Old Boudreaux. "I don't believe that for a minute."

"It's as true as I'm standing here," says Young 'Dres. "I got the second sight, me, so I see things other people don't."

"Hmpf," says Old Boudreaux, and starts back in the house.

"Wait," says Young 'Dres. "You bring your fiddle here, and I go prove it to you."

Of course, Old Boudreaux say no. But Young 'Dres got a way with him, and everybody know Old Boudreaux ain't got no more sense than a possum. So Old Boudreaux fetches his fiddle and goes to hand it to Young 'Dres. But Young 'Dres is wringing his bandana and moaning. "Mother Mary preserve me!" he says. "Can't you see its red eyes twinkling in the f-holes? Can't you smell the sulfur? You got to exorcise that devil, Old Boudreaux, or you go fiddle yourself right down to hell."

Old Boudreaux nearly drop his fiddle, he so scared. He

don't dare look in the f-holes, but he don't have to, because as soon as Young 'Dres name that devil, there's a terrible stink of sulfur everywhere.

"Holy Mother save me!" Old Boudreaux cry. "My fiddle is possessed! What am I going to do, 'Dres Petitpas? I don't want to fiddle myself down to hell."

"Well, I go tell you, Old Boudreaux, but you ain't going to like it."

"I'll like it, I promise. Just tell me what to do!"

"You give the fiddle to me, and I'll exorcise that devil for you."

Old Boudreaux so scared, he hand his pap's fiddle right over to Young 'Dres. What's more, he tell him to keep it, because Old Boudreaux never go touch it again without thinking he smell sulfur. And that's how 'Dres Petitpas get the sweetest fiddle in the parish for nothing more than the cost of the bandana he crush the rotten egg in that make Old Boudreaux believe his fiddle is haunted.

Yes, that Young 'Dres made me laugh, him. But Tante Eulalie shook her head and said, "You go ahead and laugh, 'tit chou. Just remember that people like 'Dres Petitpas are better to hear about than have dealings with, eh? You ever meet a bon rien like that—all smiling and full of big talk—you run as fast and as far as you can go."

That was Tante Eulalie. Always looking out for me, teaching me what I need to know to live in the world. By the time I could walk, I knew to keep out of the sun and stay away from traps and logs with eyes. When I got older, Tante Eulalie taught me to spin cotton and weave cloth and dye it blue with indigo. She taught me how to make medicine from peppergrass and elderberry bark and prickly pear leaves, and some little magic gris-gris for dirty wounds and warts and aching joints. Best of all, she taught me how to dance.

Tante Eulalie loved to play the fiddle, and she played most nights after supper was cleared away. The music she played was bouncing music, swaying music, twirl around until you fall music, and when I was very little, that's what I did. Then Tante Eulalie took me to the loup-garous' ball, where I learned the two-step and the waltz.

I took to dancing like a mallard to open water. Once I learned the steps, I danced all the time. I danced with the loup-garous and I danced by myself. I danced when I swept and I danced when I cooked. I danced to Tante Eulalie's fiddling and I danced to the fiddling of the crickets. Tante Eulalie laughed at me—said I'd wear myself out. But I didn't.

Then came a winter when the leaves were blasted with cold and ice skimmed the surface of the bayou. Long about Advent-time, Tante Eulalie caught a cough. I made her prickly pear leaf syrup and willow bark tea for the fever, and hung a gris-gris for strength around her neck. But it didn't do no good. At the dark of the year, she asked me to bring her the cypress-wood box from under her bed. I opened it for her, and she pulled out three pieces of lace and a gold ring and put them in my hand.

"These are all I have to leave you," she said. "These, and my fiddle. I hope you find good use for them someday."

Not long after, the Bon Dieu called and she went to Him. Her friends the loup-garous buried her under the big live oak behind the cabin and howled her funeral mass. I was sixteen years old now, more or less, and that was the end of my girlhood.

That was the end of my dancing, too, for a time. When I saw Tante Eulalie's fiddle lying silent across her cane-bottomed chair, I fell into sadness like a deep river. I lay in a nest of nutria skins next to the fire and I watched the flames burn low and thought how nobody would know or notice if I lived or died.

Some time passes, I don't know how much, and then somebody knocks at the door. I don't answer, but he comes in anyway. It is Ulysse, the youngest of the loup-garous. I like Ulysse. He is quiet and skinny and he brings me peanut butter in a jar and white bread in a printed paper wrapper; and when we dance at the loup-garous' ball, everybody stops and watches us. Still, I wish he would go away.

Ulysse sniffs around a little, then digs me out of my nest and gives me a shake. "You in a bad way, *chère,*" he says. "If Tante Eulalie see how you carry on, she pass you one big slap, for sure."

"Good," I say. "I like that fine. At least she be here to slap me."

Not much Ulysse can say to that, I think, and maybe he will go away now and let me be sad by myself. But he has another idea, him. He sniffs around again and starts to clucking like an old hen. "This place worse than a hog pen," he says. "Tante Eulalie see the state her cabin is in, she die all over again." He picks her fiddle and bow up off her chair. "Where she keep these at?"

To see Ulysse holding Tante Eulalie's fiddle gives me the first real feeling I have since it seems like forever. I get mad, me, so mad I go right up to Ulysse, who is bigger than me by a head, who has wild, dark hair and long teeth and sharp nails even when the moon is dark, and I hit him in the stomach.

"*Tiens, chère!* What is this? Why you hit your friend Ulysse?"

"Why? Because you touch Tante Eulalie's fiddle. Put it down, you, or I make you."

"Put it up, then," he says, "instead of curling up like a crawfish in winter."

I take the fiddle like it was an egg, and hang it on its hook over Tante Eulalie's bed. And then I start to cry, with Ulysse holding my shoulders and licking my hair like a wolf licks her cub till I am calm again.

After that, I clean the cabin and make myself a gumbo. I string Tante Eulalie's big loom with thread she spun and dyed, and I weave a length of pale blue cloth. The water rises to the edge of the porch and the nights get shorter. I set lines to catch fish, and make my garden with the seeds Tante Eulalie saved. The loup-garous knock on my door, and I treat them for mange and rheumatism and broken bones, as Tante Eulalie always did. But I don't dance at their balls. I take my pirogue out at sunset and paddle between the big cypress trees and listen to the frogs sing of love and the roaring of the 'gators as they fight for their mates.

One night, paddling far from home, I see lights that are not the pale *feu follets* that dance in the swamp at night. They are yellow lights, lantern lights, and they tell me I have come to a farm. I am a little afraid, for Tante Eulalie used to warn me about letting people see me.

"You know how ducks carry on when a strange bird land in their water?" she says. "The good people of Pierreville, they see that white hair and those pink eyes, and they peck at you till there's nothing left but two-three white feathers."

I do not want to be pecked, me, so I start to paddle away.

And then I hear the music.

I turn back with a sweep of my paddle and drift closer. I

see a wharf and a cabin and an outhouse and a hog pen, and a big barn built on high ground away from the water. The barn doors are open, and they spill yellow light out over a pack of buggies and horses and even cars—only cars I've seen outside the magazines Ulysse sometimes brings. I don't care about the cars, though, for I am caught by the fiddle music that spills out brighter than the lantern light, brighter than anything in the world since Tante Eulalie left it.

I paddle toward the music like a moth to a lit candle, not caring that fire burns and ducks peck and the people of Pierreville don't like strangers. But I am not stupid like Old Boudreaux. I am careful to hide my pirogue behind a button-bush and I don't come out in the open. I stalk the music like a bobcat, softly, softly, and I find a place behind the barn where I think nobody will come. And then I dance. I dance the two-step with my brown striped shawl, tears wet on my face because Tante Eulalie is dead, because I am dancing alone in the dark, because the fiddle is crying and I cannot help but cry, too.

The moon rises, the crickets go to bed. The fiddler plays and I dance as if the dawn will never come. I guess I keep dancing when the music stops, because next thing I know, there's a shout behind me. When I open my eyes, the sky is pale and gray and there's a knot of men behind the barn with their mouths gaping like black holes in their faces.

One of them steps forward. He is tall, broad-shouldered, and thick, and he wears a wide-brimmed hat pulled down low over his eyes, glittering in its shadow like the eyes of a snake in a hole. I throw my shawl around my shoulders and turn to run.

As soon as I move, all the men gasp and step back. I think that a little fear makes ducks mean, but a lot of fear makes them run. I give a hoot like a swamp owl, hold my shawl out like wings, and scoot low and fast into the cypress grove.

Behind me, there is shouting and lights bobbing here and there like lightning bugs. I creep to my pirogue and paddle away quiet as a watersnake, keeping to the shadows. I am very pleased with myself, me. I think the men of Pierreville are as stupid as Old Boudreaux to be frightened by a small girl in a striped shawl. Maybe soon I will go and hear the music again.

Next night, Ulysse comes knocking at my door. He sits down at the table and I give him coffee and then I go to my wheel and set it spinning.

"I hear tell of a thing," says Ulysse over the whirr of the wheel. "It make me think."

I smile a little. "Think?" I say. "That *is* a piece of news. You tell your friends? Old Placide, he be surprised."

Ulysse shakes his head. "This is serious, Cadence. Up and down the bayou, everybody is talking about the haunt that bust up the Doucet *fais-do-do*."

I look down at the pale brown thread running though my fingers, fine and even as Tante Eulalie's. "There weren't no haunts at the Doucet *fais-do-do*, Ulysse."

"I know that. The Doucets say different. They say they see a girl turn into a swamp owl and fly away. What you say to that, *hien*?"

"I say they drink too much beer, them."

He brings his heavy black eyebrows together. "Why you go forget everything Tante Eulalie tell you, Cadence, and make a nine-days' wonder with your foolishness?"

"Don't scold, Ulysse. The people of Pierreville for sure got more important things to talk about than me."

"Maybe so, maybe not," Ulysse says darkly. "What you doing at the Doucets'?"

"Dancing," I say, still teasing. "Who is the fiddler, Ulysse? He play mighty fine."

Ulysse is still not smiling. "He is a *bon rien*, Cadence, a bad man. Shake hands with Murderes Petitpas, you go count your fingers after."

I almost let the wheel stop, I'm so surprised. "You go to bed, Ulysse. Tante Eulalie make 'Dres Petitpas up out of her head."

"He's real, all right. Everybody say he sell his soul to the devil so he can play better than any human man. Then he fiddle the devil out of hell and keep him dancing all day and night until his hoofs split in two and the devil give 'Dres his soul back so he can stop dancing. 'Dres Petitpas is the big bull on the hill, and mean, mean. You stay away from him, you."

I maybe like Ulysse, but I don't like him telling me what to do—Ulysse, who eats rabbits raw and howls at the moon when it's full. I pinch the thread too tight and it breaks in two.

"Eh, Cadence," he says, "you going to hit me again? Ain't going to change what I say, but go ahead if it make you feel better."

I don't hit him, but I am maybe not very kind to him, and he leaves looking like a beaten dog. I hear howling, later, that I think is Ulysse, and I am a little sorry, but not too much.

Still, I do not go out again to dance. Not because Ulysse tell me, but because I am not a *couyon* like Old Boudreaux.

Two, maybe three nights after, I hear a thump against my porch and the sounds of somebody tying up a pirogue and climbing out. Not Ulysse—somebody heavier. Old Placide, maybe. I am already up and looking for my jar of fly blister for his rheumatism when there's a knock on the door.

I open it. I do not see Old Placide. I see a big man with a belly like a barrel, a big-brimmed hat, and a heavy black moustache. I try to shut the door, but 'Dres Petitpas shoves it back easy, and walks past me like he was at home. Then he sits down at my table with his hat pulled down to his snake-bright eyes and his hands spread on his thighs.

"Hey there, *chère*," he says, and smiles real friendly. His teeth are yellow and flat.

I stand by the door, thinking whether I will run away or not. Running away is maybe safer, but then 'Dres Petitpas is alone in my cabin, and I don't want that.

He eyes me like he knows just what I'm thinking. "I go tell you a story. You stand by the door if you want, but I think you be more comfortable sitting down."

I hate to do anything he say, but I hate worse looking foolish. I close the door and sit by the fire with my hands on my lap. I do not give him coffee.

"Well," he says, "this is the way it is. I am a good fiddler, me, maybe the best fiddler on the bayous. Maybe the best fiddler in the world. Ain't nobody in St. Mary's parish dance or court or marry or christen a baby without me. But St. Mary's parish is a small place, eh? I am too big for St. Mary's. I have an idea to go to New Orleans, fiddle on the radio, make my fortune, buy a white house with columns on the front."

He lifts his hands, his fingers square at the tips, his nails trimmed short and black with dirt, and he laughs. It is not a good laugh.

"You maybe don't know, little swamp owl girl, these hands

are like gold. I fiddle the devil out of hell once and I fiddle him down again. I will make those *couyons* in New Orleans lie down and lick my bare feets."

He glances at me for a reaction, but I just sit there. Tante Eulalie is right. Close to, 'Dres Petitpas is not funny at all. He wants what he wants, and he doesn't care what he has to do to get it. He can't trick me, because I know what he is. What he go do, I wonder, when he finds that out?

As if he hears my thoughts, 'Dres Petitpas frowns. He looks around the cabin, and his eyes light on Tante Eulalie's fiddle I've hung on the wall. He gets up and goes to it, takes it down from its hook, and runs his thumb over the strings. They twang dully. "Good thing you loosen the strings," he says. "Keep the neck from warping, eh? Nice little fiddle. You play?"

I don't remember getting up, but I am standing with my hands twisted in my skirts. "No," I say as lightly as I can. "Stupid old thing. I don't know why I don't throw it into the bayou."

"You won't mind if I tune her, then." He brings the fiddle to the table and starts to tighten the strings. I sit down again. "One day," he says, picking up the story. "One day, my five sons Clopha and Aristile and 'Tit Paul and Louis and Télémaque come to me. Clopha is in love, him, and he wants my blessing to marry Marie Eymard.

"Now, I got nothing against marriage. My wife, Octavie, and me been married together twenty-two years, still in love like two doves. My sons are good boys, smart boys. Clopha can read anything you put in front of him—writing, printing, it don't matter. And young Louis adds up numbers fast as I can play my fiddle. But they got no sense about women. So I tell Clopha that I will choose a wife for him, if he wants one. And when the time comes, I'll choose wives for the other boys, too. Wives are too important a matter to be left to young men.

"'My foot!' Clopha say. 'I go marry Marie without your blessing, then.'

"'You go do more than that,' I tell him. 'You go marry with my curse. Remember, I got the devil on a string. My curse is something to fear. And you see if Marie Eymard go marry together with you when she find out you don't bring her so much as a stick of furniture or a woven blanket or a chicken to start life with.'

"Well, you think that be the end of it. But my sons are hardheaded boys. They argue this way and that. And then I have an idea, me, how I can shut their mouths for once and all. I offer my sons a bet."

He stops and holds the fiddle up to his ear and plucks the strings in turn, listening intently. "Better," he says. He lays the fiddle on the table, pulls a lump of rosin from his pocket, and goes to work on the bow.

"The bet," he says, "is this. I will fiddle and my sons will dance. If I stop fiddling before they all stop dancing, I go bless their marriages and play at their weddings. If not, Clopha and Louis come to New Orleans with me to read anything that needs to be read, and Aristile, 'Tit Paul, and Télémaque go tend the shrimp boats and help Octavie with the hogs and the chickens and the cotton."

'Dres Petitpas grins under his moustache. "It is a good bet I make, eh? I cannot lose.

"My sons go off behind the hog pen and talk for a while, and when they come back, they tell me that they will take my bet—on two conditions. One, they will dance one after another, so I must fiddle out five in a row. Two, I will find a partner for them—one partner, who must dance as long as I fiddle.

"Now I am proud of my five sons, because this shows they are smart as well as strong. They know I can play the sun up and down the sky. They know I can play until the cows come home and long after the chickens come to roost. They know nobody human can dance as long as I can play." He looks away from the bow and straight at me. "They don't know you."

I turn my head away. I don't know how long I can dance. All night, for sure, then paddle home after and dance in the cabin while I do my chores. Maybe the next night, too. I might could do what I guess 'Dres Petitpas wants. But I won't. I won't show my face to the people of Pierreville, my white face and pink eyes and white, white hair. I won't go among the ducks and risk their pecking—not for anybody and for sure not for 'Dres Petitpas.

"I see you at the Doucet *fais-do-do*," he says. "I see you dance like a leaf in the wind, like no human girl I ever seen. I go to a man I know, a hairy, sharp-tooth man, and he tell me about a little swamp owl girl dances all night long at the loup-garous' ball. I think this girl go make a good partner for my boys. What you say, *hien*? You come dance with my five strong sons?"

My heart is sick inside me, but I can't be angry at the loup-garou who betrayed me. 'Dres Petitpas is a hard man to say no to. But I do. I say, "No."

"I don't ask you to dance for nothing," 'Dres Petitpas coaxes me. "I go give you land to raise cotton on and a mule to plow it with."

"No."

"You greedy girl, you," he says, like it's a compliment. "How you like to marry one of my sons, then? Any one you like. Then you be important lady, nobody dare call you swamp owl girl or little white slug."

I jump up and go for him, so angry the blood burns like ice in my veins. I stop when I see he's holding Tante Eulalie's fiddle over his head by the neck.

"Listen, *chère*. You don't help me, I take this fiddle and make kindling out of it, and I break that loom and that wheel, and then I burn this cabin to ash. What you say, *chère*: yes or no? Say 'yes' now, and we have a bargain. You help me win my bet and I give you land and a mule and a husband to keep you warm. That is not so bad a deal, *hien*?"

It sticks in my throat, but I have no choice. "Yes," I say.

"That's good," Murderes Petitpas says, and he tucks Tante Eulalie's fiddle under his chin and draws the bow across the strings. It sounds a note, strong and sweet. "The contest is set for Saturday night—that's three nights from now. We start after supper, end when the boys get tired. Make a real *fais-do-do*, eh? Put the children down to sleep?" He laughs with the fiddle, a skip of notes. "Might could take two-three days. You understand?"

I understand very well, but I can't help trying to find a way out. "I do not know if I can dance for three days and nights."

"I say you can, and I say you will. I got your fiddle, me."

"I cannot dance in the sun."

A discord sounds across the strings. "Little white slug don't like sun, eh? No matter. We make the dance in Doucet's barn. You know where it at already." Tante Eulalie's fiddle mocks me with one of the tunes he played that night. Despite myself, my feet begin to move, and he laughs. "You a dancing fool, *chère*. I win my bet, my sons learn who's boss, and I go be a rich man on the radio."

He's fiddling as he speaks and moving toward the door. I'm dancing because I can't help it, with tears of rage stinging the back of my nose and blurring my eyes. I don't let them fall till he's gone, though. I have that much pride.

The rest of that night is black, black, and the next two days, too. There are knocks at my door, but I do not answer them. I am too busy thinking how I will make Murderes Petitpas sorry he mess with me. I take my piece of blue cloth off the loom and sew a dancing dress for myself, with Tante Eulalie's lace to the neck and cuffs. Early the third morning, I make a gris-gris with Tante Eulalie's gold ring. I sleep and wash myself and put on the dress and braid my hair in a tail down my back and hang the gris-gris around my neck. Then I get in my pirogue and paddle through the maze of the swamp to the warm lights of the Doucets' farm

It is very strange to tie my pirogue to the wharf and walk up to the barn in the open. Under my feet, the dirt is warm and smooth, and the air smells of flowers and spices and cooking meat. The barn doors are open and the lantern light shines yellow on the long tables set up outside and the good people of Pierreville swarming around with plates and forks, scooping jambalaya and gumbo, dirty rice and fried okra, red beans and grits from the dishes and pots.

At first they don't see me and then they do, and all the gumbo ya-ya of talk stops dead. I walk toward them through a quiet like the swamp at sunset. My heart beats so hard under my blue dress that I think everybody must see it, but I keep my chin up. The people are afraid, too. I can smell it on them, see it in their flickering eyes that will not meet mine, hear it in their whispers: *Haunt. Devil. Look at her eyes—like fireballs. Unnatural.*

A woman steps in front of me. She is wiry and faded, with white-streaked hair in stiff curls around her ears and a flowery dress made up of store-bought calico. "I am Octavie Petitpas," she says, her voice tight with fear. "You come to dance with my sons?"

I see 'Dres Petitpas grinning his yellow-tooth grin over her head. "Yes, ma'am."

"Your partner's here, boys," 'Dres Petitpas shouts. "Time to dance!"

The fiddler turns to five men standing in an uneven line—his five sons. The first must be Clopha the reader, thin as his father is wide, with lines of worry across his forehead. Aristile and 'Tit Paul are big like their father, with trapped, angry eyes. Louis is a little older than me, with a moustache thin as winter grass. Télémaque is still a boy, all knees and elbows.

I walk up to Clopha and hold out my hand. He looks at it, then takes it with a sigh. His hand is cold as deep water.

We all troop into the Doucets' barn, Clopha and me and 'Dres and every soul from St. Mary's parish who can find a place to stand. 'Dres climbs up on a trestle table, swings his fiddle to his shoulder, and starts to play "Jolie Blonde." He's grinning under his black moustache and stamping with his foot: he's having a good time, if nobody else is.

Clopha and I start to dance. I know right away that he will not last long. He has already lost the bet in his heart, him, already lost his Marie, who I can see watching us, her hands to her mouth and tears wetting her cheeks like a heavy rain. It is hard work dancing with Clopha. I think his father tricks him so often that he is like Old Boudreaux, who doesn't know how to win. Clopha is heavy and slow. I have to set the pace, change directions, twirl under his lax arm without help or signal. He plods through five, six, seven tunes, and then he stumbles and falls to his knees, shaking his head heavily until Marie Eymard comes and helps him up with a glare that would burn me black, if it could.

Then it is Aristile's turn.

Aristile is strong, him, and he is on fire to beat me. My head barely reaches his heart, and he crushes me to him as if to smother me. Half the time, I'm dancing on tiptoe. The other, I'm thrown here and there by his powerful arms, my shoulders aching as he puts me through my paces like a mule. It's wrestling, not dancing, but I dance with wolves, me, and I am stronger than I look. Six songs, seven, eight, nine, and then the tunes all run together under our flying feet. I do not even notice that Aristile has fallen until I find myself dancing alone. Then I blink at the sun pouring in through the barn door while two men carry Aristile to a long bench along the wall. I see a girl in pink kneel beside him with a cup and a cloth for his red face, and then I go up to 'Tit Paul and the music carries us away.

'Tit Paul is even more angry than his brother, and bigger and taller. He cheats. When we spin, he loosens his grip on my waist and wrist, hoping to send me flying into the crowd. I cling to him like a crab, me, pincing his shirt, his cuff, his thick, sweaty wrist. The dance is a war between us, each song a battle, even the waltzes. I win them all, and also the war, when 'Tit Paul trips over his own dragging feet and falls full length in the dust, barrel chest heaving, teeth bared like a mink. I feel no pity for him. I think someday 'Tit Paul will find a way to shove his father's curse back into his throat.

The music doesn't stop, so I don't either, two-stepping alone as men carry 'Tit Paul to the bench where he, too, is comforted by a dark-haired girl. Through the barn doors, I see that it is dark again outside. I have danced, as 'Dres Petitpas has fiddled, for a night and a day. I am a little tired.

I dance up to Louis and hold out my hand.

Louis, who understands numbers, dances carefully, making me do all the work of turning, twisting, threading the needles he makes with his arms. From time to time, he speeds up suddenly, stumbles in my way so I must skip to keep from falling, throws me off balance whenever he can. After a time, his father sees what he's up to and shouts at him, and the spirit goes out of Louis like water draining out the hole in a bucket. There is a girl to give him water and soft words when he falls, too, a thin child with her hair in braids. I feel no pity for Louis, either, who is sly enough to beat his father at his own game when he's older.

It's light again by now, and I have danced for two nights and a day. I feel that my body is not my own but tied by the ears to Murderes Petitpas's fiddle bow. As long as he plays, I will dance, though my feet bleed into the barn floor and my eyes sting with the dust. 'Dres launches into "La Two-Step Petitpas," and I dance up to Télémaque, who is still a child, and all I think when I hold out my hand is how glad I am Octavie gave her husband no more sons.

Télémaque, like me, is stronger than he looks. He has watched me dance with his four brothers, and he has learned that I cannot be tripped and I cannot be flung. He gives me a sad, sweet smile and limps as he dances, like he's a poor cripple boy I'd be ashamed to beat. I think it is a trick lower than any of Louis's, and I turn my face from him and let myself be lost in the stream of music. The bow of 'Dres Petitpas lifts my feet; his fingers guide my arms; his notes swirl me up and down and around as a paddle swirls the waters of the bayou. Around me, I feel something like a thunderstorm building, clouds piling, uneasy with lightning, the air growing thicker and thicker until I gasp for breath, dancing in the middle of the Doucets' barn with Télémaque limp at my bleeding feet and Murderes Petitpas triumphant on his table and his neighbors around us, growling and muttering.

"The last one down!" he crows. "What you say now, Octavie?"

Octavie Petitpas steps out from the boiling cloud of people, and if she looked worn before, now she looks gray as death.

"I say you are a fine fiddler, Murderes Petitpas. There ain't a man in the whole of Louisiana, maybe even the world, could do what you done. Or would want to."

"I am a fine fiddler," 'Dres says. "Still, I can't win my bet without my little owl girl, eh?" He waves his bow arm toward the five brothers sitting on the bench with their gray-faced sweethearts. "There they are, girl. Take your pick, you. Any one you want for your husband, and land and a mule, just like I promised. Murderes Petitpas, he keep his word, *hien*?"

I touch Tante Eulalie's lace at my neck for luck, and the little bulge of the gris-gris hanging between my breasts and I say, "I do not want your land or your mule, 'Dres Petitpas. I do not want to marry any of your five sons. They have sweethearts of their own, them, nice Cajun girls with black eyes and rosy cheeks who will give them nice black-eyed babies."

An astonished wind of whispers blows through the crowd.

I go on. "I make you a bet now, Murderes Petitpas. I bet I can dance longer than you can. Dance with me, and if I win, you will give your blessing on your sons' marriages and return what you stole from me."

His eyes narrow under his broad-brimmed hat, and his fingers grip the neck of his fiddle. "No," he says. "I make no more bets, me. I have what I want. I will not dance with you."

"If you do not dance, Murderes Petitpas, everybody will think you are afraid of a little white-skin, pink-eye swamp girl, with her bare feet all bloody. What you afraid of, *hien*? You, who fiddle the devil out of hell and back down again?"

"I ain't afraid," says 'Dres through his flat yellow teeth. "I just ain't interested. You don't want to marry together with one of my sons, you go away back to the swamp. We got no further business together."

Louis gets to his feet and limps up beside me. "I say you do, Pap. If you win, you get my word I don't go run away first chance I see."

"And my word I don't go with him," says Télémaque, joining him.

Aristile comes up on the other side of me. "And mine."

"And mine," says 'Tit Paul.

"And you got my word not to make your life a living hell for taking my sons from me out of pure cussedness," says Octavie.

'Dres Petitpas looks down on the pack of us. His face is red as fire and his eyes glow hot as coals. "I see you boys still got some learning to do. I take your bet, swamp owl girl. You bring up a fiddler to play for us, and I dance the sun around again."

Everybody get real quiet, and Octavie says, "'Dres, you know there ain't no other fiddler in St. Mary's parish."

"That's it, then. I don't dance without music. The bet's off."

Someone in the crowd laughs. I'd laugh myself if this was

a story I was hearing, about Young 'Dres Petitpas and how he owns all the music in St. Mary's parish.

Then another voice speaks out of the crowd. "I will play for this dance," says my friend Ulysse.

I spin around to see him in a store-bought suit, with his wild, black hair all slicked down with oil, looking innocent as a puppy in a basket.

"I have an accordion," he says, and gives me a sharp-toothed smile, and I know, just then, that I love him.

Another man turns up with a washboard and a spoon, and he and Ulysse jump up on the table as 'Dres Petitpas climbs down. Ulysse strikes up a tune I've heard a thousand times: "T'es Petite et T'es Mignonne," which is Tante Eulalie's special tune for me. It gives my weary feet courage, and I dance up to Murderes Petitpas and take hold of his hand.

That is when the good people of Pierreville discover that Murderes Petitpas cannot dance. He has two left feet and he can't keep time, and he may know what a Window or a Cajun Cuddle or a Windmill looks like from above, but he for sure doesn't know how to do them. We stumble and fumble this way and that around the floor while the storm breaks at last in a gale of laughter. I am laughing, too, in spite of the pain in my feet, like dancing on nails or needles. I don't care if he falls first or I do. I've won already, me. The good people of Pierreville have seen 'Dres Petitpas for what he is. His sons will marry whoever they want, and he will not dare say a word against it.

Scree, scraw goes the accordion; *thunk-whoosh* goes the washboard, with Ulysse's hoarse voice wailing above it all, and I'm dancing like the midges above the water at dusk, with 'Dres stumbling after me. Somehow my feet don't hurt so much now, and my legs are light, and I enjoy myself. It is still dark outside the barn when 'Dres falls to his knees and bends his head.

As the accordion wheezes into silence, Octavie runs to her husband and puts her arms around his shoulders. His sons are kissing their sweethearts, and everybody's talking and fetching more food and slapping Ulysse and the washboard player on the back and pretending that I don't exist.

I step up to Octavie and I say, "Miz Petitpas, I'll take my fiddle now, my Tante Eulalie's fiddle your husband took from me."

She looks up and says, "Eulalie? Old Eulalie Favrot, that run away to the swamp? You kin to Eulalie Favrot?"

I nod. "Tante Eulalie take me in when I'm a baby, raise me like her own."

Octavie stands up and waves to an ancient lady in a faded homespun dress. "Tante Belda, you come here. This here's Eulalie Favrot's girl she raised. What you think of that?"

The ancient lady brought her face, wrinkled as wet cloth, right up to my lace collar so she can squint at it better. "That 'Lalie's wedding lace," she says. "I know it anywhere, me. How she keeping, girl?"

"She catch a cough this winter and die," I say.

"I sure am sorry to hear that," the ancient lady says. "'Lalie is my cousin, godmother to my girl, Denise. She marry Hercule Favrot back in the 'teens sometime. Poor Hercule. He lose his shrimp boat and his nets to 'Dres Petitpas because of some *couyon* bet they make. Hercule take to drink, him, beat 'Lalie half to death. One morning she find him floating in the duck pond, dead as a gutted fish. 'Lalie go away after the funeral, nobody know where. She never have no children."

"She have me," I say. "Can I have her fiddle back now?"

Someone brings me a plate of food while I wait, but I am too tired to eat. My legs shake and my feet burn and sting. I think maybe I should sit down, but I can't move my legs, and how will I get home before light? I feel tears rising in my eyes, and then there is an arm around my waist and a voice in my ear.

"Cadence, *chère*," Ulysse says. "Miz Petitpas bring your fiddle. Take it, you, and I carry you home to sleep."

The plate disappears from my hands and Tante Eulalie's fiddle and bow appear in its place. Ulysse picks me up in his arms like I'm a little child, and I put my head against the tight weave of his store-bought suit and let him carry me out of the Doucets' barn.

The moon's getting low, and there's a chill in the air says dawn isn't far away. Ulysse sets me in my pirogue, crawls in after, casts off, and starts to paddle. I see the Doucets' wharf get small behind us, and the people of Pierreville standing there, watching us go. The ancient lady that once was the prettiest girl in the parish waves her handkerchief to us as we slip among the cypress trees and the lights of the Doucets' farm disappear behind Spanish moss and leaves.

We do not speak as we glide through the waterways. The music echoes in my ears, accordion and washboard and fiddle all together as they play them at the loup-garous' ball. I hum a little, quietly. The sun rises and Ulysse throws me his jacket to put over my head. When we get to my cabin, Ulysse carries me and my fiddle inside and closes the door.

Not long after, we are married together, Ulysse and me, with Tante Eulalie's gold ring. We still live in the swamp, but we visit Pierreville to hear the gossip and go to a *fais-do-do* now and then. Ulysse always brings his accordion and plays if they ask him. But I keep my dancing for the loup-garous' ball and for my husband in our own cabin. We dance to the music of our voices singing and the fiddling of our eldest daughter, 'Tit 'Lalie.

And Murderes Petitpas?

Old 'Dres Petitpas fiddles no more, him. He says he fiddle himself dry in those two days and two nights. He won't go out into the swamp either, but sits on his front porch and sorts eggs from Octavie's chickens and tells his grandchildren big stories about what a fine fiddler he used to be. Aristile's got Old Boudreaux's fiddle now, and you can hear him playing with his wife's brother and two cousins on the radio. But Aristile Petitpas ain't the only fiddler in St. Mary's parish, not by a long shot. There's plenty of fiddlers around these days, and singers and accordion players and guitar players. They play Cajun and zydeco, waltzes and two-steps and the new jitterbugs, and they play them real fine. But there's none them can fiddle the devil out of hell, like 'Dres Petitpas did one time.

DELIA SHERMAN was born in Tokyo, Japan, and grew up in New York City, spending summers with her mother's family in Texas and Louisiana. She is the author of novels and short stories for adults, as well as a number of short stories for younger readers, which have appeared in the anthologies *The Green Man*, *The Faery Reel*, and *Firebirds*. *Changeling*, a novel about New York's magical underside, was published in 2006. She learned Cajun dancing in Boston, and has danced at *fais do-dos* in Lowell, Massachusetts, and Lafayette, Louisiana. She currently lives in New York City.

Visit her Web site at www.deliasherman.com.

～

AUTHOR'S NOTE

This story grows out of many different interests and parts of my life. Basically, I'm a city girl, but I love the bayou country of Louisiana: its music, and the dancing that goes with it. I've got kin in Louisiana, so I've been familiar with the landscape for a long time. My interest in Cajun music and dance is much more recent—about ten years ago, in fact, when a place down the street from me in Boston started a Cajun Dance Night. Cajun dancing appealed to me because it's both flashy and easy to learn, and I fell in love with the music. Since Cajun culture is a Creole (mixture) of different cultures, it seemed appropriate to base my plot on a British traditional ballad, "The Bonny Lass of Anglesey," which was recorded by the English folk singer Martin Carthy on his album *Crown of Horn* (1976).

A TALE FOR THE SHORT DAYS

Richard Bowes

PART ONE

The God of Thieves found himself in a vast hall filled with people rushing about laden with packages and dressed in big, heavy coats. As yet, no mortal could see him. Great glassed windows on all sides showed evening and a city. From the ceilings far above, electric chandeliers pushed back the dusk. The Trickster God is lord of the night, and all this light offended him.

Almost immediately he noticed a large sign that showed a huge diamond with the piece of coal inside it and the words BLACK STAR. Jewels always fascinated the God of Thieves. He envisioned the stone that was the model for the one on the sign. He saw facets that deflected a glance while drawing it in, the fleck of black like a lingering shred of the coal that was the diamond's origin. That jewel could hypnotize a mortal. It almost caught him.

The god knew he was in a northern city during the long, vivid nights of the solstice celebrations, and he wondered who had brought him here. People rarely summon the Sly One. Seldom does anyone offer the prayer, "Oh God of Tricksters and Thieves, come disturb my peace of mind and steal my belongings." Not just like that.

Amid the salesmen with pocket flasks and sample cases, the women laden with department store bags, he spotted clusters of young people, children of the great families. They were passing through this station, changing trains, going home from colleges, from prep schools and women's academies.

In this bustling United States on these bubbling, waning days of the year 1928, they waved their hellos and shouted their good-byes to each other over the heads of ordinary travelers.

The Trickster caught a whiff of rebellion in the air. He spied a very young woman amid a crowd of youths but not entirely of them and knew, with the instinct of a thief, that this was the daughter of a great man, a power in the land, a lord of artificial light. Her father owned Black Star Coal. It was one of his company's advertising billboards with its corporate symbol of a great diamond that the god had just seen.

The lights above, the trains that ran beneath the marble floors, were powered by coal. The young lady of seventeen, with her sleek sealskin coat and fine, dark eyes was the youngest daughter of the Coal King. The God of Thieves understood that she disliked what her father did and that it was she who had brought him here.

Charlotte Sparkman was seventeen and on her way home from Fern Hill Academy. She wanted her booming, bullying father to pause, take a deep breath, and think about what he, with his wealth and power, was doing to his employees, to his customers, to the world itself. She also wanted him to think for a moment about her, and who she was.

For a moment, the Trickster debated on the form in which he would appear to the young woman and her world. To the cunning god, a human lifetime is no more than the wink of an eye, and changing his skin is as little trouble as changing the expression on his face. Like someone trying on clothes in front of a mirror, he flashed through possible forms. He was Loki, he was the Crow, he was Mercury, he was the Fox.

Then he remembered an amusing and useful remark. At a grand soirée in a summer palace in France in 1783, Count Reynard, as he was known at that moment, paused on his way to a conquest. There, under an oak tree, he heard a savant, a most worldly and wise man, say that if one lived a very long life, one should spend the first part of it as a beautiful woman. And that seemed perfect for what he was going to do.

The children of privilege in their overcoats and scarves, some of them daringly bareheaded, waved good-bye to those friends who were getting on trains heading south, heading east, and then made their way out the doors to the taxi ramps for the trip from Pennsylvania Station to Grand Central Station.

Boys and girls from colleges and academies and finishing schools laughed and blew frosted breath as redcaps shouted and doormen's whistles shrilled. Luggage was stuffed in trunks and strapped to the roofs and the children of wealth bundled six at a time into large cabs with the youngest of them on the jump seats and maybe the smallest sitting on someone's lap.

Sunlight was all but gone and the amber-tinged streetlights were on. The early dark evoked a delicious shiver, a buried memory of their light-worshipping ancestors who saw the sun go out in the short days. So they laughed and sang in the dim interiors and urged their cabbies to race, across town, the taxis full of their friends.

~ ~ ~

Charlotte Sparkman found herself in the backseat of a cab with the youngest Borden boy and the Carson brothers coming home from Phillips Exeter and Dartmouth, and Mopsy Mildaur returning from her first semester at Miss Lowry's Finishing School.

The Sparkman girl got left out of the chatter, which she didn't mind. Young ladies who went to Fern Hill Academy made some people a bit uncomfortable. The symbol of the school was the owl, a bird sacred to the Goddess of Wisdom. And the girls of Fern Hill had a reputation for having more brains than was considered quite necessary.

She noticed the sixth member of the group. This was a young English aristocrat, a vital year or two older than Charlotte, with honey-colored hair wonderfully waved and, worn at the slightest angle, a green trilby hat that matched her eyes.

Charlotte was sure they had met before. Had it been at Newport the previous summer? She was normally so good with names. But this one was slow in coming. The young woman smiled at her and Charlotte said, "Lady Jessica Viviyan, I am so glad to see you again."

That was an amazing thing to say, because before that moment in the cab, the lovely creature she spoke to had no name and in fact did not exist. Lady Jessica had come into focus as Charlotte and the wily god invented her.

"So shy making," said Jessica Viviyan, which is what the Bright Young Things of London said about everything. "My maid is being driven up with my trunks. I came on ahead. The Harrimans are expecting me. Charlotte Sparkman," Lady Jessica said. "We two will be great friends. I am never wrong about these things."

"I would like that," said the youngest daughter of the president and chairman of Black Star Coal. And Jessica Viviyan laughed a short laugh almost like a bark.

The Coal King's daughter introduced her new friend to the others. "The daughter of the Earl of Lachmere," she said, not sure how she knew that. And the others were very impressed despite themselves.

"I came here to land a rich American," said Lady Jessica Viviyan, and they all laughed.

By the time they were out of the cab and in Grand Central Station, Lady Jessica had captured the hearts of both Carson brothers, whose family owned ocean liners. "Seafarers, I see. Young admirals. Sons of the open seas. Father would like that, I think," she said, smiling but admiring, too. They stood staring as she blew them a kiss and walked away.

Mopsy Mildaur got swept off in another band of young people who had come by calling her name. Then, on a train running beside the Hudson, Jessica Viviyan was calling the Borden boy—who some said was a tad slow—Sir Tommy, which caused him much embarrassment and delight.

Then he too was gone, and the Prince of Foxes and the King of Coal's daughter were alone, and Miss Sparkman was telling how she had come to the attention of her art instructor, who had recommended a studio class. The formidable lady who taught painting and had studied with Eakins had wondered if she would be interested in pursuing this further.

Charlotte's mother had died some years before. Her father had not yet remarried. He refused to consider his youngest daughter's request.

"There's so much in the world that I want to see. So many paintings, so many plays. And so many people I want to meet.

I want to live in Paris; I want to see Venice and Mexico and China."

"But?" asked Lady Jessica.

"My father," said Charlotte Sparkman, "has come to believe he really is a king and that he can command lives and steer the whole world."

"I shall have to speak to your father," said Jessica Viviyan.

And it seemed to Charlotte after just an hour with this person that it would be a very good thing if that were to happen. The conductor came through and announced that their next stop would be the private station at the edge of the Sparkman estate. A train steward came forward to help with her luggage.

As Charlotte rose she looked at the Cunning Lord. "There's to be a soirée at my father's house on Thursday for the lighting of the tree," she said. "Could I ask you to come?"

"That might be utterly fun making!"

The conductor passing through the car a few moments later noted that both the fine young passengers must have gotten off the train together.

The tree lighting a few nights later was probably utter fun only for a god bent on mischief and Old King Coal himself. Other guests, present for fear of offending the host, wore their best public faces and counted the minutes. A contingent of Texas oilmen, representatives of Black Diamond's new petroleum division, looked around uneasily.

Suddenly, the lights in the chandeliers went dim. James Joseph Sparkman, in his late sixties, big and bald, stood in his enormous, overheated ballroom before a twenty-foot-tall blue

Canadian pine tree. At the end of a rather long speech, he said as he had at every one of these ceremonies, "My grandfather and my father went down into the ground to dig up the coal that keeps this nation warm and alight. It's in their memory that I light this tree."

Five hundred colored electric bulbs sprang on at once. And in the moment of silence before the applause, a voice said, "So shy making that my father will never even allow electricity in the castle."

Without looking, J. J. Sparkman knew it was that Viviyan girl, Lady Jessica, that his daughter Charlotte had met, the one whose father was a lord. At dinner J. J. had heard a voice, clear and English, say, "You American men go and carve your kingdoms out of this continent. At home it was all carved up long ago."

Someone had told him that she was here to find a rich American husband. It seemed to him that she would be a wonderful catch, but Sparkman's sons were all married, and his grandsons were just children.

Unlike his ancestors, J. J. Sparkman rarely personally encountered a lump of coal. Diamonds were another matter. He had an obsession with them. They glittered on the ample front of his shirt. His collection was huge and included the famed Black Star Diamond.

In a pause in the conversation, Lady Jessica said, "A diamond is coal's way of creating art." Her voice had just the hint of throatiness in it.

From the moment Jessica Viviyan had swept through the front door, exclaiming, "How envy making, a castle bigger than dear father's!" the Trickster had been very aware that the

Black Star was on the premises. This fabulous stone legendarily contained within it the black speck that a mortal eye could glimpse but on which it could never focus.

This stone was the trademark of Black Star Coal. Its image appeared on billboards, in newspapers, on the side of coal trucks. The god saw it as a talisman and a trophy.

"Always rather thought of a diamond as a light from below the earth," remarked Lady Jessica Viviyan. And James Jacob Sparkman, who had thought of her at first as just a schoolgirl like his daughter, looked at her more closely and realized that she was a bit older than that, a woman with an understanding of the world.

Later, after the crowds had dispersed back to their estates and up to their bedrooms, Sparkman sat in his study and thought about the young Englishwoman he'd seen and listened to that evening. He even imagined himself in some not-distant future saying, "Just came back from visiting my wife's family's place. Her father the earl's a wonderful old boy, a little set in his ways. Still had the ancestral castle lighted with gas. But I talked to him, we get along really well, and he agreed to have the whole place electrified and now it can be seen for miles around."

At that moment, a side door opened and a woman in a dress of moonlight silver slipped in. "Old King Coal, you promised to show me the Black Star."

"Did I?" Sparkman tried to remember exactly when he might have said that.

"You told me you had it under lock and key"—Lady Jessica smiled playfully and imitated his voice—"that it wouldn't be prudent to leave it out."

James Joseph Sparkman unlocked a closet door and went

to a safe. He twirled the combination, reached inside, and pulled out a black velvet bag.

When he turned, he held the Black Star in his hand. The god looked upon the facets that drew the eye in. He spotted the black speck that looked like a shred of the coal from which the jewel had been formed. He knew this treasure was not something to be left in the hands of this gross mortal.

Lady Jessica smiled at Sparkman in a way no woman ever had. The smile spoke of desire and admiration, and he was utterly in the power of the God of Thieves.

The house was silent, servants and guests slept. Charlotte lay awake. She hadn't seen Lady Jessica leave that evening and yet she hadn't been able to find her. Charlotte rose, put on a robe, went out of her room and down the hall to the head of the great curving stairs.

The huge tree, still lighted, stood in the grand ballroom. Jessica Viviyan appeared in her dress of moonlight. In one hand she held a black velvet bag. Under an arm was a bundle of black-and-gray-striped cloth.

With an effortless flick, she tossed the cloth at the Christmas tree. James Jacob Sparkman's pants unfurled like a sail. The suspenders caught on the star at the treetop.

"I believe your passage to Paris is assured," Lady Jessica said. "But wouldn't you rather come with me?"

Charlotte shook her head. There was too much of this world that she hadn't seen. After the god said farewell and disappeared in a shimmer of human and animal shapes, Charlotte sat very still for a time. Then she rose, went down the stairs, got up on a chair, and unhooked the striped pants from the tree. She found her father in the closet where the God of Thieves had locked him.

Neither he nor she ever referred to the incident again. But from that evening on, she did as she wished: studied in Paris, lived in Mexico. Knew Picasso and Frida Kahlo, had several interesting liaisons. It was she, as a young American surrealist, who painted *Winter Solstice, 1928*.

It has a prominent spot in the Museum of Modern Art. Critics see the striped pants hanging on the lighted Christmas tree as symbolizing the end of the Roaring Twenties and the onset of the Great Depression. The artist herself never had anything to say about the meaning of her most famous painting.

PART TWO

Many years—a couple of generations as humans reckon such things—passed before the Trickster was again summoned to the Sparkman estate. It was on a solstice night. He stood on a hill, saw how the dark was slashed and torn apart by the headlights of cars on highways, by streetlights on every corner, by colored Christmas lights strung on the eaves of houses and on trees on front lawns. The horizon glowed with light.

This intrusion by man into the realm of darkness bothered the god greatly. Then he saw, in bright neon, a white stallion leaping over a giant diamond and the words BLACK STAR. The sign was on the roof of a huge, brightly lit gas station full of pumps and cars. He remembered the Coal King and knew he was back in that kingdom.

Guests converged on the estate, the children of the family returned from school. Vehicles arrived from all directions, passed by the gatehouse.

The God of Thieves, still invisible to mortal eyes, considered how he should appear among them. He remembered his last visit and that reminded him again of a certain night on the grounds of a summer palace in old France.

The Trickster had gone there to steal the Lilac Emerald, which he felt had too much beauty and magic for mortals to own. Madame Decamier, the mistress of the king of France, wore the emerald on a gold chain around her lovely neck.

It was on his way to a tryst with la Grande Decamier that he had overheard a wise and witty man entertaining a small audience. This savant, after telling them that one who lived a long life should spend youth as a beautiful woman, said that the middle years should be spent as a man of honor and respect: a triumphant general was the example he gave.

The Lord of Thieves had snatched that epigram out of the air and taken it with him. A few hours afterward, with the Lilac Emerald in his hand, he stepped onto the balcony of Madame Decamier's bedroom and disappeared.

More than two hundred years later, he thought it would be amusing to come to the Sparkman estate as a man of honor and fame. But as the Lord of Thieves assessed the minds of the guests, he realized that in this year of wonder, 1988, generals were of no particular interest. These people who defiled the night idolized minstrels, mimes, actors who played generals.

Charlotte was at the Sparkman mansion that night. Her father had gotten old very fast after the winter solstice of 1928. When he died a few years later, some obituaries said the great age of coal had died with its king.

Only after his death was it discovered that the fabled Black Star Diamond was missing. It was a tabloid scandal, a dead-end investigation, an unsolved mystery. His sons took over the company and diversified. Petroleum was what would run the world. They got into East Texas crude.

Charlotte was the family eccentric: an artist and a benefactor of the arts. But the family always invited her for Christmas on the Sparkman estate. And because she loved her nieces and nephews and grandnieces and grandnephews, she sometimes attended.

With each visit, she found many of her relatives, especially her eldest brother, J. J. Junior (nicknamed "Three Js"), a bit more exploitative and hubris-driven than the time before. Among the family, there were always some of the younger ones who agreed with her.

In the years since her first encounter with the Sly God, she had thought of him often and learned a certain amount about his ways. Earlier that day, she had prayed for his return, with little faith that this would do any good.

Then in the late afternoon, her young grandniece Alicia, to whom she was very close, told her, "It's so funny that everyone's excited Dane Barron is here. I didn't even know who he was at first. He wasn't even a huge star, but they're giving him the grand tour."

"And who is he?" Charlotte was a bit interested.

"The old cowboy actor, Aunt Charlotte. Don't they know about him in France?"

Charlotte thought that might be the case. She didn't pay much attention to American movies, now that they didn't have Garbo or Gable in them. But she had to see and make sure.

As she was going downstairs, she passed a cousin whom she thought was an idiot. The woman said, "Dane Barron has that same little smile I remember from that corny movie where,

I think, Burt Lancaster was the gangster and Barron was the policeman and they grew up together and the policeman character just can't help being amused when his old friend does something outrageous. I'd forgotten that I once had such a crush on him."

In the library, Charlotte found a pair of old Texas oilmen, her brothers' partners, sitting around gossiping.

"It's those westerns he did when I was a kid," one of them said. "He was from the high plains, Montana I think."

And the other added, "There was something about the way he played the rancher in that one where his daughter gets kidnapped that was just so right. Kept it all inside until the end of the movie and then let loose."

"Your brother J. J. is showing Dane the stables," said the first oilman when she asked.

"That movie, what was the name of it he was in with that young actor who was supposed to be so tough? McQueen?" someone said. "Barron played the father and just walked off with the movie. So authentic."

"Heard he's thinking about going into politics," someone else remarked as Charlotte put on a coat and went outside.

Walking past the paddocks on the earliest dusk of the year, she was reminded of another solstice and the appearance of another figure everyone thought they knew.

In the stables, Charlotte's oldest brother, J. J. Sparkman Junior, said, "And this is Constellation. His sire was the model for our corporate logo."

"You have a princely stable here. Nothing like this in Hollywood," Dane Barron said.

The big black stallion with the white diamond on his forehead looked their way and knew he was being discussed.

The leap that the horse on the logo made was an impossible one, an artist's conceit. But the Trickster saw a bit of magic in this animal. He met Constellation's eye and the two recognized each other.

You are more a king than your owner, Barron told the horse silently.

J. J. Sparkman Junior's wife said, "We bring Constellation into the house every Christmas Eve, and he has never disgraced us once."

You poor, magnificent beast, Dane Barron told Constellation. *You deserve better. You deserve to bear a god.*

Charlotte saw the tall, handsome man with the gray wings of hair. "Back when I first went out to Hollywood, they wanted to make me a singing cowboy. I told them that was perfect except for one little detail: I couldn't sing a lick," Dane Barron told Mrs. Sparkman.

The actor smiled as everyone chuckled. Charlotte saw the look of someone who told a joke but had a better one he only told himself. And now she was certain who he was.

On their way back to the house, she arranged to walk with Dane Barron. In a moment when they were alone, she said, "I'm reminded of an old friend, Lady Jessica Viviyan. Who, as it turned out, didn't exist."

Dane Barron once again smiled his smile and said, "I take it that you got to Paris and learned about painting."

"Yes, and I met many people and learned many things. Because of what I saw I became interested in tales of Count Reynard. Especially the one about Madame Decamier and the Lilac Emerald."

He said, "That is interesting."

But Charlotte's sister-in-law realized they had fallen behind and came back saying, "Laggards, keep up!"

Somewhat later, after cocktails and dinner but before the lighting of the tree, Dane Barron and Charlotte were together again briefly.

"They remember the Emerald, do they?" he asked. Mostly, the affairs of mankind were of only mild interest to the Trickster God.

"At the time," Charlotte Sparkman told him, "its disappearance caused much consternation. Especially once word spread that it was a royal gift from the king to his mistress. *L'affaire de Lilac* set off several larger scandals. Questions about the ways in which France itself was being run.

"It was one of the things that led to the revolution not that many years later. The wisdom of the savants at the garden party didn't enable them to escape the guillotine. Madame Decamier and even the king met the same fate."

All of this seemed to be news to the Sly God. Dane Barron tilted his handsome head to the side and thought about it.

"It's my brother's horse you're going after this time, isn't it?" she asked the god. "Why?"

"He's stolen the dark from me. That horse is his totem, his symbol. It appears on his standard. When I take it, I will have stolen his soul."

"The horse jumping over the diamond is a commercial logo. And Constellation himself, however beautiful, is just a horse. In the unlikely event that my brother has a soul, that's not where it is."

"I asked you once to come with me."

"I was flattered. And tempted. And now I am too old, as we

both know. When you return again, it will be because someone suitable has summoned you. I promise."

That night when the lights went down in the ballroom chandeliers and the Christmas tree lights came on, alarms went off at the stables. Despite a ground fog, the estate was well illuminated. Charlotte and her grandniece Alicia were first among the ones who hurried from the mansion in time to see the brazen theft.

Constellation sailed over the paddock gate. The rider on his back called out, "Adios, from the King of Thieves." And people could almost remember the movie where Dane Barron had said just that.

None of the police, or the private investigators Sparkman hired after the police gave up, could find a trace of the horse. None of them even knew where to start looking for anyone named Dane Barron.

"Impersonating a celebrity's not easy," one detective remarked to another. "But to invent one, then convince a hundred people that he exists and you're him! This has to be the greatest con man who ever lived."

While the law failed, the huge public relations force that Sparkman deployed did succeed in burying most of what was a thoroughly embarrassing story.

PART THREE

The old gods went about their business as they always had. But they did it more slowly, to less purpose and with less squabbling, because there seemed to be nothing worthwhile about which to squabble.

The Trickster and the Sun, as gods of night and day, had once been enemies. Now that there was so little night and so much artificial day, the Shadow God kept his horse, Constellation, stabled with the steeds that hauled the God of Light's chariot. And when they passed each other they exchanged greetings. Spoke about old times.

The Trickster, on his sojourns to the world of man, had seen the signs and totems: billboards that showed a smiling sun with beams radiating out, television commercials featuring groups of racially integrated children running barefoot past windmills and solar panels. He saw the word *SolarWind*; he heard a soft, intimate voice say, "SolarWind: energy from the earth, energy from the air, energy from the sun. Energy for all of us."

And always at the bottom of the sign, at the corner of the screen was a tiny diamond with a horse leaping over it and the words BLACK STAR. So he already knew what his enemy was up to on the solstice day when someone prayed for his presence.

"Oh, God of Thieves, a mortal has developed ideas above his station," this one had said. "He has stolen the sun and the wind. Only you can help us stop this."

For a third time the god was drawn back to the Sparkman estate. Choosing his identity, it pleased him to think once again of the wise man on that long ago night at the Château Decamier. The savant had said, "After spending the first third of one's life as a beautiful woman, and the middle third as a celebrated man, one who wishes to make the best use of a long life should spend the last third as a person who is holy and wise."

The Trickster now understood that the wise man had not been wise enough to keep his head on his shoulders during the revolution. Still he acted on the aphorism because it made the game more amusing if it had some arbitrary rules.

On a winter solstice almost a hundred years after his first visit, he floated amid the guests who congregated at the Sparkman estate and cast about to discover just what sort of holy man was honored in this time and place.

"Norville! I didn't even know he was still alive," said James Sparkman the Fourth when told that Peter Norville, author of *The Cosmology of the Entrepreneur*, had just arrived as someone's guest. "It must be fifty years since he wrote that book about God as a venture capitalist."

J4, as he was called, was the great-grandson of the Coal King. Someone, probably one of his own public relations people, had called him the man with the sun in his pocket and the wind at his back; he was rumored to be thinking of running for president. Some thought that was superfluous, since he already owned the country.

SolarWind, a wholly owned subsidiary of Black Star Energy, had a distribution lock on 80 percent of the solar power and wind energy produced in North America. It was slowly tightening the screws, raising prices. Monopoly, people said. But they didn't say it very loudly.

James Sparkman the Fourth was certain, the way he was certain of so much, that he had read Norville's book. "Twenty years back, when I had to take over the family business during the oil bust, that book laid it all out for me. I'll have to thank the author," said the man who some said owned the sun and the wind.

Diana Sparkman listened, fascinated as her distant cousin J4 talked about this legendary guru who had taught the rich to love themselves even more than they already did. Diana was the only one at the solstice gathering who understood that this celebrity had never existed before this moment. Diana was twenty-two and here to enact the legacy of her great-grandaunt Charlotte. She was the one who had prayed for the Trickster's return.

Charlotte Sparkman had been a kind of double threat, artist and patroness. There weren't a whole lot of Sparkman paintings. But her talent was real. In her later years, with her grandniece Alicia as president, she had set up a small research institute and a museum of surrealist paintings in an elegant town house just off Central Park.

The collection came to be dominated by a work found in Charlotte's studio after her death. *Into the Night* shows a horse and rider flying over a brightly lit night landscape. The horse is Constellation; the land below him is the Sparkman estate. The rider is Dane Barron.

Charlotte Sparkman had no children, but she did have disciples in her family, and they gathered at the Sparkman Institute. As Black Star Energy grew, suppressed its rivals, consolidated monopolies on solar and wind power, the members of the Institute gathered information, made contacts, bided their time.

Eventually they settled on a bright and daring great-grandniece of Charlotte's as their agent. Young Diana was trained for this moment and taught the prayer to use. When Diana saw Peter Norville, she knew the first part of her mission had succeeded.

Norville—majestic, white haired, surrounded by longtime admirers who in fact had never heard of him before—wore a slight smile. When he looked across the crowd and their eyes met, he nodded.

Later, they stood at the back of the crowd as J4 stood in

front of the Christmas tree and talked about the century-old family custom. In one hand he held a gold wand.

"I took the Black Diamond, I took Constellation," murmured the god. "I stole the family talismans and still they destroy the night." He was puzzled, almost hurt.

Diana said, "It's the difference between symbol and substance. Losing the diamond didn't destroy the coal company. Losing the horse didn't destroy the oil company.

"What you didn't have was media access. The loss of the diamond was found out only when J. J. Sparkman died. The only ones who saw you steal the horse, besides Great-great-aunt Charlotte and Cousin Alicia, were the very ones who wanted the story killed."

James Sparkman said, "And now, a moment of dark." He waved the wand, and the lights inside and outside the house went out. "And then light." The Christmas tree came on. Moving lights ran up and down the branches; stars, angels, Santas shimmered in the fir.

"I intend," said the god, "to take that wand away from him."

"It's a remote control," Diana said. "I'll take care of that. But I do have another prayer for the God of Night. A request for something only he can do."

"How goes it," the Trickster asked the Sun God who was leading his chariot horses out of the stable.

"Oh, you know"—the other shrugged—"life goes on. I guide the sun on its path. I suppose it would go anyway."

"But not as swiftly or as well as when you guide it. I've heard that down on earth there's a man who claims to control the sun and the wind, who makes others pay with their blood and sweat for their light and power. I think you should tell Brother Wind about that. Here, I'll drive those horses for you today."

It was pitch-dark as Diana drove out of the Sparkman estate. The gates hung open and useless. Ten minutes before, power to the estate had been cut. A small fire had knocked out the backup generator.

Flashlights shone inside the house. Someone had lighted a fire in a fireplace. In a bag on the seat beside her was the remote control wand J4 had used the evening before.

The radio had drive time DJs on. "Old Mr. Sun seems to be a little lazy this morning," said one with just the hint of panic.

"The news services report messages received last night saying that the dawn in the eastern United States would be seven minutes late."

"Whoa," said the other. "And here's a story that Sparkman, Mr. Sunlight himself, has a major power outage in his home."

"The message last night demanded that Black Star Energy give back the night. It was signed by the God of Thieves."

"I didn't even know they had a god."

Diana flicked off the radio. A helicopter flew overhead. A TV camera truck raced toward the estate. She knew that tabloid TV and the blogs would be alive with new sensations and old scandals.

On the morning that the sun decided to be a little late, the Sparkman estate was blacked out. By coincidence, it was exactly fifty years since the day on which Constellation was stolen. This would be a good excuse for the media to review that and the never-explained mystery of the Black Star Diamond.

The first rays of dawn outlined a hillock overlooking the

road. On it stood a horse with a diamond on his forehead and a rider who wore a diamond around his neck.

Diana felt a momentary chill as she saw the rider's face and shape change, a man in a winged helmet, a thin figure with a face like a fox, a man in a helmet with horns, a raven, a face not quite a wolf's.

She knew her disappearance would be noticed, that a search would be on. But they wouldn't find her where she was going.

Over the last twenty-plus years RICHARD BOWES has won the World Fantasy, Lambda, International Horror Guild, and Million Writer Awards. His most recent novels are *Minions of the Moon* and *From the Files of the Time Rangers*. His most recent short fiction collection, *Streetcar Dreams and Other Midnight Fancies*, was published by PS Publications in England.

His stories have been featured in the magazines *F&SF*, *Electric Velocipede*, *Subterranean*, *Clarkesworld*, and *Fantasy Magazine* and the anthologies *So Fey*, *The Del Rey Book of Science Fiction and Fantasy*, and *Naked City*.

His Web site is www.rickbowes.com.

～

AUTHOR'S NOTE

A few years ago, I wrote "The Quicksilver Kid," a story about Hermes/Mercury the Greco/Roman Trickster god and how he twisted twentieth-century American politics to his own ends. Recently, I read tales of the other European Tricksters and story cycles about the Native American Coyote god. Among the things these deities had in common was a need to defend their turf or reputation. Their enemies, who usually became their victims, were powerful: other gods, chiefs, kings. And the thing stolen, the tricks played, destroyed the honor, the "magic" of their opponents while turning them into laughingstocks. Thinking about old gods in godless times, I wondered if they had lost their powers or were just less and less able to understand the modern world and its technology.

FRIDAY NIGHT
AT ST. CECILIA'S

Ellen Klages

Rachel Sweeney came into the student lounge and threw her book bag on the couch. She smiled when she saw the backgammon board, already set up on the table by the window. She loved games, and life at St. Cecilia's would be intolerable without these Friday nights with her friend Addie.

A chittering flock of girls passed on their way to the stairs, duffels and satchels over their shoulders. Two peered in but saw that it was only Rachel and continued on. Sara had a car, and they were all off for a weekend's adventure. Rachel was grounded. Again. They wouldn't have invited her anyway.

She sat down and fiddled with the backgammon stones, black and white, making neat and ordered rows. She liked the round heft of them, liked the soft clicks as they slid together. The late afternoon light through the window blinds striped the worn wooden table, highlighting initials engraved in the varnish by decades of ballpoint pens. Rachel rolled the white dice, over and over, and watched the clock.

It wasn't like Addie to be late. But she was bringing the

pizza, since she'd lost last week. Antonio's must be really crowded. Rachel glanced over at her book bag. If she didn't come soon, they wouldn't be able to sneak a smoke before the sisters returned from vespers.

Forty-five minutes later, the room was all shadows, and Rachel was still alone. She looked at the light switch across the room, but didn't bother turning it on. She ran a hand through her short dark hair, making up excuses for Addie. None of them lifted her disappointment.

"What's this?" asked a voice from the doorway. "Sitting in the dark all by your lonesome?" The light came on.

Rachel blinked at the sudden brightness. It was the new housekeeper. "Oh. Mrs. Llewelyn. Hi."

The older woman leaned her mop against the battered couch next to the door. "Backgammon is it? I learned it as a girl. *Bach cammaun*, in the old tongue. The wee battle." She shook her head. "But as I recall, it's not much sport for one."

"Tell me about it," said Rachel. "I've been waiting for Addie, but she hasn't shown up."

"Addie. That tall girl with the glasses?" Mrs. Llewelyn frowned. "Oh dear. Did she not tell you she was going off with the others, then? She's been gone nearly an hour."

"No way. *Addie* wouldn't go with—" Rachel bit her lip, her eyes surprised with tears. When she trusted her voice again, she said, "Well, her choice, I guess. I'll go to my room. I've got a test Monday." She plunked the dice into their leather cup and reached for the first line of stones.

"Now, now, dearie. It's not as bad as all that. I'd thought to take a bit of a break about now, so if you'd fancy a game with an old woman—"

Rachel really wasn't in the mood anymore. But it would be

worse, all alone in the silent dorm. And it seemed a little rude to say no. "Sure, I'll play you."

"I accept the challenge with pleasure." Mrs. Llewelyn made a small curtsy and sat down across the table. Rachel smiled despite herself.

Mrs. Llewelyn was a dumpling of a woman, with a bun of chestnut hair going gray at the temples. She wore a white smock with ST. CECILIA's stitched over one ample breast, and *Maeve* in red script across the other. She beamed at Rachel, her cheeks filling her face, her eyes twinkling.

Rachel picked up the dice. She rolled a nine and moved two of the black stones. Mrs. Llewelyn rolled, moved a white stone, and began chattering about her neighbors and their children and other people Rachel didn't know. Rachel nodded now and then, but didn't feel the need to say anything. The click of the stones and the periodic clatter of the dice were familiar and soothing, and she was soon lost in the game.

With the last of her stones only twelve spaces away from her inner table, Rachel grinned. She was going to win. Mrs. Llewelyn rolled a three—not a good roll at all—and tossed the dice over to Rachel's side of the board.

They clipped the edge of the wooden tray and skittered across the table. Rachel grabbed for them but wasn't quick enough. They fell to the floor and rolled to the edge of the hot-air register. Rachel watched in dismay as first one, then the other, disappeared through the brass grating.

"Oh, look what I've gone and done." Mrs. Llewelyn put a hand to each cheek. "Clumsy old fool, that's what I am."

"It's okay," Rachel said after a few seconds. She looked at the backgammon board, then picked up the black stone in front of her. "It was nice playing with you, while it lasted."

She sighed. "I should go study. Church history's not my best class."

"Now, now. Hold up just a tick." Mrs. Llewelyn rummaged in the pocket of her white smock. She pulled out some crumpled tissues, the stub of a pencil, half a roll of Life Savers, and a tube of lip balm, piling them on the tabletop. "Ah, I thought as much. Here we go. They're a bit unusual, but they'll do." She handed Rachel a pair of iridescent blue-green cubes and stuffed the other items back into her smock.

"You carry *dice* with you?" Rachel asked.

"Oh, I pick things up here and there, put 'em in my pocket whilst I'm cleaning. And I like a little gamble now and then." She winked at Rachel. "Don't tell the sisters."

"Not likely."

The dice were heavier than she expected, with an odd, cold feel. Rachel rolled them across her palm, her skin tingling, and threw them onto the board. They came up double twos. Good, but not quite enough. She moved, and on the next turn, Mrs. Llewelyn set her white stone atop Rachel's black one, knocking it out of play. Rachel needed to roll a five to get back on the board, but couldn't. Three tries. She watched in frustration as Mrs. Llewelyn rolled double fours twice, then a double six to win the game. What rotten luck.

"Dear, dear. And you were so close. But that's gammon for me—double the stakes."

"Triple, actually," said Rachel. "That was *back*gammon, not gammon." She was still staring at the board, rolling the dice back and forth in her palm, reviewing the last few moves. How could she have lost? She glanced at the clock. Only seven-thirty. "Two out of three?"

Mrs. Llewelyn looked toward her bucket and mop, still

propped against the couch. "Oh, well, all right, I accept. I shouldn't, really. What if one of the sisters came by, saw me playing games—on their Lord's nickel? But I'm quite enjoying this."

"Yeah, me, too," said Rachel. "Let me just take five and go to the girls' room." She walked down the hall, still fiddling with the dice in her hand. She slipped them into the pocket of her green blazer when she entered the toilet stall. A few minutes later, she was back.

"I was having myself a think, while you were gone," Mrs. Llewelyn said. "This is such a dreary room. What say we move to my lodgings down below for the next game? No one will bother us, and we can have a nice pot of Earl Grey." She cocked her head at Rachel and smiled. "Would you play on those terms?"

"Sure." Rachel shrugged. The lounge *wasn't* particularly comfortable.

"Excellent." Mrs. Llewelyn laughed and clapped her hands. Rachel was startled by the smell of a sweet, pungent smoke, like burning cloves, as the linoleum beside the door shimmered with the same blue-green iridescence as the dice, then opened up into a large black hole.

"I can't remember if this goes to the Study or the Conservatory," Mrs. Llewelyn said. "But that hardly matters, now, does it?" A wrench appeared in her hand. She raised an arm and clipped Rachel neatly above the ear. She laughed again, the laugh turning into a cackle. Through half-closed eyes, Rachel watched as the woman's body shimmered, then folded in on itself and a huge raven hovered in the air. It tugged at the hem of Rachel's green plaid skirt and dragged her down into the impossible hole.

~ ~ ~

Rachel sneezed and opened her eyes. She was curled on her side, one cheek resting on the floral border of a wine-red Oriental rug. It smelled of tobacco. She sat up very slowly and touched the tender, walnut-size lump on her temple. Ouch. She looked around. Not in the dorm anymore, that was for sure. But the room seemed oddly familiar.

The rug lay on a floor of polished white tiles. A statue of a woman in flowing robes, a sheaf of wheat in her arms, anchored one corner. A dozen potted palms in ornate urns flanked a wall of French windows that opened onto terraced gardens—clipped precise lawns and beds of white flowers. Geometric blocks of sunshine overlaid the pattern of the rug, the sun warm on her arms.

Wait. It was nighttime. What the—?

"I'm afraid you've had a nasty tumble," said a deep, British voice.

"Huh?" Rachel startled and turned to her left. In a corner filled with more potted palms sat a bald man in a brocade armchair. He had a thick gray bristle mustache and wore a tweed jacket that seemed to have snips of twigs and moss woven into the fabric. He laid a slim leather volume on the arm of the chair.

"It was rather abrupt," he continued. "None of the usual warnings. I was immersed in one of Kipling's lesser works—not up to his usual form, really, but a compelling tale, nonetheless—quite enjoying myself, when the secret passageway opened, and down you came, knocking yourself senseless on the base of that lovely Ceres."

Rachel stared at him, her mouth open. Where *was* she? "How long have I been here?" she asked out loud.

"Not long. Not long at all. Less than five minutes, I'd imagine. I've rung for a spot of tea. I suppose smelling salts might be in order, but I'm afraid we haven't any. I say, do you like Kipling?" He held up his book.

"I don't know. I've never kippled." It came automatically, and she regretted it. This was not the time to be a smart-ass.

But the man in the chair chuckled. "Bit of a wit, eh? I shall endeavor to recall that one for the others, at supper."

"Where *am* I?" asked Rachel.

"How extraordinary! Don't you know?"

She shook her head, which hurt. "I haven't got a clue."

For some reason, this made him roar with laughter. "Oh, excellent. Excellent. What a wit you have, young lady." He wiped his eyes with a white handkerchief. "What a delightful wit."

Rachel eyed the man warily. He must be crazy. She was funny, but hardly ever made jokes that went over her own head. She stood up and moved toward the doors. Once she was outside, she'd have a better idea how to get back to the dorm.

"Look, it's been nice chatting with you, but I've gotta go. I've got a test—" She stopped in midsentence and stared at a pair of red wire-rimmed glasses lying at the base of one potted palm.

Addie's glasses.

Rachel's hand shook as she picked them up. "Where did you get these?" she asked. Her voice came out in a frightened squeak.

"I have no idea," he said calmly. "I suppose the other girl dropped them on her way out."

"What. Other. Girl."

"Why the one who tumbled down the passage last. An hour ago, at least. Tall girl, in a skirt like yours."

St. Cecilia's plaid. Rachel's stomach felt like ice. "Where *is* she, Mr.—" She let his unfinished name hang in the air.

"Plum," he said. "Professor, to be exact. Cambridge. Magdalene don, retired."

"Yeah, right," Rachel said. "Professor Plum. And I'm—" She stopped and stared at him. He *was* Professor Plum. He looked exactly like the picture on the Clue card. Impossible. Except here she was. Rachel looked around the room again, and pieces slowly fell into place. They were absurd, surreal pieces but had a certain logic to their arrangement.

"Don't tell me," she said. "This is the Conservatory."

"Naturally," replied the professor. "You took the secret passage from the Lounge, didn't you?"

Rachel shut her eyes and tried to remember the layout of the Clue board. The passage, if she could find it, would take her back to the Lounge. Or at least *a* lounge. The chances of it being the Trinity House lounge at St. Cecilia's seemed slim. The doors from this room went to the Billiard Room and the Ballroom. But which way was *out*?

"Where's Addie now?" she asked again.

"She left."

"Through the passage or the door?"

"Why, neither one. She simply disappeared. Not at all uncommon here."

"Really?"

"Yes, well, you see, Mrs. Peacock and I, Colonel Mustard and the rest, we never leave. Can't, you know. The rooms are all connected by doors, but there's no door to the outside." He sounded a little sad. "On the other hand, your kind comes and goes. You appear suddenly, traipse about until you come to a conclusion, and then poof! Off you go. As if you had never been."

"Conclusion?" Rachel thought for a moment. "Oh. Duh. Who did it, and with what."

He waved his hand impatiently. "Yes, yes, of course. I favor the knife, myself. Simple classic lines. I can't abide blunt instruments."

Like a wrench. Rachel rubbed the bump on her head and got an unpleasant image of Mrs. Llewelyn's smock-covered arm descending. The final piece fell into place. "Mrs. White. In the Lounge. With the wrench."

When she said the word *wrench*, a flash of blue-green lightning and that pungent clove smell filled the air. Professor Plum shimmered, his features as translucent as sautéed onions. Then he was gone. The solid lines of walls and furniture dissolved into pointillist colors that swirled slowly around her, wrapping her in a thick, warm cocoon that spun her away.

The garden was sunny. Alternating squares of grass and white clover stretched off as far as a city block. Rachel stood up, a little dizzy, and looked around for the French doors to the Conservatory. No building in sight. A wooden ladder stood a few yards to her right, leaning against an earthen terrace a little taller than she was. Maybe she could see better from up there.

She took a step toward the ladder but ran smack! into an invisible barrier at the border of the green grass square.

Weird.

The air shimmered and a flat cardboard disc appeared, floating waist high. It looked like the base for a pizza, painted in six colored wedges. Pinned to its center was a white plastic arrow.

Weirder by the minute.

"S-s-s-spin," hissed a tiny voice.

Rachel looked down. Next to her left heel was a thin brown snake. Great, she thought. If there's one thing Catholic school teaches you, it's never, ever listen to a talking snake in a garden.

"Go away," she said. "Shoo."

"S-spin," the snake said again. "Across squares. Slide chutes. Scale ladders-s-s."

Chutes and Ladders? The kid's game? Rachel had played it at her cousin Debbie's, years and years ago. She must have said some of that out loud, because the snake started talking again.

"She says *Snakes* and Ladders-s-s."

She? Goose bumps rose on Rachel's arms, and the side of her head throbbed. The same *she* that had turned into a black bird and dragged her down a nonexistent hole in the lounge floor? "Who is she?" Not just the housekeeper, that was obvious.

The snake tried to answer. Rachel watched it writhe and move its mouth, but no sound came out.

"Maeve?" she said, taking a guess. "Maeve Llewelyn?"

"Yes-s-s-s!" the snake hissed in relief. "It's sound snakes can't say easy."

"But what *is* she?"

"Shape shifts," said the snake.

That wasn't very useful, Rachel thought. Maybe a more practical question. "What do I have to do?" she asked the snake. She felt like Eve.

"Spin. Finish is success-s-s," it said enigmatically. "Sadly, snake stuck. Save snake?"

"Why can't you—? Oh, you can't climb ladders."

The snake shook its head slowly from side to side.

Rachel was not the sort of girl who was afraid of reptiles. "Okay, you can wrap around my arm," she said, bending down. "Don't bite."

The snake wrapped itself around the sleeve of her green cotton blazer, just under her elbow. "Thanks-s-s," it said. Its tiny red tongue flickered once, tickling her wrist a bit. Then it settled down and laid its head flat on the outside of her arm. "S-s-spin," it said.

Rachel spun the white arrow. It landed on a yellow wedge with a large 3, and she walked across into the next square easily. White, green, white. She climbed the ladder up to the top of the wall and whistled in surprise. Two hundred feet of steep hillside was terraced with stepped-back earthen walls topped with plots of green and white squares. The air was warm and fragrant with the spice of clover and newly mown grass.

Spin, move. Spin, move. Rachel landed on a square with an enormously long ladder. Thirty-two rungs later, she crawled off and flopped down in a patch of white clover.

"Exit," hissed the snake. "S-s-see?"

She looked up. On the top of the last terrace, and a few squares to the left, a brick wall surrounded a portal of soft, overlapping panels, like a rose or a sea anemone. Its center shimmered an iridescent blue-green.

"Jeez. Finally," Rachel said. "Let's get out of here." She flicked the spinner with her hand. The yellow wedge with the 3. One. Two. Threeeeeeeeeeeeeeeeee—

Rachel's feet went out from under her as she slid into a shiny red culvert, arms flailing. The metal tube twisted right, left, and right again. She banged her elbow on the first turn, then tucked her arms in. That protected her, and the snake, but physics—as usual—was not her friend. Her more streamlined body went faster and faster until the ride ended with a butt-jarring thump in a patch of green grass.

"Shit," said Rachel. She rubbed her back and her elbow and reflexively looked around for a scowling nun.

"Chutes-s-s," said the snake, sadly.

They were almost down to the bottom of the garden again. Rachel heard a faint laugh, a far-off cackle, and the spinner floated down the hillside, cresting each terrace as if it were carried on an invisible wave. It hovered next to her. She spun.

They were near the top, for the fifth time, when their current ladder ended in a patch of grass where Mrs. Llewelyn—or whoever she was—sat on a small sofa. She wore a long white dress embroidered with flowers and jewels. On her lap, she balanced a bone china cup and saucer in a delicate rosebud pattern.

"Ah, there you are. And not a moment too soon. Earl Grey gets a bit cloying when it sits too long, if you ask me." She took a delicate sip.

"Where's Addie?" Rachel demanded as she stepped off the ladder. The snake quickly slithered into the breast pocket of her blazer and disappeared behind the St. Cecilia's crest.

"Now, now. Don't you use that tone with me." Mrs. Llewelyn waggled a finger. "Remember, you're in my lodgings now, dearie."

Rachel took a deep breath. "Yes, ma'am," she said politely. She'd been dealing with nuns for three years. She knew the routine. "Where can I find Addie, ma'am?"

"Oh, she's in a safe place, never you mind. Pity she couldn't stay for tea. But you'll see her soon enough." Mrs. Llewelyn took another sip. "Care for a cup?"

"No. Thank you. I'd like to go back to my room now, if I

may." Rachel was laying it on as thick as she knew how.

"You would, would you? Just like that? Not how a wager works, dearie. You have to win your way home. Two out of three, you said." She chuckled, and her teacup shimmered. The raven flew off with a cackle.

When the bird was just a tiny speck in the blue sky, the snake emerged from Rachel's pocket and coiled around her arm again.

"I won Clue," said Rachel, talking to herself as much as to the snake. "I only have to win this, and I can go home, right?"

"Slight chance," the snake agreed.

"Well, how long have you been here?" she asked.

"Since sixty-six."

"What!?" Rachel didn't like the sound of that at all. "How come?"

"Dice hers."

"But this game doesn't use dice."

"Dice once," the snake said. "Snake eyes so easy." It looked up at her and blinked.

"Let me get this straight. Now the game has a spinner because you can roll snake eyes anytime you want?" Rachel was getting pretty good at interpretation.

"Yes-s-s."

"That's not fair. It's like loading the di— Oh." The end of the backgammon game. Double fours, double sixes. She reached into the side pocket of her blazer. "These are her dice," she said.

"Excellent." The snake's tongue flicked in and out. "Let's see."

Rachel held the blue-green cubes out on her palm. The snake undulated down her arm.

"Snake eyes," it said.

"What?"

"Show snake eyes."

"Oh, sorry." Rachel turned the two dice so that a single dot faced up on each cube. The snake butted them with its head until they were side by side. Then it opened its mouth and delicately placed one fang in the center of each dot. When it moved away, a single drop of milky venom lay pooled on each die.

"Suck," it said.

Rachel was not particularly squeamish, but poison was another matter. "Is there any other way to—"

"S-s-s-suck!" the snake commanded.

Rachel shuddered, considered her options, then lowered her head and sucked the venom off the dice. It burned her tongue, like Tabasco with an aftertaste of cloves.

"Soon, set stakes. Snake eyes," the snake said.

She had no idea what that meant. After a minute, the snake nudged her hand with its blunt head, and she put the dice back in her pocket.

"S-s-spin," it said.

She spun. Again and again and again. The muscles in her thighs felt like jelly from climbing the ladders. Worse than gym class. Her body was bruised and sore from the chutes, and she had no idea how much time had passed. Hours? Days?

Eventually she got lucky. The spinner landed on the orange 5, and Rachel stepped across the squares—One. Two. Three. Four. Five—and stood at the bottom of the short ladder that ended in the center of the anemonelike portal.

"Success-s-s-s-s-s," announced the snake.

"About friggin' time," said Rachel, wearily. She climbed to the top of the ladder. For the first time ever, she would be happy to return to St. Cecilia's.

"Yes-s-s. Snake sentence served. Assistance so nice." The snake uncoiled itself from her arm and slithered through the portal. As the last bit of its tail disappeared, Rachel saw a boy in flannel slacks and a school blazer, as fleeting as an afterimage. He tipped his cap to her, then he was gone.

In the far distance she thought she heard an angry cry.

Rachel stepped off the ladder, and everything began to whirl.

She opened her eyes, expecting to see the nubby beige couch in the lounge. But no. She was sitting on a sidewalk, her back to a telephone pole, downtown. Nowhere near St. Cecilia's. And it was morning. She'd been out all night, off campus. That wasn't good.

Across the street was a seedy brick hotel—*Rooms $2, Weekly Rates*—with a fly-specked purple sign that said Mediterranean Café. Next to it was a storefront, windows covered with plywood and graffiti. The pink neon of a corner bar buzzed on and off overhead.

Bad neighborhood. At least it wasn't another game. Maybe the bar had a pay phone. She was underage, but she could say it was an emergency. Sister Margareta would come and get her in the van. There'd be lectures, and she'd be grounded again, for the rest of the year, probably. Under the circumstances, she could live with that.

Rachel walked down to the corner, but one look inside the bar convinced her not to go in, not even in broad daylight. She waited for the light to change. The stores looked a little more prosperous—and a lot less threatening—a few blocks down.

Not a busy street. Just one parked car, and it really didn't fit the neighborhood—little silver sportster, an old two-seater

Bugatti. A miracle it hadn't been totally stripped. Rachel waited another two minutes for the light to turn green, then stepped off the curb to jaywalk. Halfway across the intersection she ran face-first into—nothing. She rubbed her nose and looked up at the street sign.

Baltic Avenue.

Baltic? Mediterranean? Not again.

Rachel beat her fists on the invisible wall. They bounced off without a sound. "I want to go home, damn it," she shouted. "I don't have to play again. I won your stupid games! Two out of three."

Her voice echoed off the grimy brick walls and the silver sports car shimmered. Mrs. Llewelyn climbed out, wearing a white silk jumpsuit with *Mab* stitched across the left breast.

"Temper, temper," she said in a scold. "You're the one set the terms. 'Twas backgammon, you said. Triple the stakes."

"So, what? I have to win"—Rachel counted on her fingers—"six out of nine? That'll take forever."

"Or so it will seem," said Mab, the Queen of the Faeries. "But I have time. All the time in the world." Her smile was warm; her eyes weren't. The shadows of the derelict buildings deepened, and somewhere in the distance, thunder rumbled. Rachel shivered.

"Now what?" she asked, trying not to sound as scared as she felt.

The queen pointed to the gutter. In a litter of broken glass and cigarette butts was a pair of white dice. "I believe it's your turn."

Yuck. Rachel picked up the dice with her fingertips and wiped them off down a dark line in the plaid of her skirt. She found a clean patch of asphalt, knelt, and rolled a four.

The queen scooped up the dice, and they crossed the street, passing an H&R Block office, closed. They stepped across a set of railroad tracks into another neighborhood, a row of rundown clapboard houses, most of them painted a pale, faded blue. On the far side of Oriental Avenue, Rachel felt the invisible wall again.

"Take a chance," the queen said, pointing.

It looked like a mailbox, except for the bright orange paint and the giant pink question mark on the side. Rachel pulled the lid open and took one of the small orange cards from the bin.

"Take a ride on the Reading," she said. "If you pass GO, collect $200."

In an instant they were moving down the sidewalk. Or the sidewalk was moving them. Hard to tell. They turned right, past a forbidding stone building, sped by a long row of brownstone apartments, and turned again at an enormous corner lot that said FREE PARKING. The sidewalk widened, the houses grew larger. The lawns on Ventnor Avenue were green and lush; they turned a third time and glided by the huge, gated mansions on Pacific and the posh condos of Park Place. Around the fourth corner, past the fly-specked hotel again, they came to an abrupt halt on the railroad tracks next to the closed tax office.

"Do you want to buy it?" The queen handed Rachel two mustard-colored hundred-dollar bills.

"What?" The ride had made her a little nauseated.

"The railroad. Do you want to buy the Reading Railroad?"

Of course. The railroad. Always buy the railroads. Best properties on the board. "Sure," she said.

The queen snatched back the two bills and handed Rachel a black-and-white cardboard deed and the dice.

Rachel sighed. She was doomed. No one ever *wins* Monopoly. You just play until it's time for dinner, or your friends have to go home. It never actually ends. She sighed again and rolled the dice—a three and a two.

Queen Mab picked them up and started down the now-familiar block. "Well, well," she said as they strolled past the clapboard houses and garish mailbox, "now you can play against your little friend." She stopped in front of the forbidding stone structure. Thick, rusty iron bars covered the single chest-high opening. JUST VISITING was stenciled in faded letters on the cracked concrete sidewalk.

"I want to go home," said a voice from inside the Jail. Freckled hands wrapped around the bars. Myopic eyes squinted at Rachel.

Addie.

Rachel started to yell, but one look at the queen's face convinced her that was not a good idea. "What have you done to her?" she said in her most polite, talking-to-nuns voice.

"Oh, she's in a bit of a pickle, truly. But she's done it all to herself, I'm afraid. Backgammon's not *her* game either. Wagered and lost. And now? Three turns and no doubles. She doesn't have the fifty dollars for the fine, and it seems she hasn't a Get Out of Jail Free card to her name." The queen shook her head in disappointment. "And we were having a lovely game up until then, weren't we dearie?"

"Not exactly," Addie said. "I had to mortgage Boardwalk, but I still own St. James Place. If you land on it, the rent will be enough to get me out of here."

"I'll try," said Rachel. "But I'm not sure—"

"Yeah, I know. We've really done it this time, haven't we, Rach?"

"Yep. Deep shit." Unless—? Rachel took a deep breath and turned around. "You let her go, right this minute," she demanded, as loud as she could.

"You're not very bright, are you?" The queen scowled. "I've warned you about using that tone with me. You Catholic girls have no respect for the old ways."

"Well, if I'm so disrespectful, shouldn't *I* be the one in jail? Addie's a good girl. Not a troublemaker like me." Rachel glared, as if she deserved to be punished. It wasn't hard.

The queen arched one chestnut brow. "You're offering to take her place?"

Rachel crossed her fingers. "I am."

"All right, dearie, suit yourself, then."

Rachel saw the blue-green flash, and in an instant she was on the other side of the iron bars. The stone wall was damp and cold against her body, and the inside of the jail smelled like piss.

Addie stared at her from the sidewalk. "What are you doing?" she asked.

"I'm a lot more used to detention than you are," Rachel said. "Trust me." She pulled Addie's glasses out of her pocket and handed them through the bars.

"Nice to see you," Addie said, putting them on.

"You, too." Rachel smiled, then looked at the queen. "I've learned a lot about keeping my word, ma'am," she said. "I suppose I'll be grateful someday."

"Not all lessons are easy," Mab agreed.

"But a wager is a wager. Rules are rules," Rachel continued.

The queen nodded. "That they are."

Rachel waited two seconds, then asked, "So, ma'am, now that I'm the one in jail, shouldn't *I* get three turns with the dice to try and roll doubles? It's only fair."

The queen considered this. "I suppose it is. You may have your three chances." She put the white dice on the window ledge.

Rachel looked at them, then back at the queen. "Want to up the stakes?"

"What now, you foolish child?" The queen sounded impatient.

"If I can roll doubles on the first try, you let Addie go home."

Mab tapped her lip thoughtfully. "Unlikely, but possible. A sporting chance. All right, I accept."

"Great." Rachel paused, counted to three in her head, and made a move to pick up the dice. She stopped, her hand in midair. "Wait a sec. Want to go double or nothing?"

The queen narrowed her eyes. "Are you daft?"

"No. I mean, what if I can roll double—oh, I don't know, how 'bout ones—on the very first roll, you let *both* of us go."

"And if you fail?"

Rachel shrugged. "I guess we stay here forever. No two out of three, no six out of nine. We're yours."

"Rach! Are you nuts?" Addie cried. "The odds are thirty-six to one. Against you."

The Queen of the Faeries laughed. "She's correct. And you have no idea what you've just done. But I accept. Roll. Your fate is in your own hands."

"Here goes." Rachel blew on her hands, shook them out, and reached for the dice again. Then she snapped her fingers.

"On second thought, I think I'll use these." She pulled the blue-green cubes out of her pocket and watched the queen's eyes widen.

"Where did you get those?" she snarled.

"You handed them to me," Rachel said. "In the lounge."

The queen clenched her fists, and Rachel could see that she was angry. She held her breath.

"'Twas a faerie gift, and freely given," said the queen with a sigh. "Roll."

The cubes were cold and heavy in Rachel's hand. She hoped the snake had known what he was doing. She wished as hard as she had ever wished for anything. Then she opened her hand and let the dice tumble onto the stone ledge.

Snake eyes.

The wall of the jail began to shimmer. Rachel stepped through the translucent stones and blinked in the sunlight. A flash of blue-green vaporized the jail behind her, obliterating the dice as well. A few wisps of smoke hung in the air and slowly dissipated.

Rachel put her arm around Addie and looked over at the Faerie Queen, standing a few feet away, her chestnut hair now streaked with white.

"You tricked me," she said, her voice thinning to a whisper. They watched her hair turn completely white, and her skin grow pale. The bird-shape became visible beneath her clothes. As she changed, the buildings and streets lost definition as well. Bricks evaporated into smoke, signs and shops misted and blurred, the horizon flickered.

"Addie, shut your eyes," Rachel said when she smelled the first strong whiff of cloves. The air crackled like sizzling rice, and she felt a breeze and the sound of flapping wings an instant before a blue-green flash so bright she could see it through closed eyelids.

Then everything was still.

Rachel sat on the linoleum floor of the student lounge, back against the ugly beige couch, her arm still around Addie. The windows were dark, and the clock on the wall said 7:45. Impossible. She'd only been gone fifteen minutes?

The lounge smelled like burning cloves.

Addie leaned over and kissed her on the cheek. "You were amazing."

"I missed you," Rachel said. She stroked Addie's brown curls for a moment, then stood up. "And now I'm starving. Let's go to Antonio's and get a pizza. Have a smoke. I *really* need a smoke."

"I thought you were grounded."

"I am." Rachel pulled a pack of Marlboros out of her book bag. "But there are worse punishments." She thought about the snake and shuddered. "Besides," she said, reaching down a hand for Addie, "the nuns are going to be a little busy for a few days."

"Yeah. How come?"

Rachel grinned. "They'll have to find a new housekeeper." She turned off the light and they walked arm in arm into the silent hallway.

Ellen Klages's story "Basement Magic" won the Nebula Award in 2005. Several of her other stories have been on the final ballot for the Nebula and Hugo Awards, and have been translated into Czech, French, German, Hungarian, Japanese, and Swedish. Her first collection of short fiction, *Portable Childhoods*, was named a 2008 World Fantasy Award Finalist.

Her first novel, *The Green Glass Sea*, won the Scott O'Dell Award for historical fiction and the New Mexico State Book Award. It was a finalist for the Northern California Book Award, the Quills Award, and the Locus Award. A sequel, *White Sands, Red Menace*, has just been published.

She was born in Ohio and now lives in San Francisco, surrounded by shelves of old board games. Her Web site is www. ellenklages.com.

~

Author's Note

Looking back, I suspect that most of my childhood was spent playing games. Card games, board games. After school, or on Saturday afternoons when it was raining or too cold to go outside and still live, I played Monopoly, Sorry, Risk, Clue, Lie Detector, Park and Shop. With my friends, I played for fun. With my family, I played for blood. (Ask my sister. She's still got the scars.)

Over the years, pieces went missing and the boxes were given away to the church rummage sale. So when I discovered eBay, that most perilous of addictions, I started gathering some of them back. Except better. The 1949 Clue game is a lovely thing—a tiny pipe made of real lead, British drawing room characters in muted lithographic colors. The earliest versions of Go to the Head of the Class have wooden game pieces named Butch and Sissy. Really. I bought reference books about old board games, discovered many I hadn't known I coveted. My living room shelves began to fill up, and friends began to hint about 12-step programs. But I am a writer. I'm allowed to have obsessions, as long as I eventually weave them into my fiction. Enter Rachel and Addie.

THE FORTUNE-TELLER

Patricia A. McKillip

Merle saw the silk trailing out from under the tooth-less pile of rags snoring in a muddy alley. She glanced around. Most in the busy marketplace were buried under hoods and shawls, eyes squinched against the drizzling rain. They paid her no attention. She knelt swiftly, tugged at the silk. Cards came with it; she felt them as she stuffed the plunder under her shawl and strode away. Oversize, they were, like her mother's cards, and knotted in threads spun by little worms on the far side of the world. The sleeping lump had probably stolen them herself, and there was no reason why Merle shouldn't have them instead. She, after all, wasn't wasting the day facedown in the mud. Fortune favored those who recognized her, and Merle had watched her mother read the cards often enough to know what to do with them.

She worked quickly and efficiently through the crowd, a tall, thin, unremarkable figure swathed against the rain like everyone, with only her eyes visible and wide open. Her long fingers caught the change rattling into a capacious coat pocket as its distracted owner bit into the sausage roll he had just purchased. Farther down among the stalls, she slid a lovely square of linen and lace, perfumed against the smells of the street, out of a lady's gloved fingers. The lady had stopped to laugh at a parrot inviting her to "Have a dance, luv, have a dance." Opening her bag to find the one-armed sailor a coin, she gave a sudden exclamation. Merle left her searching the cobbles for her lace, and disappeared back into the crush.

Another carelessly unguarded pocket in a great coat caught her eye, its shiny brass button dangling free of its loop and winking at her. She drew up close, dipped a hand in. Faster than thought another hand followed, closed around her fingers.

She drew a startled breath, gathered her wits and more breath in the next instant to raise an indignant and noisy complaint against the ruffian who had grabbed a poor, honest young girl going about her business.

Then she saw the face between the upraised coat collar and the hat. Her tirade whooshed into a laugh.

"Ansel! You gave me a moment, there."

He didn't look amused; his lean, comely face, his jade eyes were hard. "Someone will give you more than a moment," he warned, "if you don't stop this."

She shrugged that away, more interested in his clothes. "Where did you steal the coat?"

"I didn't. I'm a working man. I drive a carriage now. You—"

"I'm a working girl," she interrupted before he could get started.

"You're a thief."

"I'm a fortune-teller. Look. I even have cards now." She opened her cloak, gave him a glimpse of the cards in their silk tucked into her waistband. "I found them this morning."

He gave a sour laugh. "You stole them."

"Nobody else was using them."

"You said you were going to—"

"You know I can earn my way, telling fortunes. I've done it before. I told yours. Remember?" She shifted the shawl wrapped up under her almond-shaped eyes to remind him of the full lips and sweet, stark jawline beneath, a trifle wolfish, maybe, but then she was ravenous half the time. His own lips parted; his eyes grew vague with memory. "Remember? The day we met. You saw me and followed me to my tent; I told your fortune with tea leaves and coins made of candle wax. You stole bread and sausages and cheese for our supper. Now that I have cards, I can build a reputation like my mother had—at least when my father stayed in one place long enough."

"You told me," he reminded her softly, "that I'd meet a stranger with storm gray eyes I'd follow forever. I thought, that night, I had."

She shrugged slightly. "You liked me well enough then. But you didn't stay forever."

"You promised me you'd stop this magpie life. I stopped, but you didn't."

"Now I can," she said, tightening her cloak around the cards again. But he only made a sound between a sigh and a groan, and stepped back impatiently.

"You'll never change."

"Come and see. You know where to find me."

"Wherever they lock you away, most likely, one of these days. You can't play your tricks on the world forever."

"I'll stop, I promise," she told him, half-laughing again. He shook his head wordlessly, turning away, and so did she, with another shrug. She had coins for a meal, lace to sell; she could spend some time studying the cards now. She made her way back to her tent, pocketing a stray meat pie from a baker's busy stall along the way. Why should she pay for what the world put in her way for free?

Her fortune-teller's tent was makeshift: an abandoned shell of a wagon on the edge of the marketplace. It had a broken axle and two barrels propping up the corners where the wheels were missing. A discarded sail nailed over the ribs kept it dry. Merle had brightened the inside with dyed muslin and sprigged lawn skirts she'd separated from their drying lines. Fine shawls with gold threads, ribbons, beads of crystal and jet, left unattended in carriages or dangling too far over a lady's arm, she'd appropriated from their careless owners. She picked apart the seams and wound the swaths around the wagon ribs to make a colorful cave of embroidery, lace, ribbons, flowing cloth. She collected candle ends wherever she found them, to scatter around her while she worked. The tent was guarded by an old raven she'd found protecting a blind beggar who had fallen dead in the street. She'd coaxed it to eat; it came home with her. It had a malevolent eye, a sharp beak, and a vocabulary of two words—"Help! Murder!"—which it loosed with an earsplitting squall when it was alone and faced with a stranger.

It greeted Merle with a rustle of wind and a faint, throaty chuckle. She lit candles and shared bits of the meat pie with the bird. Then she reached outside to hang her painted sign above the wagon steps, and draped a long, dark, beaded veil over her hair and shoulders. She unwrapped the cards.

The silk was snagged and frayed, with a spill of wine along one edge. The cards themselves were creased, flecked with candle wax, and so thumbed with use that some of the images were blurring. She began to lay them out.

Scarecrow. Old Woman. Sea. Gypsy Wagon.

She paused, studying them. It was an odd deck, not at all like her mother's with its bright paintings of cups and swords, kings and queens. Those had once belonged to Merle's great-grandmother; her mother cherished them, wrapped them in spotless silk and tucked them into a cedar and rosewood box between readings. These, well-drawn and colored despite their age, said nothing at all familiar. She laid out a few more and gazed at them, perplexed. There seemed to be a lot of crows. And what would a snake curled into a hoop and rolling itself down a road possibly signify?

The curtains trembled. Merle glimpsed fingers, pale and slender, heard whisperings outside on the steps. She drew the veil across her face. No sense in getting herself into unnecessary trouble if someone happened to recognize her. When the whispering didn't go away, she lit more candles around her and waited.

The curtains opened finally. Three young women, as neatly and fashionably dressed as they could afford, stared at her anxiously.

"Come in."

Something—the exotic veil, her deep voice, which made her sound older and possibly wiser than she was, the flames weaving a mystery of light and glittering dark around her—reassured them. They ducked under the canopy, seated themselves on pilfered carriage cushions, the golden-haired one in front, the other two behind. They spent a moment eyeing the fortune-teller, the cards she had gathered up again, the motionless raven, the drifts of silk and muslin above their heads.

The one in front spoke. "I need to know my fortune."

Merle, shuffling the deck, supposed that anyone with that pretty, tired, worried face probably needed all the good news she could get.

She named her price, and when the coin lay between them, she began to turn the cards, laying them into a pattern: the rainbow arc of life and fortune.

"Wolf. Sun. Old Woman. Well." Again, nothing was familiar; she had to guess at what they should be called, keeping her voice calm and certain, no matter what showed its face. "Spider. The Blind Man. The Masked Lovers." She hesitated briefly. Who on earth was this? A blue-eyed grinning skeleton with a full head of red-gold hair, cloaked in blue and crowned, rode a pitchfork with three blackbirds clinging to the tines. "Lady Death," she guessed wildly, and the young women made various distraught noises.

One suggested timidly, "Three of crows?" which made sense when Merle remembered the other crows in the deck.

But she answered smoothly, "When a card falls into the arc of life, it no longer belongs to a suit. Don't be afraid. She doesn't always signify death. Let's see what falls after her . . ." She turned another card, hoping it wasn't more crows. Pockmarked puddles came up; that was plain enough. "Rain." She turned the next and decided it would be the last: best to end with a cheerful face. "Fool." She put the deck down. "This is good. Very good."

"It is?" the young woman who had paid said incredulously. "But it says so little about love."

Love. Of course.

"Oh, but it says a great deal." Improvising rapidly, she led the rapt watchers through it, card by card. "Wolf, at the beginning of the arc, signifies a messenger. Sun is, of course, a fortuitous message. The Old Woman in conjunction with the Well is someone you will meet who will give you strength and power—that's the well water—to achieve your heart's desire. Spider may be good or bad. When it appears in the arc, it's the web that signifies, and here it means something well planned, successful."

And so on. She could chart a fortune through twigs and broken eggshells, if she had to. Where she saw a pattern, she could find a fortune. She'd learned that much from her mother before she'd escaped from her eternally traveling family to the city. Even she couldn't see a fortune in a tinker's wagon.

"But what about Lady Death?" the young woman whispered, mesmerized by the card. "Who will die?"

"In this arc," Merle explained glibly, "Lady Death signifies protection. She guards against misfortune, malice, bad influences. Rain follows her. A little stormy weather will hamper the lovers, but that is natural in the course of true love. In the end the Fool, who signifies the wisdom of innocence, will guide your heart to achieve its innermost dreams."

The young woman, whose mouth was hanging by now, closed it with a click of teeth. She sighed and began to smile; the faces behind her brightened. "So he will love me in spite of everything."

"So the cards have shown," Merle answered solemnly, sweeping them together and palming the coin at the same time. She wondered briefly what obstacles the cards had missed. The rival lover? The deluded husband? The betrayed wife? Lack of money to wed? Mismatched circumstances: she a seamstress, he a noble who had admired too closely the shape of her lips? Merle had a hunch that, under other eyes, the cards would have suggested a darker, more ambiguous future. But the young woman had paid for hope, and Merle had earned her pay.

You see? she told Ansel silently as the women went back into the rain. I have a profession, too. Soon, with these strange cards, I'll even have a reputation. Then I can afford to be honest.

Ansel came to her that night as she knew he would. In spite of himself, she guessed wryly, taking note of his dour, reluctant expression. But she knew tricks to make him smile, others to make him laugh, which he did at last, though he sobered up too soon after that.

"You've learned a few things on the street since I saw you last," he commented, rolling onto his back in her meager bed, and stroking her hair as she laid her cheek on his chest.

"Knowledge is free," she said contentedly.

"Is it?"

"At least I don't have to steal it. Don't—" she pleaded as he opened his mouth. "Don't go back to glowering at me. You like what I learned."

She felt him draw breath, but he didn't lecture. He didn't say anything, just smoothed her hair, drew it out across his chest to watch it gleam in the candlelight, onyx dark, raven dark, true black without a trace of color in it. He laughed a little, gently, as at a memory.

"You're growing so beautiful. . . . All I could see of that the few months ago I met you was in your eyes. You were such a scrawny girl, all bones and sharp edges, and those huge eyes, the color of a mist that I wanted to walk through to see what I would find."

"And what did you find?"

He was silent again; she listened drowsily to his heartbeat.

"Someone like me," he said finally. "Which was fine until I started not liking what I was. . . . So I made myself into someone more to my liking."

Within the little cave he had made of her hair, her eyes opened. She felt a sudden, odd hollow inside her. As though he had tricked her, taken something from her that she didn't know she had until he showed her.

"So now you like me less," she said softly, and pulled herself over him until they were eye to eye in the dark fall of her hair. "But I'm going to make myself respectable with my cards."

"You stole them."

She laughed. "From some old biddy lying dead drunk in an alley. Besides, I'll hardly be the first to turn myself respectable with stolen goods. I didn't rob a bank, after all. They're only cards."

"Are they?" He eased out from under her and sat up, reaching for his trousers. "I've got to go. I'm stealing time, myself, from my job."

"Come tomorrow?"

He gave her a wide-eyed, almost startled look, as though she'd suggested leaping off a roof together, or rifling through his employer's house.

"I don't know." His face disappeared under his shirt. "I doubt that I'll have time." He reappeared. "You haven't heard a word I said."

"What word didn't I hear?" she demanded. "Tell me."

But he was withdrawing again, going away from her, even before he left the wagon.

She sighed, sitting on her pallet, naked and alone but for the raven, feeling again that strange hollow where something should have been but wasn't any longer.

"You'll come back," she whispered and reached abruptly for the cards in their stained silk to find him in her future. She shuffled them and dealt the arc: Old Woman, Spider, Rain, the Masked Lovers, Lady Death . . .

She gave a cry and flung the deck down. Candlelight glided across the Old Woman's raddled face; she seemed to smile up at Merle.

You stole a poor old woman's only means to earn a coin, the smile said. You stole her hope. And now you want to twist her cards, make them lie to you, show you how lovable you still are . . .

The rain rustled on its perch, made a sound like a soft chuckle. Merle gathered the cards together with icy, trembling fingers, wanting to cry, she felt, but not remembering how to start. She pulled on clothes, flung her cloak around her, and splashed barefoot into the rain, not sure where to find the old woman, only certain that until she returned the cards she could not change her future of webs and rain and fools and the Old Woman's knowing eyes.

PATRICIA A. McKILLIP was born in Salem, Oregon, received a master's degree in English Literature, and has been a writer ever since. Among her fantasy novels are *The Forgotten Beasts of Eld*, which won the first World Fantasy Award, *Ombria in Shadow*, which won the twenty-ninth World Fantasy Award, The Riddle-Master Trilogy, and *Od Magic*. She has also written several young adult novels, among them the SF novels *Moon-Flash* and *The Moon and the Face* (reissued as the single volume *Moon-Flash* by Firebird). Most recent books include *Harrowing the Dragon* (stories) and *Solstice Wood*; her newest novel is *The Bell at Sealey Head*.

She recently received the World Fantasy Life Achievement Award for her contributions to the field.

～

AUTHOR'S NOTE

I found writing about tricksters very difficult; they all seemed to vanish when I looked for them. I did some research into tricksters, searching for inspiration, and found, oddly enough, that just about all the great tricksters of myth and folktale were male. So I decided to make mine, whoever she was, female. The biggest hurdle for me, I think, was that tricksters are a sort of natural force: they come into your life in order to challenge you, spin you off balance, change the way you look at the world; they themselves never change. I suppose that's where the idea for my young would-be trickster came from: I wanted to write about one who could change, the trickster who could trick, could be tricked, and could even trick herself.

HOW RAVEN MADE HIS BRIDE

Theodora Goss

I. THE CHALLENGE

If you insist, said the river,
 That any of Life's daughters would accept you,
Bring me the best. If she is as beautiful
As you are boastful, I will give you
A gift, something worth having:
A basket woven of reeds, a trout.

The river laughed, and Raven
Ruffled his feathers.

But the daughters
Of the sun hid behind their brothers, the clouds,
And the mountain's daughters covered themselves
With snow. The birches on the riverbank
Shook their green fingers. Even the doe,
Who stared at him with limpid eyes,
Said no.

II. THE BRIDE

There was something charming
About him: the thin brown shoulders,

Still a boy's, and on his lips
A boy's pout.

And something alarming
In his brown eyes: the memory of lightning.

While she lay sleeping, he stole
The luminous white body of the moon
And hid it. To this day,
She searches lamenting, in anger
Turning her face first one way,
Then another.

From the porcupine, he stole her pelt, softer
Than the tassels of ripe corn. From the coyote
His color, like nightfall. From the cougar
Her mildness, and from the armadillo
His skin, as delicate as a mariposa lily.
He stole the song of the bullfrog,
All to make his bride.

For her eyes he stole the rain,
And left a desert.

Whatever Life had made
Rich and rare, he stole: for her mouth
The softness of granite, and the fragrance
Of ice.

He looked at her, entranced
And almost in love (remarkably,
Since his heart was hidden in an egg
In an eagle's nest, at the top

Of a poplar tree). He lay
Beside her and covered her with his feathers.

III. THE REWARD
The river conceded, she is splendid. And yet,
Something seems to be missing. I think
She has no heart.

Having no heart himself (you remember
That it was hidden at the top of a poplar), Raven
Had indeed forgotten.
He shrugged his brown shoulders, and his wings
Brushed against her.

What does she need one for? he asked.
I've done
Well enough without mine. And now,
You owe me.

So he stole for her
The river's laughter.

How, later, she made a heart for herself
Out of clay from the riverbank, so she could love
Her son, the first of our tribe:
That is another story.

THEODORA GOSS has been writing poetry since she can remember. Her poems have been published in magazines such as *Mythic Delirium* and *The Lyric*, and reprinted in *The Year's Best Fantasy and Horror*. She recently won a Rhysling Award. Her chapbook of short stories and poems, *The Rose in Twelve Petals & Other Stories*, was published by Small Beer Press, and a short story collection, *In the Forest of Forgetting*, is currently available from Prime Books.

She lives with her husband, daughter, and three cats in Boston, where she is completing a Ph.D. in English literature.

Her Web site address is www.theodoragoss.com.

～

AUTHOR'S NOTE

When I wrote "How Raven Made His Bride," I thought of two things. First, myths—about tricksters of course, but also about brides made by magic and the hiding of hearts in caves, or at the tops of trees, or at the bottom of the ocean. And second, that boyfriend you had in high school who was probably in Drama Club and not much else, unless he had a band, and who idolized someone impossible like Jim Morrison or Jack Kerouac, and who tied his hair, dyed black, back in a ponytail, and who was fearfully attractive but, as your mother told you, *trouble*. Yes, that one.

I want you to know that his bride became a strong and confident woman, with a story of her own—after counseling. And I wish I could show you what the armadillo looked like before Raven got to him. Like all the promises of the cosmetics companies come true.

CROW ROADS

Charles de Lint

Tartown, August 1967

"Yum," Sandra said. "Annie, you've got to check this guy out. Hair's way too long but, oh my, otherwise he's swell."

I lifted my head from last month's *16* magazine, which someone had left behind in the Laundromat, and looked across the street.

"'Swell'? I said. "Who says 'swell' anymore?"

"My sister, for one."

"And she still listens to Pat Boone."

"Would you just check him out."

"Who?"

"In front of Ernie's."

As soon as I looked again, I didn't know how I'd missed him. His hair was black and glossy like a crow's feathers, and long—longer than either Sandra's or mine, and ours was past our shoulders. Like the other guys hanging in front of the pool hall, he wore jeans and a T-shirt, but his jeans were bell-bottomed and his T-shirt had a picture of a marijuana leaf on the front.

And as Sandra had already indicated, he was drop-dead handsome.

"I think he's one of those hippies we keep hearing about," Sandra added.

I didn't think so, but I'm not exactly sure why. Maybe it was those tooled leather cowboy boots and the clear look in his eyes when he glanced our way. Weren't hippies usually barefoot and—especially considering the picture on his shirt—stoned?

"Which could be good," Sandra added. "It's all free love and fun with them, isn't it? And I'll have a helping of both, so long as he's serving."

Nothing's free, I wanted to tell her. Especially not love. But right then his gaze held mine for a long second. My mouth went dry while my body felt weirdly hot.

Beside me, Sandra giggled. "Oh god, he's looking right at us."

She bent her head down and hid behind her hair, but I held his gaze until he looked away.

Guys like him didn't come down into Tartown much. Nobody did who didn't already live here, but especially not guys like him.

People call this Tartown because the houses that aren't double-wides usually don't have much more than tar paper by way of siding. You know the kind of place. If there'd been a railway line running through town, we'd be the wrong side of the tracks. You couldn't miss the change as you walked south from the town square.

Around Henderson Street you start to see fridges in carports, patches of crabgrass growing proud and tall on otherwise bare dirt lawns, maybe a mean-eyed Doberman chained up to some old elm that has a circle of bark worn away from the constant stress of the dog's tether. By the time you've reached Jackson, there are cars up on blocks in the front yards, rusted double-wides passing for houses, and litter fluttering along the sidewalks.

And all those old clapboard houses with tar-paper siding—though some folks do manage to get aluminum or board up for the side that fronts the street.

We have a bad reputation down here: people assume that all the guys are mean and hard, the girls tough and quick to drop their panties, sometimes for money. They claim you can get pretty much any kind of intoxicant you might be looking for—from drugs to booze—if you actually have the nerve to come down here and make your buy.

Some of that's true, but most of it's just surface—a protective mask to keep the better-off at bay. You have to be born poor to know how quick kids will turn on you if they think that living in a fancy house, or having parents who work, somehow makes them better than you. And there's diddly-squat you can do about it. But if you can get them a little scared of you, mostly all they've got to throw at you is trash talk—and even then it's behind your back. Unless they're in a big enough crowd. Then they get a little fearless.

I'm not saying our toughness is a complete front. Live with a certain attitude long enough and that's who you become. But nobody starts out that way. It's like a dog. Treat it bad, day after day, and sooner or later it's going to turn on you. That's what happened to us growing up here.

And sure, there are genuinely bad kids living here, the same way there are bad parents. But mostly we're just poor, and being poor doesn't automatically make you bad. My dad's unemployed, but he doesn't drink and it's not like he's ever lifted a hand to Mom or any of us kids. There's just no work. *Nobody* living in Tartown has any real work—just makeshift jobs, doing handy work, picking fruit and vegetables in season, shoveling snow for the town in winter. Whatever puts a meal on the table.

And living in a place like this doesn't leave much for us kids to do. We don't have a spiffy soda shop or the town park to hang out in. All we've got is Ernie's and the Wash 'n' Go.

But we don't really miss what we never had. All we want is to be left alone. So when someone like this handsome hippie stranger comes wandering down into our territory . . . well, they're just asking to become entertainment, aren't they?

"Travis is so going to whup his ass," Sandra said.

I nodded. Not by himself, maybe, but he had a half-dozen friends hanging with him today. The stranger didn't stand a chance.

I've never really cared for Travis, though unfortunately, he felt differently about me. He was everything I didn't like about the worst of Tartown. Hair slick with Brylcreem and combed back into a ducktail. Stocky and tough, with a chip on his shoulder and no imagination. I don't know why, but that long-haired boy—he seemed full of imagination. Or maybe he was just filling mine.

"I want to hear what they're saying," I said.

I left the *16* magazine on the Formica table at the front of the Laundromat and went outside with Sandra trailing behind me. We crossed over and stood under Ernie's window—the pane so caked with dust that you can never see in, not even at night when the lights are on inside and it's dark out on the street. Standing here, we were close enough to the front steps so that we could hear and see everything.

"Yeah, well, we don't much care for your kind around here," Travis was telling the stranger.

Either the long-haired boy was clueless, or braver than he should be, because he obviously wasn't ready to back down from Travis.

"What? People with black hair?" he asked.

I liked the sound of his voice. There's was a little burr of an accent to it—like the British bands you'd hear on *The Ed Sullivan Show*. Not a British accent, just something different. Pleasant.

"People with *long* black hair, smart-ass," Travis told him.

"Not much I can do about it."

"You could cut it and stop looking like a girl."

The stranger shrugged. "It'd just grow back. And what's wrong with girls?"

He glanced our way and winked. Sandra giggled, and I found myself holding my breath.

"You're some kind of weird freak, aren't you?" Travis said.

He looked at his friends, and they grinned back at him. Tension lay thick in the air. Fists were going to fly any minute. Everybody seemed aware of it, except for the stranger.

"You got a name, buddy?" Travis asked.

"That'll do."

"What?"

"Buddy. That'll do for a name. Why do you need one?"

Travis smiled. I'd seen that smile before—just before he kicked a dog, or took down one of the smart-mouthed kids at school.

"I like to know the name of a guy," he said. "You know, before I beat the crap out of him."

"And here I thought you wanted to shoot some pool."

It was the weirdest thing. Everybody just stood there looking at him, trying to figure him out. Travis's animosity didn't disappear, but even he was curious.

"You on some kind of drugs?" he asked.

"I don't think so. You mean like nicotine or caffeine?"

"What?"

"Smokes and coffee."

"They're not—"

"Tell you the truth, I wouldn't mind a hit of either. *And* a game of pool." He smiled at Travis. "You know, before you beat the crap out of me."

"You want to play pool with me?"

Buddy shrugged. "Or whoever can give me a decent game."

Travis prided himself on his playing and couldn't resist the challenge. He fixed Buddy with one of the patented tough-guy looks that he'd picked up from watching endless spaghetti westerns, eyes squinted, lip curled in an Elvis sneer. Clint Eastwood he was never going to be, but no one ever told him that to his face.

"For money?" he asked.

"I don't gamble. But I'll play for the cost of the table."

"You're on, chump."

Travis started up the steps into Ernie's, pausing when Buddy didn't move.

"What's your problem?" he asked.

"I think I prefer 'Buddy' to 'Chump.'"

There was a long moment of silence. I was pretty sure Travis was just going to tear into the guy, but then he smiled.

"Okay," he said. "Buddy it is. Now do you want to play, or do you need to go brush your hair and make yourself pretty first?"

"My hair's fine the way it is," Buddy told him.

They all went inside, and Sandra and I hurried around to the back. We opened the screen door and slipped inside, moving quietly so that Ernie wouldn't notice us. We didn't have to be so cautious. Like everybody else, Ernie was focused on Buddy and Travis as they set up a table.

Sandra had snuck in here before but this was my first time. It was about as dirty as I'd imagined—smoke-stained walls, the smell of sweat in the air—but there was something almost pretty about the lawn green felt of the tables, each with its own light swinging overhead. I could see why my brothers liked to hang out here. They could go on forever about a game—which is how I know anything about pool—but mostly I think they liked the fact that it was such a guy place.

The boys were all gathered at a table near the front. Travis made a show of taking down what I guess was his favorite cue, but Buddy just picked one at random.

"Who breaks?" he asked.

"If I was sporting," Travis said, "I'd say you do. But I'm not. We'll flip for it. Call it in the air."

He took out a quarter and spun it into the air, catching it and slapping it down on the back of his hand. It came up tails. Buddy had called heads.

"Here's where the weeping starts," Travis said.

He set up his cue ball and made the break, sinking a striped ball in a corner pocket. He managed to sink another before missing an easy cross-side. But he'd left the table safe.

"Three ball," Buddy called. "Cross-corner."

It was a long, hard shot, made more difficult by the eight ball being partially in the way of his cue ball. But he just leaned on the table, set up, and took his shot. The cue ball did a little swerve around the eight, struck the three with a solid click, then set itself up for an easy shot in a side pocket. Meanwhile the three bounced off the end cushion and went rolling up the table to drop into the corner pocket. Just as he'd called it.

"Nice shot," Billy Chambers said.

Travis shot him a dirty look. His mood darkened more when Buddy ran through the rest of his balls, then sank the eight in a double-cross-side.

Buddy gave him an innocent look.

"Best out of three?" he asked.

"You some kind of shark, Buddy?"

"We're not playing for money, are we?"

"There's still the cost of the table."

Buddy shrugged. "If that's all you're worried about, I'll cover it."

"So now you're made of money?"

"Nope." He took a crumpled five-dollar bill from his pocket and laid it on the side of the table. "But I've got a five-spot. Think that'll cover it?"

Travis had a dark look in his eyes that was way more scary than when he was just playing at being tough.

"Rack 'em up," he said.

Buddy won the coin toss and this time Travis didn't get a turn. Buddy sank three striped balls on the break, then ran through the remainder, one by one, finishing with the eight.

Looking up from the table, he smiled. Not a good move.

Travis had never been a good loser. Without warning, he took a swing at Buddy with his pool cue. If it had connected with Buddy's head, that would have been all she wrote, as my dad would say. But it didn't come close.

I never saw Buddy move. One moment he was bent over the pool table, looking up, the next he was standing beside Travis. I couldn't really see what he did. He just seemed to touch Travis on the side of the neck, or maybe his shoulder. Whatever it was, Travis went down like a puppet with its strings cut. He would have smashed his head on the side of the table, or at least the floor, if Buddy hadn't caught him and laid him down on the wood planking.

The pool room was absolutely still—until we all heard the double click of two hammers being cocked on a shotgun. On the other side of his counter, Ernie stood with a cigar in the corner of his mouth, the twin barrels of his shotgun pointed at Buddy.

Billy Chambers and Woody Thompson had been starting for Buddy, but they—along with everybody else—backed away, out of the line of fire. Buddy seemed no more concerned about the shotgun than he had been of the threat that Travis had represented on the street outside.

"Oh. God," Sandra said from beside me, her voice so hushed that I could barely hear it.

Her hand was on my upper arm, fingers gripping me so tight it hurt. I didn't turn to look at her. I couldn't have looked away if my life depended on it.

Buddy regarded Ernie for a long moment. Leaning casually on the pool table, he gave a slow shake of his head.

"Guy takes a swing at me with a pool cue," he said, "and you're blaming me."

Ernie's hand was steady, his gaze hard. He was a big man who didn't have to pretend at toughness. Everybody knew he'd done time, and it wasn't for unpaid parking tickets.

"Travis may be a little shit," Ernie said, "but he's one of our own. You're not."

"That makes him right?"

"Right or wrong doesn't mean crap to me, you hippie freak. My place, I make the rules. Walk out, or they'll be carrying you out."

If it wasn't so real, the tension so thick in the air that I could hardly breathe, I would've had to laugh at how stupid all of this sounded.

But the shotgun was real. I didn't doubt that Ernie would use it. Nobody did.

Except Buddy, I guess, or he wouldn't have mouthed off the way he did.

"Well, now," he said, his voice soft, almost friendly. "You try and use that thing, old man, and I'll have to beat you senseless and burn this place to the ground."

Nobody even breathed.

"Your funeral," Ernie said.

I never saw Buddy move—and this time I was really looking. I don't think anybody did. He was leaning on the pool table, then he was standing beside Ernie, plucking the shotgun from his stunned hands. Ernie took a swing at him. Buddy shifted his head slightly, and the blow went by his ear. Then he did whatever it was he'd done to Travis, except this time he didn't bother to catch Ernie. It was only blind luck that Ernie didn't crack open his head when he went down.

Buddy stood behind the counter and looked around the pool room.

"Anybody else think they have balls?" he asked.

Nobody said a word. Nobody made a move.

Buddy nodded. "Didn't think so." He looked down at Ernie, then back up once more. "You better make sure you get him out of here, because tonight this place is going to burn."

Then he walked around the counter and started for the door. Just before he stepped out, his gaze caught mine. He gave me a quick smile, tipping his finger against his brow, and then he was gone.

It was a long thirty seconds or better before anybody even moved. Then Woody knelt by Travis, trying to rouse him. Somebody else went behind the counter to see to Ernie. The whole room was a hubbub of noise.

I didn't stay to listen to any of it.

I slipped out the screen door with Sandra, catching the door so it wouldn't bang closed.

"God, that was something," Sandra said. "Wasn't that something?"

I nodded. It was something, all right. I just wasn't sure what. All I could remember was his gaze meeting mine, holding some kind of promise that I wasn't sure made me feel good or scared. More like a bit of both.

"I have to go home," I said.

"But—"

I cut her off. "Mom told me I had to look after Jane this afternoon."

Sandra nodded.

"Call me later," she said, then hurried around the side of the building toward the front of the pool hall.

I waited until she was gone, then cut across the empty lot behind Ernie's, picking my way through the trash and weeds, heading for anywhere but home. I'd lied about having to look after my little sister Jane. What I really needed was time on my own. I hated all the cock-of-the-roost posturing that went on with the boys of Tartown and whoever was unfortunate enough to get in their way when they decided to have some fun. I hated any kind of violence.

So why was I so intrigued by the stranger? From the moment Travis had taken a swing at him, I'd sensed a fierce potential for violence in the stranger that I'd never seen in any Tartown boy or man. Not even Ernie.

Except the stranger hadn't hurt anybody, a part of me argued. He could have, but he'd just stopped them from doing anything to him.

He really could have. I didn't doubt it for a moment.

That was what bothered me. And he'd said he was going to burn down the pool hall. I got the sense he'd really do that, too, whether there was anybody in there or not.

There's no railway running through town, but there is a track south of Tartown, passing through abandoned farmlands. They used to ship coal and lumber on the old freights, down from the mountains. Now the track doesn't carry anything except people like me, walking along the wooden ties, kicking at the weeds growing up through the gravel.

"I didn't start it, you know."

The voice caught me by surprise. It wasn't that I didn't recognize Buddy. Or even that I wasn't half-expecting him, considering the look he'd given me before he left the pool room. It was more this weird feeling that I'd called him up out of the thin air by thinking about him so hard.

I turned to find him sitting on a granite outcrop a few yards from the tracks. Still long-haired. Still handsome.

I don't have a thing for bad boys—not like Sandra and

some of my other friends, always mooning over the next James Dean or Elvis. Oh, I liked "Leader of the Pack" as much as the next girl. I just didn't want to live it. And whatever else the stranger might be, I knew he was trouble. One way or another, a boy like him was always going to be trouble.

"Back there, I mean," he added when I didn't say anything.

"I know."

Did I? I thought I did, but maybe I just wanted to believe it. Because he'd been awfully quick to deal with the trouble when it came his way. And hadn't he come down into Tartown of his own accord? Nobody'd dragged him. Who came to Tartown and didn't expect trouble?

"You're different from the other girls," he said. "What's your name?"

"Annie. What's yours?"

"Turns out it's Buddy."

"But not 'Chump.'"

We both smiled.

"No, what's your *real* name?" I asked.

"What makes you think that isn't my real name?"

"You don't look like a Buddy."

He didn't look like anybody I'd ever seen before except in the stories you could find in *Life* and *Time* about the hippies out on the West Coast.

"What?" he said. "I'm not friendly enough?"

"C'mon. I told you mine."

"I'm still waiting for someone to give me one I like enough to keep."

I was ready to blow him off. If he was going to be like this, I wasn't going to waste my time talking to him, I didn't care how handsome he was. But his eyes were guileless. Those eyes . . . I'd never seen their like before, a peculiar mix of gold and green, flecked with little speckles of rust.

Either he was a really good liar, or he was telling the truth—I couldn't tell which—but I found myself willing to give him the benefit of the doubt, and so I stayed.

"Well," I said, "then tell me where you're from, this place where people don't have names."

That made him smile again, but I didn't catch the joke this time. He answered my question with one of his own.

"Have you ever watched the way crows fly?"

I shrugged. "I guess. But what's that got to do with anything?"

"They look like they're flying helter-skelter through the air, but they're often following patterns—especially when they're heading to roost in the evening."

"And your point is?"

"The places where their shadows fall on the ground make . . . I don't know. Let's call them ghost roads. Crow roads. All those shadows, day after day. The echo of them builds up so much after a while that you can almost see them, if you're looking the right way."

I found myself wondering if he'd lied when he said he didn't use drugs.

"Well, that's nice," I told him and got ready to start walking again.

"If you follow along one of those roads with an open enough mind, they can take you somewhere else."

"Crow roads," I said, not even trying to hide my skepticism. "Made by shadows."

"The memory of those shadows, yes. The crows don't actually make them. They're already there, patterns of . . . energy, deep in the ground. Their flight just follows them and makes them easier to see."

"And they take you where?"

He shrugged. "Some of them can take you to a place where people don't have names."

I just looked at him for a long moment.

"You know," I said finally, "you seem kind of nice, and you've got to know you're handsome, but tell me honestly. Does a crap story like you're telling me now ever really work on anybody?"

"I'm just answering your questions. I can't help it if the answers seem enigmatic to you."

"Oh, you're way past enigmatic."

He shrugged, then leaned back on the stone.

"No, seriously," I said. "What do you expect me to think when you tell me something as stupid as that?"

"I tell you what. Why don't you give me a name? Maybe you'll come up with one I can keep."

I shook my head. "Okay, I know you're stoned. Which explains the way you're talking right now, and how you just came sauntering into Tartown like it's no big deal. Like nobody like Travis was going to come down hard on you. I get that. What I don't get is what you did to him and Ernie. You hardly seemed to touch them and they just dropped to the floor."

"That's no big deal. It's just knowing where the pressure points are and how to use them. They'll be fine. Though I can't say the same for your Ernie's place of business."

"He's not my Ernie. He won't even let girls in."

"His loss."

"Yeah, well, he's kind of old for us anyway." Ernie had to be in his thirties, which was positively ancient. "So," I went on, "you just did something to these pressure points . . ."

He nodded, but didn't explain any more.

"Is it like that Kato guy on TV?" I asked.

I made a couple of lame chopping motions with my hands. My brothers love shows like *The Green Hornet* and were so bummed when it went off the air this summer.

"It's complicated," he told me. "People have energy patterns in them—just like the earth does—so if you exert pressure in one place, it can affect another, seemingly unrelated part. Right now I'm getting rid of some toxins in my kidneys."

He held up his hand as he spoke and pressed his thumb into various parts of the open palm, as if that was supposed to explain anything. And it didn't. And the way he was goofing was really starting to bug me. But I have to admit, I didn't really mind. Sure, I didn't really care for *what* he was saying, but I couldn't seem to come close to getting tired of that odd accent in his voice, and he was *so* easy on the eyes.

But still . . .

Still what? So he was a little out there. It sure made him more interesting than Travis, or Les at the corner garage, whose idea of a date was asking me if I wanted to go to a dogfight behind the Carters' barn. Yuck. Mind you, talking about kidneys was only a few steps up from that.

"You really know how to sweet-talk a girl," I told him.

"Yeah?" he said. "I didn't think I was so good at talking."

"You seem to do pretty good."

"But I'm not winning you over."

"Winning me over to what?"

He pushed himself up from the rock and ambled over to me.

"Don't you dare knock me out with some magic finger poke," I told him.

"I'd never. I just wanted to know if I can kiss you."

I heard Mrs. Gear's voice in my head. She's our high school English teacher, and she's always saying, "I don't know, *can* you?" when someone misuses "can I" for "may I." But I didn't correct him like she would have. With him standing so close to me, I was back to my mouth going dry and my body feeling all weirdly hot again.

This was so far from the fumbling attempts at a kiss—usually immediately followed by a hand groping its way up the front of your top. That was all the local boys were good for. This was . . . romantic.

If I'd tried to say anything, I would have had to clear my throat, and that would have spoiled everything. So I just nodded. He leaned in closer, lips soft against mine, one hand going to the back of my head and tangling in my hair, the other caressing the small of my back and pulling me closer to him.

You know how you read about someone's knees going weak? I knew just what that meant now.

I put my arms around his neck and let myself fall into the unfamiliar heat that was building inside me like a pressure cooker.

If I was Sandra, I suppose it would have been inevitable that I'd sleep with him. But I'm not, so it surprised me that I ended up doing just that. I wasn't saving myself for when I was married or anything. But I did want it to mean more than just being out with some Tartown boy.

This felt like more. Way more.

So I let him lead me away from the railroad tracks, into

the woods, and you know what? Turns out that thing he does with his fingers is good for a lot more than knocking some guy out in a fight.

"I'm not going to see you again, am I?" I said later.

I was snuggled in the crook of his arm where we lay on the grass with only the sun to cover our skin, twisting a lock of that long hair of his around a finger. It was so thick and so soft. Up close his eyes were even more amazing. I felt like I could just swim away in them.

"You could come with me," he said.

I thought of all those runaway kids in their bare feet and raggedy clothes, holding flowers and making peace signs at the cameramen from *Life* magazine. I'm not saying I'm the most practical of girls—witness me lying here in the arms of a boy whose name I didn't know, who claimed to not even *have* a name unless I gave him one. But I knew I wanted more out of life than whatever it was those kids had found.

I'd already chosen the academic rather than the commercial stream when I got to high school. Everybody thought I was making a big mistake—from my parents and friends to the administrators at school. Tartown girls either left school pregnant before they graduated or they got jobs as secretaries and beauticians and the like. But I had my guidance counselor on my side. He'd told me about scholarships and student loans. If I kept my grade average up, I could actually do it. I could go on to university. I could get out of this place—not as a hippie, hitchhiking to nowhere, but with a future ahead of me.

My long-haired lover was cute, but cute wasn't enough to make me want to give up my dreams.

"I can't," I told him.

"Can't or won't?"

I sat up and looked for my clothes.

"I don't want to," I said.

I pulled my top on over my head. When I pushed my hair out of my eyes, I saw he was just lying here, head cradled on his elbow, looking at me.

"You're not trying very hard to convince me to come with you," I said.

Not that it would work, but couldn't he at least try?

"Where I'm going, you can only go when you're ready. No sooner."

So we were back to enigmatic.

"The place where people don't have names," I said.

He nodded.

"That you get to by following these crow roads."

"It's not just crows," he said. "Most birds and animals use them."

"Which is what makes them magic."

"I didn't say that."

"Well, then what are they? Where *do* they go?"

He sat up, long hair falling down his chest, and gave me a serious look.

"I don't know," he said. "I don't have words to describe it."

"You just pop a pill, and there you are."

He shook his head. "It's like names. We don't need names or words to describe what just *is*. What we know in here." He touched that beautiful chest of his, right in the middle, where his heart would be.

I finished getting dressed, and he did the same.

"Are you really going to burn down the pool hall?" I asked.

He nodded.

"I wish you wouldn't."

"Why's that?"

"The boys around here don't have much, but at least they've got that. Take it away, and who knows what kind of bad trouble they'll get into."

I was thinking more of my brothers than of Travis and his gang.

"Then for you, I won't do it," he said.

"You weren't really going to do it, were you?"

Something flashed in his eyes then, hard and unrelenting.

"Oh yeah," he told me. "I always try to do what I say I will."

Okay, I didn't want to be here where everything felt dark and tense again, like it had back at Ernie's.

"Don't," I said.

"Don't what?"

"Don't look like that. I want to remember your kindness."

His features softened.

"I'd never hurt you. You know that, don't you?"

I nodded. I don't know why, but I did.

He stepped close and kissed me, then pulled away when I tried to hang on to him.

"I have to go," he said. "But you know where to find me."

"I don't know any such thing."

"Follow the crow roads."

"But that's just a—"

"It's not just a story. It's not something you can use now, but you can hold on to it against a time when maybe you'll feel you need something just like that."

"I really don't know what you're talking about."

"I know you don't. But I hope you'll remember all the same. And Annie? Bring me a name when you do come."

He started back toward the railway tracks and I followed along behind him, but somewhere between the little meadow where we'd been lying and the wooden ties held down by those long steel rails, he just wasn't there anymore.

I stopped dead in my tracks and looked around.

"Buddy?" I called. "C'mon, Buddy. Don't mess around like this."

But his name wasn't Buddy, was it? He came from a place where people don't have names. He . . .

I'd say, maybe he hadn't been here at all, but I still had a satisfied tingle that seemed to fill every nook and cranny of my body, and . . . I pulled my bra from my pocket where I'd stuck it because I'd liked the feel of my small breasts pressing against the fabric of my top. I hadn't been in the woods satisfying myself. I had a bedroom for that.

I looked up and down the tracks. Overhead, a crow cawed, and I followed the path of its shadow on the ground.

Crow roads.

But I still wasn't ready to give up my own dream.

I started for home.

The funny thing was, nobody really remembered Buddy. Or at least not the way I did. Sandra, when we were talking on the phone that night, remembered Travis knocking him to the floor of the pool hall and Ernie throwing the both of them out, threatening to call the cops if they kept fighting outside his place. So Travis had just let him go.

"But he was handsome, right?" I said.

"Well, sure he was, long hair and all. But it did make him

kind of girly, and he sure couldn't stand up for himself."

I didn't argue. I didn't want to get into how not girly he really was. That was going to be a secret between him and me.

I don't know what Ernie or Travis remembered—I didn't really have any reason to talk to either of them and I wasn't about to start now. But I overheard Woody and Les at the corner store a couple of days later, laughing about the hippie they'd sent packing, so I could guess.

"I think maybe he pissed his pants when Travis hit him," Woody said.

I didn't understand what was going on until a few months later, when I came across a reference to both someone like Buddy and this whole misremembering business. I'd taken an interest in our local folklore after that afternoon, and there was any number of books on the subject in the reference section of the public library, which means you can't sign them out, but you can read them in the library. Not that Tartown kids have much luck getting library cards. They always find some excuse not to give them to us—the odd time one of us actually comes in trying to get one.

I'm sure it's illegal—and it's certainly not right—but what's a kid to do? I don't want to sound mean, but most of their parents wouldn't care one way or another, so who's going to fight it or even complain? Mine would have, but I didn't want to bother them with it. My grandma always said to pick your battles, and not being able to get a library card didn't seem to be one worth fighting. And to tell you the truth, I kind of liked the excuse of having to go and spend the time at the library when I wanted to read the books they have in there.

According to the folklore, people often don't remember encounters they have with things they can't explain. It's easier for them to just pretend it never happened, or slip on a new set of fake memories that make more sense. It's not that anyone does it on purpose. Apparently, it's this subconscious thing.

The book that had the reference to Buddy—or someone who could be Buddy—was written back in the thirties. It was a collection of folktales from the area, with annotations by the guy who'd done the fieldwork. The bit about Buddy was thrown in with a bunch of other sections on strange men coming out of the woods.

There was the one about this blacksmith with a horse and cart, who just shows up, ready to fix a thrown shoe, but he's really sent out by the fairies to seduce young women into their fairy mound. Why? The book didn't say. They usually had an old-fashioned name like Daniel or Benjamin or Elijah, and the girls they went after were always alone at the time.

Another was about this Wild Boy, living in the woods, in the branches of trees. He'd keep you there for one day that was actually a year, telling you stories. I wondered if that was a euphemism for making out. He had all these different names, too, like Luke or Johnny.

And then there were these people, particular to our area, who would just show up at odd times, to mingle with humans. They were usually dark-haired, and the thing about them was that however you treated them, they'd treat you back the same, only more so. They especially liked to either fight with the local men or seduce the young women—which made them like the blacksmith, I guess, because they were forever offering to take the girls back to some hidden world with them.

Some girls didn't go and regretted it. Some girls went with them, or followed them later, and were never seen again. But one of the old women who were the sources the author found for these stories told him that those girls who did go away were just fine, you didn't need to worry about them. If a girl had a name to give the stranger, and love in her heart, he would never hurt her.

"How do you know that?" the author had asked her.

"I just do," she'd said. "If you have faith, you'll come to no harm."

"Faith in God, you mean?"

He wrote that the old woman had just laughed. And then she said, "No, faith in the power of love."

Which made him think that she was one of the ones who regretted not going, but she never admitted to it.

I didn't regret not going. I knew how to go. I just wasn't ready yet.

But I took to watching birds a lot—especially crows—following the paths their shadows make on the ground when they fly by overhead. Buddy was right. They fly the same routes more often than they don't.

So why don't I go?

I still have things I want to do in this world. I want to prove that a Tartown girl can be more than everybody's already decided she can be. I want to be part of the changes I can see coming, where women will be in charge of their own bodies and their own destinies. Things are already in motion. Like NOW, the National Organization for Women, pushing for passage of an Equal Rights Amendment to the Constitution.

Everybody seems to think Women's Lib is just some big joke. Even Mama shakes her head when it comes up.

But I know it's going to happen.

It has to.

And I'm going to be part of it.

But unlike that old lady in the book, I'm not going to grow old and fill up with regrets. I'll do the things I need to do, as much as I can, but one day, I'll go.

One day, I really will. I'll just up and go, following those crow roads to where a boy with long black hair is waiting for me.

The only thing I'm still missing is his name. I know I have to have a name for him when we meet again. So far it hasn't come to me, but you know what? I have the faith that it'll come to me when the time is right.

It's just sleeping in my heart for now.

CHARLES DE LINT is a full-time writer and musician who currently makes his home in Ottawa, Canada, with his wife, MaryAnn Harris, an artist and musician. His most recent novels are *The Blue Girl*, *Widdershins*, and *Little (Grrl) Lost*. Other recent publications include *Dingo* and the collections *The Hour Before Dawn*, *What the Mouse Found*, and *Triskell Tales 2*.

For more information about his work, visit his Web site at www.charlesdelint.com.

∾

AUTHOR'S NOTE

"Crow Roads" gave me the opportunity to present a strong, independently minded young woman in a time when the concept of such went against the grain of general thinking. Of course, there were plenty of strong women in the time the story is set, and before it as well, but the sixties was when the struggle for true equality really took off and women began to make the inroads that brought us to where we are today: still not a perfect time, but without a doubt, it's a more egalitarian society than we had fifty years ago.

Annie is a young woman caught on the threshold of all those changes, and I loved having this opportunity to meet her and discover the choices she would make through the course of the story.

THE CHAMBER MUSIC
OF ANIMALS

Katherine Vaz

Sophie Wilder tore through her closet like mad. Laundry and shoes flew backward. When she tried to move aside the box from her college days, it ripped open and she stared at what was inside. Platform sandals! Jeans with hems big enough to fit over her head! Good God—a black-light Grateful Dead poster!

"I'm so sorry, Rangy," she said, lifting her stuffed orangutan from the bottom of this time capsule. When she carried him to the kitchen, his extra-long arms, draped over her shoulders, swayed and patted Sophie on her back, until it felt like the sort of quiet dance her husband, Ray, had enjoyed with her when he was alive. She fished in a drawer for some batteries, unzipped Rangy's spine, and snapped them into the transistor radio he harbored inside.

Rangy had two knobs, kidney height, and she clicked one of them: Static . . . crackling. She tuned his second knob. Music! Scarlatti! Rapid breathless scales. Rangy chattering at full speed, scolding her.

He made her grin and forget for a second that she was in

a nightmare equal to the one when Ray's crop-dusting plane had crashed.

"I have an important job for you, Rangy," she whispered.

His stare was glassy—that was her fault, for letting him drop off a shelf and lie neglected in her closet. Rangy remained elegantly clean-shaven, and he'd kept his thick, reddish brown fur—a cherrywood-under-mahogany shade that Sophie had tried to dye her own hair without as much success.

She tiptoed with Rangy into Philip's bedroom. He was sleeping; the doctors warned that the radiation would keep him drowsy. She set Rangy on the pine dresser crowded with bottles of water, pill vials, a tin of mint Sucrets, and books her son was too dizzy to read. Rangy struggled to confine "Ode to Joy" to a low volume. Sophie had read many studies declaring that music helped cure the sick. Music took everything physical and lifted it until it got attached to invisible wires, where it could be shocked clean with grace. If anything could come to the rescue, it would be the medicine of Bach, Mozart, Puccini.

"Mom?" Philip woke up and turned over in bed to face her. She admired that he'd turned out angular and thin like his dad—though the leukemia was paring his flesh down to the bones—but she was especially fond of Philip's green eyes, since he'd invented those on his own. How had so much time passed? He was already twenty-one. Her eyes were a sky blue; Ray's had been brown. She pressed a palm to Phil's forehead to drink up his fever. When she saw her tiny, upside-down reflections pasted to the mirrors over his irises, she was annoyed. Either those twins of herself should whirl around, dive inside him, and fix what was wrong, or they should scram out of the way so she could gaze farther in.

"Hey, Mom?" He reached up to hold her hand. "It's okay to leave me by myself. Really. Whoa, is that Rangy? Where'd you find him?"

"He'll keep you company while I'm at work," said Sophie. Philip's CD player might produce sharper notes, but only for a few hours at a time. Rangy could sing on his own without stopping—and every piece would be a surprise. "Maybe he'll teach you how to carry a tune."

Philip said, "Sure, as long as Rangy has a wheelbarrow handy."

They started giggling.

Sophie opened a curtain. The hibiscus was tapping at the pane—salmon and orange trumpet-shapes that shook in the breeze and tossed layer after layer of their coats onto Philip's eyelids to weight them shut. The calico cat, Dinah, entered the room with her fashion-model-on-the-runway sashay before jumping onto the bed. She squinted at Rangy.

"Behave yourself, Dinah," said Sophie. She turned Rangy's knobs to a medium-high volume.

Rangy soared into some music that caused Sophie to kiss Philip good-bye in a hurry. Dinah offered one of her "go-away-now-and-leave-the-house-to-me" growls.

It was only while driving past the artichoke fields—the air beige with dust, as if the angels were peeved at being forced to cart the rugs of heaven down to the clouds for cleaning and were thrashing them with extra fury—that Sophie cried. She'd left Rangy serenading Philip with *An American in Paris*. Going to Europe on a backpacking trip—London, Paris, maybe Barcelona—was supposed to have been Philip's present for graduating from UCLA with top honors in botany. She'd been working extra shifts at the artichoke factory for years to save up, despite Philip insisting that she please not bother. Right now the two of them were supposed to be in Maine, with Sophie's mother, Alice, who'd helped with the funds, for a farewell party. A good and happy farewell.

She stopped and rolled down her car's window. A spongy arm of ocean air stretched over the fields, over her Chevrolet so dusted and caked it looked ready to be fried. She flicked on her car radio to the classical station as *An American in Paris* wafted away, and a piece she could not name—Philip devoured music; he'd know—eerie but grand, speckled the inside of her car and her skin with black notes.

Out of the rain of whole, half, quarter, sixteenth, and grace notes in Philip's room, several stuck together and fell hard on Rangy's head. "Ah!" he said, blinking. "Was that the famous mystic chord of Scriabin?" His back ached . . . surgery? Again? He also recalled a box, a closet, screams fading to silence. In his younger days, Rangy could have named any musical piece without hesitation. But was it his fault he had been drugged and discarded, just because CD players got invented—wait! That was one right there! The enemy! In the corner! He lurched at the sight of a banner of a UCLA Bruin (*nasty fatsos*, why were *they* a mascot, instead of intelligent, slender, trapeze-artist musical apes with red highlights?) and haystacks of T-shirts that made him shudder; they were of a palette (lime green, sunny yellow) that hunters wore in the woods to keep their nutty friends from shooting each other. . . . And *who* was this person splayed under a striped comforter? Rangy recalled a boy in the Wilder house . . . who'd tired of him.

The first sight to meet his approval was the alluring feline curled on the bed. Her eyes were slit like pistachios ready to be eaten, and she was sporting haute couture peach-tinted patches on her alabaster fur. Love, thought Rangy, but aloud he said only, "It's good to be alive."

The cat hunched and her tail quivered like a lightning rod zapped in a storm. "There'll be no monkeying around here!" she yowled.

How rude. "I am an ape, not a monkey," he said. He had his pride. His face and dried-apricot-size ears burned as the cat lolled around, laughing. Rangy did not wish to abandon his usual becoming modesty, but this was too much. He shouted over "La Réjouissance" from *Music for the Royal Fireworks* that *orangutan* was of Malayan origin and meant "man of the forest," so you see, though gorillas got most of the press coverage, he was of a tribe considered the lifeblood and sensibility, as it were, of the animal kingdom, and . . . *oof.*

The cat sprang, knocked him flat, and bashed at him until he was stuck on a *talk show*! And people accused *apes* of jabbering?

Rangy writhed on his back to return himself to the classical station and used the ceramic flamingo lamp to pull himself up. The cat grinned from her perch on the boy in the bed. Rangy let Handel's Concerto for Harp in B-Flat Major reply for him. He was not, after all, full of the slop of human or cat bodies. His innards were pure beauty, and he could easily, invisibly invade and inhabit any creature alive. His heart was a box carrying the world's greatest artists. And yet Sophie had given him away, to her son who'd one day discarded him, too. Philip . . . yes, this was grown-up Philip, snoring and sopping up—hoarding!—Rangy's music.

Rangy was thirty-five. He'd been robbed of his prime years.

Dinah's mouth dropped open as Rangy curled his toes around the edge of the dresser. He raised his arms until his fingers met in a flame shape over his head. He was quite pleased with his arc—matching a swelling of the music—as he executed a perfect dive into Philip's ear to collect the notes and clefs—everything—of the harp concerto.

Rangy only wanted to reclaim what was rightfully his.

His jungle instincts came to his aid as he surveyed the mucky dark that was inside Philip and ate a few bubbling oxygen molecules, and he snatched five harp notes floating past—easy as grabbing fruit off a plantain tree. He needed them; with the radio waves cut off, his chest was muffled.

Ah! The bass clef, caught around a vein! He used it as a hook to corral more notes, like a croupier at a gambling table hauling in the chips. He juggled the harp sounds before reminding himself that he was not a zoo prisoner, performing tricks. He could picture the hideous sign: WATCH APE HANDLE HANDEL! (No, some idiot would probably write: WATCH MONKEY HANDLE HANDEL.)

He invented his own xylophone tune by tapping the rib cage with the prongs of a sixteenth note, but he stopped to watch some blob-shaped cells glowing white and surrounding a whole note. Curious: the cells bit the note to pieces and then swallowed the crushed parts. They got fatter. And more fluttery.

The largest glowing cell spotted Rangy. It devoured a C note and trapped some musical bars and hung them as tentacles to turn itself into a Monster Jellyfish.

It jetted through the blood right at Rangy.

He darted through the slats of Philip's rib cage and found a horde of quivering harp notes stuck to the heart. When he nestled into the bed of them, a swarm of melody sprayed outward to seal the spaces between the ribs. The seals were shimmering and transparent but kept the Monster out, since even jumbled music has the kind of beauty that resists what is ugly. Staring through the gauzy curtain, Rangy trembled as the Monster lashed its tentacles at the ribs and at the spaces between the ribs sealed up with Handel. Smaller white blobs ganged up near the Monster Jellyfish and took turns cracking their whip arms, too. One of them ripped the musical curtain, and Rangy flung a B-flat note at the fissure to seal it again.

He had no idea how to bang out of this new cage. Snickering jellyfish were—one by one—lining up in the tunnel leading from Rangy to the ear, where at the very top the light of the room was shining like a coin.

They were slowly assembling. Rangy's breathing grew shallow. A few more jellies swam up. Then a clot more: the passageway back into the room was a millimeter more narrow now. Two millimeters.

Three.

Soon enough, they would entirely block his escape. The Monster Jellyfish stayed vibrating right outside the rib cage.

Rangy ate a C, an A, a G, and an E note, but that only reminded him of when Philip won the California State Spelling Bee Championship. Sophie had baked a lemon cake and cut and frosted it into a bee shape, with a chocolate Kiss for the stinger. The neighbors arrived and told Philip how far he would go one day, and Rangy was inspired to belt out "The Flight of the Bumblebee," and everyone applauded, including Philip; he wasn't afraid to share the limelight. Rangy had tried to take a bow, and when he tumbled off the kitchen counter, it was Philip who'd rescued him.

Rangy rested his head on Philip's heart and cried. The muscle was thumping out its own brave music—Philip must still love him very much—to soothe Rangy to sleep, but Rangy first used a grace note to floss his teeth, because Rangy, like all good primates, unlike disgusting jellyfish, was always careful with grooming.

Philip's heart was burning.

Sophie put her hand over her chest while the factory's noises drowned out the *Stabat Mater* on the radio. She'd consumed nothing but coffee all day; no wonder she ached with heart-burn. She slumped on one of the chairs around the work-table where they clipped the claws off dried baby artichokes and decorated them as ornaments to be sold in the gift shops throughout the valley. Martin and Clara were the most artis-tic, piling on glitter and gems.

A dried baby artichoke looks like a monkey's paw. If you find one, isn't it supposed to grant you three wishes? She thought, Wish #1: I wish Ray had stayed home sick the day his crop-dusting plane's engine failed. Wish #2: I wish a miracle for Philip. Wish #3: If someone must be taken once again, please take me.

"Honey," said Miriam Ruiz, Sophie's supervisor, "go on home." Sophie had saved up several weeks worth of sick days. Martin, Clara, Miriam, and the rest of the crew handed Sophie a check: a little extra, to help out. She hugged them all. It was enough that they'd volunteered to work extra, to cover for as long as she needed . . . no one came out and said, "Until your only child dies."

She took a long detour home—not through the fields, but along the Pacific Coast Highway. The sea was flat and covered with lace, as if moths had attacked a thin white coverlet over a turquoise blanket.

She found Philip tossing, holding his gut . . . and Rangy missing. "Dinah!" Her screech was half a sob. "What did you do with Rangy?"

The cat arched, twirled around, and skittered away.

Sophie whispered into Philip's ear, "Don't worry, baby, we'll fight this. I've heard lots of stories about people beating leukemia."

Rangy got wide-eyed at the shapes of the sounds of the words (quavering whole notes) tumbling down the shaft of Philip's ear. They knocked aside some of the horrible cells in the passageway. But more swam up to take their place. He looked out the rib cage. The Monster Jellyfish was laughing. Not just because Rangy was trapped, but also because Rangy now knew who the monsters really were.

Alice was using kitchen tongs to agitate the photos in their chemical-bath trays in her darkroom. The tongs were blackened from the time she'd had to fry about a hundred chickens at the Rangeley Moose Festival. What a relief to have her photo lab in the laundry room instead of the basement, since her broken leg would prevent her from gallivanting down any stairs. She was anxious to develop her newest roll and send the pictures to California, to amuse Philip. She leaned on her crutch and shifted her weight; it felt like she'd dined on stones. Her white hair was knotted and skewered in place with some year-old chopsticks from the Soon King Chinese Take-Out. With this broken shin, she not only couldn't drive into town, but she also couldn't get on a plane and fly to California.

She shook a tray and frowned at the shot of red squirrels

hooting at her from the bark of an evergreen. She'd been flat on her back when she'd snapped it. She'd mistaken a stump in a thicket for a moose and tripped while hurrying to capture it on film, and that's when she'd broken her damn fool leg.

Tongs in hand, she was scratching off a squirrel's face when the phone rang. Her "Hello?" was crabby, but it was unbearable to glance around her big, drafty kitchen with the banner—now sagging—that said "Congratulations, Philip!" and the balloons—shriveling—from Jordan Gibson's Party Store, stamped with "Bon Voyage!"

"Mother?"

"Aha, Sophie! Calling to say you're sorry? I got into a lot of trouble with that sangria recipe you sent. Emily McPhee and I thought it tasted like fruit punch and we drank too much and spent an evening trying to hit the high notes in 'Auld Lang Syne.' It was jolly fun except for the headache." *Good night*, she was chattering worse than a red squirrel! She loved teasing her daughter about leaving the hilarities of Maine to be a hippie in California long ago and marrying and only visiting a few times a year . . . but this was hardly the time for blathering. She just didn't want to hear any bad news.

"Mother? I think Philip is worse. No—I know he's worse." Sophie's voice cracked, and what she'd been holding in flooded out and soaked into the telephone wires and poured into Alice's ear.

Alice gazed out her window at her blueberry patches. When Philip was to have been here for his farewell party, she'd planned to ask him, since he was a wizard with plants, why the berries were getting so destroyed by bugs. There wouldn't be much of a jam season this summer.

"Ma? Did you hear me? Is your leg okay?"

"It's not as broken as the rest of me, darling," said Alice. "Please tell Philip I love him to pieces." She wasn't sure what else got said before they said good-bye. She opened a window and hurled a spoon at a squirrel in a tree. Insects, worms, predators! The squirrel tossed back a hectoring cackle when the spoon missed by a mile. Why were so many of her neighbors proud of being nature lovers? Nature! FAH! It was guerrilla warfare!

When Adam Drabble knocked at Alice Gardner's back door and got no reply, he wiped his muddy shoes on the fleur-de-lis rubber mat, set down the box of groceries (with the lottery ticket on top, because Alice liked to grab it, scrape off the silver, and give him immediate hell for it being a zero), and tiptoed in. Was it his imagination, or had her moose decor—ceramic bookends, dish towels, doorstops—multiplied overnight? "Mrs. Gardner?" he called. "I've got your delivery."

He found her hunched over in her Queen Anne wing chair, gripping her crutch with both hands, and her hair falling loose with chopsticks stuck in like antlers, while her shoulders shook with weeping.

"Mrs. Gardner!" Adam knelt and patted her hand. "Is this about your grandson? We were all looking forward to his party."

"No, I'm crying because my audition for the ballet fell flat."

Adam grinned. "Listen, sweet pea," he said. "I have an idea."

Adam was a philatelist. He told Alice that a "Cinderella" was a category of stamps that collectors invented, creating their own designs for make-believe countries.

If they couldn't send Philip Wilder to Europe, they could bring Europe to him.

~ ~ ~

Alice phoned Jordan Gibson in Madrid, Maine, and Emily McPhee, her best friend, in Lisbon, Maine. Adam lived in Paris, Maine; Kate and Joseph Goshen lived in Berlin, New Hampshire. And for good measure, Alice called the Dickinsons, Ellen and Christopher, in Mexico, Maine, to tell them that she was in charge of a Cinderella Contest.

In Madrid, Lisbon, Paris, Berlin, and Mexico, the midnight oil burned and offered extra pinpricks of light you'd see if you were way up in the sky over Maine and New Hampshire and peering down through the darkness, because no one wanted to sleep until he or she had painted or drawn a Cinderella that would make a sick young man fall inside his dreams.

Jordan Gibson was the first to bring his Cinderella artwork to Alice. She was glad to see him in his overalls; he was a widower and had once taken Alice out, to dine on baked scrod for the purpose of suddenly acting like sappy teenagers instead of staying pals. Just because he lived close to Rangeley was no reason for them to ruin a friendship by getting married, now that both their spouses were gone. "Heavens, Jorrie," she'd said. He'd done himself up in a string tie, and his hair showed the furrows where he'd raked his hair with grease. "You look like someone from *Bonanza*."

"Careful, Ally," he'd said. They'd been sick with mirth and horror; what on earth were they thinking? "You might hurt my feelings."

His Cinderella stamp said MADRID, MAINE, and displayed a small plasterboard with a moose cut from a magazine, and pasted over the animal were clippings of a matador's outfit and a mouse-eared matador's cap, glued at a tilt. Over his collage, he'd stretched Saran Wrap to represent the rain of Maine.

"Jordan," said Alice, "you're my homegrown Picasso."

"Thank you, my dear," he said, kissing a bare patch on her scalp.

Philip was being lifted up and away. He and Rangy were traveling. The road was mostly smooth but sometimes jarring.

Rangy heard the word *radiation* right before a flash of light set off a swirl of cells and notes brilliantly stunned, as if someone had thrown an electrical switch. Philip's heart turned into a trampoline. Rangy got bounced out of the ribcage with a force that burst him through the thin, protective curtain of music, past the conduit of escape through the ear, through the throat . . . the Monster Jellyfish, shocked, cast a tentacle toward Rangy but missed, and the little monster cells were either dissolving in the bright light or glomming together . . . the harp notes formed a funnel streaming into Philip's brain. They were sinking into his memory. Rangy wasn't fast enough to grab them. Those were *his* notes, *he'd* been the one locked away, *his* chest had played the harp!

The Monster Jellyfish, boiling with fury, in spasms from the electric light, zoomed upward to trap Rangy behind Philip's eyes. The throat was too narrow for the Monster to enter, but it also meant that Rangy was more trapped than ever.

Some of Philip's hair follicles died. Rangy threw some harp notes to poke through the scalp as black hair, and he noticed that his own fur was molting.

Sophie brought in a Federal Express package, opened it, and set out an array of placards. Dinah was prancing around, and Philip sat up. Perching on the bed and holding Philip's hand was a young, redheaded woman in a denim skirt, pink flip-flops, and a T-shirt as striped as the comforter. Philip's girlfriend? Rangy was enraged that she ignored his cry for help; redheads were supposed to stick together! His fur—or what was left of it—was a much more vibrant, glossy shade than hers.

"It's a Cinderella contest from Grandma Alice, and you're the judge, Phil," Sophie said. "If you can't go to the cities, the cities will come to you. Pick the one you like best."

"Get me out of here, Red!" shouted Rangy.

"Oh, let's go to Paris," said Martha, laughing. Rangy scowled as she pointed at a painting of squirrels in sequined outfits, hanging off trapezes in branches (ha! Rangy could swing through trees without any phony setup) as if they were in the Cirque du Soleil. An evergreen was trimmed to look like the Eiffel Tower. Perforations around the edges of the artwork made it into a stamp. In the top right corner, "39 cents (highway robbery)" was hand-lettered in, and PARIS, MAINE, was written on the bottom. Someone had scratched out the eyes of the squirrels and replaced them with glitter. "I think your grandmother added her own touch to this one," said Sophie.

"I can hear her saying, 'Take that, you monsters! If you look at me, you have to be dazzled,'" said Philip.

Well, Rangy was saying exactly that to the monsters inside Philip, wasn't he? Only they weren't getting dazzled, just angry.

Martha squeezed Philip's hand until his blood surged in a way that knocked the Monster aside a bit, and some of the pulse of Martha's love bloomed toward Rangy. Then the Monster roared back into place. But Martha had managed to send Rangy some Redness . . . he had to admit it.

Another stamp featured a moose as a matador, covered

with glimmering plastic wrap. Rangy wanted to weep from being this near to the animal world.

"Rain!" said Sophie. "The rain of Maine stays mainly in the Maine!"

"Unless it comes here!" said Martha.

"Look what else came to us," said Philip. "Germany."

BERLIN, NEW HAMPSHIRE, was a stamp worth 52 Euros, showing a wall fallen down around a blueberry patch.

"From the Goshens? Remember when Mr. Goshen tried to pour a birdbath out of concrete and it collapsed into rubble?" said Philip.

"I remember," said Sophie. "Too much sand."

Oh, for heaven's sake; now Sophie was wet-eyed. If it went on like this, Rangy was going to be a wreck.

"Should it count if it's from New Hampshire?" said Martha.

Philip said that probably the fun of travel was going to places that weren't part of the original plan or country.

The hibiscus outside the window swayed, craning to get a better look inside at the Cinderellas.

LISBON, MAINE, showed boats and oarlocks. Martha exclaimed that the American and the European Lisbons were famous for water . . . lakes and rivers, and the sea.

MEXICO, MAINE, pictured a moose holding maracas.

"It's all beautiful and maybe that's what's making my eyes hurt," said Philip. "It's like I have double vision."

Martha kissed Philip's forehead, her lips brushing against Rangy.

"It's hard to pick one winner," said Philip, his eyelids dropping so that Berlin, Lisbon, Madrid, Mexico, and Paris disappeared. "They're each of them by themselves and all of them together really wonderful."

Alone at night, in darkness, Rangy used his jungle night vision to stare along with Philip at the moose under the cooling plastic rain: Why did Rangy feel wrapped in ribbons of harp music? He glanced around and saw, sprinkling down out of Philip's memory, a replaying of the music, making it alive again. Drifting down, too, were other memories being called back, like translucent snapshots.

Floating past Rangy was Grandma Alice, here in California, long ago . . . Philip—skinny, wild-haired—kept Rangy on his lap as they drove by the artichoke fields, with Philip's dad at the wheel and Sophie next to him. They were on their way to Carmel and were playing the game of What Does That Cloud Look Like? Grandma Alice, in the backseat, shouted that the clouds looked like lint, and Ray said, "There's the beard I wore as Santa at that stupid artichoke-farmers' Christmas party."

Philip had no idea what to describe as being in the heavens until Rangy sang the "Toreador Song" from *Carmen*, prompting Philip to think of Spanish dancers . . . "Castanets!" he yelled. Grandma Alice shouted, "That's where thunder comes from!" and Sophie said laughing, "Cloud castanets!" and Ray said, "Could you please see them as lobsters with huge claws, Phil? I'm hungry."

Rangy groped at the memory of the cloud castanets, and he seized an armful of the memory of Handel's harp concerto . . . he was damp, as if he were in a rain forest, with a tide rising over his ankles . . . the level of water was growing until it threatened to cut him in two: Philip was crying. His tear ducts were pouring outward.

Ah! Rangy clutched his armful of freshly remembered harp music. He could swim out through the open tear ducts, sliding to the safety of the room with most of the Handel in his possession.

He glanced at the Monster guarding the throat; it fluttered, drunk with light, and under its wings a small jellied army was amassing.

Rangy glanced at the duct . . . narrowing. Philip was starting to dry his eyes.

Another snapshot hailed down: redheaded Martha singing opera one night in the Wilder living room, "O mio babbino caro." Rangy had missed it by being trapped behind a box, but thanks to Philip's memory, Rangy could accompany her now, changing *babbino* to *baboon-o*.

And another: Philip at his dad's funeral, putting his collection of baseball cards in the casket for his father to take to trade with God.

Maybe Rangy had missed his young adulthood by being in a closet, but Philip's dad hadn't survived long . . . and Philip might have no prime years at all.

Rangy turned a last time toward the river flowing to freedom in the room, and he stopped Philip's crying by seizing the duct and spraying the Monster Jellyfish with sorrow and brine, and for half a second—long enough for the creature to be stunned as if with a fire hose and blown aside—Rangy found his chance to dive back toward the heart and the core of the body where the cells were winning the battle.

He was still upset at Dinah for calling him a monkey . . . he'd show her! Apes and monkeys are always being admired for their inventive use of tools! While the Monster Jellyfish shook off its drenching and reared back up, Rangy imagined vines as he swung with his exceedingly long arms from vein to artery (okay, he was born in a factory, but it had pipes overhead), and he was so inspired by Philip's bathing them in memories that he conjured his own: Rangy had been a glorious musician, and he plucked the notes sticking to his mange and realigned them into proper bars and measures and stretched them around the cells of disease. Corralled like that, the cells burst into flames, and the music pounded the flames until they were smoke.

He hurled half notes to combust the cells guarding the passageway to the ear; while swinging with one arm through Philip's insides, he kept reassembling the sounds tucked under his other arm, and though he got some of the patterns wrong, he pitched the musical phrases everywhere. Rangy stopped to catch his breath in the dark interior now lit by bonfires, but as the haze cleared, the King Monster appeared right before him, and with one whip of a tentacle, Rangy was caught.

He whimpered. The last of the notes in his grip sailed away. The Monster was going to squeeze him until he burned to death.

But the notes, free-floating, inspired, decided to reproduce like memory upon memory. They wound their bars through the fluttering wings of the Monster and tore off pieces. Rangy, quaking, looked up to see a chain of notes forming a spear from a glissando. He screeched when it hurtled toward his head . . . until he realized that the music was tossing him a weapon, and he grabbed the note-spear in his singed paw and stabbed the

Monster with the fierce glissando from Handel. The Monster bellowed, and other notes overhead circled in a ring that crashed down like a cut chandelier right as Rangy leapt through their open center . . . and the Monster Jellyfish Cell, the warlord of disease, burst like a bad Roman candle, scattering its poisonous light . . . but more notes lit sharply down on those flares, and they died away while putting them out.

Rangy patted where his ears hurt. They'd been burned. He looked over the field of dying fires and dying notes, and though a few quivers of harp strings floated toward him, he said, No, stay here where you belong. And he stretched his arms over his head and swam through Philip's ear—the narrowed tunnel was littered with embers as he shot through to the light of the room, where a moose stood glazed in rain, telling him that safety gleamed within reach. Rangy hurled toward freedom, but the fires and hooks left by the dead cells tore at him. He burst through Philip's ear into the safety of the room, but he screamed in pain. He put his hands up to cover the wounds on the sides of his head only to discover that his narrow escape had torn off his ears. He waited for someone to pick him up; Philip slept soundly, and the room was dark. No one came for him, and he blacked out on the floor.

When Rangy awoke, Sophie was patting his mottled fur. He winced when she touched where his ears had been. Oh, great . . . there was Dinah. It sounded as if his volume was on its lowest setting when Sophie said, "Dinah! You chewed up Rangy! You ate his ears!"

What was Martha saying? She was smiling. Balloons bobbed near the ceiling—red and blue, like the colors of the blood that goes in and out of the heart—and on every one of the Cinderellas was a cobalt ribbon, as if Rangy were at a children's party, where everyone wins a prize so no one's feelings get hurt. "It's a miracle," Martha said. Philip's face was flushed, but he was sitting up and grinning.

Right when Rangy thought he'd faint, Sophie set him next to Philip, who draped one of Rangy's arms over himself and the other over Martha and said, "I don't need Europe, Mom" . . . and then something about having the world right there with him. Rangy couldn't make out the words, because Sophie clicked him on to Beethoven's Ninth Symphony, and as the soaring faded to nothing, Rangy understood that, like the great composer, he, too, was deaf now.

Sophie patched his fur with reddish brown yarn, and she sewed apricot-colored silk ears onto him. They didn't cure his deafness, but he felt very attractive in them. He was put on the shelf over Philip's bed, and often he tumbled forward so that Philip could keep him near. A pulse, a heartbeat: these go through the skin, and though the deaf cannot hear music, they can feel it. Beat and beat; quicken and slow; close enough, close enough. You are mine.

Grandma Alice stomped around outside with her crutch. Her leg was almost mended. What perfect timing, now that Philip would also soon be well! The crutch indented the ground of the blueberry patch as she walked. Philip had told her to set out these strange metal things that billowed out music—inaudible to humans—that kept the bugs away. He was a genuine wizard with plants.

She was showing her restored garden to Jordan and Emily, when Jordan said, "Hold on, Ally." He copied the arrangements of circles and half circles and quarter circles that Alice had punctured into the earth with her crutch. It read like a few bars of music. Emily picked out the tune on Alice's piano.

"Oh, my stars," said Emily. "With a few hiccups and notes backward, I do believe this is the harp concerto by Handel."

"Huh," said Alice.

"Shh," said Jordan. "Listen."

Because that's how music roams, via the air but also through bodies and the earth, where it clamors. That's why we say that grass sings. Wind murmurs. Emily played the Blueberry Patch Music again while Jordan inclined his head. Alice looked westward. Philip getting out of his bed; that was a reason for the instrument associated with angels to pluck itself from a distance, as if extra-long arms had far and wide to fling it, as if the heart need not travel far to go where it's needed.

KATHERINE VAZ, a Briggs-Copeland Fellow in Fiction at Harvard and a current Fellow of the Radcliffe Institute, is the author of *Saudade* and *Mariana*, picked by the Library of Congress as one of the Top Thirty International Books of 1998. Her collection *Fado & Other Stories* won the 1997 Drue Heinz Literature Prize, and her short fiction has appeared in numerous magazines.

Vaz's children's stories have been published in the anthologies *A Wolf at the Door* and *Swan Sister* and her young adult stories in *The Green Man* and *The Faery Reel*.

~

AUTHOR'S NOTE

My father taught a "History of the Far East" course in high school; he kept a statue of Buddha in his study, and we'd sometimes take trips across the Bay to San Francisco's Chinatown for lunch or for ginseng, incense, and books. We learned that the monkey was a famous trickster in Chinese lore.

When my brother Patrick was a child, he was given a stuffed orangutan with a transistor radio inside, and not long ago he agreed with me that Rangy—he's kept him—was sort of our family trickster (though I hasten to add before I get into trouble that orangutans are *apes*). Rangy lost his ears early on, so almost from the start he was a bit of a Beethoven, too, playing music he couldn't hear.

My story is a tribute to how much we treasure the boon-companion animals who kept us company in sickness and in health when we were young; they really did always sing to us. May they continue their shape-shifting as we age so that we can carry them in secret.

UNCLE BOB VISITS

Caroline Stevermer

First we knew of Uncle Bob's visit, Denny Otto refused to diagram a sentence. The sentence was already up on the blackboard, written neatly along the top. It was *Make hay while the sun shines.*

Denny Otto answered Miss Lillegren's summons to the front of the room, took the piece of chalk she offered him, and even set the chalk against the blackboard at the exact angle to make it squeak. Then he put the chalk back in the tray and stepped away from the blackboard. "I can't. Uncle Bob don't like it."

Miss Lillegren was having none. "Denny. Diagram the sentence."

"No."

It went on like that until Denny Otto's knuckles had a taste of Miss Lillegren's steel-edged ruler, and Denny Otto had to stand in the corner.

None of us made a sound. There was no giggling, no jiggling around in our seats. We all knew that the worst part of standing in the corner is being laughed at. None of us wanted to laugh at Denny Otto. While flat-out disobedience was no novelty from him, it wasn't like him to hold out so stubbornly for no apparent reason. We figured he was maybe coming down with something, or ailing in some less obvious way, because you don't just refuse to diagram sentences for no reason. It doesn't pay.

Miss Lillegren made Cheryl Thorson diagram the sentence about making hay. We went through some more sentences, taking turns while Miss Lillegren read the sentences out loud, easy sentences for the younger kids, full-bore howlers for us older ones.

When Miss Lillegren judged enough time had passed, she called Denny Otto back from his corner. "I think you should diagram this next sentence. *Whoso loveth instruction loveth knowledge: but he that hateth reproof is brutish.*"

That's from the Bible, so Denny Otto had to try. He reached for the chalk. It rolled away from his hand, rattling in the tray as it went. Not just the big piece either—three or four tag ends and a bit of colored chalk skittered away from him, too. They sounded like sleet on a picture window in the perfect silence of our schoolroom.

"See there. I told you." Denny Otto turned to Miss Lillegren. "Uncle Bob don't like it."

Miss Lillegren was staring at the chalk as if she thought she'd maybe seen a snake. Still, her voice kept dead steady. "I'll read the sentence again."

"I can't diagram it if Uncle Bob won't let me have the chalk." Denny Otto tried again to pick up a piece. He had no better luck. The blue stick of chalk rolled away from him so fast, it fell out of the tray and broke in two when it landed on the floor.

Denny Otto turned to Miss Lillegren. He looked a bit scared of what the chalk was doing, but much more worried by what Miss Lillegren might do about it.

We were saucer-eyed. None of us could see how Denny Otto was doing it. Rapt, we waited for the conflict of will to play out.

When Miss Lillegren couldn't stare at Denny Otto any longer, she unlocked her desk and brought the box of chalk out of the supply drawer. "You may have a whole new stick of chalk, Denny, and I will read the sentence out again."

But when Miss Lillegren opened the box of chalk, there weren't any sticks of chalk inside, just chalk dust. It sifted out like flour across Miss Lillegren's desk, the skirt of her brown dress, and the floor that Miss Lillegren had to sweep and wax and polish herself.

Miss Lillegren did not say a word. Denny Otto didn't either. In silence we watched as Denny Otto walked back to his corner without even being told.

Only when he was face to the wall again did Denny Otto speak. "Uncle Bob don't like grammar."

Miss Lillegren set us all to doing arithmetic. No blackboard necessary for that. We worked out twenty extra-credit problems from the back of the book. My long division was longer and crookeder than usual, but I think that was understandable. We all had a lot to think about.

By the next morning, Miss Lillegren had more chalk from somewhere, and we went back to working at the blackboard, same as ever. Two days later, Randy Schumacher had to put a list of states and a list of state capitals on the board. He was only as far as *Lincoln, Nebraska*, when he got fed up and said, "Uncle Bob doesn't care much for geography, I bet."

Just exactly then, the big dictionary fell off Miss Lillegren's desk.

We all jumped and giggled, a scared little titter.

Miss Lillegren looked around at the whole schoolroom, and she had that look in her eye, the cold self-possession that could quell farm boys twice her size. "Do any of you have anything rational to say? No? Then go on, Randy."

That was when the books on the top shelf of the bookcase tipped over one by one, like dominos. If they'd done it all in a single slump, it might have been a mishap. As it was, they fell over slow, just enough time between to make you doubt the next was going to move—until it did. Seven volumes of the *Book House* books. Seven thumps.

Uncle Bob did it—that was the mood of the room, although no one dared say it right out loud. We couldn't help wriggling in our seats, hunkering down to see how Miss Lillegren would take it. Something was right there with us in the schoolroom, we knew that for sure. All it meant to us was that Miss Lillegren had someone new to deal with. Someone her own size to pick on.

A sense of anticipation ruled the room. We could almost see what wasn't there. I don't know how the others thought Uncle Bob looked, but I had a fixed idea he was a boy, dark and lithe as an otter, just a bit taller than Denny Otto.

Maybe we were pretending, but Miss Lillegren was pretending, too. She acted like there was nothing going on. She ignored our restlessness and paid no attention to the sudden snorts and stifled grunts of amusement we emitted.

One by one she put us through our paces, grade by grade. Lesson after lesson, there wasn't a story problem that wasn't punctuated by Uncle Bob. If nothing fell on the floor, there would come a knock on wood that sounded as if it came from inside Miss Lillegren's desk, or a sound like brushing, high up in the corners of the room, as if a bat or a bird had flown in.

Miss Lillegren kept on pretending. She turned a deaf ear to the sounds with no source, the objects mislaid, and the doors that weren't locked yet would not open. As the days passed, the atmosphere thickened and set. Uncle Bob took on substance for us with every knock and rattle.

When a page was missing from the encyclopedia, it was Uncle Bob who had torn it out. When the bologna sandwich in Sharon Minge's lunch box had six box-elder bugs inside its waxed paper wrapping, we all knew how they got there. By the time the oil stove quit working and the schoolroom got so cold we could see ourselves breathing, Uncle Bob was fixed solid in our belief.

It's no hardship to have the oil stove go out on a fine sunny afternoon in early fall. Fall moves on fast, though. The blackbirds go south, then the ducks, then the Canada geese. The high blue sky goes heavy and gray. The rain makes the road mud underfoot, and the wind peels the leaves off the branches. Orange construction paper pumpkins yield to brown construction paper turkeys. Pretty soon it was too cold to be in an unheated schoolroom all day long. Finally the school board sent Donald Voldt over to see about fixing the stove.

Donald Voldt doesn't talk much, but when he does, he's loud. Donald Voldt is large, from his earflap hat to his nine-buckle overshoes. If there is anything broken that you can't fix, you send for Donald Voldt. If Donald Voldt can't fix it, you know it can't be fixed.

The oil stove in the schoolroom took him all day, and the repairs didn't last through the night. The following morning, Donald Voldt was back, and he had a considering look. "I haven't thought of him in thirty years, but I know him when I don't see him. Uncle Bob is here, isn't he?"

Miss Lillegren soured remarkably, given that a minute before she'd been thanking Donald Voldt for starting up the stove again. "Please don't egg the children on. They are bad enough without your encouragement."

Donald Voldt gathered up his tools. "Suit yourself. But in my day, Mrs. Brisbois had to take care of it. You should talk to her, see what she thinks you should do."

Miss Lillegren didn't say anything, but somehow we all knew that Mrs. Brisbois was going to be the very last person Miss Lillegren talked to about Uncle Bob.

The second repairs to the oil stove took better hold. It was nice to come indoors after recess, hang up our coats on the hooks in the cloakroom, and enjoy the prickly smell of our wet mittens drying on the stove.

As the afternoons turned dark, the world outside our turkey-decked windows looked blue. Inside, the two big white glass ceiling fixtures made us an island of glowing light, and the bulky oil heater made us an island of warmth in a world of bare fields and gray sky.

Tooth decay was our science project. Under Miss Lillegren's direction, we had formed a scientific hypothesis: soda pop rots human teeth. We had an empty canning jar. Denny Otto brought in one of his baby teeth. We put the tooth in the jar, poured a whole bottle of Spring Grove cream soda over it, and screwed the lid down tight. Once a week, we took the lid off and fished the tooth out to see how rotted it was. On the Wednesday before the second repairs, Denny Otto's tooth was holding its own, no cream soda damage visible.

On the Wednesday after, there were two teeth in the jar. Suspicion fell on Denny Otto, but he showed us his teeth. We could see he had no fresh gaps. Nor did any of the rest of us.

That Thursday, even though we weren't supposed to check our experiment again for another six days, Sharon Minge held the jar up to the light. There were four teeth in the jar, all more or less human-looking. Friday morning, there were eight.

"At this rate, someone will have a hard row to hoe chewing his supper," Miss Lillegren said as she locked the jar in her desk.

Denny Otto knew what Miss Lillegren was talking about. "Oh, those aren't his own teeth. Uncle Bob steals them."

At about two that afternoon, the oil stove went out again. It was cold outside, rain blowing sleet, and the schoolroom chilled as fast as if we'd left the door open.

"Uncle Bob wants school to let out," said Denny Otto.

"School lets out at four-thirty and not a moment sooner," Miss Lillegren stated, but she let us put on our coats so we could stay warm enough to think. "We'll diagram sentences, shall we?"

"Uncle Bob won't like it." No sooner had Denny Otto said the words than a small blue book fell off the bookcase. I was the one Miss Lillegren told to put it back. It was *Adrift on an Ice Pan*.

"There is no Uncle Bob." As we were out of chalk again, Miss Lillegren started us off diagramming sentences in our grammar notebooks. Instead of going one by one, we each had to do every sentence, whether it was too advanced for us or not. It was hard to hold a pencil with cold fingers, but harder wearing mittens. The schoolroom got colder and colder. If there had been a breeze, we would have been warmer outdoors.

At four o'clock, the schoolhouse door opened. The wind stirred every construction paper turkey in the room. We looked up, half grateful for the interruption, half scared that Uncle Bob had found a new way to freeze us out.

Footsteps in the cloakroom, and then Donald Voldt came in, big as a barn in his heavy coat. He had a little woman beside him, all bundled up in an old coat, clean overshoes, and a bright blue head scarf. "I saw from the chimney that your stove went out again," said Donald Voldt, "so I got Mrs. Brisbois. She'll fix you up."

Miss Lillegren introduced herself to Mrs. Brisbois and made us go all around the room and introduce ourselves according to the proper rules of etiquette. Most of us knew Mrs. Brisbois already, and those who hadn't met her yet had heard about her. When her boys were students at our country school, they set records for being bad. When they got old enough, they joined the U.S. Air Force. Whatever they did after that, no one knew for sure, but one had been given a medal.

Mrs. Brisbois didn't seem to pay any attention to our formal introductions. She looked around the room the whole time, and she looked especially hard at the corners of the ceiling. She kept on looking even after the last of us said our name. Silence filled the room. Even Miss Lillegren kept still as Mrs. Brisbois conducted her inspection.

When Mrs. Brisbois spoke, her voice was quiet, but it carried. "Everyone sit down."

Donald Voldt was way too big for one of our desks, so he leaned against the long side table. Looking more sour than ever, Miss Lillegren sat at her desk up front. The rest of us were already sitting down, most of us with our hands folded, as if we were going to pray any minute.

Despite her overshoes, Mrs. Brisbois didn't make any sound at all when she walked. She moved as silent as could be to Miss Lillegren's desk and looked over her shoulder. "You were diagramming sentences. What's the next one?"

"Now is the winter of our discontent," said Miss Lillegren stiffly. She broke off, as if anyone would know what came next.

"Go on," Mrs. Brisbois prompted.

"Made glorious summer." Miss Lillegren sounded as sulky as Denny Otto. "By this son of York."

"Good. That's a hard one." Mrs. Brisbois turned from Miss Lillegren to Denny Otto. "You mustn't call him Uncle Bob. Call him Grandfather."

"My grandpa lives in town," Denny Otto protested.

"You're lucky." Mrs. Brisbois kept looking at Denny Otto. "We all are. We have many grandfathers, some we know and some we don't. Show respect." She left Denny alone and looked at the rest of us. It was like being looked at by the district nurse when she came around on inspection.

Mrs. Brisbois let us go and looked back at the ceiling. We all craned our necks and looked, too, but it was the same as ever up there.

"Children have to learn, Grandfather," Mrs. Brisbois said to the ceiling. "If you like this place so well you've come back, you must study, too.".

Miss Lillegren's steel-edged ruler fell off the desk and slid across the floor until it bumped into one of Mrs. Brisbois's five-buckle overshoes.

"We are diagramming sentences," Mrs. Brisbois said to the ruler. "Your turn, Grandfather." Mrs. Brisbois picked up the ruler and took it with her to the blackboard. There was nothing but chalk dust left in the tray, but Mrs. Brisbois rubbed her finger in the dust. When she touched the blackboard, her finger left a long white horizontal line.

"Now is the winter." With the tip of her finger, Mrs. Brisbois wrote *winter* on the line. Then she made a short vertical stroke to set the verb off from the subject and wrote *is*. "Of our discontent." She paused for another look around the room, as if to make certain we were paying close attention, then went back to the blackboard. "Made glorious summer." She wrote *made* after *is* on the horizontal line. Another quick look, this time at the ceiling, another vertical stroke to divide the verb from the object, and she wrote *summer* on the horizontal line. "By this son of York."

The words glowed white against the blackboard: *winter / is made / summer.* No chalk manufactured ever looked like that. The words burned so bright that for once the blackboard really looked black by contrast.

Huddled in our heavy coats, shivering in the icy schoolroom, we watched in wonder. Neat as dicing a carrot, Mrs. Brisbois put the rest of the words in, slanting lines for the adjectives and prepositional phrases, but subject / verb / object shone out like a promise. She held up the ruler and stepped back. "Now, Grandfather, take your turn."

There was a space of silence while nothing whatsoever happened. Nothing fell over. Nothing made a sound.

The oil stove started up. Warmth edged into the room.

In one of those too little too late moments common in late autumn and early winter, the sun came out just at the end of the afternoon. It dropped below the cloud cover at last, and the angled light filled our schoolroom with a color like honey. For a full silent minute, the light and the warmth made the schoolroom feel like a cozy island again. Then the sun went back under the clouds, and the lines and letters on the blackboard were just chalk dust and finger smears.

Mrs. Brisbois took the eraser to the blackboard and rubbed out every trace of her work. Winter made summer hadn't lasted long, but the peacefulness of the schoolroom lingered. The oil stove kept on working. Mrs. Brisbois took the steel-edged ruler and went to inspect the books in the bookcase. Nothing shifted, let alone fell. There wasn't a sound that didn't belong.

When it was warm enough, we started to take off our coats, but Miss Lillegren stopped us. "School is dismissed for today, children. I'll see you bright and early Monday. Mrs. Brisbois, if you could spare me a few minutes, I have some questions."

Mrs. Brisbois handed Miss Lillegren the steel-edged ruler. "Of course."

Donald Voldt shepherded us all out of the schoolhouse ahead of him. We never got to hear what Mrs. Brisbois told Miss Lillegren. We never proved our scientific hypothesis either, so we don't know that soda pop rots teeth, not for certain. But I sometimes wonder where the teeth come from, and who misses them.

CAROLINE STEVERMER grew up miles from anywhere on a dairy farm in southeastern Minnesota. After high school, she attended Bryn Mawr College in Pennsylvania, where she earned a B.A. degree in the history of art. She lives in Minnesota. Her third collaboration with Patricia C. Wrede, a sequel to *Sorcery and Cecelia* and *The Grand Tour*, is *The Mislaid Magician*.

Visit her Web site at http://members.authorsguild.net/carolinestev.

～

AUTHOR'S NOTE

On both sides of my family tree one finds schoolmarms in profusion. That's why it seemed natural to me to set a story about a trickster in a schoolhouse like the one I attended for four years.

Diagramming sentences was how we learned grammar. At the time, I believed that the importance adults attached to what I thought of as an utterly pointless skill was just another instance of their inexplicable wrongheadedness about what to teach and how to teach it. Years later, I learned the truth.

Here is a note from deep within the brackets of the *Compact Oxford English Dictionary*'s definition of *grammar*: "In the Middle Ages *grammatica* and its Rom. forms chiefly meant the knowledge or study of Latin, and were hence often used as synonymous with learning in general, the knowledge peculiar to the learned class. As this was popularly supposed to include magic and astrology, the O.F. *gramaire* was sometimes used as a name for these occult sciences. In these applications it still survives in certain corrupt forms, F. *grimoire*, Eng. Glamour, Gramarye."

And here is the definition of *Gramarye*: "1) Grammar, learning in general; 2) Occult learning, magic, necromancy. Revived in literary use by Scott."

So studying grammar was tantamount to studying magic. If only they'd explained that to me at the time, I would have paid better attention.

UNCLE TOMPA

Midori Snyder

The sky sits, a bright turquoise stone
  Resting on the prongs of the mountains.
Below, the high plateau spreads out its cloth
Embroidered with towns and villages.

Uncle Tompa traverses on his horse,
And beneath a brocade hat lined in marmot,
His cheeks are butter-smooth, and hairless,
His eyes, sharp obsidian.

He is a man with skills; with intelligence:
A weaver, a scripture reader, a servant to rulers,
A trader of most unusual goods, a humble porter,
A strong man, willing to carry a boulder if enough can be
found to lift it on his back.

With these skills he separates
The grasping miser from his money,
The arrogant ruler from his power,

The overly pious from their prayers,
The foolish girl from her virginity.

Trickster, rascal, fox, and wag,
When Uncle Tompa rides into a village
His stomach rumbles, hungering for mischief
His fingers twitch to turn the handle of a prank.

Above, the Khandromas laugh and
Peals of colors arc across a rainbow.
Below Uncle Tompa grips the hem of the plateau,
Shakes, and sends fools tumbling over the edge.

Note: Khandroma: otherwise known as "rainbow-clad, sky-going goddesses."
These are female tricksters who manipulate weather, travel the skies in rainbows, and are known to be very helpful to worthy young heroes.

MIDORI SNYDER has published numerous fantasy novels, including *The Flight of Michael McBride*, which combined Irish folklore with the legends of the American West; a high fantasy trilogy, *New Moon*, *Sadar's Keep*, and *Beldan's Fire*, set in the imaginary world of Oran; and *Hannah's Garden*, about a young violinist and her trickster relatives. Snyder lives in Milwaukee, Wisconsin, and when she isn't teaching English or writing, she is the webmistress for the Endicott Studio for Mythic Arts (www.endicott-studio.com).

~

AUTHOR'S NOTE

One of the best gifts my mother, a Tibetan scholar, ever gave me was a collection of Uncle Tompa stories called *Tales of Uncle Tompa: The Legendary Rascal of Tibet*, compiled and translated by Rinjing Dorje. Rinjing first heard these tales as a boy herding yak in Tibet, probably when he was about the same age I was when I received the book. Though separated by continents, cultures, and language, I am certain that we two guffawed aloud in the same places in the tales, deliciously scandalized by Uncle Tompa's terrible pranks and sexual adventures. Uncle Tompa wasn't that sort of illustrious culture hero whose cosmic tricks shape a universe. He was a trader, an itinerant weaver, a scripture reader, a servant, in short a working man whose pranks often leveled the playing field for the common folk. The vain, wealthy man seeking a cure for baldness finds himself paying for a punishing "cure"; the prudish mother, failing to educate her daughter about sex, discovers too late that Uncle Tompa has proven an apt instructor; a cruel and abusive abbot worships Uncle Tompa's frozen turd, tricked into believing it is a celestial offering. Although it has been many years since I received the book, I still reread these hilarious tales and am reminded by Uncle Tompa to keep my heart free from pettiness and my eyes open if I want to survive as nobody's fool.

CAT OF THE WORLD

Michael Cadnum

"I got the cat, Bobby!" cried the big bald man as he thrust the burlap bag containing my material form into the pickup truck.

"He's going to get out," asserted Bobby, a thin man in glasses, as he thrust the key into the ignition and started the engine. "Look out, Nick—the knot is coming undone."

Indeed the bag was a shabby weave, and the knot poorly tied. I could see out of it easily, and I was using the skills I had developed eluding asps along the Nile four thousand years ago. I writhed and very nearly escaped the confines of my porous prison.

"Hit him with something," said the lean, gear-shifting Bobby, and sure enough his bald-headed colleague began rummaging in the floor of the truck for a truncheon worthy of the task.

I am not easy to injure, being divine—a being from beyond the centuries, an immortal in feline form, worshipped in Alexandria long before Caesar tossed dice, and lauded in Rome long before a pope so much as prayed.

But for all my immortal nature I confess that it is possible to cause me some small pain—or even worse. At the sight of a large black plumber's wrench in Bobby's fist, I fell quite still. As I lay there feigning despair I heard bald and burly Nick say, "We'll use the bungee cord this time—Tank tore the last cat to pieces in about a half second."

I considered this unpleasant statement.

Tank I took to be some companion or associate, but it was the *tore to pieces* phrase that had my full attention.

While I first set paw upon sand in the Egypt of the Ancients, I have traveled the world. My current sojourn on the West Coast of North America was my first since Caruso was so badly frightened by the 1906 San Francisco earthquake. I had been enjoying the sight of the sunset through the Golden Gate Bridge from beside the bay when these two local characters seized me, mistaking me for a mortal feline. Now here I lay, surmising—as I parsed their conversation—that they had in mind a scheme of no little horror.

Indeed, a plan of both horror and brutality.

It seemed that they owned a fighting dog, known as Tank. They trained this beast by swinging captured cats overhead while the still-maturing canine developed his taste for blood. How many stray and innocent cats had succumbed to this regime I could not guess. However, as the pickup pulled up before a garage door I committed myself to a challenge. I would see that no further such harm was ever done by these two members of the working class—as dim and unfeeling as any I had eluded during the French Revolution.

My plan was smart, and sure to work: I would deceive them into doing violence against each other.

"I deem you to be little more than a dog, Nick," I opined in an excellent imitation of Bobby's reedy, ill-bred accent.

"What?" asked Nick, tossing the wrench onto the floor of the truck.

"I judge your nature to be as doglike as any cur I have encountered," I said in perfect-Bobby tone and inflection as the actual Bobby gaped, too surprised to utter a sound.

"Are you out of your mind, Bobby?" asked Nick, and I realized that for all my voice-throwing skill, and cunning mimicry, I had badly misjudged my choice of words. "Furthermore, I believe your mother to have been a dog as well," I said, still imitating Bobby's unschooled accent, and dimly recalling the sort of insult I used to hear on Mississippi riverboats. "Indeed, a veritable female dog."

"What are you saying?" asked Nick, his large, shiny head cocked to one side, in a very tense and quiet voice.

"Issue of a dog's litter, you!" averred my mock-Bobby as the real Bobby at last found his voice and said, as he clenched the steering wheel, "I didn't say that!"

I added, "You're the offspring of a mongrel female, Nick. You, you, you. A dog's scion. A bitch's whelp," I continued, trying to hit the exact epithet that would confound Nick and set him to thrashing Bobby so I could make good my escape.

Nick thrust a meaty fist right across the seat.

It crashed into Bobby, knocking Bobby's glasses off, and sent him sprawling out of the truck. I tumbled part of the way out, still somewhat tangled in the tattered sack. By then the garage door had wheezed open and a pit bull on a chain was barking and bounding, ignored by Nick as the big man climbed from the truck and strode to a metal box in a dark corner of the building.

He found a handgun, a large black automatic. By now Bobby was on his feet and letting off a stream of invective entirely on his own, without any prompting from me. He was much less fluent than I had been, limiting his vocabulary to repetitive obscenities. Bobby threw his broken spectacles into the half-dark garage and hit Nick in the face.

Nick examined his gun and said, in an intense, low voice, "I'm out of bullets or I'd shoot you dead, Bobby. When I come back from the gun shop I don't want you here."

Big Nick strode off down the street. Bobby brushed himself off, climbed into the truck, and drove with no little haste, even without the aid of his glasses. As he and the truck vanished up the street, I at last extracted my form entirely from the burlap. I flexed my limbs in the pleasant evening air.

The dog pulled crazily on his chain, barking and growling. This caused me no alarm at all, at first. But then he gave a spirited lunge and slipped free of his brass-spiked collar. He leaped in my direction, and—to my dismay—he was very fast.

As it happens, I can speak both high and low Dog as well as any dachshund, just as I can discourse in both ancient and modern Greek. But the speed of this fighting animal—all teeth and muscle—gave me not a moment for conversation.

The animal seized me by the scruff and commenced to shake me from side to side with a force that would have sundered my neck—if I had not been trained in the arts of martial cunning by a master in Kyoto at about the same time the haiku was in its early stages of perfection.

Under the cold stars
the warm tongue
of my neighbor's pup.

I made it up at the moment the dog was just beginning to tire. The syllable count was imprecise, and the *neighbor* a bit of poetic license, but it was not a bad literary offering under the circumstances. The pit bull Tank turned out to be an overgrown pup, in truth, of boundless but clumsy ferocity.

"Stay your efforts, my dear fellow," I said in formal, even legalistic Dog, my voice somewhat strained. "I am neither prey nor master."

I spoke a slightly rusty Dog vocabulary, I realized. My words had the effect, however, of startling Tank into dropping me.

I took pleasure in stretching myself to my full height, and I exaggerated my size even more by lifting the hair along my spine and hissing. I put on a brave display of both divine and feline wrath.

Tank was so genetically compressed, however—and so inexperienced at suffering defeat—that he lunged at me again, and it was only by slashing the dog several times on his wet and freckled snout that I forced him to retreat.

He yelped, cowering, long before I was done. A few choice Dog-epithets, and another swipe of my claws across his nose, and Tank would never think of doing harm to any catlike being ever again.

As I finished with the dog, a buxom human female opened the side door to the garage and inquired—in the wheedling, mindless tone humans often use on animals—"Tankie, what is going on?"

The poor dog was shivering and broken-spirited, but I, on the other hand, was by now feeling quite buoyed by my extemporaneous adventures.

"My good young woman," I said, flourishing my tail, "could I trouble you for a dash of refreshment?"

"Who's there?" asked the young lady.

"Cicero called me Little Leo," I told her with a silken chuckle, "and Charlemagne said that I was his Leopard *sans* Spots. Call me what you will, my dear mortal lass, while you serve me a taste of something sweet."

I have a way with humans, and an especially winning mastery of ladies, and yet this woman and I were getting off to an unusually awkward introduction. Speechless and wide-eyed, she backed into her well-lit house, leaving the door ajar.

No sooner had I insinuated myself into her living room, talking of pleasant subjects, than she began to throw things in my direction. She waved her arms and yelled. When she seized a telephone, pushed some numbers, and called into it that a mountain lion was leaning on her sofa I was complete in my understanding of her misapprehension.

"I am no local predator, my dear woman," I demurred, "but an immortal out of the pagan past." I added, "I am prepared, indeed, to be your lover, however exotic I may strike you."

Do I need to recount my blandishments, my exalted praise of her beauty? All my eloquence was met by her screams, until she heaved the phone itself in my direction and held up a chair, keeping the furniture's four spindly wooden legs between my polite person and her by now red-faced and increasingly less attractive countenance.

By the time Nick thumped sweating and cursing through the front door, holding the dark and heavy-looking pistol, I was beginning to tire just a little of her company.

She threw the chair to one side and insisted to Nick, her out-thrust finger trembling in my direction, "It's a talking cat!"

"Mary Jean, what's the matter?" asked Nick, with a con-fused opening and closing of his eyes.

"It talks!" said Mary Jean.

Big Nick was holding the automatic in two hands, the gun resting across his open palms, as though he was afraid he might break it. I recognized his mood as one of a man who had just loaded and cocked a firearm, and now was having second thoughts about using it. Nick was of quick temper, I saw, but not without a sense of consequence.

Not wanting to see any further violence on this fine night, and not absolutely certain that my physical incarnation could comfortably survive contact with a forty-five or nine-millimeter projectile, I rejoined, "Bobby put me up to it—it was all his idea."

The accent of my unaffectedly spoken English has been described as sounding like that of an Egyptian wine steward. For this reason, perhaps, before I could continue my utterly fictional charge against the absent Bobby, Nick apparently needed to have my assertion clarified.

He asked, "Bobby did what?"

I continued, in a much more American—indeed, subur-ban—accent, "That's right, Nick. Bobby said, 'Pretend to be a cat, and indulge in carnal affection with Mary Jean.'"

In his surprise—consternation might describe his reac-tion more accurately—Nick dropped the gun.

The pistol went off with a deafening report.

Very nearly at once the police arrived, and sheriff's deputies joined them, a half dozen or more armed with shotguns and rifles and tranquilizer darts—and nets in case a wild animal had to be gathered in.

"Where's the lion?" was the cry from nearly every voice.

Calm fell immediately. Paramedics were summoned to attend to the bullet wound in Nick's leg, and counselors were called to provide balm to the shattered nerves of the young Mary Jean.

All the while I made my physical apparition as small and harmless as possible, and perched myself on the sofa. I received a gentle tickle under the chin by a quite nice policeman, and a series of very pleasant strokes up and down my back by a sweet-natured female officer.

"It's just a kitty," said the female constable, rubbing my ears. "Look how frightened he is."

Not long afterward I melted away into the night. The proletarian neighborhood of stucco houses and chain-link fences was peaceful and pretty in a run-down sort of way, and I felt quite pleased with the evening's drama.

Once I was down the street and around the corner I returned to my usual jaunty profile—just as I encountered a woman struggling with a punctured tire.

"Young lady," I said, putting on my gentlest manner, "please allow me to be of assistance."

"I don't need any help, thanks," she said, quite out of breath.

I gave a sweet-natured laugh.

"Oh!" she exclaimed, startled when she saw me in the illumination from the streetlight.

She laughed, embarrassed at herself, and reached down to give me the kindest of tickles, right under my chin.

I purred.

MICHAEL CADNUM is the author of thirty books, including the novels *The Book of the Lion*, *In a Dark Wood*, and *Nightsong*.

A former Fellow of the National Endowment for the Arts and a National Book Award Finalist, Cadnum has also published several collections of poetry, including *The Cities We Will Never See* and *Illicit*, and a picture book for children, *The Lost and Found House*. His short stories were recently collected in *Can't Catch Me and Other Twice-Told Tales*.

Cadnum lives in Albany, California, with his wife, Sherina, and his parrot, Luke.

His Web site is www.michaelcadnum.com.

~

AUTHOR'S NOTE

The main character of my story is neither a real cat nor a genuine god any longer, but seems to have evolved into a creature of liveliness and imagination, with a spirit that will not accept a moment of defeat. Perhaps my cat-immortal is, in his subtle and vital way, very much like the rest of us.

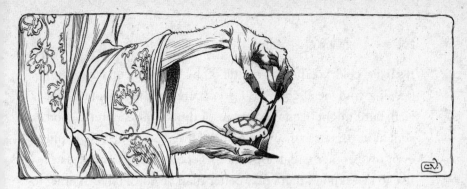

HONORED GUEST

Ellen Kushner

I have met very few evil people in my life, but my grandmother is one of them. When my mother died, Omama told
my father that she would support him and my brother and me,
but only if he gave up all his and my mother's friends, her family, and his work in their studio, to return to Omama's family
compound.

There was no reason for this. She already had other sons
and cousins working for her. There had been one more, but
my uncle Great Light had taken his own life right before the
Harvest Festival. Maybe she needed father back to make up a
propitious number. That's not what he says. When I asked why
we could not visit my weaver grandmother and all the cousins
anymore, he sighed. "Omama has never learned to share."

"She's so rich she never had to."

"Wealth is not a disease, Bright Phoenix," my father said
sternly. "You may be rich yourself someday, so I want you to
remember that."

That may be so, but I think being rich can make you selfish.

It's like a cold: you have to fight it off by wrapping up warm and keeping your head covered. I don't care so much about being rich, but I might like to be famous. I think I have a pretty good shot at it, because since I was five I have played the *kchin*, and even my brother Great Joy, who is good at games and doesn't like to lose, knows that I play better than he does. I like to practice. When I kneel before my instrument, and my fingers bend and dance on the strings, I feel as if I know things no one has ever known before. It isn't just pretty sounds, it's like entering another world. Some of the great *kchin* players played for years in solitude before letting anyone else hear them, but I don't mind playing for others. I like their admiration well enough, but even better I like to think that somehow my music has changed them, as it changes me.

It isn't really decent for a well-bred girl to be famous, I know. Even my weaver grandmother used to *tut!* and bite off threads with a snap when the subject came up. "A decent girl doesn't get herself talked about," she'd say. So maybe I won't be famous in my own lifetime. It's different after you're dead; it's all right for people to talk about you then. In the *Annals of the Ancestors*, which we are reading with our tutor, it says very nice things about the poet Lady Glorious Spring, the painter Pure Delight, and the calligrapher Lady Sweet Water—not only were they all virtuous, but some are even relatives, and Lady Sweet Water was the prince's own concubine.

My omama likes to hear us play. When she has guests, Great Joy and I are often summoned to the Phoenix Chamber to perform for them after a meal, while she and her guests sit on their cushions around the rosewood tables, drinking tea and munching sweets. Unless instructed otherwise, we play old favorites, nothing new or original: "The Bridge of Sighs," "Maiden's Fancy," things like that. Joy always wants us to do "Spring Sowing" because he gets to do the show-offy bit imitating the lark.

"Of course I had great talent when I was a girl," our grandmother says when we are done. Somehow she manages to make it sound as if she was much better than we are. "The great Yellow Tortoise himself invited me to play a duet with him when he attended my father's birthday feast. What an event that was! Everyone was there. Lady Sweet Water kissed my cheek, and the Crown Prince himself honored me with a bow. Oh, yes, I was quite something. Though you wouldn't know it to look at me now." She holds out her huge, knobby hands, crusty with rings, and of course all the guests say that, No, her hands are wonderful, lovely, she must honor them with a tune . . .

All except one. The red-haired woman in the fancy trousers, sitting at the end of the table, says quietly, "Wisdom comes with age. Pain comes with wisdom." Her foreign accent is musical. Even sitting, she is very tall. I have been watching her as she surreptitiously shifts her long legs under the table, trying to get comfortable.

My grandmother looks sharply at her. "What book taught you to say *that*, Honored Miss?"

"An old one," says the visitor. "As you know, I collect antiquities."

"Antiquities?" Uncle Green Tea asks. "Then perhaps you have come to admire our famous crystal tortoise?"

But Omama shushes him. "Pray continue, Honored Guest."

"Today we like to view the world as an endless progress

toward a perfect now. And so we scorn those who came before us as unenlightened fools. But I know this of the riches I traffic in: their age often reveals great wisdom."

"Maybe your barbarian kindred scorn the past," says Omama rudely. "In this house, we respect the ancestors."

"And pain?" A young poet my grandmother likes to flirt with leans forward, challenging the stranger. "Does the wisdom of your antique writings also reveal pain and its cure?"

The red-haired woman takes a long sip of tea before she answers. "True wisdom conquers pain." She keeps her eyes lowered, as if her spiky eyelashes are shielding some secret. But I have noticed already that they are vivid green, the color of cress in the stream, of moss in the wood—all colors found in nature, but I have never seen them looking out from a human face. And her hair is a fox's hair, though much softer, and braided with jewels. Her nose is long and sharp, and her fingers are tapered, a musician's hands. Strange that she collects antiquities. I wonder what she is doing here? Perhaps she is selling us something. Omama likes to have the best and the rarest of everything.

The foreign woman turns her strange eyes to Omama's poet. "Since pain is not a disease," she says, "there is no one cure for the suffering it causes. Each pain demands its own cure."

My uncle Green Tea smiles politely. "As the pain of toothache is helped by willow bark and syrup of poppy?"

("Idiot," Omama snarls.)

"Exactly, Honored Sir," the stranger says smoothly. "But you would never take that for the pain of childbirth."

"And the pain of love?" asks the poet daringly.

"Why," she says, contriving to look up at him through her lashes, even though she is taller than he, "the lover saying *yes*, that is the cure to that pain."

Even though she speaks our language slowly and thoughtfully, her voice is pure music. The poet flushes a little. Omama's clawed ringed hand descends on his wrist. "More tea?" She speaks with great refinement, but the words croak in her throat. If her voice was ever beautiful, it isn't now.

But the stranger has the poet in thrall. He leans toward her, past Omama's hand, so far that he is in danger of knocking over the table. "And the road to that *yes*?" he breathes. "Where do we find that?"

She smiles demurely—"Where but in music?"—and slides her eyes over to me, seated silent at my *kchin*. "Even more than words, poetical sir, music unlocks the heart, does it not?"

"Ah!" gasps the poet, because my grandmother's claws have dug into his wrist for real this time. Great Joy is about to giggle; I kick him under the low table our *kchins* rest on. Unbidden, he starts to play, and I join him, to make it look planned. All right, it's "Spring Sowing" again, but it's a sprightly tune, bound to cheer up even the most disgruntled of guests . . . and even, I hope, their more disgruntled hostess.

But it's a disaster. Even though we take the piece too fast, and almost crash into the ending, the poet is full of praise for our playing. He compliments my grace and charm particularly. He doesn't know he's digging himself a hole so deep he'll never be invited back again. Omama doesn't like to hear anything praised but herself, and sometimes her collections, because she chose them.

Although she is a newcomer, the strange guest is wise

enough to know this. "Oh, bah!" she says dismissively. "Any girl may look charming and graceful posed over such a rare and gorgeous instrument as that—and dressed as she is, too, in such lovely robes. Cloth like that would lend beauty to a block of wood. I tell you, I have traveled the length and breadth of these islands, and nowhere have I seen such weaving."

The cloth of my robes was made by my weaver grand-mother, but Omama doesn't say so. "Of course you haven't." She gestures to the maid to offer the woman more sweets. "Our weavers are the finest and most subtle. Their work em-bodies the very spirit of the land. Patterns laid down by tradi-tion, passed through the generations. I have only the best in my household, of course; I chose that stuff for Bright Phoe-nix's robe. She has a muddy complexion, but the right colors can work wonders. Stand up, child, and turn around."

I feel so hot that I can barely breathe. I don't know if it's an-ger or embarrassment or what. Maybe I'm getting sick. I force myself to rise to my feet slowly. I am standing in the center of the tables, on the mat above them all.

"Look at the child!" Omama cackles. "Clumsy as an ox. You'd never know she was of my family, would you? Of course, in my day, we learned deportment. People always remarked on the grace of my walk. Seeing me in the garden, the poet Violent Cloud said, was like seeing a peony drift down the path, cut loose from its stem . . ."

"May I?" murmurs the foreign woman. She reaches out to finger the cloth of my robe. When she touches it, I feel some-thing vibrate deep in me, as if she has just plucked a string. "They say there is magic woven into your fabrics, as well, mag-ic that must be given freely."

Omama chuckles. "As to that . . . I don't know anything about that. But it will take a deal of magic to turn this ox into a swan, clumsy thing! That's enough, girl, sit down. Are you interested in cloth, Honored Guest? I have an unparalleled collection of weavings. What Phoenix wears is mere trash next to them."

"Weaving?" the foreigner says vaguely. She fiddles with the ruby in her ear. "Oh, no. Carvings and manuscripts are more my line; I have clients all over the islands of the most discriminating tastes; what would they want with cloth?"

"Barbarians," Omama mutters under her breath, so everyone can hear her.

She waves at my brother and me, as if she were shooing chickens out of the yard. We bow and then wrap up our instruments in their layers of special cloth and carry them out with us.

As we walk out, I hear the foreigner say, "Any crystal that you have chosen, Honored Lady, must naturally be of the best."

I am grateful to the moss-eyed woman for soothing Omama's ruffled feathers; but for some reason, I am sad that she did not think me worthy of praise.

The next morning, Omama sends for me.

She is sitting on her couch, surrounded by beautiful objects—precious carvings of wood and stone, fine glazed vases, and even enameled urns, as well as rich hangings—while her maids put the finishing touches on her makeup and her hair. She looks as though she herself is being turned into an object of art.

"Girl." She does not ask me to sit, and so I stand. "I have decided. You spend too much time alone, or with your brother. You will spend mornings with me, from now on. You will read aloud to me, and refine your embroidery skills, which are lamentable. You will lunch with me unless I have guests, and in the afternoon, after my nap, you will observe the way that I do business. It is time you learn something of how the family makes its money; you know nothing of trade, or money lending, or influence, for that matter. You do not know the world. It is time you began."

My head is spinning, and my mouth hangs open, but nothing comes out, which is good, because I hear nothing in her plans for me that allows for time to study, or to practice, unless she is asleep. And as for business—

"Close your mouth, girl, you look like a stuffed trout. And say, *Thank you, Omama.* It's not every girl gets a chance like this."

"Thank you, Omama," I parrot while my heart pounds in panic. "What about Father? Surely he can teach me about business."

"Ah . . ." She looks into a mirror, frowns, and shakes her head at the maid who is holding it. "Not the wisteria hairpiece, you idiot girl!" The maid flushes, but Omama doesn't notice; it's as if no one has any feelings in the world but her. "Your father is very busy these days. Now that he is in a responsible position, he cannot possibly waste his time on you."

"But Father has always taught me!"

I have gone too far. You do not argue with Omama. "Taught you what?" she blazes. "Taught you disrespect? Taught you to waste your time? Or to spend it on useless frivolity, on wastrels and vulgar craftsmen like your mother's trashy family?" She spits and hisses like fire. "Look at you—ugly as sin and day-old mold, standing there gaping like a beached fish. Look at her!" she instructs all the maids. "Children are supposed to be a blessing, but mine only bring forth curses like this one! Born in the garbage, what can you expect—a merchant's daughter wasn't good enough for him, he had to go against my wishes and marry down in the gutter, and what do they bring forth but gutter trash?"

"You're wasting your time," says a musical voice from the doorway.

It is the tall woman, the stranger who collects antiques. How did she get here without being sent for? "Forgive me—I'm early, aren't I? But I so wanted to see the crystal tortoise. And instead I stumble on you being vexed by ungrateful relatives."

Omama laughs bitterly. "Wasting my time, am I?"

"Afraid yes." The woman slips into the room like a whispered tune. Today she is wearing our style of dress: a robe of gray, cross-woven with green threads that shimmer when she moves, bound up with a sash in a seashell pattern. Her wild hair is modestly coiffed, stuck through with two sticks topped with shells as well. It's as though she is a cool breeze come in; for the first time, I feel like I can breathe again. Even though she proceeds to insult me: "Children are born to be a heartbreak to their parents. I certainly was. You can no more *affect* them with your own wisdom than you can *infect* a stone with a head cold."

Omama laughs, and the whole room breathes again. "You're right about that. A stone is exactly what this one's got for brains."

The woman shrugs. "What do you expect? Girls are a curse—when they're young." She makes it sound as if she's old herself, as old as Omama, although she is nowhere near. "Fortunately, Miss Bright Phoenix is most ornamental, which makes up for a lot."

Oh, dear. First she says I'm a curse, and now she's praising me. I feel myself prickle with pleasure, even as I dread what's coming. I want to tell her, *Stop! You'll set her off again!* My hands are shaking a little, still, from the last tirade. When Omama starts spitting poison at me, there is nothing I can do but wait till she is done. I have learned not to cry, no matter what she says. But it can be so hard.

"The women of our family have always been beauties," Omama says smugly. She presses her crimsoned lips together as if she's just eaten a tasty sweet. "It's a pity about her feet." Omama thinks only peasants have big feet. My feet are not that large. I am glad to see that today I am wearing my prettiest slippers, embroidered with peonies. "Sit down, girl, so we don't all have to look at them." I sit on the cushions across from her. "So, Honored Guest, you are eager to see my tortoise, are you? Amaranth," she tells a maid, "fetch out the crystal tortoise—and be sure you don't drop it with your donkey's hands."

Another maid kneels and pours out the tea into translucent porcelain cups. The guest is about to drink when my grandmother smacks it out of her hand and it spills all over the silk pillows. "Clumsy idiot!" Omama barks at the poor maid. "What do you think you are doing? How can you serve jasmine tea before noon?"

I try to catch the maid's eye, to offer her a sympathetic glance, but she won't meet my look.

"Honestly," Omama says, "they get stupider every year. I don't know why they can't keep it straight, something as simple as that."

Our guest doesn't bat an eye; she just mops up the tea with her handkerchief. "The Sultan of Uru served jasmine tea for *breakfast*," she says. "Shows you what he's made of, eh?" With her other hand she turns the ruby in her ear.

Is she laughing at us? Omama doesn't think so. She nods approval. "I hear the only taste he's got is in ivories. I don't suppose you picked up any of those in Uru . . . ?"

"One or two," the merchant says nonchalantly. "Nothing up to your standards, I expect, but I could show them to you if you like."

I feel like a ball being batted between two tigers. What will the strange woman do next? Does she like me, or not? And why should I care? Surely she is just trying to get on Omama's good side. She is a merchant, after all, and Omama is rich. Maybe she has something to sell her. Maybe she is hoping to buy the crystal tortoise and thinks she'll get a bargain if she flatters my grandmother. I wonder if Omama has noticed the ruby that glitters in the guest's right ear. It isn't very large, but the color is very true. Maybe that's why the strange woman puts her hand to it so often, to hide it lest Omama be jealous.

Amaranth presents the crystal tortoise on its silken cushion.

The guest looks at it with hungry eyes. "May I?" She picks it up and examines it in the light. "Remarkable. Flawless, as you say. One of the treasures of the house."

"A real artist made this." Omama's lacquered claws reach for the tortoise, and tap its crystal shell. "Notice the curve, an almost perfect sphere . . ."

"Mm, yes. Old, too, I'd say."

"Plenty old, Honored Guest. Does it please you?"

"How could it not? If I may—" She takes it back, and strokes the crystal with her tapered finger. Her nails are short as a boy's. "They say the tortoise lives a thousand years, and grows wiser with each one. To own such a thing . . . surely the owner is happy and will also live well beyond his allotted span. How lucky you are to possess it!"

"Hardly lucky." Omama sighs gustily. "It is beautiful, yes, but the thing is a curse to me." The merchant sits forward and looks interested. I wonder, is this the business I am supposed to be learning, this bargaining over the tortoise? "Yes, a curse. My husband gave it to me before he died—just before."

"How sad. That such a lovely thing should be twined with such grief!"

Omama strikes a noble attitude. "Sad, indeed. Grief and I are old friends." I could just smack her.

"Such a brave woman," the visitor says. "To live with such memories!"

Omama has the tortoise on her lap and is stroking it like a kitten. "Sometimes I think I should just get rid of it. As you say, it would fetch a pretty price. It is, I'm sure, worth ten times what I paid for it. But then I think, no, I must keep it in the family."

"To pass on to your lovely granddaughter, perhaps?"

Omama chuckles. "Perhaps. If she pleases me."

"At least you have taken great pains to train her to be a decent musician."

"Would you like Miss Phoenix to play for you again?" She claps her hands to the maids. "Buttercup! Fetch Miss Phoenix's instrument."

No one moves. "Buttercup, I said!"

The youngest maid flutters a bow. "You sent Buttercup away last year. I'm Goldenrod, madam."

"I know who you are! There's nothing wrong with my memory."

Goldenrod brings the *kchin*. The maid wants to unwrap it for me, but I never let anyone else do that. It is wrapped in cloth my weaver grandmother gave me when I left her house, when my mother died. Ancient cloth, the forerunner of the pattern my grandmother and her sisters are famous for. The weaving is subtle, with hints of clouds and cranes and mountaintops. "Your future is not in crafting such as this," my mother's mother told me, "but it will protect your chosen instrument." It still has the smell of the house I grew up in, buried deep in its folds.

I play "Maiden's Fancy" with all the variations. If I can go far enough into the music, I can forget about what's going on, the two tigers battling with me in the middle, sure as always to get hurt. If the stranger is cruel, I'll suffer. And if she is kind, Omama will punish me for it. Don't think about it. Think about the music.

Knowing the piece by heart, I sneak a look up through my lashes as I play. Omama is frowning into her teacup. The visitor is sprawled back on her cushions, her body loose with pleasure. Her red head is tilted back, her long neck stretched out like a melody. She is listening, though; there is a furrow of concentration between her brows. When I finish, she doesn't move. "Ah," she sighs. "That was worth traveling for."

For the first time, she addresses me directly. "Now how did a young girl learn to play like that?"

"It's nothing."

"It's everything. Art like that is everything. All I can do is appreciate; you create. What's that song called?"

"'Maiden's Fancy.'"

"Well that explains it. A young girl's hopes and dreams and wishes, ice and fire, power and helplessness . . . that is what is meant by *fancy*, yes?"

"Yes," I breathe.

"And you know it all in your own heart. And make me feel it, remember it, in mine. That is what art does. It makes us remember, yes?"

Omama laughs a brittle laugh. "I don't need music to remember. My memory is flawless."

"Oh, come, now, madam; all of us forget from time to time. And as the years pile on each other, with so many memories to keep track of, it is easy to misplace one or two, no?"

"Flawless," Omama rasps again. "Do you not know the story of the Immortal Tortoise of the Blessed Isles? To capture one is to ensure a hundred years of vigorous youth." And, indeed, she has her fingers clasped around the tortoise like a jeweled cage.

"Truly," the guest says politely, "so fine is the carving that one might almost imagine this to be one of the Immortals turned to crystal. Do you not think so, Miss Phoenix?"

Before I can answer, Omama snorts, "Please! Bright Phoenix has no eye for art or beauty of any kind."

"How can a girl live surrounded by so much beauty here, and yet be insensitive to it?"

I'm not! I want to tell the stranger. *I know beauty; I live for it. Don't listen to her.*

"I have no idea. But there she is, fit only to moon about and noodle on the strings. She knows nothing of the world. I am trying to teach her to be practical, for all the good it does."

"Ah, no." The foreign woman shakes her shapely head. "This one will never be practical. She is not like us. A dreamer and a maker, that one. Decorative and diverting, yes, but no more."

My hand flies to my heart, as if to press it back in. The poet writes: *Hard words from a friend cut glass; they are glittering diamonds of pain.* But this woman is not my friend; why do her words cut me so?

"Now, the Tortoise of the Blessed Isles," she goes on. "There are many who scoff at such tales. People like us, practical people who know the world. They even scoff at the thought of your weaver women, putting power into their cloth. They say only the ignorant are wont to perceive artists as magic makers, miracle workers, beyond the run of ordinary folk. I was one such scoffer . . . once. I had heard of the Immortal Tortoise; who hasn't? I had heard . . . but now I have seen."

"Seen?" Omama's eyes are sharp and bright. "How, seen?"

"I have sailed the seas for many years. Some say its color has even got into my eyes. Such voyages are not without a price. Once, long ago, I encountered a storm so fierce that all my ship was lost. I battled through the waves to an island. And there, in the pearly dawn, thirsty and aching, I woke to such a sight . . ." She looks off into the distance, as though seeing it again, and turns the ruby in her ear. "Tortoises on the beach. Hundreds of them, it seemed. They move very slowly. You can stand and watch, and think that one is standing still, until you see its tracks in the sand and realize that it has moved, indeed."

"Is old age slowing them down?"

"Far from it. Wisdom, maybe. I watched them for a long, long time. They permitted me to survive, as if their wisdom was also a gift."

My grandmother nods thoughtfully. "The wise move slowly, is that it?"

The guest demurely lowers her eyelids. "Maybe more slowly even than old age."

Omama looks sharply at her face. "How old did you say you are?"

"I didn't."

"And where was this island of yours?"

"No one knows."

"You were rescued."

"I was rescued at sea. Despairing of being found there after so long, I built myself a raft, and cast myself upon the mercy of the waves. And for weeks, maybe months, I drifted, sustained only by . . . tortoise flesh."

"How much?"

"Ten, twenty . . ."

"No. How much do you want for it?"

I don't believe it. Omama is bargaining for magic tortoise flesh. She is too impatient even to observe the niceties. It's as if, seeing the cure for old age within her reach, my grandmother doesn't want to let even another minute go by without it.

The woman pulls a kerchief from her purse and unwraps it to show a piece of leather. "There is no price for such as this," she says. "But, Gracious Lady, I will give it to you, gladly, for the gift of the tune your sweet granddaughter played me. It is a privilege to watch her soft young face, and her art has given me back my youth more surely than any magic can."

I can hardly breathe. I don't even want to imagine what's coming next. But Omama only smiles a cutting smile. "I am so glad the music pleased you."

"Very much so."

"My dear," Omama says poisonously to me, "our Honored Guest has praised you well beyond your feeble merit. We must make an equally generous gift to thank her."

"Not at all," the woman says. But I can feel her quivering like a cat on the hunt, her gaze fixed on the crystal tortoise glowing on its silk cushion. Oh, the rogue! She doesn't care about me at all.

I kneel as gracefully as I can. I stretch out my hand for the crystal, but Omama's voice stops me like a whip. "No, my dear. For a gift to be of real value, it must come from the heart."

In that moment, we both understand clearly. The expression on the stranger's face is nearly comical, surprised and baffled. She is not very good at hiding her feelings after all. But I hide mine, although I cannot speak, for fear my voice will betray me. Omama knows my heart too well. I bow to the stranger, so low my hair brushes the pillow at her feet. *This is what comes of trying to be clever,* I want to tell her. *This is what comes of trying to outplay Omama. You, beautiful stranger, with your grassy eyes and foxy hair, your sweet voice and razored words, you are no match for her. And neither am I.*

"Come, child," Omama says stickily, like honey. "You, who have been given so much, must learn to be generous."

I cannot stop my hands from shaking just a little as I lift the *kchin*. The woman receives it awkwardly, like someone being given a baby to hold who's afraid she'll drop it. "Such a fine instrument should be protected," she stammers awkwardly. She tries to wrap it in the end of her sash, which of course is ridiculous.

I find I have my grandmother's cloth twisted round my hands, the cranes and mountains chasing each other amongst the clouds. At a signal from Omama, I slowly unbind myself from it, and gently drape it around the *kchin*. Omama nods, and I bow and go, finding the way to the door by memory, since my eyes are blind with tears.

"I may not live a thousand years," I hear her tell the woman, "but I have enough wisdom to know a treasure's worth. More tea, Honored Guest? My goodness; tortoise tastes much like shoe leather."

I sit in my room, very still. I eat nothing and drink nothing. I am going to die here. Hour by hour and piece by piece, I am going to be forced to give up more and more of myself, until all that is left is a sad lady with rich robes and too many pairs of embroidered slippers to hide her big feet. If I'm lucky, I will be married off to some dignitary; if I'm not, I'll be kept at Omama's side until she dies—*Or until I kill her*, a small voice whispers inside me. But that is nonsense. When I dreamed of fame, it was not as a murderer. Those are not the books I long to be in, the lists of awful tragedies and wicked deeds. I wanted something else.

There are poems about the way I feel: tears staining silk, and loss like a hole that cannot be filled. But their very images imply a kind of loveliness. I don't feel lovely. I just feel dead, and tired, and very sad. The strange merchant is surely gone by now. She sent me no token of thanks, not even a note.

The moon enters my window like a thief, but unlike any thief it leaves a bar of silver in my lap.

And into the bar of silver falls a pebble, a rough little stone, and then another. I look up to the window and see a slender hand, with short nails like a boy's. "Hist!" she whispers. "Come out."

I follow the voice out into the moonlit garden.

"There you are," she says. Her face is white. The moon turns her hair the color of dried blood. "Cost me a fortune to find out which one's your window. Good! I wanted to thank you."

"Don't thank me."

"Wait until you see what form my thanks take." She steps closer to me, and I do not turn away. She cannot hurt me anymore; she has already taken what I love most. "You were generous."

"Against my will."

The stranger woman looks down at me, long and hard, so that I look up to meet her cress green eyes. "Your grandmother's a fool, you know. She can no more keep you from your art than that stupid tortoise can keep her from her death."

"You wanted that stupid tortoise!"

"Is that what you think? I wanted something else."

"What?"

"Kiss me and find out."

I raise my face to her. Her breath smells of sweet almonds. And when she kisses me, it's—nothing like music, it's like nothing but itself, as if there were a whole new part of my body I've never known about till now, and a whole new art form waiting for it to master.

"There," she murmurs. "I have taken the most valuable thing in her house, and she doesn't even know it. Sweet girl, I've got something for you." I am expecting a locket or a ring— but she turns away to the bench behind her and lifts up something large. The strings of my *kchin* shine in the moonlight. "Here you go."

I clutch it to me as if it were my heart.

"The cloth," I say. "It was wrapped in a cloth."

"Ah," she says. "Now, that, I'm afraid I must keep." I stare at her. "Oh, come on, Bright Phoenix; what do you think I went to all that trouble for?" I still don't understand. "You know the old bat. She can never have enough of anything, because nothing is enough to fill her miserable hungry heart. She was never going to sell me something I wanted; the moment I wanted it, she had to want it more. If I was going to get what I came for, I was going to have to make her give it to me."

"You wanted my other grannie's cloth?"

"You really don't know what it is, do you? These cloths stay in families for generations; they almost never leave this island. It's the real thing, child, ancient and beautiful and maybe even powerful, if you know what you're doing. I don't. But there are those who do, or think they do, and they'll pay a lot for something like that, if they think it was given freely and its power intact."

"But it wasn't hers to give. It's mine."

She pulls my cloth from her hanging sleeve, and unfolds it and drapes it around her shoulders. Wrapped in the scent and colors of my past, the stranger looks at me, and I seem to see what she sees: a young girl with dark hair sleek as ebony, lips stung with kisses moist and lightly parted, revealing teeth like pearls; even her eyes gemmed with unshed tears.

"Will you give me your cloth?" she asks.

"No."

"Will you sell it to me?"

I think of what she's given me already. I'm seized with a longing like pain—for her kisses, for her freedom . . . "Take me with you," I whisper. "Please."

"No. Not yet. You're too young yet to give yourself freely."

"That is my price."

She slides the fine weaving from off her shoulders, begins folding it up for me. She's going to leave me with nothing.

"Wait," I say. "Wait. I want three things from you. Give me three things, and the cloth is yours."

"Tell me."

"First, your name."

"Jessica. It's Jessica Campion."

"What does that mean?"

"In my language? Nothing, really. Campion is some kind of flower, but in my land we carry our fathers' names. Like you, I am the daughter of a great house. I left my home and my family to pursue other things that pleased me more."

"That's the first thing."

"And the second?"

I blush, but say it: "A lock of your hair."

Hair is strength and spirit. She takes a tiny silver scissors from her belt. She cuts a long lock from the crown of her head and winds it round and round my fingers. I close my hand on it.

"And the third?"

"The third is a promise. I want your promise to return."

"How do you know I'll keep it?" she mocks gently.

"Because you're going to give me something precious."

She smiles, so that the lines around her eyes dance. How old is she really? Ten years older than I am, her face toughened by weather and the sea? "A gift of the heart?"

"No, indeed, Jessica Campion." I like using her name; it makes me feel powerful. "I'm from a merchant's house, re-member? I'll take something real, something you value enough to come back for. How about that jewel in your ear?"

Her hand flies to it. "Oh, this? It's not worth much—not even a fraction of the value of your *kchin*, let alone that cloth—"

"That's why I want it, Jessica Campion."

"Oh?" She looks a little cold, a bit displeased. But I am used to that. So I persist. "You always touch it," I say, "when-ever you are thinking hard. I do not think you'll want to be without it long."

Her moonlit face breaks into a grin. "You wretch!" she says. "You're a quick study. All right, here. But be careful with it—it's one of the family rubies. I don't dare go home without it."

I wonder if she has an Omama, too.

I reach up my hand to her, the hand wrapped with her hair. I touch her cheek. It is warm. She bows her head to me, and nuzzles my face, and moves to my lips. Our kisses are so many I lose count of them. When at last I get my breath I say to her, "There is your promise, sealed. Don't stay away too long."

"You'll hardly know I'm gone."

I fold the cloth for her, and place it in her sleeve myself. Like a shadow I have kissed, she leaves the garden then, taking with her all my past. But I have gotten my future in return.

ELLEN KUSHNER grew up in Cleveland, Ohio, but visited her grandparents in the Bronx every summer, and now lives in New York City. Her novel *Thomas the Rhymer* won the World Fantasy Award. Her first novel, *Swordspoint*, is considered a classic of the "Mannerpunk" or "Fantasy of Manners" style. She went back to that setting and wrote several short stories (including this one) and two more novels about it. As a public radio host in Boston for many years, she created the national series *Sound & Spirit*, which has led to various albums and live performances, including *The Golden Dreydl*, a subversive Chanukah story with subversive music by the band Shirim, which will appear as a chapter book in time for the holidays in 2007. She may or may not be married to Delia Sherman, depending on which of the fifty states they find themselves in.

Her Web site is www.ellenkushner.com.

～

AUTHOR'S NOTE

I like making people up. Before I wrote this story I had never done what some writers live for, which is to take someone who really annoys you, put them in a story, and do something really nasty to them. But Omama is based entirely on someone (*not* one of my relatives, I hasten to say!) whom I actually knew. I am delighted to have been able to get her down on these pages here, where she can merely entertain us and do no lasting harm to anyone.

Jessica Campion is a character who first appeared in the novel I wrote with Delia Sherman, *The Fall of the Kings*. Once they'd met her, readers started asking when Jessica would get a book of her own. I thought about it for a while, and came to the conclusion that Jessica, an unmitigated trickster, cannot be relied on to carry an entire novel. I think she is much more the sort of person who pops up in other people's stories, so here she is. (At the end of my new book, *The Privilege of the Sword*, Jessica does make a *sort-of* appearance when her mother unexpectedly becomes pregnant with her!)

The world of Bright Phoenix is based on a setting I fell really hard for when I first read the Chinese epic *The Story of the Stone* in the lively translation by David Hawkes and John Minford.

ALWAYS THE SAME STORY

Elizabeth E. Wein

Two weeks before Gus Gimpel's boarding school broke up for the summer, the front-page headline on the morning paper announced, "Bullfinch's Circus Heads West for Windy City." There was a picture of Emilia and her three wire-walking bears, and of Gus's own father smirking proudly behind his moustache and the shadow of his tall silk hat. They stood in front of the circus train's new steam engine, ready to go.

Gus looked at the picture and thought he could not possibly waste one more second of this green June at Capital Academy. At night in his dorm Gus would hear the lonely train whistles blowing a mile away across the river, or the freight cars clanking and shifting in the nearby Furnacetown sidings, and it gave him a homesick feeling. Gus had learned to walk to the rhythm of the rails as Bullfinch's Circus moved from town to town. He had been born in his parents' private coach. So now, when he found himself longing for his circus family, Gus decided he would join them early this year.

He put on a ragged and inconspicuous sports jersey and signed out his intention to visit the boathouses. Once off campus he pulled his cap low over his thick glasses in what he hoped was gangsterlike self-assurance and walked seven blocks east to the Furnacetown train yard. It was not the first time Gus had used the boathouse ruse. He was familiar with all the trains that rumbled through day and night, stopping north of the city to take on water, and the hoboes who rode the freight cars following available work. There was always traffic coming and going with coal and steel and lumber here in Pennsylvania, even in the middle of the Depression.

Gus was friendly with the crumb boss who did the cooking at the hobo camp by the Furnacetown water tanks. Traveling workmen, and women, too, sometimes, had been welcome to hitch rides on the Bullfinch's circus train for as long as Gus could remember, and he thought of hoboes as extended circus family.

"Saw the papers today," the crumb boss said to Gus. "You looking for a ride home? There's a side-door Pullman with your name on it heading west this very morning. The big C & O with the three two-eight-four Berkshire engines. The brakeman's a good guy, he's expecting a few extras. Tell him you're with Bullfinch's, and he'll see you get the right connection. You better hurry, though; they're nearly finished filling up the boilers."

So Gus got a free ride home for the summer. It took him three days to catch up with his father's private train. What Gus forgot about was telling his parents what he had done. There was a terrible scene when he turned up. The shouting seemed to go on for hours.

"There are police in three cities, Augustus Gimpel, *police in three cities*, looking for you!" his father thundered. And his mother added, "Didn't it occur to you your *school* might notice you were gone?"

It had not occurred to him. As the ringmaster's son of Bullfinch's Circus, Gus had always been a sort of visiting hero in the patchwork of temporary schools he attended in the towns where the circus also happened to be. But at Capital Academy the only thing his schoolmates noticed about Gus were his spectacles as thick as your thumb, and his ability to do long division in his head. They thought his circus background was all made up, tall tales and fish stories designed to impress them. Gus did not care whether or not they noticed he was gone.

"It's always the same story with you," his mother complained. "You never think about real consequences!"

"And you read too much," added his father. "Life's not like a Kipling adventure! Happy endings are not guaranteed!"

Mr. Gimpel was certainly right in that Gus was a fan of Kipling. Gus longed for the exotic life of Kim, the young English-born, Indian-bred, British Empire spy; or to be like Mowgli, raised by wolves; or like Harvey Cheyne in *Captains Courageous*, rescued from drowning in the North Atlantic and growing to manhood aboard a cod schooner a thousand miles at sea.

Mr. Gimpel could see that his son was not perturbed. His voice rose in a long crescendo, like a train whistle. *"You could have been kidnapped!"*

Gus nearly laughed. He would have laughed, if his father had not been so angry. "Why would anyone do that?"

"Because there's a depression on, and this circus brings in plenty, and you're the circus owner's son!"

"I wouldn't be kidnapped by *hoboes*," Gus said loyally. "Anyway, where's the adventure in riding a train? We do that every day."

His mother sighed. "What a world for a child to feel at home in. We should have sent him to school five years ago."

So he was grounded for the summer. Or as grounded as it was possible to be, traveling with a circus. Gus was not allowed to leave his father's coach when they were in town, and on the rails he always had someone minding him, like a babysitter. There were a lot of sitters available.

They were scheduled to reach Chicago in a week. Gus sat on the roof of the caboose with his legs dangling over the edge of the cupola, riding backward. The train was trundling along at the breathtaking speed of about five miles an hour, and this was a nice place to sit, far from the stink and steam at the front. Gus was reading *Captains Courageous* aloud to his friend Jiri Jezek, the trapeze artist. Jiri could not read English, though he was literate in several other languages, and a font of obscure and original ideas. His circus trick was to hurl himself a dozen times over his shoulder while dangling by his wrist on the end of a wire thirty feet above the ground, which he did blindfolded. Jiri said it built confidence to work in the dark.

Gus's mind was wandering as he read. Crossing Ohio on the Bullfinch's Circus train, comfortable and familiar though it was, the wide, flat fields of sprouting soybeans were dull in comparison with Kipling. Gus sighed and stopped reading for a moment.

"I know just how Harvey feels," he said, "when the fishermen don't believe his stories about his rich father. None of the kids at school believe anything I tell them! Wire-walking bears—oh, sure. The other boys just laugh and pretend to growl when they see me coming. And Mother and Dad don't believe I'm safe riding freight trains."

"Well, what if you lost your glasses?" Jiri reminded him, making a face and waggling a finger.

"I keep 'em on pretty tight," Gus said. He tied them to his head with rubber bands.

Jiri had always worried about Gus's glasses. Jiri had taught Gus to climb up the access ladders on the train cars with his eyes shut. It was a good thing to know how to do, because if you were caught in a cloud of steam you were blind anyway.

"It would be a problem if I was Harvey Cheyne and lost my glasses out at sea," Gus conceded. "But not on a train. I can cross the roof of a moving train with my eyes shut. I was born and bred on a train."

Once, on a trip across the Allegheny Mountains, Jiri and Gus and three of the other trapeze artists had rattled through the six-mile-long Harp's Hill tunnel lying on the roof of the lions' wagon, while the big cats roared beneath them in the pitch-black.

"Born and bred on a train," Gus repeated, and liked the sound of it. "Born and bred on a train!"

Jiri laughed. "You sound like Turtle, in the folktale. 'Born and bred in the river!' says Turtle."

"Brer Rabbit says something like that, too," said Gus, "in *Uncle Remus*. When Brer Fox catches him, Brer Rabbit begs and begs not to be thrown into the briar patch. So Brer Fox finally throws him in the briar patch, and then Brer Rabbit can escape, because he was 'born and bred in the briar patch!'"

"There are many like that," said Jiri. "The crayfish that begs not to be drowned; the thief that begs not to be put over the fence. And so, his captors put him over the fence, and he legs it!"

Gus laughed, and so did Jiri.

"It is always the same story. Storytellers all use the same ideas," the showman added. "Like circus performers. I do the same trick Lilian Leitzel did; but I am not so pretty as she was, so not so famous, either."

Gus laughed. "But you do your trick blindfolded. So who needs glasses?"

"We are soon arriving in Olympus," Jiri said. Bullfinch's was going to stop in Olympus for three days to take on water and give a couple of performances. "I must supervise them setting up my rig. Will you come with me?"

"Sure," said Gus. "If Dad lets me."

Gus was so carefully watched over the three days that they stayed in Olympus that he began to feel like a real prisoner. His favorite sitters were the roustabouts, the men who did the loading and hauling of the tents and equipment. They guarded him in pairs, and although Gus was supposed to be grounded the roustabouts found a way to sneak him into town to the drugstore for a flavored phosphate soda during the circus parade. Only Jiri noticed, but he just smiled and waggled his warning finger and said nothing.

Bullfinch's Circus finished its run in Olympus and packed up to move on. As the train was shifting off the sidings to go out onto the main track, Gus showed the most attentive of this year's rookie roustabouts, Red and Ray, how to ride on the end sills of the shunt locomotive that was pushing the train from behind. There was another train parked alongside Bullfinch's, a row of fancy old passenger cars, and Gus and the new men had to hug tight to the side of their engine to get by. Halfway along the row of carriages, Red lost his grip. He grabbed at Gus for balance and fell away from the side of the locomotive, taking Gus with him.

The engine had not been going very fast, and neither one of them was hurt. Gus knew how lucky they had been. The other roustabout, Ray, must have jumped down when he saw them fall and now came scrambling over to them as they untangled themselves in the twilight gloom between the trains. The cars of the Bullfinch's Circus train rumbled thunderously past above them; they always seemed bigger when you were on the ground. Gus lay flat along the bed between the rails; he knew they would not be able to get up, or out, until the train had passed.

"C'mon, this way." Ray darted beneath the train that was parked still on the siding. "Get up, kid." He held a hand out to Gus.

"That's not a good idea," said Gus. "It's dangerous to climb between the wheels."

"This old coach isn't going anywhere," Ray said. "Come on." And the other one, Red, picked up Gus by the back of his collar and the seat of his pants and bustled him headfirst toward Ray.

The two men hauled Gus across the rails beneath the carriage. They were on the other side of the train so quickly that Gus did not have time to protest. He sat up blinking in the sunlight on the far side of the siding, thick glasses askew. He untangled the elastic band and took his glasses off to wipe them on his shirttail. While he was doing it he looked up at the blurs that were Ray and Red, sitting on either side of him, and said calmly, "That sure was a dumb thing to do."

What happened to Gus now was exactly what happened to Harvey Cheyne on his first encounter with the skipper in *Captains Courageous*. Ray socked him in the jaw so hard it knocked him cold.

Gus woke up in the dark. And in an automobile. In the back-seat of a big saloon car, to be exact, with a big dark body sitting on either side of him, and his first thought was: Where are my glasses?

He did not know what was going on, so it did not occur to him either to be scared or that he might be in danger. But some little inkling of instinct told him to keep quiet (after all, the last time he had spoken someone had punched his lights out), so he sat with his eyes adjusting to the dark, wondering where he was, who was with him, and where he was going.

There was nothing to be seen or heard outside the car but the dark shadows and swish of passing telegraph poles. The men on either side of him were silent, and after a few seconds Gus decided that they were asleep. There were three of them, not two, as he had first thought, sitting with him in the back; plus another in the front, and the driver. The two in front and the one between Gus and the door seemed to have enormous heads. No, they were wearing hats. And the driver was smok-ing, because Gus could smell it, and he could see the orange glow of the cigarette, an occasional beautiful blur like a dis-tant campfire.

"Hey," Gus said experimentally, and discovered that it hurt

considerably to talk. "Excuse me, Mr. Driver, but do you happen to know where my glasses are?"

The driver and the backseat passenger with the hat, who was apparently not asleep after all, burst out laughing.

"Because I can't really see without my glasses," Gus explained defensively.

"Probably back in Olympus," said the one with the hat sitting next to him. It was an unfamiliar voice, and though Gus could not see his companions, he had a sudden sure feeling that he did not know any of the other men in the car, either: he had been handed over to them while he was out cold.

"Where are we going?" Gus asked.

"Can't tell you that," Driver said evenly, drawing on his cigarette.

Gus's mind skipped fleetingly over Harvey Cheyne the ship's boy and Kim O'Hara the British spy, and dismissed them both. His thoughts settled like a wake of buzzards over Mowgli, picked up while sleeping and rushed over the treetop highways by the Bandar-Log: *the people without a Law, the eaters of everything.* What had his father shouted? *You could have been kidnapped.* And Gus had nearly laughed.

He tried to imagine Emilia's bears coming to his rescue, like Baloo rescuing Mowgli in *The Jungle Book.* For a moment it made him feel better. But only for a moment. Gus knew he was on his own.

Ray and Red must have been paid off, he thought. The dirty double-crossers! What did they have to go and do a thing like this for? It'll give the roustabouts a bad name.

Gus sat quietly between the big strangers and assessed his situation.

He could not see the faces of his kidnappers (it was dark anyway). He could see absolutely nothing outside that might give him any clue of where he was. If they stopped and he tried to run away he would have a pretty hard time seeing where he was going, and chances were that even if he did not stumble he would be slow enough to catch.

So, Gus wondered, how serious are they? Will they kill me if they don't get paid? How much am I worth? If I see their faces, what will happen? Maybe I'm safer if I can't see them. Maybe they took my glasses away on purpose, so that I can't recognize them for the police later. I'd recognize Red and Ray, but I'll bet they've made themselves scarce.

I'll bet there are police in three cities looking for me again.

But maybe not, this time, Gus realized unhappily; maybe they'll just say I've run away again, like the boy who cried wolf. *Always the same story.*

A train whistle let out its soaring wail into the dark. A few moments later the automobile shook as the wind of the train caught it, overtaking them on tracks that must be running parallel to the road.

Holy cow, that's a fast one, Gus thought. A flyer. And all lit up, so it's a passenger train.

Within thirty seconds it had flashed past in a rush of clattering rails and lighted windows. The train whistle let out another series of mournful screams, taking on a different note as the train sped ahead of them into the night and fading as it got farther away.

How fast are we going? Gus asked himself. A mile a minute? That train must have been doing ninety. Unless I've been knocked out for a day or more, there's only one train that could be at this time of night, and that's the Pennsylvania Zephyr, from Chicago to New York. And it can't go that fast in Pennsylvania, 'cause of the mountains, so we're still in Ohio. And that means we're on the Conestoga Highway heading for Pittsburgh.

This wildly deductive detective work made Gus feel hot and cold all over, all at once. His face hurt. He did not realize how widely he was grinning until Driver suddenly said, "Geez, kid, could you stop smiling? I can see your teeth in the mirror. You're giving me the creeps."

Gus pressed his lips together and swallowed. His sore jaw felt a little better when he was not smiling.

They stopped at a grade crossing. They had to wait fifteen minutes while a freight train lumbered past in the dark, car after car after endless car. The crossing lights blinked furiously, but Gus could not see the train.

I know where I am, he thought. Sort of. That's fine.

They stopped again so Driver could get out and kick all the tires, checking for something. He went off into the dark for a few minutes and Gus sat in the suddenly quiet car, missing the sound of the big engine and the concrete highway joists thunking under the wheels. One of the sleeping men snored lightly, but the man between Gus and the door was still awake. He lit a cigarette. Even in the flare of his match Gus could not make out any of the features of his face.

Driver came back, got in, and said to the one in the backseat, "Left front tire's leaking again."

"Flat?" the man next to Gus asked briefly.

"No, a little soft. It's the spare, y'know. We should've got it fixed before we started—"

"You said that." The speaker dragged on his cigarette, and Gus strained to get a look at him. The man turned his head sharply and blew a cloud of smoke into Gus's face. Gus turned away, choking.

"I know we didn't have time," Driver said apologetically. "We would've missed the pickup. But we'll have to do something soon—"

"Keep going."

"Okay, Boss." He started the car.

They drove for another twenty minutes, and then even Gus could tell the tire was flat, because they were clunking and flumping all over the road. The sleeper in the front seat sat up, as did the two on the other side of Gus. They pulled over again. The engine died.

There was silence for a minute or two. Gus was still not exactly scared. He reckoned he was worth more to these people alive than dead, and he could see that a small part—or maybe a large part—of their plan had gone awry.

"Well, get out," the man next to Gus said to Driver. "Change it."

"Can't change it, Boss. It's the spare. We'll have to stop another car. Or I could walk; I reckon we're still sixty miles from the city, but there's got to be a gas station nearer than that."

One of the other men muttered, "So much for our head start."

Gus thought, *Good*. He wriggled nervously between his captors. Boss laid his arm conspiratorially across Gus's shoulders.

"You're not going anywhere," he said.

"Maybe if you wait, someone will come along and help you fix the car," Gus suggested.

"You'd like that, wouldn't you, kid? A chance to make a break for it."

"We can't just sit here waiting," one of the men pointed out.

"You got a better idea?"

"We passed a couple of water tanks not too far back," said Driver. "There was a big locomotive filling up. I might be able to hop a train. The rails are fenced off here. A couple of you give me a hand to put me over the fence, and I'll leg it."

Gus's heart leaped. The words reminded him of something. He thought, suddenly, of Brer Rabbit and the briar patch.

"Don't hop a train!" Gus said, his voice sounding high and thin in the dark.

The men all burst out in wild laughter.

Gus improved on himself.

"Don't make me hop a train!" he squeaked. It still hurt to talk.

"Who said *you* were going to?" one of them asked, and they all roared with laughter again until Boss rumbled slowly, "We could all hop a train."

"Yeah, that would work all right," another agreed. "Keep us together. Keep the law guessing where we are. Take one going back west, pick up a new automobile in Fort Hamilton or someplace, and they'll be looking for us in the wrong direction."

Gus had been waiting, calculating his moment. Now he put in angrily, *"This isn't fair!* How'm I going to jump on a freight train without my glasses?"

Boss's large hand on Gus's shoulder lifted and fell in a reassuring pat.

"You worry too much," he said. "Get out."

The men began to swing the doors open, and to spill from

the big car like clowns. Boss locked his arm around Gus's neck as he opened his own door. He pulled Gus after him out of the car.

Gus, with his head held down, followed obediently but protested vociferously aloud. "I'm not going!"

"Shut up, kid," his captor hissed, "or I'll have to knock you out again." Gus shut up.

They hoisted him over the fence so they could cross the tracks and walk on the other side of the railway line, where they were less likely to be seen from the road. A gangster escorted Gus on either side, each locking one of his arms with their own; and Gus could make out nothing but shadows in blackness, and the occasional orange gleam of someone's cigarette. If there were stars, he could not see them. It was hard going to walk on the crushed rock ballast of the railroad bed, and whenever Gus stumbled it gave his jaw such a jolt that he began to think it must be broken. But he knew that every step was taking him closer to the watering station, with its attendant hobo jungle and familiar freights.

"Shh," Driver warned. They all fell on Gus, holding him still and silent with strong arms binding down his limbs and someone's hands clamping his sore mouth so firmly shut it made his eyes water. They crouched down around him and waited for a watchman to pass along the tracks.

"C'mon," Boss hissed. "Now."

They hustled Gus along the rails in the shadow of the looming freight cars.

"Up here," Driver whispered. "Flatbed load of Pennsylvania white pine. There's space at the end. Not much. We'll make it—" He hauled himself aboard and beckoned to Boss to hand up Gus.

"Oh, please, sir," implored Gus with a gulp, "don't put me on this train!"

His captors chuckled quietly, and three of them picked him up and lifted him aboard.

It was an hour before the train began to move. They lay low against the flatbed beneath the uneven ends of massive tree trunks. They all stayed very quiet as they waited, the kidnappers out of fear of discovery, and Gus out of self-preservation, confident that his chance would come when they were moving.

At last the cars began to groan and clank and shift, and then finally they were rolling back westward in the blue prelight of a clear June morning. Gus's spirits soared. *And we're even heading in the right direction,* he thought. His captors were sleepy gray blobs against the lighter gray of the fresh timber. Boss still sat vigilant with his arm around Gus's neck, and Gus could feel that the train was going too fast for any of them to move from their precarious perch. He waited.

As the sky grew lighter, and Gus sat small and unresisting, the man's hold on him relaxed. Boss had, after all, been awake all night. After some time Gus was able to lift the protective arm away, and laid the heavy hand on the shoulder of one of the other sleeping kidnappers as a decoy.

No one was holding him, now. The long train slowed, then crept. They crossed a bridge and clicked slowly through fields that were a blinding green in the low, early-morning sunlight. Gus stood up quietly and began to climb the log pile.

He tried to look around when he reached the top. The felled trees stretched out before him like a solid highway, lashed securely to the flatbed with mighty chains. Gus could not see where they ended. He began to crawl cautiously toward the other end of the car. His hands and feet found knobs and twigs that gave good holds. He reached the other end of the tree trunks and squinted at the next car, studying it carefully. It was a boxcar, and Gus could just make out the ladder at the back. He climbed down from the trees and swung himself across to the ladder. This was more like it; this was familiar. He climbed up and crept along the over-running board on the roof.

Gus climbed over three more cars, putting space between him and his kidnappers, and then he found an open door. He could not see it, but he could hear it below him, a hollow, empty sound. The train was still crawling through the green fields, more slowly than a man walking. Gus did something he would not normally have considered safe: he lowered himself over the roof and half-shinned, half-slid down the open door frame, as though it were a drain spout. He fell into the boxcar and lay on his back, gasping. The train began to pick up speed; it occurred to Gus that he could have killed himself with that last performance.

But there seemed to be no harm done. A new blurred face, not gray but brown this time, gazed into his inquiringly.

"What kind of a trick was that!" The hobo looked up at the roof of the car, and then out the open door. "Are those your friends? Say, they're not even trying to get on. Just running around out there in the sugar beets like headless chickens, looking for you. What'd you jump down for? Better wave goodbye to them—" He waved, himself. "So long, folks!"

Gus joined him at the boxcar door. He could not see his captors; the beet field was all a haze of green. If there were blurred creatures moving among the green waves, they could have been anything: men or foxes or headless chickens.

"You stole something from them or something, kid? They look mad as hornets!"

Gus leaned out the door. *"Always the same story!"* he shouted. He knew they could not hear him.

But he yelled after them anyway, at the top of his voice.

"Born and bred on a train!" he yelled. "I learned to walk on a moving train! I can cross the roof of a moving train with my eyes shut! *I was born and bred on a train!"*

The hobo laughed. "Pipe down, Brer Rabbit," he said. "You've got a long ride ahead of you."

ELIZABETH E. WEIN is the author of *The Winter Prince*, *A Coalition of Lions*, and *The Sunbird*, young adult novels that chronicle the lives of King Arthur's children. Set in sixth-century Britain and Ethiopia, the cycle continues in the two-part work The Mark of Solomon, consisting of *The Lion Hunter* (2007) and *The Empty Kingdom* (2008). *The Lion Hunter* was short-listed for the 2007 Andre Norton Award.

Wein has a B.A. in English from Yale and a Ph.D. in folklore from the University of Pennsylvania. She lives in Scotland with her husband and two small children. She frequently squanders writing time on keeping her pilot's license current.

Her Web site is www.elizabethwein.com.

～

AUTHOR'S NOTE

Before I wrote "Always the Same Story," I wrote twenty pages of something else and was utterly disgusted with it. So I asked my seven-year-old for a new idea. Her suggestion for a trickster story was "something about a clown," which put the idea of a circus in my head, which put the idea of a circus child in my head. As it happens, a friend of mine had been such a child. His father owned a very prestigious circus that traveled by rail throughout Britain before and after World War II. DSM rarely talked about his family, but he told me several times of the delicious childhood sensation of being lulled to sleep in his berth to the rhythm of a moving train. "Always the Same Story" is not about my friend, but it was inspired by his memory of feeling at home in a circus train.

DSM, who loved me, was not a fan of my writing and was forthright enough to say so. I don't know what he'd have thought of "Always the Same Story." But he was a bit of a trickster himself, and I hope he would have liked it.

THE SEÑORITA AND
THE CACTUS THORN

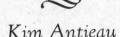

Kim Antieau

Once upon a dusty time a young woman walked down a long dirt driveway toward the earth-colored house with a long, wide front porch. Beside the house was a paloverde tree, all green to gather in and process the sun, and a mesquite tree, whose roots reached clear down to springs that gurgled up and became rivers in China, or so some supposed; on the other side of the house, a saguaro stood, two arms up, as if a bandit were asking for all its cash and bonds. Behind the house in a tall palm tree, an owl asked the young woman, "Who, who?" She held a white umbrella over her head with one hand and carried a small suitcase in her other hand. She wore a long white dress that kept wiping the dirt off her buttoned leather shoes as she walked.

The Woman Who Lived in the House stepped outside, wiping her hands on her apron, and thought, "This woman—this girl—from the city will never last in the desert long enough to marry my *mijo*. No, no."

Everyone who lived anywhere near knew that the Woman

Who Lived in the House was a force to be reckoned with. She had lived here for as long as anyone could remember and maybe before. All kinds of stories had circulated about her previous life, before she became the Woman Who Lived in the House. Some said she had been La Llorona, wandering the wash in front of the house wailing, until she spotted the Señor on the porch. He looked cool on the verandah, comfortable, drinking his watermelon juice. He asked her to join him, so she did.

Another tale goes around that she was once Coyote. Before she ran the nearby hills, most coyotes were loners, but she knew where to get the food for the least amount of trouble, and oh, the songs she sang. All the coyotes wanted to be part of her chorus. When she was Coyote, she had known all the magic of the desert and how to trick anyone or anything out of whatever they held precious. One woman said she even tricked her grandmama out of her gold teeth, then gave them back when she couldn't figure out what to do with them. Then she met Señor. Once again he sat on that porch, drinking his juice. And she was smitten. Being that time of month and everything—the full moon—she decided to come and sit for a spell. She had been here ever since.

Whatever story anyone told, everyone believed the Woman Who Lived in the House had once been full of magic. Maybe still was. They didn't take any chances. No one crossed her. All of them would have advised the young woman to go home, no doubt. No man, no matter how beautiful or well groomed, was worth it.

When the young woman reached the porch, she said, "Señora, I am—"

"I know who you are," the Woman said. "You are the woman who wishes to marry my *mijo*."

"And he wishes to marry me," the Señorita said.

The Woman nodded. "Well, we have three nights to see how suited you are to be his wife and live in this desert."

The Señorita hesitated, still standing on the dusty ground.

"Come," the Woman said, almost as an afterthought, "you are most welcome to my house."

The Señorita smiled and stepped up onto the porch. "I am glad to be here," she said. "I'm looking forward to learning more about your son's life out here. I can't wait to see him."

"He has gone away with his father," the Woman said, "to buy horses on the other side of the mountain. They will not return until three nights have passed. I have much to teach you. You must know how to wash my son's clothes, cook his favorite foods, and survive in the desert. Only then can you be a good wife to my son."

The Woman took the suitcase from the girl, and they stepped out of the bright sun into the cool house. Outside smelled faintly of mesquite, inside of allspice.

"Your son knows how to wash his own clothes and cook his own favorite meals," the Señorita said. "You have taught him well. He will be a good husband. Still, I am eager to learn all that you can teach me."

"I am not concerned about whether he will be a good husband or not," the Woman said as she led the younger woman down a long hallway to a bedroom. A large window took up most of the east wall, giving the Señorita an excellent view of the desert. The Woman put the suitcase on the bed. "First, you cannot wear those clothes. Look, your dress is already gray at the hem."

"I will change," the Señorita said.

"Yes," the Woman said. "Then we will cook."

After the Señorita put on a darker and shorter dress, she wandered through the long house until she came to the kitchen, where her future mother-in-law waited. The woman handed her an apron, which the younger woman put on.

"You are too skinny," the Woman said. "You have to have meat on your bones. You should be bigger, fatter, stronger. More meat keeps the bruises away when you run into things or they run into you."

"I can eat," the Señorita said. "I will gain weight. And I am strong."

"I have already asked for the blessings of the directions," the Woman said, "so we may begin. We'll make masa first, then tortillas. Later mole."

"Masa for tortillas?" the Señorita asked. She smiled. She had made tortillas many times with her mother. Perhaps her first test would not be so difficult.

"Over there is the ash," the Woman said.

"Ash?"

The Woman looked at her. "You haven't made tortillas before?"

"We always use masa harina," she said.

The Woman shook her head. "No, we must have the blessings of the desert, the trees. Their spirit—their ash—is what brings the tortillas into being."

The Señorita resisted the impulse to shrug. She looked into three bowls: one contained water, the other corn, so the third must be ash.

"Mix the ash with the water," the Woman said.

While the ash and corn boiled, they began chopping chiles for the mole: poblanos, serranos, *pasillas*. Twice the Señorita forgot she was chopping chiles and rubbed her eyes. She tried not to cry out—or cry—but the pain was awful. She felt so stupid. She chopped chiles all the time in the apartment she shared with her mother and grandmother in the city. Well, at least, she watched while they chopped.

The Woman and the Señorita stood in the kitchen for many hours. The Woman asked about the Señorita's family. She said her mother and grandmother thought it was good she was coming out to the desert. They had been desert people once, too, but had had to move away.

"My grandmother says the desert is full of magic," the Señorita said.

"Hmph, the desert is full of danger," the Woman said as they prepared the masa. "No, no, that's too much water. It can't be too sticky or too dry."

The Señorita was tired at the end of the day. She tried to enjoy the tortillas and mole they had made as they ate a silent dinner together. They had also prepared beans and refried beans, flour tortillas, bread, flan, and a couple of other desserts for another time. She was glad to go to bed.

The Woman Who Lived in the House had to admit—to herself—that the woman from the city had followed her directions very well. She was too skinny and sometimes thoughtless, but she could be a good cook if she tried. She still did not think she was the woman for her son. The Woman started to get into her bed, when suddenly she heard a shriek. And then another. She stepped out of her room to see the Señorita running down the hallway toward her.

"Señora! This house is haunted," she said. "I have heard a ghost. And there are monsters snorting around under the window."

The Woman calmly followed the girl back to her room. She stepped to the window.

"There! Do you hear it?" the Señorita said.

"That is no ghost, you foolish girl," the Woman said. "That is an owl! You've never heard an owl before?"

"And what is that horrible snuffling noise?" the Señorita asked.

"Look, can't you see? They are javelinas! What kind of wife are you to be if a bird and a pig terrify you? They are nothing! We have rattlesnakes and scorpions and heat that'll scorch your skin off. Now those are things to scream about. Good night!"

The Woman went back to her room, leaving the Señorita in the dark. The young woman shut her window and climbed into bed once again. She felt like crying, but she didn't. Tomorrow she would do better.

The next day, the Woman awakened the Señorita early. They went into the desert and gathered prickly pear pads, mesquite pods, cinchweed, and some verbena. Although the Señorita did not know what any of these plants were, she learned quickly and gathered up her fair share. She also seemed to get pricked by a cholla or prickly pear every other step she took. She even got pricked by a saguaro.

At the end of their trek, she felt bruised and battered. She stood on the porch for a long time while the Woman plucked the thorns from her shoes, shirt, and jeans. She put them all in a bowl that was nearly overflowing by the time they were finished.

"What kind of desert wife can you be if you become a

porcupine every time you step off this porch?" the Woman said, setting the bowl of cactus thorns on the kitchen counter. "You are too fragile for this place."

"I am not fragile," the Señorita said. "I just need to learn to be more observant."

"Hmph," the Woman Who Lived in the House said. "Let's observe some horse manure then. The barn needs cleaning."

This was not something the Woman ever did, but she was more and more convinced that this girl from the city was not suitable for the desert, so she showed her how to muck out the stalls and waited for her to refuse such dirty work. The young woman did not refuse. The Woman returned to the house and prepared dinner alone.

That night as the Woman was getting into her bed, the Señorita once again cried out. The Woman went to the room and asked her what was wrong.

"Wild dogs are trying to get into my room," she said. "Listen. They're right at hand."

"Those are not wild dogs," the Woman said. "Those are coyotes. Have you never heard a coyote? They are far away. None would want to come into this room. It is stifling hot." She flung open the window. "How do you suppose you can live in the desert if a coyote howl terrifies you?"

The Señorita said nothing. The sounds of the owl, javelinas, and coyotes seemed to fill the room. How would she ever sleep? She had barely slept the night before. Even though the Woman had told her the noises she heard were only javelinas and an owl, the sounds still kept her awake. Now tonight the coyotes were calling out!

"I am sorry to have troubled you, Señora," she said. "I will go to sleep now."

~ ~ ~

The Señorita did not sleep well. She even cried a little, putting her pillow over her face so that she could not be heard. She loved the Woman's son very much, but she did not even know if they would live in the desert. Why was she putting herself through all of this? So far, she did not like the desert, and she wanted to go home. She sighed. Still. She did not want to fail. Maybe the desert wasn't so bad. She did like the birds. She noticed Gila woodpeckers in the saguaros, calling out for all the world to hear. The thrashers were noisy, too, watching them with yellow eyes. And quail ran in front of them, seeming to chastise the women for disturbing them. She liked all the bird chatter; it was more conversation than she got from the Woman.

She got out of bed and helped cook breakfast with the Woman. Then she cleaned the kitchen. Laundry was next. She did not wince as she and the Woman lifted the tubs of water onto the stove, even though her arms and legs shook. After lunch, they went into the garden and gathered squash, beans, and chiles. She listened to everything the Woman said and did as she was told. She didn't put her fingers in her eyes once after working with the chiles.

After dinner, the Señorita said, "I would like to make you breakfast in the morning, Señora, to show you my appreciation for all you have taught me."

"It has to be early," the Woman said. "We have much to do before the men return tomorrow."

"I will be up before you," the Señorita said. "Before the sun."

"Hmph," the Woman said. She knew the Señorita would never get up before she did. Still, if she did manage to get up and make her breakfast, how could the Woman convince her son that the Señorita would never survive out here? He needed to find another woman, someone more appropriate. The Woman heard the front door open. The Señorita must have gone out to the porch. The Woman hurried into the kitchen and got the bowl filled with the cactus thorns. She went into the Señorita's room, lifted the covering over her mattress, and sprinkled the cactus thorns over the mattress. This way, even if the owl, javelinas, and coyotes didn't keep her awake, the thorns would. She dropped the cover back down, hesitated, then left the room.

The Señorita stepped off the porch into the desert. It was a warm night, and the moon was up. The owl started asking, "Who, who, who." The Señorita knew—now—that it would fly away soon, to go hunting, and return in the morning. If she could learn the habits of an owl in only three days, what else could she learn? Her mother and grandmother had urged her to come out here, to find her roots. Look for magic.

She sighed and waved at the moon.

"Hello," she said softly. "I know I'm new to this place and I don't understand much. I do know I love a man, and his mother isn't quite sure I'm up to living out here. I'm not sure either, but I'd like a fair chance. I'm new at this. I guess I said that, didn't I? I need to get a good night's sleep, so I can wake up early. I wonder if you all could help me? I seem to have trouble sleeping with the noise—with the music—of the night. Coyotes, could you maybe croon me a lullaby? And javelinas, could you dig and snort somewhere away from the house? And anything else anyone can do to help me sleep—and wake up early—I'd really appreciate it. *Gracias!*"

The Señorita went to sleep. The Woman waited for her to cry out again, but she heard nothing. In fact, the sound of the coyotes seemed more distant tonight, or toned down. Something different. She stood by the window and waited for the javelinas, but they didn't come. And the owl must have already left to go hunting. The desert was strangely quiet, almost melodic, soothing.

The Señorita had the best sleep of her life. She awakened just before the sun came out when something pricked her foot. She reached down and found a single tiny thorn sticking out of the blanket.

"Thank you," she said as she got out of bed and got dressed. She dropped the thorn into the empty bowl that had been filled with thorns only the day before; then she went out into the morning to collect eggs.

The Woman got out of bed, put on her clothes, and went into the kitchen. The Señorita stood at the table, waiting. Steam rose from plates of blue corn tortillas, fried potatoes, beans, and eggs.

"*Buenos dias, Señora,*" the Señorita said.

"Good day," she said as she sat at the table. The Señorita sat with her. "How did you sleep?"

"Very well," the young woman said. "I don't think I would have awakened on time except a thorn pricked me. We must have missed one when we pulled them out the other day." She laughed.

The Woman began eating. The food was delicious!

The Woman pushed away from the table. What mischief was this? She hurried to the girl's room and lifted up the cover over the mattress. Where she had sprinkled thorns now lay feathers: all different colors and sizes of feathers.

The Woman dropped the cover and nodded. It was a good

trick. A true one. To survive in the desert one needed magic. How could she have forgotten that?

The Woman Who Lived in the House returned to the kitchen and sat at the table with her future daughter-in-law.

"After breakfast, I'll show you my linens," the Woman said, "and you can pick which ones you'd like to use at the wedding."

"Thank you, Señora," she said. "That is most generous."

"You may call me Mama," the Woman said.

"Tell me, Mama," the Señorita said, "how did you end up here?"

"Ahhh," she said. "Now that is a story. It all started in the wash. Can you sing?"

"A little," the Señorita said.

"Well, wait and see," the Woman said. "I have a chorus or two I can teach you."

KIM ANTIEAU is the author of several novels, including *The Jigsaw Woman, Coyote Cowgirl,* and two books for young adults: *Mercy, Unbound* and *Broken Moon.* She has recently finished work on an adult novel, *Church of the Old Mermaids.* More information about her work can be found on her Web site: www.kimantieau.com.

～

AUTHOR'S NOTE

My husband, Mario Milosevic, and I were staying at a writers' retreat in Arizona. I kept waking up nights after being pricked by a cactus thorn. One morning I said, "I feel like the princess and the pea!" Mario said, "Wouldn't that be the señorita and the cactus thorn?" I laughed, and the story began to unfold in my mind. I didn't see the mother-in-law as the villain, however. I liked the idea of her being a trickster even though she had retired from that role. Because of the "trick," both women were able to come to terms with their true wild natures.

BLACK ROCK BLUES

Will Shetterly

He's running above the sun-splashed ocean, leaping from cloud to rainbow and back again, grinning because no one can catch him, when someone walks up beside him, smiles in the smuggest way, and says, "Wakey-wakey."

He says, "G'way," and pulls the sleeping bag over his head.

The smug walker is a beautiful young woman with skin the color of the deepest sea and hair the color of the darkest night. She's naked. Street would like that if her smile wasn't so annoying. She says, "Time to wake up, Trickster."

He sits up fast, thinking something's terribly wrong if he has a visitor in his hideaway, but at least the smug walker from his dream will be gone.

Only she's not. She's in his room. Or, to be precise, she's in a storage room at the back of the Dupree Building that's full of cartons of Hi-John's Good Luck Lawn and Garden Spray. She's wearing a blood-red jacket and purple jeans and low gray boots, and her head has been shaved and her skin is only as dark as a plum, but her smile is at least as annoying in reality as it was in the dream. She looks remarkably familiar for someone he's never seen. Maybe it's just that her smile reminds him of someone, but he can't remember who. He wants to say something clever. What falls from his lips is, "Hunh?"

Her smile gets even more annoying. "Yes. You were always loveliest in the morning."

He blinks three times. She refuses to disappear like the dream, so he says, "Wha—Who're you?"

She shakes her head. "Now, that'd be telling, wouldn't it?"

He wants to get out of his sleeping bag because he doesn't like looking up at her. But when he found this room, he arranged the cardboard boxes so six formed a bed and two made a table and four made a chair with a back and a footstool. His clothes are on top of the remaining stacks across the room. "What do you want?"

"And that'd be telling, too."

He frowns, then sees that this poor girl is trying to play the player. He grins and stretches. "What'd you call me?"

Her smile falters. She says, "All right. You get one. Trickster."

His grin is so wide he has to crank it down for fear of hurting his face. "Well, now and then, I s'pose." He points at his clothes. "I'm putting those on." He points at the door. "A lady would wait outside."

She points at the window. "While a two-bit grifter takes the back door? My thought is not."

He stands and tries not to shiver as he walks across the cold concrete floor. "O ye of little trust."

She taps the side of her head. "O me of much smart."

He tugs on gray silk boxers but leaves his socks off because there's no way to put them on without the annoying girl seeing the holes in the heels. "They call me Street."

"Unless they're looking for a light-fingered fool or a punk to run a cheap-ass scam. Then they ask for Trickster."

"And when they ask for you?"

She hesitates, then shrugs and says, "Oh."

"Mystery woman."

She smiles. "That, too."

"Oh!" He has to laugh. "They call you O!"

"Now I've given you two."

He nods. "O'Riley. Odegaard. Oprah. Eau Claire. Open Sesame. Oh, what a pain."

O shakes her head. "Wasting time, T."

Street frowns as he buttons up a black guayabara. "So, O, how'd you find—" Her smile makes him hear himself, and he gets the grin back to say in time with her, "That'd be telling, wouldn't it?" He puts one leg into his tan chinos. "You didn't tell the cops—"

"Of course not."

He pauses with the chinos half on. "You're all right, O. Y'know, if you snuck in hoping for some quality time with a fine young fellow like myself—"

"I told Bossman Sevenday."

With one leg halfway into the chinos, Street looks at her instead of what he's doing and falls, landing hard on his hands. "What the—" As she laughs, he pushes himself up, jerks up his pants, and glares at her. "Why would you—"

"Things've been too easy, T. You need some spice in your life."

He yanks his belt tight, grabs a turquoise silk jacket, and steps into dark red loafers. "What'd I ever do to you?"

She smiles coolly.

He gives her a mocking smile in return and says, "That'd be telling, wouldn't it?"

O nods. "They'll be here in two minutes. We better take the fire esc—"

Street frowns. "We?"

Which is when the storage room door swings in as if it were kicked by a mule. The mule is a huge man so tall that he has to duck when he steps inside. His T-shirt says LOOKING FOR SOMEONE TO HURT.

O says, "They *would* be early."

Street wrenches open the storage room window. "Come on! If—"

A little man in a dark red suit drops onto the fire escape with a friendly smile and a large pistol. "Tut, tut, my tricksy. A gent pays his bills afore making his departure. And it's true you'll be making the big departure soon, but Bossman Sevenday'll have what's his first, now, won't he?"

Mr. Big and Mr. Small don't offer answers, so Street doesn't ask questions. They drive from the Dupree Building in Flash-town to the country homes of Hillside while Big and Small sing Tin Pan Alley songs in perfect harmony. O follows the black limousine in a small silver roadster with the top down. Street thinks she must be working with his captors, but he can't figure out why she was acting more like audience than actor, and he doesn't like thinking about her. So he joins Big and Small on the choruses, and he smiles as they wince whenever he goes off-key.

They pass many walled homes before Mr. Big turns toward a high gate like gleaming ivory. It swings back at their approach. The limousine rolls over a long white cobblestone driveway and stops beside a bone white mansion. Small leaps out to open Street's door, saying, "If you'd be so kind, my tricksy." Street feels safer staying where he is, until Small nods at Big and adds, "The kindness is for my compatriot. He must clean the car if a guest is reluctant to leave it."

Big grins sheepishly, and Street leaps out.

O parks her roadster beside the limousine and walks over to them. For the drive, she added racing goggles and a white scarf. She pushes the goggles up on her forehead. Street thinks she's the finest thing he's ever seen, then wishes he hadn't thought that.

"On with the show!" O calls, waving the others toward the back of the mansion.

Street asks, "Do I get paid?"

Big says in a very gentle voice, "Oh, you should hope you don't, Mr. Trickster."

O leads, and Big and Small follow, and Street sees no choice but to be escorted around the mansion. In the back, a man lounges by an enormous pool, drinking a piña colada. He wears a black top hat, smoky round glasses, a black Hawaiian shirt printed with silver skulls, gray pinstriped surfer shorts, and black flip-flops. He looks up and laughs. "Trickster! O! So very good to see you!"

Street, knowing who this must be, says, "And I couldn't imagine anyone better to see me, Mr. Bossman Sevenday, sir. I'm just afraid there's a teensy misunderstanding—"

"A misunderstanding?" says Bossman Sevenday. "When Trickster is involved? Oh, no. How could that be?"

As Bossman Sevenday and Big laugh heartily, Small

whispers, "He's not happy, my tricksy. You should make him happy."

Street desperately wants to do precisely that and has no idea how. He looks at the swimming pool, an elongated hexagon, then looks closer. It's the shape of a coffin.

Bossman Sevenday laughs harder and says, "You like my pool, Trickster? You may swim in it anytime. Some people like it so much, they go in and never want to leave."

Street swallows and says, "I love your pool, Mr. Bossman Sevenday, sir. But I was thinking how happy I would be if I could do something for you. Whatever you liked. All you'd have to do is tell me what you wanted, and I'd be on my way to do that this very second, Mr. Bossman Sevenday, sir."

Bossman Sevenday stops laughing and says, "The rock."

"The rock?" Street says.

Bossman Sevenday nods.

"That's it?" says Street.

Bossman Sevenday nods again.

Street looks at O. She says, "He wants the rock."

Street says, "Of course he wants the rock! I'll go get it now." He begins to back out of the yard. "Mr. Bossman Sevenday, sir, I'm very, very grateful for the chance to get you a rock. I mean, the rock."

Bossman Sevenday begins laughing again. "Of course you are, Trickster. You have twenty-four hours."

Street says, "I might need a little—"

Bossman Sevenday frowns.

Street says quickly "—less time than that. You never know. Twenty-four hours, that's plenty. You'll have it in a day, at the very latest."

"Good Trickster," says Bossman Sevenday. And, as he laughs and Street backs away, the flesh from Bossman Sevenday's face drips like candle wax from his skull.

Street trips and leaps up and runs. Bossman Sevenday's laughter follows him around the bone white mansion and down the cobblestone drive. The cobblestones sound hollow like drums beneath Street's feet. As he reaches the front gate, he thinks the cobblestones are skulls and imagines people buried together, packed as tightly as cigarettes. He leaps onto the gleaming ivory gate to climb it, but it swings inward. He drops from it, runs into the road, then hears a car racing down the driveway.

The silver roadster pulls up beside him. O says, "Faster if you ride with me."

Street doesn't slow down. "No," he puffs. "Way."

O says, "I'm not about to take you back. Not without the rock. If you want to get away from here—"

Street jumps over the side of the roadster and buckles himself into the passenger seat. "Go!" O puts the speedometer exactly at the posted speed limit. Street says, "Faster!"

O says, "If a cop stops us, we'll go a lot slower."

Street nods. "Right. Good thinking. I'm cool with that." But Street breathes fast and sweats profusely. He knows he doesn't smell like he's cool with anything. He says, "Back there. Did you see anything odd?"

"Odd?" O grins. "Nope."

The melting face must've been a freak of the sunlight. The cobblestones must've only sounded hollow. Street says, "Me neither. Just wanted to show the Bossman I'm dedicated to finding his rock."

O says, "I think he knows that."

"Except I don't know what it is," Street admits. "Or who took it. Or why he expects me to find it."

O says, "Why doesn't matter as much as the fact he expects it."

"True. You know where it is?"

O shakes her head. "If you were looking for something that people wanted, where would you go?"

Street frowns, then grins.

Street leads O through Meandering Market. Today, it's in a freight lot near the docks. His grin is back, because people are nodding and smiling, saying, "Howzit, T-man!" and "Yo, the Streetdog!" and "Tricks baby, lookin' so fine!" The impromptu aisles are thick with people who like bargains and don't care about sales slips. Street usually moves through the Market like a prince, perusing each dealer's wares, looking over clothes, tunes, shows, tech, gems, and all the sweet distracting things of the world. Now he's moving just fast enough not to make anyone wonder why he's moving fast.

The crowd is full of people who want to be seen in their bright colors and careful hair. Picking any of them out would be a challenge, but Street's challenge is greater. He looks where he thinks no one is, in shadows and quiet places. He spots the little brown man at the tent and aluminum trailer called Pele's Cafe. Mouse sits on a stool near the back, nursing a cup of the house java.

Mouse spots Street just as quickly. He sets the coffee cup down, looks around, and Street knows Mouse is doing the math, distance to aisles and number of obstacles and the length of Street's stride and the speed of Mouse's. Then Mouse smiles at Street, telling Street two things: Mouse figures he can't get away, and Mouse would really, really like to get away.

Mouse says, "How ya, Tricks? You and the lady seeking a seat? You can have mine in half a mo, if you fancy."

Street says, "Ah, Mouse! How long has it been?"

Mouse shrugs. "There's just dead time between deals. You looking for a ride? I know someone with a lead on a silver Zephyr, good as new—"

O says, "If it's parked by Dingo's newsstand, you don't."

Mouse says, "Or a bulletproof vest? Only one hole in it."

Street says, as if he knows exactly what he's talking about, "I'm after the rock."

Mouse's eyes don't change at all, meaning he's much more guilty than if he looked scared. Mouse says, "The actor? Plymouth? The Hope Diamond? Not my speed, Tricks. You know me. Sweet and small, nothing memorable. I so hate trouble."

Street says, "Mouse, you got to know yourself. Take me, for example. I am a very smooth liar."

O snorts, but if it might have turned into a laugh, she stifles it when Street glances at her.

He tells Mouse, "You're a smooth facilitator. Someone wants to sell and someone wants to buy, no one's better than you at making it happen. But you're not a smooth liar. No shame there. Perfection in all things is a gift given to few of us."

"Very few," O agrees. "Very, very few." Street glances at her again. She says, "So very few—"

Street tells her, "Should I need your help, you'll know because I'll have ripped out my tongue and used it to hang myself to spare me from asking you."

O says, "Ooh! Looking forward to that!"

Street puts a hand on Mouse's shoulder to keep him from sidling away. "So. The rock."

Mouse says, "Haven't seen it."

Street says, "And if you had, what would you have seen?"

Mouse shrugs. "A black rock. I don't know. I just hear what you do."

"And if you were looking for the black rock, where would you go?"

"You got me confused with the library reference desk, Tricks."

"Fair enough. Should I receive anything of value, you take ten percent."

Mouse shrugs. "But I don't know anything."

Street nods.

Mouse says, "And I take fifteen."

Street nods again.

Mouse says, "Mama Sky."

O's mouth opens, as if she's going to say her nickname, but she closes it.

Mouse says, "See you in better times," and slips away, a faint shadow that dissolves in the surging sea of Market shoppers.

As the Zephyr speeds up Sunset, Street says, "You got to admit that went well."

O keeps her eyes on the road. "True. If there's one thing you know, it's how to deal with scumbags."

Street glares at her, but she's not looking, so he laughs. "Got us a name, didn't I?"

"A name's not the rock."

"Anyone else get this far?"

O says grudgingly, "No."

Street laughs.

O says, "How're you going to find Mama Sky?"

Street smiles. "I'm not."

O glances at him as a truck comes around the corner. O takes the shoulder of the road, spraying dirt, then swings back onto the road, and says, perfectly calmly, "You're not."

Street shakes his head. "Saw your face when Mouse said the name. You know her."

"True."

"I'm thinking we're heading there now."

"You're thinking right."

"So. Who is she?"

"My mother." O's voice says it would be a good idea not to ask more questions, which makes Street want to ask a lot more. Then he looks at her face and decides that while she's probably twice as annoying as any annoying person could be, he can wait until she's ready to talk again.

O slows at the top of Sunset, then speeds along High Road and parks. For a moment, Street thinks they've stopped at a garden with a view of the city and the ocean. Then he sees they're in front of a small house that's the same blue as the sky. A large woman in a loose housedress of the same blue comes out of the front door to stand perfectly still with a perfectly calm expression. Her skin is as dark as O's. Her white hair billows around her round face like clouds.

Street looks at O and the large woman. The light dims, and he glances up. Heavy clouds are gathering in front of the sun. As the sky darkens, so does the color of the house and the woman's robes.

Street says, "If it's about to rain, it'd sure be nice to go inside or put up the top."

A drop of rain hits him, then another, and water begins to fall more heavily.

O says, "Mother."

Mama Sky says, "Daughter."

O says, "Is this necessary?"

Mama Sky says, "Am I happy?"

O says, "You have the rock."

Mama Sky says, "Why would I have the rock?"

O says, "You never tell me what I want to know."

Mama Sky says, "I always tell you what you need to know."

O says, "How do you know what I need to know?"

Mama Sky says, "Because I'm your mother."

O says, "I don't know why I came here!" and reaches to start the car.

Street catches her hand. "Because of the rock."

"I don't care about the rock!"

Street says, "I wish I could say that." The rain is a cold torrent. He's soaked, like O and the roadster. He gets out, splashing through deep puddles to stand at the bottom of the porch. "Mama Sky, ma'am? I'm—"

She says coldly, "I know who you are."

Street says, "Oh. Well, I'm powerful sorry you don't like what you've heard. I hate the notion that a fine-looking woman like yourself isn't glad to see me."

Mama Sky squints at him, then laughs. "You are a most foolish young man who thinks that flattery excuses most of his faults."

As the rain slackens, Street says, "When a fine-looking woman with a laugh as big as the world thinks a man has faults, he hopes telling her the truth will excuse all of them."

Mama Sky shakes her head. "What my daughter sees in you, I'll never know."

O says, "Mama!"

Mama Sky smiles again, and the rain stops. Street thinks that Mama Sky knows what a young woman might see in him. Then he wonders if that means O sees something in him that isn't as annoying as what he sees in her. He glances at her and sees only annoyance.

Mama Sky says, "You children come in."

The return of bright sunlight feels good on Street's skin, but he says, "Thank you, ma'am," quickly to keep O from saying anything. He grins at O, then heads inside.

The living room is small and comfortable and filled with furniture in every shade of dawn and dusk and clouds and rainbows.

Mama Sky says, "Let me get you some tea," and O says almost as quickly, "We can't stay," and Street says just as quickly, "Tea would be lovely."

O glares at him. Mama Sky beams and goes into the kitchen. Street circles the living room, ignoring O and looking for anything that might be called a black rock. The only things in the room as dark as an overcast midnight are a pillow and a plate stand and the bindings of some books.

Mama Sky returns with a blue tray, a blue teapot, and a blue plate heaped high with macaroons and meringues. Street says, "Allow me," and hurries to help her.

She smiles and shakes her head and sets the tray on a coffee table painted with children flying kites and sailing in boats. "I'm not so helpless." She pours a cup of tea for each of them.

Street's afraid that O will refuse hers, but she accepts it and says quietly, "Thank you, Mother."

Street takes a deep drink. It's green tea with ginger, and he doesn't have to lie when he says, "Delicious!" He crams a meringue into his mouth, swallows, sips tea, crams a macaroon, swallows, sips tea, and then notices the women staring at him.

Mama Sky says, "When did you last eat?"

Street opens his mouth to answer. When he thinks about the past, he remembers playing tricks, sometimes for money, sometimes for fun. He remembers running and hiding because few people have as finely developed a sense of humor as he. He remembers eating and drinking things that had to be consumed quickly because they tasted terrible or he had to get someplace quickly. But he can't remember when he last sat still and ate. "I've been kind of busy today." He eats six more cookies, but more slowly, savoring each bite.

Mama Sky says, "Let me fix you a sandwich."

Street says, "I'd surely love that some other time, but I'm under a deadline. With the emphasis on dead."

Mama Sky frowns. "Whose deadline?"

Street says, "Bossman Sevenday's."

The room darkens. Street thinks it will rain again. Then everything lightens, and Mama Sky says, "You're trying to find this rock for Bossman Sevenday?"

Street says, "Yes, ma'am."

Mama Sky says, "I wouldn't have anything belonging to that, that—" She spits into a flowerpot. "But Ms. Brigitte's a fine lady, and I'd help you for her sake, if I could. But I can't."

O stands. "Dead end, T. Let's go."

Street asks Mama Sky, "Do you ever shop at the Meandering Market?"

Mama Sky says, "Why would I? I have my garden. Visitors bring me things. I have much more than I need."

O says, "See, T? All done here. Let's go."

Street says, "Did anyone bring anything like a rock? Maybe something for your garden?"

Mama Sky says, "No, I assure you, that is not the case."

O says, "Wasting time, T. You got free food. Time to move."

Mama Sky says, "But you know, someone did bring me something last week. That Stormboy." She looks at O. "He's quite proper, and dependable, too." She looks at Street, then laughs. "All kinds of dependable, though. Sometimes dependable fun is best."

O says, "Stormboy isn't dependable fun. He's dependable un-fun."

Mama Sky says, "Maybe I shouldn't have pushed you to take up with him."

"Maybe not," O agrees.

"Trickster's not so bad," Mama Sky says. Then she looks at Street and says, "But I'll count my silver when you leave." Then she laughs.

Street says, "I wouldn't take anything from you, Mama Sky."

Mama Sky says, "You know, I believe you, which proves I have some foolishness in me. But you took something from Bossman Sevenday."

Street shrugs. "I don't like him." Then he frowns. "But I didn't take anything from him."

Mama Sky says, "Why does he want you to find his rock?"

Street says proudly, "Because I can." Then he frowns. "Bossman Sevenday seems to think I'm responsible. But I'd remember—"

O says, "What?"

Street says, "That's mad."

O says, "What is?"

Street says, "I remember everything I did for the last six days. I don't remember a thing before. It's like the world started then."

Mama Sky smiles. "World's much, much older than that, Trickster."

Street shakes his head, then says, "What did Stormboy bring you?"

Mama Sky goes to a shelf covered with little things like white twigs and seashells and porcelain statues of white and black pugs. She picks up a blue cloth bag tied with blue string and says, "Stormboy said this brings luck in love. So long as I don't look in it, there's hope for him to court my O. But if I think he's not the one to encourage, I might as well open it and keep what's in it." Mama Sky looks at O. "And since you're so set on not having him—" She starts to pull the end of the string that's tied around the bag.

Street and O yell together, "No!"

Mama Sky looks at them. "Don't you want to know if it's this black rock?"

Street says, "If I was playing a trick, I'd set up something like that." As the women frown at him, he adds, "Only it'd be a subtler, smarter, and much kinder trick than I'd expect someone like Stormboy to play."

O says, "Yours are hardly ever subtle, smart, or kind." Then she adds, "But Stormboy's idea of subtle is a mud slide or a lightning strike." She holds her hand out to Mama Sky. Mama Sky sets the blue bag in O's palm. O traces the shape of the thing in the bag, then nods. "It's the rock."

Street says, "And it's a trick?"

O nods. "Stormboy is an even more despicable weasel than you."

Street grins. "You like someone less than me?"

O says, "Now you only have to move higher in my opinion than everyone else in the world."

Street laughs. "A start is a start."

As O drives down Cigarillo Canyon, Street lifts the blue bag off the console. The rock inside is the size of a small chicken egg. It feels familiar in his hand.

O says, "Put it back."

"I was thinking I'd take a little peek."

"You were not."

"Okay, I was thinking I'd pretend to take a little peek to trick some information from you."

"Like?"

"Like what would happen if I took a little peek."

"Why would I know?"

"Because you stopped your mother as fast as I did. Maybe faster."

"Maybe I had the same thought you did."

Street tugs the string to untie the bag.

O says, "No!" and reaches for it.

Street dangles it just beyond her reach. "Here's what I think. I think there's all kinds of things you're not telling."

"As if that's hard to figure out."

"And something stole my memories six days ago. This rock."

O laughs. "A rock takes people's memories. Yeah, right."

"Last, I think if I take the rock out, I'll lose six more days, but you'll lose everything up to this moment. And we'll be equal."

O glances from the road to him. "That'd be a dirty trick."

Street nods. "Yeah." He ties the bag up and sets it back on the console.

At the end of Cigarillo, O turns onto Tree Lizard. Street can't read what's going on behind her smooth expression. He thinks that she's her mother's daughter, then wonders why he likes knowing that. He says, "I don't know if it means anything to say you're sorry for something you don't remember, but I am sorry."

O flicks her cool eyes to him, then back to the road. They're driving through Flamingoville, a neighborhood that's nice for nothing special except being nice: bright little houses, friendly shops, good cheap restaurants, sidewalks filled with lazy, happy people.

Street says, "I think I did something stupid, and you tracked me down, and now you're trying to help and punish me at the same time."

"What do you think you did?"

"Since you're too fine for me to have gone chasing someone else, um, I stole the black rock from Bossman Sevenday?"

O nods. "You're such an idiot."

Street hits the glove compartment with the flat of his hand. "Oh, man! I am such an idiot!"

"I told you that."

"I was hoping you'd say someone framed me. I really stole it?"

"They say you were drunk at the Talon with a little box, telling our crowd you were the best thief ever because you could steal the black rock from Bossman Sevenday and put it back before he noticed. And you had the rock to prove it."

"He caught me putting it back?"

O shakes her head. "Everyone laughed and said anything could be in that box. How could you know what you had in it? So you got angry and looked inside—"

"Am I that stupid?"

O nods. "Then you wandered off, looking twice as drunk. No one knew what happened after that. So I started asking for the word on Trickster, and I heard about a kid called Street who went by that handle. The rest is history."

Street grins. "So, um, does that mean you and I are—?"

O says, "Were."

Street grins wider. "I may be stupid, but I do have great taste."

"Did you hear the past tense?"

Street keeps grinning. "I still have great taste."

O shakes her head sadly. "I still have terrible taste." Then she finally smiles at him. The wait was worth it

When O turns the smile back to the road, Street says, "What bothers me is why a man would have a rock that makes people forget everything?"

O says, "Who said a *man* had a rock like that?"

Street swallows. "So, Bossman Sevenday is—?"

O says, "Who would you steal from to prove you're the best thief ever?"

"Not the All One. No way it's the All One. Tell me I'm not that stupid."

O says, "You're not that stupid."

Street stares ahead and feels his eyes stretching wide, and he wants to scream. He closes his mouth and says quietly, "Death. I'm stupid enough to steal from Death."

O nods. "All the newly dead still have their memories, thanks to you. Bossman says they're making quite the ruckus. He'll be glad to get the rock back."

Street looks at the blue bag. "He's getting it back. He'll be glad." Street laughs. "Nothing to be worried about, then."

O says, "He's Death."

Street says, "Is there someplace else we can go?"

"Where Death can't find you?"

Street tries to swallow again, but his throat is dry. He says in a rough whisper, "Then let's take him the rock."

"Good," says O, and she turns off Memorial into the big ivory gates of Bossman Sevenday's home.

As they walk up the white marble steps, the door is opened by an elegant dark woman in a dress as black as the heart of a cave. She says, "You're early."

O says, "Yes, ma'am."

Street says, "You're Ms. Brigitte? I'm—"

"Trickster," says the dark woman. "Indeed, you are. I shall tell my husband—"

Bossman Sevenday's voice booms from deep within the mansion. "Trickster! Oya! So good of you to return so soon!"

Ms. Brigitte steps back, opening the door wide. A pale hall with many closed doors along its sides stretches into murky shadows. Street's focus is on Bossman Sevenday, striding toward them in impeccable evening wear. Even the near end of the long hall is dim. There's a reddish glow to the west, though Street was sure he came into the house from midafternoon.

Ms. Brigitte says, "Business tires me," and leaves the hall, closing a pair of white doors behind her. The air smells of cigarettes and perfume and oranges and peanut butter and all the other smells that Street has ever known, but muted. He hears music and laughter and crying and gasps that are the sound of loving or dying, equally muted. He looks at O. "Oya?"

She nods.

He says, "A good name. I'm sorry I forgot it."

She smiles, and he thinks that if nothing is good after this moment, he could be content. And then he thinks that's the stupidest thought he has ever had, because he wants everything to be even better. He calls, "Mr. Bossman Sevenday, sir? I've got your rock." He holds out the cloth bag.

As Bossman Sevenday reaches for it, Street thinks about jerking the stone out. But it belongs to Bossman Sevenday, who must know how to show it to the dead without forgetting who he is. Maybe his dark glasses let him look on the stone. Street could knock off the glasses. The idea is tempting, but it doesn't seem like a good idea to risk making Death like him even less. Letting Bossman take the bag, Street says, "I'm glad to have this straightened out. Taking something from Bossman Sevenday! You know only a fool would do that."

"Yes, I do," says Bossman Sevenday, laughing as he takes Street's arm. "Walk with me."

O says, "The gem's back. Everything is back the way it should be now."

Bossman Sevenday says, "Not quite. Someone stole from me."

Street almost smiles in pride, then stops himself. "Not really, Mr. Bossman Sevenday, sir. You've got the rock back. And if you've got it, it's like it was never gone, so no one could say anything was taken. Not really. If you see what I mean."

Bossman Sevenday laughs. "They'll talk, Trickster. Which is why you must come with me now."

Street says, "Oya, want to wait outside for me? I shouldn't be long."

Bossman Sevenday shakes his head and laughs louder. "Ah, Trickster, don't ask her to be that patient."

Street says, "You're taking me now?"

Bossman Sevenday nods.

"And I'm not coming back?"

Bossman Sevenday nods again.

"I didn't expect this."

Bossman Sevenday says, "Expecting things is not one of your gifts, Trickster."

O says, "Bossman, I'm asking—"

Bossman Sevenday shakes his head. "Some things I must do with no thought of others."

Street says, "I can't believe it. No one'll believe it at first."

Bossman Sevenday says, "Believe what?"

Street drops to his knees. "Oya! See me here before the Bossman!"

As O squints at him, Bossman Sevenday says, "Begging won't save you."

"I'm not begging." Street clasps his hands together.

Bossman Sevenday says, "Sure looks like—"

Street cries, "Thank you, Mr. Bossman Sevenday, sir! Thank you!"

Bossman Sevenday frowns.

Street glances at O. "You see how happy I am? You tell everyone of Bossman Sevenday's kindness! You tell 'em to stop fearing him, because he's the most forgiving gentleman there could be!"

O nods hesitantly.

Street looks back up at Bossman Sevenday. "I was terrified

you'd kick me out in the world without my memories, and folks would laugh at me for the rest of my life as the poor fool who tried to steal from you. I thought I'd suffer and suffer as the proof that no one should mess with you."

Bossman Sevenday says, "You will—"

Street cries louder, "Now Oya's seen how you'll even forgive a trickster who was fool enough to steal from you. People will come up to you and say you're the gentlest gentleman of all!" Street leans forward and kisses Bossman's cold shoes. "See, Oya! Tell 'em how grateful I was when you left me!" He kisses Bossman's shoes again. The leather is even colder against his lips. "Bless you, Bossman Sevenday! Bless you!"

Bossman Sevenday looks at O, then at Street. Smoke comes from behind his round sunglasses, and they begin to glow red, and he says, "Get. Up."

Street says, "Are we going now, Bossman?" He scrambles to his feet and grins. "I can't wait!"

Bossman Sevenday's face is a flaming skull as he screams, "Get out! You get out of here this instant!"

Street says, "But, Bossman, haven't you forgotten—"

O grabs his wrist and jerks him toward the door.

Street says, "No, O! I beg you! Don't make me go back!"

They stumble down the long hall. The tiles rock beneath them as the earth quakes. Doors blow open. Harsh winds like arctic storms and scorching desert gales buffet them from each door that they pass, and they hear screams and wails of despair. And as they run, Street shouts, "Let me go back, O! Please!"

Ms. Brigitte stands at the front door. She glares at them, then throws the doors wide and shouts, "You deserve no less!"

"No! Please, no!" cries Street. He and O plunge down the steps and leap into the Zephyr and race away from Bossman Sevenday's home.

And as they go, Street is not sure whether the sound that he hears is Bossman's rage or his laughter.

Street stretches in the car as they cruise into the city. O looks at him and says, "I don't think you know the meaning of subtlety."

Street nods. "I'm not the only one."

O says, "You don't have your memories."

Street says, "I know life's good, and you're the best there is. What else do I need to know?"

O laughs. "Not one thing at all."

Street says, "So everyone in our crowd has a purpose?"

O nods. "More or less. And duties with the purpose."

Street says, "What about me?"

O shakes her head.

Street laughs. "So my only purpose"—he smiles smugly at O—"is to be."

O smiles back. "A pain."

He shrugs. "Well, yes. Everyone's good at something."

WILL SHETTERLY's *The Gospel of the Knife*, a sequel to *Dogland*, was named a 2008 World Fantasy Award Finalist for Best Novel. He can usually be found in beautiful Tucson, Arizona, with his beautiful wife, Emma Bull, and their beautiful cat, Toby.

～

AUTHOR'S NOTE

As a writer, I hate afterwords. All that's important about a story should be in it. But as a reader, I love them. It's the chance to go backstage at the magic show. If you go, you'll be less impressed with the magic, but more impressed with the show. So, if you think my story is a fine little thing (and, I confess, I'm quite proud of it), don't read any more of this afterword.

You were warned.

When I was a boy, I loved superhero comics. *The Flash* had one of my favorite villains: the Trickster, a laughing thief whose shoes let him walk on air. As an adult, I sent a proposal to DC Comics to use their Trickster, but DC wasn't interested, so I put the proposal away.

When Terri and Ellen invited me to write a story, I racked my brains for an idea that was worthy of them. Then I remembered my comic book proposal. I sat down, expecting to write a supernatural gangster thriller with gunfights and ghastly doings. But Trickster isn't a fighter. He's just a guy who leaps before he looks, and who often gets away with things that he shouldn't because he causes more problems for himself than for anyone else. And for all that he's shortsighted and selfish, his impulsive nature makes him do good things, too. As gods go, Trickster is about as human as they come.

It seems right that his story turned into something I never expected. Somewhere, Trickster is laughing.

THE CONSTABLE OF ABAL

Kelly Link

They left Abal in a hurry, after Ozma's mother killed the constable. It was a shame, too, because business had been good. Ozma's mother had invitations almost every night to one party or another in the finest homes of Abal. Rich gentlemen admired Ozma's mother, Zilla, for her beauty, and their wives were eager to have their fortunes told. Ozma, in her shiny, stiff, black-ribboned dress, was petted and given rolls and hot chocolate. The charms and trinkets on the ends of the ribbons that Ozma and her mother wore (little porcelain and brass ships, skulls, dolls, crowns, and cups) were to attract the attention of the spirit world, but fashionable ladies in Abal had begun to wear them, too. The plague had passed through Abal a few months before Ozma and her mother came. Death was fashionable.

Thanks to Ozma's mother, every wellborn lady of Abal strolled about town for a time in a cloud of ghosts—a cloud of ghosts that only Ozma and her mother could see. Zilla made a great deal of money, first selling the ribbons and charms and then instructing the buyer on the company she now kept.

Some ghosts were more desirable than others of course, just as some addresses will always be more desirable, more sought after. But if you didn't like your ghosts, well then, Ozma's mother could banish the ones you had and sell you new charms, new ghosts. A rich woman could change ghosts just as easily as changing her dress and to greater fashionable effect.

Ozma was small for her age. Her voice was soft, and her limbs were delicate as a doll's. She bound her breasts with a cloth. She didn't mind the hot chocolate, although she would have preferred wine. But wine might have made her sleepy or clumsy, and it was hard enough carefully and quietly slipping in and out of bedrooms and dressing rooms and studies unnoticed when hundreds of ghost charms were dangling like fishing weights from your collar, your bodice, your seams, your hem. It was a surprise, really, that Ozma could move at all.

Zilla called her daughter Princess Monkey, but Ozma felt more like a beast of burden, a tricked-up pony that her mother had laden down with secrets and more secrets. Among Ozma's ghost charms were skeleton keys and tiny chisels. There was no magic about how Ozma got into and out of locked desks and boudoirs. And if she were seen, it was easy enough to explain what she was looking for. One of her ghosts, you see, was playing a little game. The observer saw only a small solemn girl chasing after her invisible friend.

Zilla was not greedy. She was a scrupulous blackmailer. She did not bleed her clients dry; she milked them. You could even say she did it out of kindness. What good is a secret without someone to know it? When one cannot afford a scandal, a blackmailer is an excellent bargain. Ozma and Zilla assembled the evidence of love affairs, ill-considered attachments,

stillbirths, stolen inheritances, and murders. They were as
vigilant as any biographer, solicitous as any confidante. Zilla
fed gobbets of tragedy, romance, comedy to the ghosts who
dangled so hungrily at the end of their ribbons. One has to
feed a ghost something delicious, and there is only so much
blood a grown woman and a smallish girl have to spare.

The constable had been full of blood. a young man, quite pretty to look at, ambitious, and in the pay of one Lady V_____.
Zilla had been careless, or Lady V_____ was cleverer than she
looked. For certain, she was more clever than she was beautiful, Zilla said, in a rage. Zilla stabbed the constable in the neck
with a demon needle. Blood sprayed out through the hollow
needle like red ink. All of Ozma's ghosts began to tug at their
ribbons in a terrible frenzy as if, Ozma thought, they were
children and she were a maypole.

First the constable was a young man, full of promise and
juice, and then he was a dead man in a puddle of his own
blood, and then he was a ghost, small enough that Zilla could
have clapped him between her two hands and burst him like
a pastry bag, had he any real substance. He clutched at one of
Zilla's ribbon charms as if it were a life rope. The look of surprise on his face was comical.

Ozma thought he made a handsome ghost. She winked
at him, but then there was a great deal of work to do. There
was the body to take care of, and Zilla's clothes and books and
jewelry to be packed, and all of the exceedingly fragile ghost
tackle to wrap up in cotton and rags.

Zilla was in a filthy temper. She kicked the body of the constable. She paced and drank while Ozma worked. She rolled
out maps and rolled them back up again.

"Where are we going this time?" Ozma said.

"Home," Zilla said. She blew her nose on a map. Zilla had terrible allergies in summer. "We're going home."

On the seventh day of their journey, outlaws shot and killed Neren, Zilla's manservant, as he watered the horses from a stream. From inside the coach, Zilla drew her gun. She waited until the outlaws were within range and then she shot them both in the head. Zilla's aim was excellent.

By the time Ozma had the horses calmed down, Neren's ghost had drifted downstream, and she had no ribbons with which to collect trash like the outlaws anyway. Zilla had made her leave most of her ghosts and ribbons at home. Too many ghosts made travel difficult: they frightened horses and drew unwelcome attention. And besides, it was easy enough to embroider new ribbons and collect new ghosts when one arrived in a new place. Ozma had kept only three favorites: an angry old empress, a young boy whose ghost was convinced it was actually a kitten, and the constable. But neither the empress nor the little boy said much anymore. Nothing stirred them. And there was something more vivid about the constable, or perhaps it was just the memory of his surprised look and his bright, bright blood.

She's a monster, the constable said to Ozma. He was looking at Zilla with something like admiration. Ozma felt a twinge of jealousy, of possessive pride.

"She's killed a hundred men and women," Ozma told him. "She has a little list of their names in her book. We light candles for them in the temple."

I don't remember my name, the constable said. *Did I perhaps introduce myself to you and your mother, before she killed me?*

"It was something like Stamp or Anvil," Ozma said. "Or Cobble."

"Ozma," Zilla said. "Stop talking to that ghost. Come and help with Neren."

Ozma and Neren had not liked each other. Neren had liked to pinch and tease Ozma when Zilla wasn't looking. He'd put his hand on the flat place where her breasts were bound. Sometimes he picked her up by her hair to show how strong he was, how little and helpless Ozma was.

They wrapped Neren's body in a red sheet and wedged it between the branches of a tree, winding the sheet around and around the branches. It was what you did for the dead when you were in a hurry. If it had been up to Ozma, they'd have left Neren for dogs to eat. She would have stayed to watch.

I'm hungry, said the constable's ghost. Ozma gave him a little bowl of blood and dirt, scraped from the ground where Neren had died.

After that, they traveled faster. The horses were afraid of Ozma's mother, although she did not use the whips as often as Neren had.

Ozma sat in the carriage and played I Spy with the constable's ghost. *I spy with my little eye*, said the constable.

"A cloud," Ozma said. "A man in a field."

The view was monotonous. There were fields brown with blight, and the air was foul with dust. There had been a disease of the wheat this year, as well as plague. There *were* no clouds. The man in the field was a broken stalk in a clearing, tied with small dirty flags, left as a piece of field magic. A field god to mark the place where someone had drawn the white stone.

Not a man, the constable said. *A woman. A sad girl with brown hair. She looks a little like you.*

"Is she pretty?" Ozma said.

Are you pretty? the constable said.

Ozma tossed her hair. "The ladies of Abal called me a pretty poppet," she said. "They said my hair was the color of honey."

Your mother is very beautiful, the constable said. Out on the coachman's seat, Zilla was singing a song about black birds pecking at someone's eyes and fingers. Zilla loved sad songs.

"I will be even more beautiful when I grow up," Ozma said. "Zilla says so."

How old are you? said the constable.

"Sixteen," Ozma said, although this was only a guess. She'd begun to bleed the year before. Zilla had not been pleased.

Why do you bind your breasts? said the constable.

When they traveled, Ozma dressed in boy's clothes and she tied her hair back in a simple queue. But she still bound her breasts every day. "One day," she said, "Zilla will find a husband for me. A rich old man with an estate. Or a foolish young man with an inheritance. But until then, until I'm too tall, I'm more useful as a child. Zilla's Princess Monkey."

I'll never get any older, the constable said, mourning.

"I spy with my little eye," Ozma said.

A cloud, the constable said. *A wheel of fire.* The dead did not like to say the name of the sun.

"A little mouse," Ozma said. "It ran under the wheels of the carriage."

Where are we going? the constable said. He asked over and over again.

"Home," Ozma said.

Where is home? said the constable.

"I don't know," Ozma said.

Ozma's father was, according to Zilla, a prince of the Underworld, a diplomat from distant Torlal, a spy, a man with a knife in an alley in Benin. Neren had been a small man, and he'd had snapping black eyes like Ozma, but Neren had not been Ozma's father. If he'd been her father, she would have fished in the stream with a ribbon for his ghost.

They made camp in a field of white flowers. Ozma fed and watered the horses. She picked flowers with the idea that perhaps she could gather enough to make a bed of petals for Zilla. She had a small heap almost as high as her knee before she grew tired of picking them. Zilla made a fire and drank wine. She did not say anything about Neren or about home or about the white petals, but after the sun went down she taught Ozma easy conjure tricks: how to set fire dancing on the backs of the green beetles that ran about the camp; how to summon the little devils that lived in trees and shrubs and rocks.

Zilla and the rock devils talked for a while in a guttural, snappish language that Ozma could almost understand. Then Zilla leaned forward, caught up a devil by its tail, and snapped its long neck. The other devils ran away and Zilla chased after them, grinning. There was something wolfish about her: she dashed across the field on all fours, darting back and forth. She caught two more devils while Ozma and the ghosts sat and watched, and then came strolling back to the camp looking flushed and pink and pleased, the devils dangling from her hand. She sharpened sticks and cooked them over the campfire as if they had been quail. By the time they were ready to eat, she was quite drunk. She didn't offer to share the wine with Ozma.

The devils were full of little spiky bones. Zilla ate two. Ozma nibbled at a haunch, wishing she had real silverware, the kind they'd left behind in Abal. All she had was a tobacco knife. Her devil's gummy boiled eyes stared up at her reproachfully. She closed her own eyes and tore off its head. But there were still the little hands, the toes. It was like trying to eat a baby.

"Ozma," Zilla said. "Eat. I need you to stay healthy. Next time it will be your turn to conjure up supper."

Zilla slept in the carriage. Ozma lay with her head on the little pile of white petals, and the constable and the empress and the kitten boy curled up in her hair.

All night long the green beetles scurried around the camp, carrying fire on their backs. It didn't seem to upset them, and it was very beautiful. Whenever Ozma woke in the night, the ground was alive with little moving green lights. That was the thing about magic. Sometimes it was beautiful and sometimes it seemed to Ozma that it was as wicked as the priests claimed. You could kill a man and you could lie and steal as Zilla had done, and if you lit enough candles at the temples, you could be forgiven. But someone who ate little devils and caught ghosts with ribbons and charms was a witch, and witches were damned. It had always seemed to Ozma that in all the world there was only Zilla for Ozma, only Ozma for Zilla. Perhaps home would be different.

Ozma thought that Zilla was looking for something. It was four days since Neren had died, and the horses were getting skinny. There was very little grazing. The streambeds were mostly dry. They abandoned the carriage, and Zilla walked while Ozma rode one of the horses (the horses would not carry Zilla) and the other horse carried Zilla's maps and boxes. They went north, and there were no villages, no towns where Zilla could tell fortunes or sell charms. There were only abandoned farms and woods that Zilla said were full of outlaws or worse.

There was no more wine. Zilla had finished it. They drank muddy water out of the same streams where they watered their horses.

At night Ozma pricked her finger and squeezed the blood into the dirt for her ghosts. In Abal, there had been servants to give the blood to the ghosts. You did not need much blood for one ghost, but in Abal they'd had many, many ghosts. It made Ozma feel a bit sick to see the empress's lips smeared with her blood, to see the kitten boy lapping at the clotted dirt. The constable ate daintily, as if he were still alive.

Ozma's legs ached at night, as if they were growing furiously. She forgot to bind her breasts. Zilla didn't seem to notice. At night, she walked out from the camp, leaving Ozma alone. Sometimes she did not come back until morning.

I spy with my little eye, the constable said.

"A horse's ass," Ozma said. "My mother's skirts, dragging in the dirt."

A young lady, the constable said. *A young lady full of blood and vitality.*

Ozma stared at him. The dead did not flirt with the living, but there was a glint in the constable's dead eye. The empress laughed silently.

Ahead of them, Zilla stopped. "There," she said. "Ahead of us, do you see?"

"Are we home?" Ozma said. "Have we come home?" The road behind them was empty and broken. Far ahead, she

could see something that might be a small town. As they got
closer, there were buildings, but the buildings were not re-
splendent. The roofs were not tiled with gold. There was no
city wall, no orchards full of fruit, only brown fields and ricks
of rotted hay.

"This is Brid," Zilla said. "There's something I need here.
Come here, Ozma. Help me with the packhorse."

They pulled out Ozma's best dress, the green one with silver embroidery. But when Ozma tried to put on her dress, it
would not fasten across her back. The shot-silk cuffs no longer
came down over her wrists.

"Well," Zilla said. "My little girl is getting bigger."

"I didn't mean to!" Ozma said.

"No," Zilla said. "I suppose you didn't. It isn't your fault,
Ozma. My magic can only do so much. Everyone gets older, no
matter how much magic their mothers have. A young woman
is trouble, though, and we have no time for trouble. Perhaps
you should be a boy. I'll cut your hair."

Ozma backed away. She was proud of her hair.

"Come here, Ozma," Zilla said. She had a knife in her hand.
"It will grow back, I promise."

Ozma waited with the horses and the ghosts outside the town.
She was too proud to cry about her hair. Boys came and threw
rocks at her and she glared at them until they ran away. They
came and threw rocks again. She imagined conjuring fire and
setting it on their backs and watching them scurry like the
beetles. She was wicked to think such a thing. Zilla was probably at the temple, lighting candles, but surely there weren't
enough candles in the world to save them both. Ozma prayed
that Zilla would save herself.

Why have we come here? the constable said.

"We need things," Ozma said. "Home is farther away than I thought it was. Zilla will bring back a new carriage and a new manservant and wine and food. She's probably gone to the mayor's house, to tell his fortune. He'll give her gold. She'll come back with gold and ribbons full of ghosts and we'll go to the mayor's house and eat roast beef on silver plates."

The town is full of people, and the people are full of blood, the constable said. *Why must we stay here outside?*

"Wait, and Zilla will come back," Ozma said. There was a hot breeze, and it blew against her neck. Cut hair pricked where it was caught between her shirt and her skin. She picked up the constable on his ribbon and held him cupped in her hands. "Am I still beautiful?" she said.

You have dirt on your face, the constable said.

The sun was high in the sky when Zilla came back. She was wearing a modest gray dress, and a white kerchief covered her hair. There was a man with her. He paid no attention to Ozma. Instead he went over to the horses and ran his hands over them. He picked up their feet and rapped thoughtfully on their hooves.

"Come along," Zilla said to Ozma. "Help me with the bags. Leave the horses with this man."

"Where are we going?" Ozma said. "Did the mayor give you gold?"

"I took a position in service," Zilla said. "You are my son, and your name is Eren. Your father is dead, and we have come here from Nablos. We are respectable people. I'm to cook and keep house."

"I thought we were going home," Ozma said. "This isn't home."

"Leave your ghosts here," Zilla said. "Decent people like we are going to be have nothing to do with ghosts."

The man took the reins of the horses and led them away. Ozma took out her pocketknife and cut off her last three ribbons. In one of the saddlebags, there was a kite that a lady of Abal had given her. She tied the empress and the kitten boy to it by their ribbons, and then she threw the kite up so the wind caught it. The string ran through her hand, and the two ghosts sailed away over the houses of Brid.

What are you doing? the constable said.

"Be quiet," Ozma said. She tied a knot in the third ribbon and stuck the constable in her pocket. Then she picked up a saddlebag and followed her mother into Brid.

Her mother walked along as if she had lived in Brid all her life. They stopped in a temple and Zilla bought a hundred candles. Ozma helped her light them all, while the priest dozed, stretched out on a prayer bench. Couldn't he tell how wicked they were? Ozma wondered. Only wicked, wicked people would need to light so many candles.

But Zilla, kneeling in front of the altar steps, lighting candle after candle, looked like a saint in her gray dress. The air was thick with incense. Zilla sneezed, and the priest woke up with a snort. This would be a very dull game, Ozma thought. She wished that Zilla had charmed the constable instead of killing him. She had not been at all tired of their life in Abal.

Zilla led Ozma through a public square where women were drawing water from a well, and down a narrow street. The gutters smelled of human sewage. In Abal the finest houses had been outfitted with modern plumbing. There had been taps and running water and hot baths. And a public bath— even if Brid had such a thing, Ozma realized—would be out of the question, as long as she was a boy.

"Here," Zilla said. She went up to the door of a two-story stone house. It did not compare to the house they had lived in, in Abal. When Zilla knocked, a woman in a housemaid's cap opened the door. "You're to go around to the back," the woman said. "Don't you know anything?" Then she relented. "Come in quickly, quickly."

There was a vestibule and a front hall with a mosaic set in the floor. The blue and yellow tiles were set in a spiralling pattern, and Ozma thought she saw dragons, but the mosaic was cracked and some of the tiles were missing. Light fell down through a vaulted skylight. There were statues standing in paneled niches in the wall, gods and goddesses looking as if they had been waiting for a long time for someone to bring their coats and hats. They looked dowdier than the gods in Abal did, less haughty, less high. There were ghosts everywhere, Ozma saw. Somehow it made her miss Abal less. At least Brid was like Abal in this one way.

She didn't care for the gods. When she thought of them at all, she imagined them catching people the way that Zilla caught ghosts, with charms and ribbons. Who would want to dangle along after one of these household gods, with their painted eyes and their chipped fingers?

"Come along, come along," said the housemaid. "My name's Jemma. I'm to show you your room and then I'll take you back down to the parlor. What's your name, boy?"

Zilla poked Ozma. "Oz—Ozen," Ozma said. "Ozen."

"That's a foreign name," Jemma said. She sounded disapproving. Ozma stared down. Jemma had thick ankles. Her shoes looked as if they pinched. As she hurried them along, little eddies of ghosts swirled around her skirts. Zilla sneezed.

Jemma led them through a door and then up and up a winding staircase. Ghosts drifted after them lazily. Zilla pretended they were not there and so Ozma did the same.

At the top of the stairs was a hall with a door on either side. Their room had a sloped roof, so there was barely room to stand up. There were two narrow beds, a chair, a basin on a small table, and a window with a pane missing.

"I see there's a fireplace," Zilla said. She sank down into the chair.

"Get up, get up," Jemma said. "Oh please, Miss Zilla, get up. I'm to show you down to the parlor and then I must get back to the kitchen to start dinner. It's a mercy that you've come. It's just been the two of us, me and my da. The house is filthy and I'm no cook."

"Go on," Zilla said. "I'll find the parlor. And then I'll come find you in the kitchen. We'll see what we can do for dinner."

"Yes, Miss Zilla," Jemma said, and made a little bob.

Ozma listened to Jemma thumping down the stairs again as if she were a whole herd of maids. Some of the ghosts went with her, but most remained crowded around Zilla. Zilla sat in the chair, her eyes shut tightly.

"What are we doing here?" Ozma said. "How could there be anything in this place that we need? Who are we to be?"

Zilla did not open her eyes. "Good people," she said. "Respectable people."

The constable wriggled like a fish in Ozma's pocket. *Good liars*, he said quietly. *Respectable murderers.*

～ ～ ～

There was water in the basin so that Zilla and Ozma could wash their hands and faces. Zilla had a packet of secondhand clothing for Ozma, which Ozma laid out on the bed. Boy's clothing. It seemed terrible to her, not only that she should have to be a boy and wear boy's clothing but that she should have to wear clothes bought from a store in Brid. In Abal and in the city before Abal, she'd had the most beautiful dresses and gloves and cloaks, and shoes made of the softest leather. It was one thing to dress as a boy on the road, when there was no one to admire her. She slipped the constable out of the pocket of her old clothes and into the pocket of her shirt.

"Stop sulking or I'll sell you to the priests," Zilla said. She was standing at the window, looking out at the street below. Ozma imagined Brid below them: dull, dull, dull.

Ozma waited just outside the door of the parlor. Really, the house was full of ghosts. Perhaps she and Zilla could start a business here in Brid and export fine ghosts to Abal. When Zilla said, "Come in, son," she stepped in.

"Close the door quickly!" said the ugly old man who stood beside Zilla. Perhaps he would fall in love with Zilla and beg her to marry him. Something flew past Ozma's ear: the room was full of songbirds. Now she could hear them as well. There were cages everywhere, hanging from the roof and from stands, and all of the cage doors standing open. The birds were anxious. They flew around and around the room, settling on chairs and chandeliers. There was a nest on the mantelpiece and another inside the harpsichord. There were long streaks of bird shit on the furniture, on the floor, and on the old man's clothes. "They don't like your mother very much," he said.

This was not quite right, Ozma saw. It was the ghosts that followed Zilla and Ozma that the birds did not like.

"This is Lady Rosa Fralix," Zilla said.

So it was an ugly old woman. Ozma remembered to bow instead of curtsy.

"What is your name, child?" said Lady Fralix.

"Ozen," Ozma said.

"Ozen," Lady Fralix said. "What a handsome boy he is, Zilla."

Zilla sneezed sharply. "If it meets with your approval, Lady Fralix, dinner will be served in the small dining room at eight. Tomorrow Ozen and Jemma and I will begin to put your house in order. Shall we begin here?"

"If Ozen will agree to help me cage my friends," Lady Fralix said. "We can go over the schedule tomorrow morning after breakfast. I'm afraid there's been too much work for poor Jemma. There are one or two rooms, though, that I would prefer that you leave alone."

"Very well, madam," Zilla said in her most disinterested voice, and *aha!* thought Ozma. There were birds perched on Lady Fralix's head and shoulders. They pulled at her thin white hair. No wonder she was nearly bald.

Zilla was a good if unimaginative cook. She prepared an urchin stew, a filet of sole, and because Jemma said Lady Fralix's teeth were not good, she made a bread pudding with fresh goat's milk and honey. Ozma helped her carry the dishes into the dining room, which was smaller and less elegant than the dining rooms of Abal, where ladies in beautiful dresses had given Ozma morsels from their own plates. The dining room was without distinction. It was not particularly well appointed. And it was full of ghosts. Everywhere you stepped there were ghosts. The empty wineglasses and the silver tureen in the center of the table were full of them.

Zilla stayed to serve Lady Fralix. Ozma ate in the kitchen with Jemma and Jemma's da, a large man who ate plate after plate of stew and said nothing at all. Jemma said a great deal, but very little of it was interesting. Lady Rosa Fralix had never married as far as anyone knew. She was a scholar and a collector of holy relics and antiquities. She had traveled a great deal in her youth. She had no heir.

Ozma went up the stairs to bed. Zilla was acting as lady's maid to Lady Fralix, or rifling through secret drawers, or most likely of all, had gone back to the temple to light candles again. Jemma had started a fire in the grate in the dark little bedroom. Ozma was grudgingly grateful. She used the chamber pot and then bathed as best she could in front of the fire with a sponge and water from the basin. She did all of this behind a screen so that she was hidden from the constable, although she hadn't been so modest while they were traveling.

The constable did not have much to say, and Ozma did not feel much like talking, either. She thought of a thousand questions to ask Zilla, if only she were brave enough. When she woke in the night, there were strange cracking sounds and the fire in the grate was shooting out long green tongues of flame. Zilla was crouched before it, adding things to the blaze. She was burning her ghost tackle—the long needles and the black silk thread, the tubes and ointments and all of her notebooks. "Go back to sleep, Ozma," Zilla said, without turning around.

Ozma closed her eyes.

Zilla woke her in the morning. "What time is it?" Ozma said. A thin gray light was dribbling through the window.

"Five in the morning. Time to wake and dress and wash your face," Zilla said. "There's work to do."

Zilla made a porridge with raisins and dates while Ozma located a broom, a brush, a dustpan, and cloths. "First of all," Zilla said, "we'll get rid of the vermin."

She opened the front door and began to sweep ghosts out of the front hall, through the vestibule, down the front steps and into the street. They tumbled in front of her broom in white, astonished clouds. "What are you doing?" Ozma said.

"This is a respectable house," Zilla said. "And we are respectable people. An infestation of this kind is disgraceful."

"In Abal," Ozma said, "fashionable homes were full of ghosts. You made it the fashion. What is different about Brid? What are we doing here?"

"Sweeping," Zilla said, and handed Ozma a brush and a dustpan.

They went through the smaller dining room and the larger dining room and the breakfast room and two sitting rooms, which seemed to Ozma pleasant at best. Everywhere there were souvenirs of Lady Fralix's travels: seashells, souvenir paperweights, music boxes, and umbrella stands made from the legs of very strange animals. They all seethed with ghosts. There was a ballroom where the ghosts rinsed around their ankles in a misty, heatless boil. Ozma's fingers itched for her ribbons and her charms. "Why are there so many?" she said.

But Zilla shook her head. When the clocks began to strike eight o'clock, at last she stopped and said, "That will do for now. After Lady Fralix has dressed and I've brought her a tray, she wants your help in the front parlor to catch the birds."

But Lady Fralix caught the birds easily. They came and sat on her finger, and she fed them crumbs of toast. Then she

shut them in their cages. She didn't need Ozma at all. Ozma
sat on the piano bench and watched. Her hands were red and
blistered from sweeping ghosts.

"They need fresh water," Lady Fralix said finally.

So Ozma carried little dishes of water back and forth from
the kitchen to the parlor. Then she helped Lady Fralix drape
the heavy velvet covers over the cages. "Why do you have so
many birds?" she said.

"Why do you have a ghost in your pocket?" Lady Fralix
said. "Does your mother know you kept him? She doesn't seem
to care for ghosts."

"How do you know I have a ghost?" Ozma said. "Can you
see ghosts, too? Why is your house so full of ghosts? In Abal,
we caught them for ladies to wear on their dresses, but the
ladies only pretended that they could see their ghosts. It was
fashionable."

"Let me take a look at yours," Lady Fralix said. Ozma took
the constable out of her pocket. She did it reluctantly.

The constable bowed to Lady Fralix. *My lady*, he said.

"Oh, he's charming," said Lady Fralix. "I see why you
couldn't give him up. Would you like me to keep him safe for
you?"

"No!" Ozma said. She quickly put the constable back in her
pocket. She said, "When I first saw you I thought you were an
ugly old man."

Lady Fralix laughed. Her laugh was clear and lovely and
warm. "And when I saw you, Ozen, I thought you were a beautiful young woman."

After lunch, which was rice and chicken seasoned with mint
and almonds, Zilla gave Ozma a pail of soapy water and a pile

of clean rags. She left her in the vestibule. Ozma washed the gods first. She hoped they were grateful, but they didn't seem to be. When she was finished, they had the same sort of look that Zilla wore when she was bamboozling someone: distant, charming, untrustworthy.

Ozma's back and arms ached. Twice she'd almost dropped the constable in the pail of water, thinking he was a clean rag.

Zilla appeared in the vestibule. She reached up and touched the robe of one of the gods, a woman with a wolf's head. She left her hand there for a moment, and Ozma felt a terrible jealousy. Zilla rarely touched Ozma so gently.

"Be careful with the tiles," Zilla said. She did not look particularly dirty or tired, although she and Jemma had been beating bird shit out of the carpets and upholstery all afternoon.

Lady Fralix came and watched from the balcony while Ozma cleaned the mosaic. "Your mother says she will try to find tiles to replace the ones that have been broken," she said.

Ozma said nothing.

"The artist was a man from the continent of Gid," Lady Fralix said. "I met him when I was looking for a famous temple to the god Addaman. His congregation had dwindled, and in a fit of temper Addaman drowned his congregation, priests, temple and all, in a storm that lasted for three years. There's a lake there now. I went swimming in it and found all kinds of things. I brought the mosaic artist back with me. I always meant to go back. The water was meant to cure heartsickness. Or maybe it was the pox. I have a vial of it somewhere, or maybe that was the vial that Jemma thought were my eyedrops. It's so important to label things legibly."

Ozma wrung dirty water out of a rag. "Your mother is very

religious," Lady Fralix said. "She seems to know a great deal about the gods."

"She likes to light candles," Ozma said.

"For your father?" Lady Fralix said.

Ozma said nothing.

"If your ghost needs blood," Lady Fralix said, "you should go to the butcher's stall in the market. I'll tell your mother that I sent you to buy seeds for the birds."

There was nothing to do in Brid. There was no theater, no opera, no chocolate maker. Only temples and more temples. Zilla visited them all and lit hundreds of candles each day. She gave away the dresses that she had brought with her from Abal. She gave away all her jewels to beggars in the street. Zilla did not explain to Ozma about home or what she was planning or why they were masquerading in Brid as a devout, respectable housekeeper and her son. Zilla used only the most harmless of magics: to make the bread rise, to judge whether or not it was a good day to hang up the washing in the courtyard.

She made up simple potions for the other servants who worked in the houses on the street where Lady Fralix lived. She told fortunes. But she only told happy fortunes. The love potions were mostly honey and sugar dissolved in wine. Zilla didn't charge for them. Neighborhood servants sat around the kitchen table and gossiped. They told stories of how the mayor of Brid had been made a fool of, all for love; of accidental poisonings; who had supposedly stuffed their mattresses with bags of gold coins; which babies had been dropped on their heads by nursemaids who drank. Zilla did not seem to pay any attention.

"Lady Fralix is a good woman," Jemma said. "She was

wild in her youth. She talked to the gods. She wasn't afraid of anything. Then she came to Brid to see the temples and she bought this house on a whim because, she said, she'd never been in a town that was so full of sleepy gods. She claims that it's restful. Well, I don't know about that. I've never lived anywhere else."

"There's something about Brid," Zilla said. She looked cross, as if the word *Brid* tasted bad. "Something that drew me to Brid, but I don't know what. I don't know that I'd call it peaceful. Ozen finds it dull, I'm afraid."

Ozma said, "I want to go *home*." But she said it quietly, so that Jemma wouldn't hear. Zilla looked away as if she hadn't heard either.

Ozma developed calluses on her hands. It was a good thing that there was nothing to do in Brid. She spent all her time mopping and dusting and carrying firewood and beating upholstery. Zilla's nose was always pink from sneezing. The constable grew bored. *This was not what I expected death to be like*, he said.

"What is death like?" Ozma said. She always asked the ghosts this, but they never gave satisfactory answers.

How do I know? the constable said. *I'm carried around all day in a young girl's pocket. I drink the stale blood of market cattle. I thought there would be clouds of glory, or beautiful lecherous devils with velvet bosoms, or a courtroom full of gods to judge me.*

"It will be different when Zilla has done what she needs to do," Ozma said. "Then we'll go home. There will be clouds of glory, and my pockets will be lined with lavender and silk. Everyone will know Zilla, and they'll bow to her when we drive by in our carriage. Mothers will frighten their children with stories about Zilla, and kings will come and beg her to give them kisses. But she will only love *me*."

You think your mother is a blackmailer and a thief and a murderer, the constable said. *You admire her for what you think she is.*

"I know she is!" Ozma said. "I know what she is!"

The constable said nothing. He only smirked. For several days they did not speak to each other until Ozma relented and gave him her own blood to drink as a peace offering. It was only a drop or two, and she was almost flattered to think that he preferred it.

It was hard work keeping Lady Fralix's house free of ghosts. Ozma said so when she brought Lady Fralix's breakfast up one morning. Zilla and Jemma had gone to a temple where there was a god who, according to his priests, had recently opened his painted mouth and complained about the weather. This was supposed to be a miracle.

"Your mother wants me to let my birds go free," Lady Fralix said. "First the ghosts, now the birds. She says it's cruel to keep things trapped in cages."

This did not sound at all like Zilla. Ozma was beginning to grow tired of this new Zilla. It was one thing to *pretend* to be respectable; it was another entirely to *be* respectable.

Lady Fralix said, "It's considered holy in some places to release birds. People free them on holy days because it pleases the gods. Perhaps I should. Perhaps your mother is right to ask."

"Why do the ghosts come back again and again?" Ozma said. She was far more interested in ghosts than in birds. All birds did was eat and shit and make noise. "What do you want to wear today?"

"The pink dressing gown," Lady Fralix said. "If you let me keep your ghost in my pocket today, I'll give you one of my dresses. Any dress you like."

"Zilla would take it away and give it to the poor," Ozma said. Then: "How did you know I'm a girl?"

"I'm old but I'm not blind," Lady Fralix said. "I see all sorts of things. Ghosts and girls. Little lost things. You shouldn't keep dressing as a boy, my dear. Someone as shifty as you needs some truth now and then."

"I'll be a boy if I want to be a boy," Ozma said. She realized that she didn't really think of herself as Ozma anymore. She had become Ozen, who strutted and flirted with the maids fetching water, whose legs were longer, whose breasts did not need to be bound.

Be a girl, said the constable, muffled, from inside her pocket. *Your hips are too bony as a boy. And I don't like how your voice is changing. You had a nicer singing voice before.*

"Oh, be quiet," Ozma said. She was exasperated. "I've never heard so much nonsense in all my life!"

"You're an insolent child, but my offer stands," Lady Fralix said. "When you're ready to be a girl again. Now. Let's go down and do some work in my collection. I need someone with clever fingers. My old hands shake too much. Will you help me?"

"If you want me to," Ozma said, ungraciously. She helped Lady Fralix out of bed and into a dressing gown and then she combed what was left of Lady Fralix's hair. "How old are you?"

"Not as old as your mother," Lady Fralix said, and laughed at Ozma's look of disbelief.

There was no door to the room in which Lady Fralix kept her collection, but Ozma felt sure she had never noticed this room before. There were four or five ghosts brushing against the door that wasn't there. They stayed on the threshold as if tethered there. "What are they doing?" Ozma said.

"They want to go inside," Lady Fralix said. "But they're afraid. Something draws them. They want it and they don't know why. Poor little things."

The room was very strange. It was the size of a proper ballroom in Abal, only it was full of paintings on stands, altars, and tables piled high with reliquaries and holy books and icons. Along the far wall there were gods as large as wardrobes and little brass gods and gods of ivory and gold and jade gods and fat goddesses giving birth to other gods and goddesses. There were bells hanging from the ceiling with long silk ropes, bells resting on the floor so big that Ozma could have hidden under them, and there were robes stiff with embroidery, hung about with bells no bigger than a fingernail.

Where are we? said the constable.

Lady Fralix had stepped inside the room. She beckoned to Ozma. But when Ozma put her foot down on the wooden floor, the board beneath her foot gave a terrible shriek.

What is that noise? said the constable.

"The floor—" Ozma said.

"Oh," Lady Fralix said. "Your ghost. You had better tie him up outside. He won't want to come in here."

The constable trembled in Ozma's hand. He looked about wildly, ignoring her at first. She tied him to the leg of an occasional table in the hallway. *Don't leave me here*, the constable said. *There's something in that room that I need. Bring it to me, boy.*

"Boy!" Ozma said.

Please, boy, said the constable. *Ozma, please. I beg you on my death.*

Ozma ignored him. She stepped into the room again. And again, with each step, the floor shrieked and groaned and squeaked. Lady Fralix clapped her hands. "It's almost as good as going to see the orchestra in Oldun," she said. She walked in a quick odd pattern toward an altar carved in the shape of a winged fish.

"Why don't you make any sound when you walk?" Ozma said.

"I know where to place my foot," Lady Fralix said. "I keep my most precious relics here. All the things that belong to gods. There. Put your foot down there. There's a pattern to it. Let me teach you."

She showed Ozma how to navigate the room. It was a little like waltzing. "Isn't this fun?" said Lady Fralix. "An adept can play the floor like a musical instrument. It comes from a temple in Nal. There's an emerald somewhere, too. The eye of a god. From the same temple. Here, look at this."

There was a tree growing out of an old stone altar. The tree had almost split the altar in two. There was fruit on it, and Lady Fralix bent a branch down. "Not ripe yet," she said. "I've been waiting almost twenty years and it's still not ripe."

"I suppose you want me to dust everything," Ozma said.

"Perhaps you could just help me go through the books," Lady Fralix. "I left a novel in here last summer. I was only halfway through reading it. The beautiful gypsy had just been kidnapped by a lord disguised as a narwhal."

"Here it is," Ozma said, after they had hunted for a while in companionable silence. When she looked up, she felt strange, as if the room had begun to spin around her. The gods and their altars all seemed very bright, and the bells were tolling, although without any sound. Even Lady Fralix seemed to shimmer a little, as if she were moving and standing still at the same time.

"You're quite pale," Lady Fralix said. "I'd have thought you wouldn't be susceptible."

"To what?" Ozma said.

"To the gods," Lady Fralix said. "Some people have a hard time. It's a bit like being up in the mountains. Some people don't seem to notice."

"I don't care for gods," Ozma said. "They're nothing to me. I hate Brid. I hate this place. I hate the gods."

"Let's go and have some tea," Lady Fralix said. She did not sound in the least bit perturbed to hear that Ozma was a heretic.

In the hallway, the constable was tugging at his ribbon, as if the room were full of blood.

"What is it?" Ozma said. "There's nothing in that room, just boring old gods."

I need it, the constable said. *Be kind, be kind. Give me the thing I need.*

"Don't be tiresome," Ozma said. Her head ached.

Before Ozma could put him in her pocket, Lady Fralix took hold of her wrist. She picked up the constable by his ribbon.

"Very curious," Lady Fralix said. "He's so lively, such a darling. Not the usual sort of ghost. Do you know how he died?"

"He ate a bad piece of cheese," Ozma said. "Or maybe he fell off a cliff. I don't remember. Give him back."

"It's a good thing," Lady Fralix said, "that most people can't see or talk to ghosts. Watching them scurry around, it makes you dread the thought of death, and yet what else is there to do when you die? Will some careless child carry me around in her pocket?"

Ozma shrugged. She was young. She wouldn't die for years and years. She tried not to think of the handsome young constable in her pocket, who had once thought much the same thing.

By the time Zilla and Jemma returned from the temple, Lady Fralix had made up her mind to let the birds go, as soon as possible.

"I only kept them because the house seemed so empty," she said. "Brid is too quiet. In the city of Tuk, the god houses are full of red and green birds who fly back and forth carrying holy messages."

Zilla and Jemma and Ozma carried cage after cage out onto the street. The birds fussed and chattered. Lady Fralix watched from her bedroom window. It was starting to rain.

Once the birds were free, they seemed more confused than liberated. They didn't burst into joyful songs or even fly away. Ozma had to shoo them out of their cages. They flew around the house and beat their wings against the windows. Lady Fralix closed her curtains. One bird flew against a window so hard that it broke its neck.

Ozma picked up its body. The beak was open.

"The poor little things," Jemma said. Jemma was terribly tenderhearted. She wiped rain off her face with her apron. There were feathers sticking out of her hair.

"Where do the ghosts of birds and animals go?" Ozma said quietly to Zilla. "Why don't we see them?"

Zilla looked at her. Her eyes glittered and her color was

high. "I see them," she said. "I can see them plain as anything. It's good that you can't see them, Ozen. It's more respectable not to see any kind of ghosts."

"Lady Fralix knows I'm a girl," Ozma said. Jemma was chasing the birds away from the house, flapping her own arms and her sodden apron. The rain fell harder and harder but Zilla didn't seem to notice. "She said something about how I ought to be careful. I think that perhaps I'm becoming a boy. I think she may be right. I stand up when I piss now. I'm shaped differently. I have something down there that I didn't have before."

"Let me take a look at you," Zilla said. "Turn around. Yes, I see. Well, it has nothing to do with me. You must be doing it yourself somehow. How enterprising you've become. How inconvenient."

"Actually," Ozma said, "it's more convenient. I like standing up when I piss."

"It won't do," Zilla said. "It's not very respectable, that's for certain. We'll take care of it tonight."

I liked you better as a girl, the constable said. *You were a nice girl. That girl would have given me what I wanted. She would have found what I needed in that room.*

"I wasn't a nice girl!" Ozma said. She stood naked in the attic room. She wished she had a mirror. The thing between her legs was very strange. She didn't know how long it had been here.

Ever since we came to this house, the constable said. He was sitting in the corner of the grate on a little heap of ashes. He looked very gloomy. *Ever since your mother told you to be a boy. Why do you always do what your mother tells you?*

"I don't," Ozma said. "I kept you. I keep you secret. If she knew about you, she'd sweep you right out of the house."

Don't tell her then, the constable said. *I want to stay with you, Ozma. I forgive you for letting her kill me.*

"Be quiet," Ozma said. "Here she comes."

Zilla was carrying a small folded pile of clothes. She stared at Ozma. "Get dressed," she said. "I've seen all that before. It doesn't particularly suit you, although it does explain why the housemaids next door have been mooning and swanning around in their best dresses."

"Because of me?" Ozma said. She began to pull her trousers back on.

"No, not those. Here. Lady Fralix has lent you a dress. I've made something up, although only a liar as good as I am could pull off such a ridiculous story. I fed Jemma some confection about how you've been dressing as a boy as penance. Because a young man had fallen in love with you and committed suicide. You're handsome enough as a boy," Zilla said. "But I don't know what you were thinking. I never cared much for that shape. It's too distracting. And people are always wanting to quarrel with you."

"You've been a man?" Ozma said. The dress felt very strange, very confining. The thing between her legs was still there. And she didn't like the way the petticoats rubbed against her legs. They scratched.

"Not for years and years," Zilla said. "Gods, I don't even know how long. It's one thing to dress as a man, Ozma, but you mustn't let yourself forget who you are."

"But I don't know who I am," Ozma said. "Why are we different from other people? Why do we see ghosts? Why did I change into a boy? You said we were going home, but Brid isn't home, I know it isn't. Where is our home? Why did we come here? Why are you acting so strangely?"

Zilla sighed. She snapped her fingers, and there was a little green flame resting on the back of her hand. She stroked it with her other hand, coaxing it until it grew larger. She sat down on one of the narrow beds and patted the space beside her. Ozma sat down. "There's something that I need to find," Zilla said. "Something in Brid. I can't go home without it. When Neren died—"

"Neren!" Ozma said. She didn't want to talk about Neren.

Zilla gave her a terrible look. "If those men had killed you instead of Neren . . ." she said. Her voice trailed off. The green flame dwindled down to a spark and went out. "There was something that I was supposed to do for him. Something that I knew how to do once. Something I've forgotten."

"I don't understand," Ozma said. "We buried him in the tree. What else could we have done?"

"I don't know," Zilla said. "I go to the temples every day and I humble myself and I light enough candles to burn down a city, but the gods won't talk to me. I'm too wicked. I've done terrible things. I think I used to know how to talk to the gods. I need to talk to them again. I need to talk to them before I go home. I need them to tell me what I've forgotten."

"Before *we* go home," Ozma said. "You wouldn't leave me here, would you? You wouldn't. Tell me about home, oh please, tell me about home."

"I can't remember," Zilla said. She stood up. "I don't remember. Stop fussing at me, Ozma. Don't come downstairs again until you're a girl."

～ ～ ～

Ozma had terrible dreams. She dreamed that Lady Fralix's birds had come back home again and they were pecking at her head. Peck, peck, peck. Peck, peck. They were going to pull out all of her hair because she had been a terrible daughter. Neren had sent them. She was under one of Lady Fralix's bells in the darkness because she was hiding from the birds. The constable was kissing her under the bell. His mouth was full of dead birds.

Someone was shaking her. "Ozma," Zilla said. "Ozma, wake up. Ozma, tell me what you are dreaming about."

"The birds," Ozma said. "I'm in the room where Lady Fralix keeps her collection. I'm hiding from the birds."

"What room?" Zilla said. Her hand was still on Ozma's shoulder, but she was only a dark shape against darkness.

"The room full of bells and altars," Ozma said. "The room that the ghosts won't go in. She wanted me to find a book for her this afternoon. The floor is from a temple in Nal. You have to walk on it a certain way. It made me feel dizzy."

"Show me this room," Zilla said. "I'll fetch a new candle. You've burned this one down to the stub. Meet me downstairs."

Ozma got out of bed. She went and squatted over the chamber pot.

So you're a girl again, the constable said from behind the grate.

"Oh, be quiet," Ozma said. "It's none of your business."

It is my business, the constable said. *You'll go and fetch the thing that your mother needs, but you won't help me. I thought you loved me.*

"You?" Ozma said. "How could I love you? How could I love a ghost? How could I love something that I have to keep hidden in my pocket?"

She picked up the constable. "You're filthy," she said.

You're lovely, Ozma, the constable said. *You're ripe as a peach. I've never wanted anything as much as I want just a drop of your blood, except there's something in that room that I want even more. If you bring it to me, I'll promise to be true to you. No one will ever have such a faithful lover.*

"I don't want a lover," Ozma said. "I want to go home."

She put the constable in the pocket of her nightgown and went down the dark stairs in her bare feet. Her mother was in the vestibule, where all the gods were waiting for dawn. The flame from the candle lit Zilla's face and made her look beautiful and wicked and pitiless. "Hurry, Ozma. Show me the room."

"It's just along here," Ozma said. It was as if they were back in Abal and nothing had changed. She felt like dancing.

"I don't understand," Zilla said. "How could it be here under my nose all this time and I couldn't even see it?"

"See what?" Ozma said. "Look, here's the room." As before, there were ghosts underfoot, everywhere, even more than there had been before.

"Filthy things," Zilla said. She sneezed. "Why won't they leave me alone?" She didn't seem to see the room at all.

Ozma took the candle from Zilla and held it up so that they could both see the entrance to the room. "Here," she said. "Here, look. Here's the room I was telling you about."

Zilla was silent. Then she said, "It makes me feel ill. As if something terrible is calling my name over and over again. Perhaps it's a god. Perhaps a god is telling me not to go in."

"The room is full of gods!" Ozma said. "There are gods and gods and altars and relics and sacred stones, and you can't go

in there or else the floorboards will make so much noise that
everyone in the house will wake up."

Bring me the thing I need! shouted the constable. *I will kill
you all if you don't bring me the thing I need!*

"Ozma," Zilla said. She sounded like the old Zilla again,
queenly and sly, used to being obeyed. "Who is that in your
pocket? Who thinks that he is mightier than I?"

"It's only the constable of Abal," Ozma said. She took the
constable out of her pocket and held him behind her back.

Let me go, the constable said. *Let me go or I will bite you.
Go fetch me the thing that I need and I will let you live.*

"Give him to me," Zilla said.

"Will you keep him safe while I go in there?" Ozma said. "I
know how to walk without making the floor sing. The ghosts
won't go in there, but I could go in. What am I looking for?"

"I don't know," Zilla said. "I don't know, but you will know
it when you see it. I promise. Bring me the thing that I'm looking for. Give me your ghost."

Don't give me to her, the constable said. *I have a bad feeling
about this. Besides, there's something in that room that I need.
You'll be sorry if you help her and not me.*

Zilla held out her hand. Ozma gave her the constable. "I'm
sorry," Ozma said to the constable. Then she went into the
room.

She was instantly dizzy. It was worse than before. She concentrated on the light falling from the candle, and the wax
that dripped down onto her hand. She put each foot down
with care. The ropes from stolen temple bells slithered across
her shoulders like dead snakes. The altars and tables were

absolutely heaped with things, and all of it was undoubtedly
valuable, and it was far too dark. How in the world did Zilla
expect her to come out again with the exact thing that was
needed? Perhaps Ozma should just carry out as much as she
could. There was a little wax god on the table nearest her. She
held up the hem of her nightgown like an apron and dropped
the god inside. There was a book covered in gold leaf. She
picked it up. Too heavy. She put it back down again. She picked
up a smaller book. She put it in her nightgown.

There was a little mortar and pestle for grinding incense.
They didn't feel right. She put them down. Here was a table
piled with boxes, and the boxes were full of eyes. Sapphire eyes
and ruby eyes and pearls and onyx and emeralds. She didn't
like how they looked at her.

As she searched, she began to feel as if something was pulling at her. She realized that it had been pulling at her all this
time, and that she had been doing her best to ignore it, without
even noticing. She began to walk toward the thing pulling at
her, but even this was hard. The pattern she had to walk was
complicated. She seemed to be moving away from the thing
she needed, the closer she tried to get. She put more things in
the scoop of her nightgown: a bundle of sticks tied with strips
of silk; a little bottle with something sloshing inside of it; a
carving of a fish. The heavier her nightgown grew, the easier it
became to make her way toward the thing that was calling her.
Her candle was much shorter than it had been. She wondered
how long she'd been in the room. Surely not very long.

The thing that had been calling her was a goddess. She felt
strangely annoyed by this, especially when she saw which goddess it was. It was the same wolf-headed goddess who stood in
the vestibule. It seemed to be laughing wolfishly and silently

at her, as if she, Ozma, was small and insignificant and silly. "I don't even know your name," Ozma said, feeling as if this proved something. The goddess said nothing.

There was a clay cup on the palm of the goddess's hands. She held it as if she were offering a drink to Ozma, but the cup was empty. Ozma took it. It was old and ugly and fragile. Surely it was the least precious thing in the entire room.

As she made her way back toward the hall, she began to smell something that was both sweet and astringent, a fragrance nothing like Brid. Brid smelled of cobblestones and horses and soap and candles. This fragrance was more agreeable than anything she had ever known. It reminded her of the perfumed oils that the fashionable ladies of Abal wore, the way their coiled, jeweled hair smelled when the ladies bent down like saplings over her and told her what a lovely child she was, how lovely she was. A drowsy, pearly light was beginning to come through the high windows. It settled on the glossy curves of the hanging bells and the sitting bells, like water. The two halves of the stone altar and the tree that had split them were in front of her.

All the leaves of that strange, stubborn tree were moving, as if in a wind. She wondered if it was a god moving through the room, but the room felt hushed and still, as if she were utterly alone. Her head was clearer now. She bent down a branch and there was a fruit on it. It looked something like a plum. She picked it.

When she came out of the room, Zilla was pacing in the hallway. "You were in there for hours," Zilla said. "Do you have it? Let me have it."

The plum was in Ozma's pocket and she didn't take it out. She pulled the things from Lady Fralix's room out of the gathered hem of her nightgown and put them on the floor. Zilla knelt down. "Not this," she said, rifling through the book. "Not this either. This is nothing. This is less than nothing. A forgery. A cheap souvenir. Nothing. You've brought me trash and junk. A marble. A fish. A clay cup. What were you thinking, Ozma?"

"Where is the constable of Abal?" Ozma said. She picked up the clay cup and held it out to Zilla. "This is the thing you wanted, I know it is. You said I would know it. Give me the constable and I'll give you the cup."

"What have you got in your pocket?" Zilla said. "What are you keeping from me? What do I want with an old clay cup?"

"Tell me what you did with the constable," Ozma said, still holding out the empty cup.

"She swept him out the door with all the other ghosts," said Lady Fralix. She stood in the hallway, blinking and yawning. All her hair stood out from her head in tufts, like an owl. Her feet were bare, just like Ozma's feet. They were long and bony.

"You did what?" Ozma said. Zilla made a gesture. Nothing, the gesture said. The constable was nothing. A bit of trash.

"You shouldn't have left him with her," Lady Fralix said. "You should have known better."

"Give it to me," Zilla said. "Give me the thing in your pocket, Ozma, and we'll leave here. We'll go home. We'll be able to go home."

A terrible wave of grief came down on Ozma. It threatened to sweep her away forever, like the ghost of the constable of Abal. "You killed him. You murdered him! You're a murderer and I hate you!" she said.

There was something in her hand and she flung it at Zilla

as hard as she could. Zilla caught the cup easily. She dashed it at the floor, and it broke into dozens of pieces. The nothingness that had been in the cup spilled out and splashed up over Zilla's legs and skirts. The empty cup had not been empty after all, or, rather it had been full of emptiness. There seemed to be a great deal of it.

Ozma put her hands over her face. She couldn't bear to see the look of contempt on her mother's face.

"Oh, look!" Lady Fralix said. "Look what you've done, Ozma," she said again, gently. "Look how beautiful she is."

Ozma peeked through her fingers. Zilla's hair was loose around her shoulders. She was so beautiful that it was hard to look at her directly. She still wore her gray housekeeper's uniform, but the dress shone like cloth of silver where the emptiness, the *nothing*, had soaked it. "Oh," Zilla said. And "oh" again.

Ozma's hands curled into fists. She stared at the floor. She was thinking of the constable. How he had promised to love her faithfully and forever. She saw him again, as he was dying in Zilla's parlor in Abal. How surprised he had looked. How his ghost had clung to Zilla's ribbon so he would not be swept away.

"Ozma," Zilla said. "Ozma, look at me." She sneezed and then sneezed again. "I have not been myself, but I am myself again. You did this, Ozma. You brought me the thing that I needed, Ozma, I have been asleep for all this time, and you have woken me! Ozma!" Her voice was bright and joyful.

Ozma did not look up. She began to cry instead. The hallway was as bright as if someone had lit a thousand candles, all burning with a cool and silver light. "Little Princess Monkey," Zilla said. "Ozma. Look at me, daughter."

Ozma would not. She felt Zilla's cool hand on her burning cheek. Someone sighed. There was a sound like a bell ringing, very far away. The cool silver light went out.

Lady Fralix said, "She's gone, you stubborn girl. And a good thing, too. I think the house might have come down on us if she'd stayed any longer."

"What? Where has she gone? Why didn't she take me with her?" Ozma said. "What did I do to her?" She wiped at her eyes.

Where Zilla had stood, there was only the broken clay cup. Lady Fralix bent over and picked up the pieces as if they were precious. She wrapped them in a handkerchief and put them in one of her pockets. Then she held out her hand to Ozma and helped her stand up.

"She's gone home," Lady Fralix said. "She's remembered who she is."

"Who was she? What do you mean, 'who she is'? Why doesn't anyone ever explain anything to me?" Ozma said. She felt thick with rage and unhappiness and something like dread. "Am I too stupid to understand? Am I a stupid child?"

"Your mother is a goddess," Lady Fralix said. "I knew it as soon as she applied to be my housekeeper. I've had to put up with a great deal of tidying and dusting and mopping and spring-cleaning, and I must say I'm glad to be done with it all. There's something that tests the nerves, knowing that there's a goddess beating your rugs and cooking your dinner and burning your dresses with an iron."

"Zilla isn't a goddess," Ozma said. She felt like throwing more things. Like stamping her foot until the floor gave way and the house fell down. "She's my mother."

"Yes," Lady Fralix said. "Your mother is a goddess."

"My mother is a liar and a thief and a murderer," Ozma said.

"Yes," Lady Fralix said. "She was all of those things and worse. Gods don't make very good people. They get bored too easily. And they're cruel when they're bored. The worse she behaved, the more she forgot herself. To think of a god of the dead scheming like a common quack and charlatan, leading ghosts around on strings, blackmailing silly rich women, teaching her daughter how to pick locks and cheat at cards."

"Zilla is a god of the dead?" Ozma said. She was shivering. The floor was cold. The morning air was colder, somehow, than the night had seemed. "That's ridiculous. Just because we can see ghosts. You can see ghosts, too, and I can see ghosts. It doesn't mean anything. Zilla doesn't even like ghosts. She was never kind to them, even when we were in Abal."

"Of course she didn't like them," Lady Fralix said. "They reminded her of what she ought to be doing, except she couldn't remember what to do." She chafed Ozma's arms. "You're freezing, child. Let me get you a blanket and some slippers."

"I'm not a child," Ozma said.

"No," Lady Fralix said. "I see you're a young woman now. Very sensible. Here. Look what I have for you." She took something out of her pocket.

It was the constable. He said, *Did you bring me what I need?*

Ozma looked at Lady Fralix. "The fruit you picked from the tree," Lady Fralix said. "I see it ripened for you, not for me. Well, that means something. If you gave it to me, I would eat it. But I suppose you ought to give it to him."

"What does the fruit do?" Ozma said.

"It would make me young again," Lady Fralix said. "I would enjoy that, I think. It gives back life. I don't know that it would do much for one of the other ghosts, but your ghost is really only half a ghost. Yes, I think you ought to give it to him."

"Why?" Ozma said. "What will happen?"

"You've been giving him your blood to drink," Lady Fralix said. "Powerful stuff, your blood. The blood of a goddess runs in your veins. That's what makes your constable so charming, so unusual. So lively. You've kept him from drifting any further away from life. Give him the fruit."

Give me what I need, the constable said. *Just one bite. Just one taste of that delicious thing.*

Ozma took the ghost of the constable from Lady Fralix. She untied him from Zilla's ribbon. She gave him the fruit from the tree and then she set him down on the floor.

"Oh yes," Lady Fralix said wistfully. They watched the constable eat the fruit. Juice ran down his chin. "I was so looking forward to trying that fruit. I hope your constable appreciates it."

He did. He ate the fruit as if he were starving. Color came back into his face. He was taller than either Ozma or Lady Fralix and perhaps he wasn't as handsome as he had been, when he was a ghost. But otherwise, he was still the same constable whom Ozma had carried around in her pocket for months. He put his hand to his neck, as if he were remembering his death. And then he put his hand down again. It was strange, Ozma thought, that death could be undone so easily. As if death was only a cheat, another one of Zilla's tricks.

"Ozma," the constable said.

Ozma blushed. Her nightgown seemed very thin, and she wondered if he could see through it. She crossed her arms over her breasts. It was odd to have breasts again. "What is your name?" she said.

"Cotter Lemp," said the constable. He looked amused, as if it were funny to think that Ozma had never known his name. "So this is Brid."

"This is the house of Lady Fralix," Ozma said. The constable bowed to Lady Fralix, and Lady Fralix made a curtsy. But the constable kept his eyes on Ozma all the time, as if she were a felon, a known criminal who might suddenly bolt. Or as if she were something rare and precious that might suddenly vanish into thin air. Ozma thought of Zilla.

"I have no home," Ozma said. She didn't even know she had said it aloud.

"Ozma, child," Lady Fralix said. "This is your home now."

"But I don't like Brid," Ozma said.

"Then we'll travel," Lady Fralix said. "But Brid is our home. We will always come back to Brid. Everyone needs a home, Ozma, even you."

Cotter Lemp said, "We can go wherever you like, Ozma. If you find Brid too respectable, there are other towns."

"Will I see her again?" Ozma said.

And so, while the sun was rising over the roofs of the houses of the city of Brid, before Jemma had even come downstairs to stoke the kitchen stove and fetch the water to make her morning tea, Lady Fralix and the constable Cotter Lemp went with Ozma to the temple to see her mother.

KELLY LINK is the author of three collections: *Stranger Things Happen*, *Magic for Beginners*, and *Pretty Monsters*. Her work has won three Nebulas, a Hugo, and a World Fantasy Award. She once won a free trip around the world by answering the question "Why do you want to go around the world?" ("Because you can't go through it.")

Link lives in Northampton, Massachusetts, where she and her husband, Gavin J. Grant, run Small Beer Press, co-edit the fantasy half of *The Year's Best Fantasy and Horror*, and twice yearly produce the zine *Lady Churchill's Rosebud Wristlet*.

Her Web site is www.kellylink.net.

~

AUTHOR'S NOTE

I wrote this story first of all for Ellen Datlow and Terri Windling, and second of all for Holly Black, who wanted a happy ending (it hadn't even occurred to me that there could be a happy ending until she asked). Thank you, Holly!

I read P. C. Hodgell's strange and excellent novel *God Stalk* when I was a teenager, and I loved the city of Tai-tastigon, which was full of gods. So that was one inspiration. I had originally intended to write a story about a woman and her daughter, set just after the Great Depression, going from town to town and setting up as spiritualists and healers, and eventually as housekeepers to an old, rich man. But the story was shifty and changed as I wrote it, much as Ozma and her mother change. The name Ozma just seemed right to me. I suppose it's partly because Frank L. Baum wrote *The Wizard of Oz,* the humbug wizard being one of the best trickster characters ever. I've always wanted to have a green curtain for my office, to write behind.

A REVERSAL OF FORTUNE

Holly Black

Nikki opened the refrigerator. There was nothing in there but a couple of shriveled oranges and three gallons of tap water. She slammed it closed. Summer was supposed to be the best part of the year, but so far Nikki's summer sucked. It sucked hard. It sucked like a vacuum that got hold of the drapes.

Her pit bull, Boo, whined and scraped at the door, etching new lines into the battered wood. Nikki clipped on his leash. She knew she should trim his nails. They frayed the nylon of his collar and gouged the door, but when she tried to cut them, he cried like a baby. Nikki figured he'd had enough pain in his life and left his nails long.

"Come on, Boo," she said as she led him out the front door of the trailer. The air outside shimmered with heat, and the air conditioner chugged away in the window, dribbling water down the aluminum siding.

Lifting the lid of the rusty mailbox, Nikki pulled out a handful of circulars and bills. There, among them, she found a stale half bagel with the words BUTTER ME! written on it in gel pen and the crumbly surface stamped with half a dozen stamps. She sighed. Renee's crazy postcards had stopped making her laugh.

Boo hopped down the cement steps gingerly, paws smearing sour cherry tree pulp and staining his feet purple. He paused when he hit their tiny patch of sun-withered lawn to lick one of the hairless scars along his back.

"Come *on*. I have to get ready for work." Nikki gave his collar a sharp tug.

He yelped and she felt instantly terrible. He'd put on some weight since she'd found him and was looking better, but he still was pretty easily freaked. She leaned down to pat the solid warmth of his back. His tail started going, and he turned his massive face to lick her cheek.

Of course that was the moment her neighbor, Trevor, drove up in his gleaming black truck. He parked in front of his trailer and hopped out, the plastic connective tissue of a six-pack threaded between his fingers. She admired the way the muscles on his back moved as he walked to the door of his place, making the raven tattoo on his shoulder ripple.

"Hey," she called, pushing Boo's wet face away and standing up. Why did Trevor pick this moment to be around, when she was covered in dog drool, hair in tangles, wearing her brother's gi-normous T-shirt? Even the thong on one of her flip-flops had ripped out, so she had to shuffle to keep the sole on.

The dog raised his leg and pissed on a dandelion just as Trevor turned around and gave her a negligent half wave.

Boo rooted around for a few minutes more and then Nikki tugged him inside. She pulled on a pair of low-slung orange pants and a black T-shirt with the outline of a dachshund on it. Busy thinking of Trevor, she cut through the self-service car wash that stood between the trailer park and the highway. As she waded through the streams of antifreeze-green cleanser and gobs of snowy foam bubbles, Nikki realized she still wore her broken flip-flops.

There were a couple of people waiting on the bench by the bus stop, the stink of exhaust from the highway not appearing to bother them one bit. Two women with oversize glasses were chatting away, their curled hair wilting in the heat. An elderly man in a black-and-white houndstooth suit leaned on a cane and grinned when she got closer.

Nikki took a deep breath of the sour cherry spatter mixed with the car wash liquids that make the Jersey summers smell like a chemical plant of rotten fruit. She tried to decide if the bus was going to come before she ran back for some sandals.

Just then, Nikki's brother Doug's battered gray Honda pulled into the trailer park. He'd bought the car two weeks ago even though he didn't have a job; he anticipated a big winning in another month and seemed to think he was already made of money.

Nikki ran over to the car and rapped on the window.

Doug jumped in his seat, then scowled when he saw her. His beard glimmered with grease as he eased himself out of the car. He was a big guy to begin with, and over four hundred pounds now. Nikki was just the opposite—skinny as a straw no matter what she ate.

"Can you take me to work?" she asked. "It's too hot to take the bus."

He shook his head and belched, making the air smell like a beach after the tide went out and left the mussels to bake in the sun. "I got some more training to do. Spinks is coming over to do gallon-water trials."

"Come on," she said. It sucked that he got to screw around when she had to work. "Where were you anyway?"

"Chinese buffet," he said. "Did fifty shrimp. Volume's okay, I guess. My speed blows, though. I just slow down after the first five to eight minutes. Peeling is a bitch and those waitresses are always looking at me and giggling."

"Take me to work. You are going to puke if you eat anything else."

His eyes widened and he held up a hand, as if to ward off her words. "How many times do I have to tell you? It's a 'reversal of fortune' or a 'Roman incident.' Don't *ever* say puke. That's bad luck."

Nikki shifted her weight, the intensity of his reaction embarrassing her. "Fine. Whatever. Sorry."

He sighed. "I'll drive you, but you have to take the bus home."

"Deal!" Nikki shouted, running for the trailer. She kicked off her flip-flops and picked up some sandals, then ran back. Sitting in the cracked backseat of his car, she brushed a tangle of silvery wrappers off the leather. A pack of gum sat in the grimy brake well and she pulled out a piece.

"Good for jaw strength," Doug said.

"Good for fresh breath," she replied, rolling her eyes. "Not that you care about that."

He looked out the window. "Gurgitators get groupies, you know. Once I'm established on the competitive eating circuit, I'll be meeting tons of women."

"There's a scary thought," she said as they pulled onto the highway.

"You should try it. I'm battling the whole 'belt of fat' thing—my stomach only expands so far—but the skinny people can really pack it in. You should see this little girl that's eating big guys like me under the table."

"If you keep emptying out the fridge, I might just do it," Nikki said. "I might have to."

Nikki walked through the crowded mall, past skaters getting kicked out by rent-a-cops and listless homemakers pushing baby carriages. At the beginning of summer, when she'd first gotten the job, she had imagined that Renee would still be working at the T-shirt kiosk and Leah would be at Gotheteria and they would wave to each other across the body of the mall and go to the food court every day for lunch. She didn't expect that Renee would be on some extended road trip vacation with her parents and that Leah would ignore Nikki in front of her new, black-lipsticked friends.

If not for Boo, she would have spent the summer waiting around for the bizarre postcards Renee sent from cross-country stops. At first they were just pictures of the Liberty Bell or the Smithsonian with messages on the back about the cute guys she'd seen at a rest stop or the number of times she'd punched her brother using the excuse of playing Padiddle—but then they started to get loonier. A museum brochure where Renee had given each of the paintings obscene thought balloons. A ripped piece of a menu with words blacked out to spell messages like "Cheese is the way." A leaf that got too mangled in the mail to read the words on it. A section of newspaper folded into a boat that said, "Do you think clams get seasick?" And, of course, the bagel.

It bothered Nikki that Renee was still funny and still having fun while Nikki felt lost. Leah had drifted away as though Renee was all that had kept the three of them together, and without Renee to laugh at her jokes, Nikki couldn't seem to be funny. She couldn't even tell if she was having fun.

Kim stood behind the counter of the Sweet Tooth candy store, a long string of red licorice hanging from her mouth. She looked up when Nikki came in. "You're late."

"So?" Nikki asked.

"Boss's son's in the back," Kim said.

Kim loved anime so passionately that she convinced their boss to stock Pocky and lychee gummies and green tea and ginger candies with hard surfaces but runny, spicy insides. They'd done so well that the boss started asking Kim's opinion on all the new orders. She acted like he'd made her manager.

Nikki liked all sweets equally—peanut butter taffy, lime green foil-wrapped "alien coins" with chocolate discs inside, gummy geckos and gummy sidewinders and a whole assortment of translucent gummy fruit, long strips of paper dotted with sugar dots, shining and jagged rock candy, hot-as-hell Atomic FireBalls, flat squares of violet candy that tasted like flowery chalk, giant multicolored spiral lollipops, not to mention chocolate-covered malt balls, chocolate-covered blueberries and raspberries and peanuts, and even tiny packages of chocolate-covered ants.

The pay was pretty much crap, but Nikki was allowed to eat as much candy as she wanted. She picked out a coffee toffee to start with because it seemed breakfast-y.

The boss's son came out of the stockroom, his sleeveless T-shirt thin enough that Nikki could see the hair that covered his back and chest through the cloth. He scowled at her. "Most girls get sick of the candy after a while," he said, in a tone that was half grudging admiration, half panic at the profits vanishing through her teeth.

Nikki paused in her consumption of a pile of sour gummy lizards, their hides crunchy with granules of sugar. "Sorry," she said.

That seemed to be the right answer, because he turned to Kim and told her to restock the pomegranate jelly beans.

Nikki's stomach growled. While his back was turned, she popped another lizard into her mouth.

It was pouring when Nikki finished her shift. Rain slicked her skin and plastered her hair to her neck as she waited for the bus in front of Macy's. By the time it finally came, she was soaked and even more convinced that her summer was doomed.

Nikki pushed her way into one of the few remaining seats, next to an old guy who smelled like a sulfurous fart. It took her a moment to realize he was the houndstooth suit-and-cane guy from the bus stop that morning. He'd probably been riding the bus this whole time. Still jittery from sugar, she could feel the headache-y start of a postcandy crash in her immediate future. Nikki tried to ignore the heavy wetness of her clothes and to breath as shallowly as possible to avoid the old guy's stink.

The bus lurched forward. A woman chatting on her cell phone stumbled into Nikki's knee.

"'Scuse me," the woman said sharply, as though Nikki was the one who fell.

"I'm going to give you what you want," the man next to her whispered. Weirdly, his breath was like honey.

Nikki didn't reply. Nice breath or not, he was still a stinky, senile old pervert.

"I'm talking to you, girl." He touched her arm.

She turned toward him. "You're not supposed to talk to people on buses."

His cheeks wrinkled as he smiled. "Is that so?"

"Yeah, trains, too. It's a mass-transportation thing. Anything stuffed with people, you're supposed to act like you're alone."

"Is that what you want?" he asked. "You want everyone to act like you're not here?"

"Pretty much. You going to give me what I want?" Nikki asked, hoping he would shut up. She wished she could just tell freakjobs to fuck off, but she hated that hurt look that they sometimes got. It made her think of Boo. She would put up with a lot to not see that look.

He nodded. "I sure am."

The 'scuse-me woman looked in their direction, blinked, then plopped her fat ass right on Nikki's lap. Nikki yelped, and the woman got up, red-faced.

"What are you doing there?" the 'scuse-me lady gasped.

The old pervert started laughing so hard that spit flew out of his mouth.

"Sitting," Nikki said. "What the hell are you doing?"

The woman turned away from Nikki, muttering to herself.

"You're very fortunate to be sitting next to me," the pervert said.

"How do you figure that?"

He laughed again, hard and long. "I gave you what you wanted. I'll give you the next thing you want, too." He winked a rheumy eye. "For a price."

"Whatever," Nikki muttered.

"You know where to find me."

Mercifully, the next stop was Nikki's. She shoved the 'scuse-me woman hard as she pushed her way off the bus.

～ ～ ～

Doug sat on the steps of the trailer, his hair frizzy with drizzle. He looked grim.

"What's going on?" Nikki asked. "Only managed to eat half your body weight?"

"Boo's been hit," he said, voice rough. "Trevor hit your dog."

For a moment, Nikki couldn't breathe. The world seemed to speed up around her, cars streaking along the highway, the wind tossing wet leaves across the lot.

She thought about the raven tattoo on Trevor's shoulder and wished someone would rip it off along with his skin. She wanted to tear him into a thousand pieces.

She thought about the old pervert on the bus.

I'll give you the next thing you want, too.

You know where to find me.

"Where's Boo now?" Nikki asked.

"At the vet. Mom wanted me to drive you over as soon as you got home."

"Why was he outside? Who let him out?"

"Mom came home with groceries. He slipped past her."

"Is he oka—?"

Doug shook his head. "They're waiting for you before they put him down. They wanted to give you a chance to say good-bye."

She wanted to throw up or scream or cry, but when she spoke, her voice sounded so calm that it unnerved her. "Why? Isn't there anything they can do?"

"Listen, the doctor said they could operate, but it's a couple thousand dollars and you know we can't afford it." Doug's voice was soft, like he was sorry, but she wanted to hit him anyway.

Nikki looked across the lot, but the truck wasn't in front of

Trevor's trailer and his windows were dark. "We could make Trevor pay."

Doug sighed. "Not going to happen."

Now she felt tears well in her eyes, but she blinked them back. She wouldn't grieve over Boo. She'd save him. "I'm not going anywhere with you."

"You have to, Nikki. Mom's waiting for you."

"Call her. Tell her I'll be there in an hour. I'm taking the bus." Nikki grabbed the sleeve of Doug's jacket, gripping it as hard as she could. "She better not do anything to Boo until I get there." Tears slid down her cheek. She ignored them, concentrating on looking as fierce as possible. "You better not either."

"Calm down. I'm not going to—" Doug said, but she was already walking away.

Nikki got on the next bus that stopped and scanned the aisles for the old pervert. A woman with two bags of groceries cradled to her chest looked up at Nikki, then abruptly turned away. A youngish man stretched out on the long backseat shifted in his sleep, his fingers curled tightly around a bottle of beer. Three men in green coveralls conversed softly in Spanish. There was no one else.

Nikki slid into her seat, wrapping her arms around her body as though she could hold in her sobs with sheer pressure. She had no idea what to do. Looking for a weird old guy who could grant wishes was pathetic. It was sad and stupid.

If there was some way to get the money, things might be different. She thought of all the stuff in the trailer that could be sold, but it didn't add up to a thousand dollars. Even sticking her hand into the till at the Sweet Tooth was unlikely to net more than a few hundred.

Outside the window, the strip malls and motels slid together in her tear-blurred vision. Nikki thought of the day she'd found Boo by the side of the road, dehydrated and bloody. With all those bite marks, she figured his owners had been fighting him against other dogs, but when he saw her he bounded up as dumb and sweet and trusting as if he'd been pampered since he was a puppy. If he died, nothing would ever be fair again.

The bus stopped in front of a churchyard, the doors opened, and the old guy got on. He wore a suit of shiny sharkskin and carried a cane with a silver greyhound instead of a knob. He still stank of rotten eggs, though. Worse than ever.

Nikki sat up straight, wiping her face with her sleeve. "Hey."

He looked over at her as though he didn't know her. "Excuse me?"

"I've been looking for you. I need your help."

Sitting down in the seat across the aisle, he unbuttoned the bottom button on his jacket. "That's magic to my ears."

"My dog." Nikki sank her fingernails into the flesh of her palm to keep herself calm. "Someone hit my dog and he's going to die . . ."

His face broke into a wrinkled grin. "And you want him to live. Like I've never heard that one before."

He was making fun of her, but she forced a smile. "So you'll do it."

He shook his head. "Nope."

"What do you mean? Why not?"

A long sigh escaped his lips, like he was already tired of the conversation. "Let's just say that it's not in my nature."

"What is that supposed to mean?"

He shifted the cane in his lap, and she noticed that what

she had thought of as a greyhound appeared to have three silver heads. He scowled at her, like a teacher when you missed an obvious answer and he knew you hadn't done the reading. "You have to give me something to get something."

"I've got forty bucks," she said, biting her lip. "I don't want to do any sex stuff."

"I am not entirely without sympathy." He shrugged his thin shoulders. "How about this—I will wager my services against something of yours. If you can beat me at any contest of your choosing, your dog will be well and you'll owe me nothing."

"Really? Any contest?" she asked.

He held out his hand. "Shake on it and we've got a deal."

His skin was warm and dry in her grip.

"So, what it going to be?" he asked. "You play the fiddle? Or maybe you'd like to try your hand at jump rope?"

She took a long look at him. He was slender, and his clothes hung on him a bit, as though he'd been bigger when he'd bought them. He didn't look like a big eater. "An eating contest," she said. "I'm wagering that I can eat more than you can."

He laughed so hard she thought for a moment he was having a seizure. "That's a new one. Fine. I'm all appetite."

His reaction made her nervous. "Wait—" she said. "You never told me what you wanted if I lost."

"Just a little thing. You won't miss it." He indicated the door of the bus with his cane. "Next stop is yours. I'll be by tomorrow. Don't worry about your dog for tonight."

She stood. "First tell me what I'm going to lose."

"You'll overreact," he said, shaking his head.

"I won't," Nikki said, but she wasn't sure what she would do. What could he want? She'd said "no sex," but he hadn't made any promises.

The old guy held out his hands in a conciliatory gesture. "Your soul."

"What? Why would you want that?"

"I'm a collector. I have to have the whole set—complete. All souls. They're going to look *spectacular* all lined up. There was a time when I was close, but then there were all these special releases and I got behind. And forget about having them mint-in-box. I have to settle for what I can get these days."

"You're joking."

"Maybe." He looked out the window, as if considering all those missing souls. "Don't worry. It's like an appendix. You won't even miss it."

Nikki walked home from the bus stop. Her stomach churned as she thought over the bargain she'd made. Her soul. The devil. She had just made a bargain with the devil. Who else wanted to buy souls?

She stomped into the trailer to see her mom on the couch, eating a piece of reheated pizza. Doug sat next to her, watching a car being rebuilt on television. Both of them looked tired.

"Oh, honey," her mother said. "I'm so sorry."

Nikki sat down on the shag rug. "You didn't kill Boo, did you?"

"The vet said that we could wait until tomorrow and see how he's doing, but he wasn't very encouraging." Long fingers stroked Nikki's hair, but she refused to be soothed. "You have to think what would be best for the poor dog. You don't want him to suffer."

Nikki jumped up and stalked over to the kitchen. "I don't want him to die!"

"Go talk to your sister," their mother said to Doug. Doug pushed himself up off the couch.

"Show me how to train for an eating contest," Nikki told him, when he tried to speak. "Show me right now."

He shook his head. "You're seriously losing it."

"Yeah," she said. "But I need to win."

The next morning, after her mother left for work, Nikki called herself out sick and started straightening up the place. After all, the devil was the most famous guest she'd ever had. She'd heard of him, and what was more, she was pretty sure he knew a lot of people she'd be impressed by.

He knocked on the door of the trailer around noon. Today, he wore a red double-breasted suit with a black shirt and tie. He carried a gnarled cane in a glossy brown, like polished walnut.

Seeing her looking at it, he smiled. "Bull penis. Not too many of these around anymore."

"You dress like a pimp," Nikki said before she thought better of it.

His smile just broadened.

"So are you *a* devil or *the* devil?" Nikki held the screen door open for him.

"I'm *a* devil to some." He winked as he walked past her. "But I'm *the* devil to you."

She shuddered. Suddenly, the idea of him being supernatural seemed entirely too real. "My brother's in the back, waiting for us."

Nikki had set up on the picnic table in the common area of the trailer park. She walked onto the hot concrete and the devil followed her. Doug looked up from where he carefully counted out portions of sour-gummy frogs onto paper plates. He looked like a giant, holding each tiny candy between two thick fingers.

Nikki brushed an earwig and some sour cherry splatter off a bench and sat down. "Doug's going to explain the rules."

The devil sat down across from her and leaned his cane against the table. "Good. I'm starving."

Doug stood up, wiping sweaty palms on his jeans. "This is what we're going to do. We have a bag of one hundred sixty-six sour-gummy frogs. That's all we could get. I divided them into sixteen plates of ten and two plates of three, so you each have a maximum of eighty-three frogs. If you both eat the same number of frogs, whoever finishes their frogs first wins. If you have a . . . er . . . reversal of fortune, then you lose, period."

"He means if you puke," Nikki said.

Doug gave her a stern look but didn't say anything.

"We need not be limited by your supply," said the devil. A huge tarnished silver platter appeared on the table. It scuttled over to Nikki on chicken feet, and she saw that it was heaped with sugar-studded frogs.

The candy on the paper plates looked dull in comparison with what glimmered on the table. Nikki picked up an orange-and-black gummy candy poison dart frog and put it regretfully down. It just seemed dumb to let the devil supply the food. "You have to use ours."

The devil shrugged. With a wave of his hand, the dish of frogs disappeared, leaving nothing behind but a burnt-sugar smell. "Very well."

Doug put a plastic pitcher of water and two glasses between them. "Okay," he said, lifting up a stopwatch. "Go!"

Nikki started eating. The salty-sweet flavor flooded her mouth as she crammed in candy.

Across the table, the devil lifted up his first paper plate, rolling it up and using the tube to pour frogs into a mouth that seemed to expand. His jaw unhinged like a snake's. He picked up a second plate.

Nikki swallowed frog after frog, ignoring the cloying sweetness, racing to catch up.

Doug slid a new pile in front of Nikki, and she started eating. She was in the zone. One frog, then another, then a sip of water. The sugar scraped her throat raw, but she kept eating.

The devil poured a third plate of candy down his throat, then a fourth. At the seventh plate, the devil paused with a groan. He untucked his shirt and undid the button on his dress pants to pat his engorged belly. He looked full.

Nikki stuffed candy in her mouth, suddenly filled with hope.

The devil chuckled and unsheathed a knife from the top of his cane.

"What are you doing?" Doug shouted.

"Just making room," the devil said. Pressing the blade to his belly, he slit a line in his stomach. Dozens upon dozens of gooey half-chewed frogs tumbled into the dirt.

Nikki stared at him, paralyzed with dread. Her fingers still held a frog, but she didn't bring it to her lips. She had no hope of winning.

Doug looked away from the mess of partially digested candy. "That's cheating!"

The devil tipped up the seventh plate into his widening mouth and swallowed ten frogs at once. "Nothing in the rules against it."

Nikki wondered what it would be like to have no soul. Would she barely miss it? Could she still dream? Without one, would she have no more guilt or fear or fun? Maybe without a soul she wouldn't even care that Boo was dead.

The devil cheated. If she wanted to win, she had to cheat, too.

On her sixth plate, Nikki started sweating, but she knew she could finish. She just couldn't finish before he did.

She had to beat him in quantity. She had to eat more sour gummy frogs than he did.

"I feel sick," Nikki lied.

"Don't *you know*." Doug shook his head vigorously. "Fight it."

Nikki bent over, holding her stomach. While hidden by the table, she picked up one of the slimy, chewed-up frogs that had been in the devil's stomach and popped it into her mouth. The frog tasted like sweetness and dirt and something rotten.

The nausea was real this time. She choked and forced herself to swallow around the sour taste of her own gorge.

Sitting up, she saw that the devil had finished all his frogs. She still had two more plates to go.

"I win," the devil said. "No need to keep eating."

Doug sunk fingers into his hair and tugged. "He's right."

"No way." Nikki gulped down another mouthful of candy. "I'm finishing my plates."

She ate and ate, ignoring how the rubbery frogs stuck in her throat. She kept eating. Swallowing the last sour-gummy frog, she stood up. "Are you finished?"

"I've been finished for ages," said the devil.

"Then *I* win."

The devil yawned. "Impossible."

"I ate one more frog than you did," she said. "So I win."

He pointed his cane at Doug. "If you cheated and gave her another frog, we'll be doing this contest over and you'll be joining us."

Doug shook his head. "It took me an hour to count out those frogs. They were exactly even."

"I ate one of the frogs from your gut," Nikki said. "I picked it up off the ground and I ate it."

"That's disgusting!" Doug said.

"Five-second rule," Nikki said. "If it's in the devil for less than five seconds, it's still good."

"That's *cheating*," said the devil. He sounded half-admiring and half-appalled, reminding her bizarrely of her boss's son at the Sweet Tooth.

She shook her head. "Nothing in the rules against it."

The devil scowled for a moment, then bowed shallowly. "Well done, Nicole. Count on seeing me again soon." With those words, he ambled toward the bus station. Pausing in front of Trevor's trailer, he pulled out a handful of envelopes from the mailbox and kept going.

Nikki's mother's car pulled into the lot, Boo's head visible in the passenger-side window. His tongue lolled despite the absurd cone-shaped collar around his neck.

Nikki hopped up on top of the picnic table and shrieked with joy, leaping around, the sugar and adrenaline and relief making her giddy.

She stopped jumping. "You know what?"

Doug looked up at her. "What?"

"I think my summer is starting not to suck so much."

Doug sat down on a bench so hard that she heard the wood strain. The look he gave her was pure disbelief.

"So," Nikki asked, "you want to get some lunch?"

HOLLY BLACK is the author of *Tithe: A Modern Faerie Tale*; *Valiant: A Modern Tale of Faerie*, which was the recipient of the Andre Norton Award; and *Ironside: A Modern Faery's Tale*. She collaborated with Tony DiTerlizzi to create the internationally best-selling *Spiderwick Chronicles*. She is currently working with Ted Naifeh on a graphic novel entitled *Good Neighbors*. You can visit her at www.blackholly.com.

～

AUTHOR'S NOTE

One of the most recognized trickster figures around is the devil. In folklore, the devil's attempts to steal souls often involves humorous and impossible contests. I watched the Glutton Bowl this past Thanksgiving and was captivated by the absurdity of competitive eating. More research revealed fascinating details, like the controversial belief that skinnier contestants have a strategic advantage, due to the "belt of fat" that prevents a stomach from expanding and the taboo around the word *puke*. I wondered how the devil would cheat at such a contest and wound up writing "A Reversal of Fortune."

GOD CLOWN

~

Carol Emshwiller

Mud slides, landslides, earthquakes . . . We know what Great God Clown does. We hear him laughing right in the middle of doing it. Sometimes he sounds just like a donkey.

He loves the desert. We all do. It's an acquired taste, and we all acquired it. At first the desert scared us but now it's Great God Clown that scares.

Last year crops dried up. All the grapes turned to raisins on the vine. This year it's the opposite. Water runs right into the house even though I dug a ditch in front of the door.

Abby's house slid down. Skidded right across the road. It now sits on Ramsey's property. We propped it up so it didn't slant and it's good as new, but Ramsey may not like it when he finds out it's at his place. It's in a grove of trees. A pretty spot. Much nicer than where it used to be. The stream is nearby. I hope Ramsey lets it stay.

We think something should have happened to Ramsey's place but nothing did. It's not even off-kilter. That's not fair. Abby is much nicer than Ramsey. She saves animals and hands out food to whoever or whatever needs it. I don't know how many cats she has. Though only one dog. Even the dog loves cats. Abby'd save a bug if she could. I've seen her pick up beetles and take them outside where they belong. I don't think she ever squashes anything.

And she saved me. That was a long time ago. I didn't know she was that type when I came, I just went where I saw cats and the dog. I could tell the dog wouldn't hurt me. He's like Abby. Or maybe he knows the difference between a robber and a visitor. Except I *was* a robber. I came there to rob.

Nobody was home and I knew it. I'd walked all the way from Middle Fork. It was a hot day. First I stopped at the spigot in the front yard for a drink and to fill my water bottle. Then I knocked on the door and called, though I knew there was nobody home. I walked all around the house. I petted the dog. I petted the cats. Some of them. I tried to count them but I couldn't. I told them all that I was only going to steal some food and a drink, then I broke a window and crawled in. I made myself a peanut butter sandwich. I was a kid and that's what I liked best. Abby only had one good chair. I sat in it in the tiny living room, cats on my lap, as I ate.

Abby's rickety pickup drove in just as I was climbing back out. I heard her coming a long way off. If I hadn't stopped to steal another piece of bread for later I'd have made it out and away before she got back.

All the donkeys with eel stripes and striped socks belong to Great God Clown. In the yard there was just such a one. Also one goat, one sheep, and a nasty rooster.

Great God C.—just when you think all's well, he'll trip you up. I don't know what he wants. Mostly to laugh—at the way we try to eke out a living in among all these stones and on the slopes too steep for planting. He sends our terraces down whenever he feels like it.

Abby didn't say a word when she saw me. I was stuck, one leg on one side of the windowsill and one leg on the other, bread in one fist, water bottle in the other. No wonder I fell out and squashed her marigolds.

She looked at me hard and then turned around and grabbed two bundles of groceries, came over and handed them to me—can you believe it? Me with my bread and water bottle?—and went back to the truck for more. We took them inside. (The door had been unlocked all along. Now that I know her I know she never locks anything.)

She went ahead and put things away. I could have run away right then, but I just stood there.

Abby is a small, skinny person. Even back then I was bigger than she is, and yet she scared me. I didn't dare move.

Finally, after everything was put away, she turned and stared me up and down. I was dusty from the long walk. I hadn't even combed my hair when I left home four days ago. My top was my nightgown, tucked into my brother's worn-out work pants, but she knew I was a girl right away, though some along the way had called me Boy and Sonny.

Her very first words to me were, "How'd you like a bath?"

She didn't even ask me what my name was or tell me hers. I don't think she cares much about names. I'll bet she thinks: do ravens have names? Hummingbirds? Jackrabbits? And what about all these cats? And I suppose she didn't care what name I gave her.

But names are useful. Afterward she told me hers was Abby.

~ ~ ~

I've seen God Clown. I really have. (I don't lie, now that I've been with Abby. Lots of people do though. Many say they've seen him but haven't.) But you spend your life in the hills, you see things. He doesn't like to be seen. One of these days I'll be washed over the side of a terrace myself, or come down in a big sweep of scree or snow. Those are his favorite ways.

I'll bet Abby's seen him. I'll bet more than once.

And so I took a bath, and Abby gave me one of her loose men's shirts to wear after. I was too big to fit her jeans or T-shirts. And while I took a bath she washed out my nightgown and my brother's pants. After that we went out and fed every creature for half a mile around, and after that we fed ourselves.

Even though I'd had a big sandwich, I was still hungry enough to eat lots of split pea soup.

I slept on a pad on the floor in her living room and was happy for it. In fact I slept better than I had since I left. I felt safe with Abby, even with the door unlocked.

We didn't talk much until next morning at breakfast. Actually, not so much even then. First we went out for eggs and thanked the chickens—every single one. Then we sat down to scrambled eggs with cheese.

"So," she said, "do you want to tell me how you got those bruises?"

I thought they didn't show much. And after all it had been four days and most were where you couldn't see. Maybe she watched me as I took a bath. I wouldn't put it past her. I wouldn't put anything past her.

I couldn't answer.

"Look here," she said, and lifted her T-shirt to show me her back. "I had that same problem, but a long time ago. That's all over with. Maybe yours is, too."

I couldn't answer—even more. Or, rather, even less.

It was a black T-shirt and had a picture of mountains on the front and under them it said GET LOST. I wondered if she wore it to tell me what to do next. Now that I know her I know she wouldn't say that. Yesterday she was wearing one that had a book and under it was written READ SLOWLY. In a way I know she meant them both.

(Later on I *did* get lost in the mountains, but on purpose.)

"Well," she said, "it's not that hard to guess. Your dad or who?"

So then I said, "My dad's dead."

"So it's got to be a who."

But that was all I could say. And Abby said, "I don't need to know. Besides that's three towns back." (I'd already told her I'd walked four days.) Then she said, "Let's get to work." And so we did, and afterward we went to town and got me some jeans and T-shirts of my own. Abby said I'd already earned them with my work and I could do more work tomorrow if I felt the need to earn more.

I said I wanted boys' T-shirts because they had pockets, but I really wanted boys' because they were boys'. And I still did like wearing my brother's old worn-out work pants.

I didn't have breasts yet and I didn't want them. Back then I thought maybe I'd be lucky and that would never happen.

I never did tell her who did it—all those bruises. I mean it's not a unique story that has to be told over and over in slightly different ways and with different people. Abby'd be the first to say that, especially since she had whip marks on her back and wasn't about to ever tell me how she got them.

Of course there wasn't room for me to stay with Abby very long. All she has is one room with a sleeping alcove for herself. She didn't say anything—she never would—but I could tell it was hard for her. First I lived in a house of thatch . . . *all* thatch . . . that we made for me out in back of hers, and later I moved way up above everybody else. Onto the steep places where they bring their goats sometimes.

Talk about an off-kilter house! Mine was that way the minute we nailed it up.

I was happy all the time out here . . . every single minute. Not like home. I did a lot of work for everybody, even Ramsey sometimes. I got me my own cat. I had me a sheltering boulder and a pretty good tree.

I learned how to grow things, take care of animals, and avoid roosters. (Not a one of us, including Abby, who wasn't afraid of them.) And I did get breasts after a while in spite of myself.

But I don't like how things are going in our valley these days. Ramsey (of course) made Abby move back to her little spot that's a long ways from the stream. (Not that she hasn't a pretty good ditch.) He even tried to get her to pay rent for the two weeks she spent on his land before she could get her house dragged back.

And now these last things, rattlesnakes all over this year, people's dogs dead, houses full of stinkbugs, Ramsey being Ramseyish.

Abby's too old for this kind of aggravation. Not that she would ever tell anybody how old she is. She says your age is in how hard it is to hop around, whether you can still repair the roof without falling off, and whether you can see the leaves at the tops of trees. "And," she says, "I'm getting to that age."

And this, now, is the last straw. My own house slid right on down—*all* the way down in the middle of the night . . . That wouldn't be so bad if it hadn't landed on top of Abby's. She heard me coming, sprained her wrist rescuing her new puppy. It was hard enough for her, getting around before, and *now* look.

Her house is okay, but mine is a mess. We—Abby, even with her bad wrist, and a couple of her neighbors—dragged it back up, piece by piece, and propped it against my boulder, but I spent the night with Abby. Helped her feed everything. Helped her cook a stew. We thanked the vegetables.

The very next morning a hailstorm ruins everybody's gardens. Talk about last straws! This has got to stop. I say, "Abby, we have to do something. Have things ever been this bad?" And she says, "This is the way it is. Sometimes worse and sometimes better." And I say, "I don't think so."

And yet another bad thing: Now the neighbors warn me that Ramsey found out where I used to live and told them I was here. My stepfather's going to come and get me once he gets the truck working. Wouldn't it be nice if Great God Clown would have something happen to the truck on the way here? Like all of a sudden too much water in the ford or another mud slide down by the forks?

Sometimes I think to go on up to meet him—God Clown, I mean. He's got to be pretty old by now, and maybe even meaner and more crotchety than ever. It sure seems so.

Abby would go, I bet, if she still could. She'd take him a present. Food most likely. Or a kitten. Though what would he do with a kitten? Considering what's been happening, a rooster would be more fitting, and Abby's got a nasty one she could well do without.

I'll do it. Bring gingerbread and the rooster. Enough lemonade for both of us. God Clown and me, I mean. I won't tell Abby. She might worry.

I take the hardest, least-used path, the one that goes straight up. In spots it's almost gone altogether. Trust him to have a path just exactly like this, all rocks and ruts. Some places I have to crawl. Some places are completely washed out. Where else could it lead except to him?

I didn't bring enough food, so I eat some of the gingerbread. I drink half the lemonade and then water it down from the stream. Maybe Great God Clown won't notice. It's still pretty good, even if weak.

A couple of times I think I'm lost, but I always take the worst and least used trail. It's got to be the right way.

It's afternoon before I get anywhere that seems like anyplace at all—a ledge and not much of a cave behind it, but all the more reason this has got to be his.

My legs are shaky. I'm used to climbing, but not so far, so fast, and so steep. I flop down, but the ledge is kind of scary—narrow and a drop-off on two sides—so I go on in.

After all that sunshine I can't see very well in here. Everything gleams of mica and fool's gold. (Of course!)

~ ~ ~

All things with glitter and with stripes or spots belong to Great God Clown. Also horned toads, owls that shriek in the middle of the night, sidewinders because of how they move . . .

There's just about room in here for three or four friendly people to lie down. I sit. I treat myself to more of his lemonade. I think of what to say.

Pretty soon I can see a little better.

His glinting eyes. Just like the fool's gold.

He has a permanent smile. Like a clown has. Well, of course he does.

I knew he'd look odd, but I didn't think he'd look like this: a little the color of granite, a little the color of a rooster. And much smaller than I thought. I thought he'd have to be big to do all the things he does. Of course I could probably start a landslide myself. Even Abby could.

"You're an old man. How do you do it? All these disasters? And you look as if you need your sleep."

"Mmmm."

I don't scold. After I get a good look at him . . . well, not that good a look . . . I realize scolding isn't what's needed.

"You don't do it for fun, do you. Even though you smile. Even though you laugh."

"Mmmm."

"This place is so hard to find. You let me find you, didn't you?"

"Mmm-mmm."

An mmm that sounds like a maybe.

Then I think about how Abby has never said a single word against him no matter what happened.

I tell him everything I practiced up to say. I tell him Ramsey has four big dogs that roam all over and scare people. I say Ramsey has a house bigger than he needs for just one messy man. I tell him Ramsey found out where I used to live and told them I was here and I may have to go back home. I say Ramsey still thinks I'm a boy even though I have breasts. I guess he never looks at me closely and never wonders why I never grow up from being a boy.

Great God Clown doesn't answer anything a rooster wouldn't have answered.

Then I ask him . . . just as if I had three wishes, which of course I don't . . . I say: number one, I wish that Abby should have the life she deserves. Doesn't he know her by now? Doesn't he care? Number two, there's . . . well, there's me. I don't want to have to go back where I got beat up just about once a week no matter what I did. There's no number three. I say, "Maybe I can work out some tit for tat. I can bring you things. I can help."

There's thunder and a sprinkling of rain outside, but it doesn't bother us. The sun is still shining, coming under the clouds. If I tip my head sideways, I can see a little bit of a rainbow.

Great God Clown is quiet for so long I know something's going to happen. There's just too much silence for too long a time.

Then he says, "You do it."

"What?"

"You. You do it. But no cruelty. Just what's needed. There's no going back, you know. You can't."

"You don't do it for fun, do you?"

"It's a necessity. Just keep things the way they have to

be. The mountain trickling down. Trees blowing over. Boulders crashing off cliffs. Sometimes right on top of things. On people. It has to be."

Great God Clown is just like Abby. He says exactly what she always says: "This is the way it is, sometimes worse, sometimes better."

I see now how it's all inevitable. Slides and such. Hail. Droughts. Everything is exactly as it's supposed to be. I say, "It'll be a hard job."

"That's the way it is."

All the lemonade is gone by now and most of the gingerbread (he liked it), but he tells me I won't need much. He says, "There's moss and miner's lettuce . . . Solomon's seal. Elderberries this time of year. They're good just plain. You'll have the weather to keep you company. And stars."

"I'll do the best I can."

He's hopping to the front of his cave. Cawing, cackling. Quack, quack, quack. Off he goes, happy as could be. I can't imagine where. Where could he go?

I yell out a thanks for me not having to go home. At least I got that wish.

Actually I never did get a good look at him. The rooster was always in the way, and the fool's gold glittered so. Mostly I was watching the clouds outside his doorway, backlit by lightning. I saw the rain stop. I saw the rainbow over the top of a mountain. I saw a hawk fly by.

There's no such thing as luck or hope. Things are as they have to be. There's nothing but Great God Clown sitting up here deciding who gets what, all the way down to marmots and spiders. But now it's me, having to do what has to be done to keep it like it is. You can't be mean about it. And you have to be spry and clever and sly and quick. You have to smile. *Have to!* That's the main thing. It's all one big joke.

I sneak back once in a while and, funny thing, I think I see him right in Abby's yard. She's put out a lawn chair and there he sits in a big floppy hat. Or somebody just like him. Imagine that, both of them!

Two sides of the same thing. I should have known because she never said a word against him.

CAROL EMSHWILLER has won a Nebula for her story "Creature" and also for her story "I Live with You." She has a Lifetime Achievement award from the World Fantasy Convention.

She has received a National Endowment for the Arts grant and two New York State grants. Her short fiction has appeared in many literary and science fiction magazines. Her most recent books are the novel *The Secret City* and the collection *I Live with You.*

Carol Emshwiller grew up in Michigan and in France and currently divides her time between New York and California. Her Web site is www.sfwa.org/members/emshwiller.

～

AUTHOR'S NOTE

I wrote this because Ellen asked for trickster stories. But I can never write "on demand." I tried, though, and got about two pages and then got stuck. It just wouldn't move. I put it aside and thought I'd never come back to it, but this spring I took it out and looked at it. I guess it had "ripened" or maybe "festered" enough to begin to move.

I didn't write it for any other reason than that Ellen suggested it. I can't think of anything that might have influenced it. Well, yes, when I was writing my historical western *Ledoyt,* I put in the word *trickster,* but the editor said that word wasn't used till much later by anthropologists, but I knew there was Coyote. For *Ledoyt,* I changed the word trickster to Great God Clown. So I thought of those words right away for this story.

Of course . . . *of course,* it takes place in my beloved mountains. I try to get them in whenever I can.

THE OTHER LABYRINTH

Jedediah Berry

THE MAZE OF WHITE ROSES

He would hack through them with his sword were they not so beautiful. The thorns and snowy blossoms, still dripping last night's rain, cover every inch of the trellis walls, and the walls are high. The odor alone is enough to get lost in.

But Jacques Cordon, emissary of the Marquise, is no stranger to secret passages and winding roads. He has parleyed with princes and kings, and spied on them, too. He is never late, and he never loses his way. Not even, he tells himself, while the guest of the labyrinth builder.

The night before, *le labyringénieur* had shown him to a low-ceilinged room at the rear of the château, and left him there with no wood for the fireplace, no oil for the lamp. The mattress was hard and the blanket thin. Jacques slept fitfully, and when dawn came he flung himself from bed and dressed quickly, hoping, at least, for a warm breakfast. Instead he found that his door had been locked from the outside. He threw his weight against it, but the door held fast; he shouted but his cries were ignored. Jacques's only escape, he saw, was through the window and into the château gardens. He climbed onto a chair and hoisted himself over the sill, tearing his shirt on the latch before tumbling to the stone path below.

No mundane gardens, these, but a tortuous puzzle-place, as beautiful as it is confounding. The morning fog has yet to lift, and he can see no farther than ten paces in front of him. Roses, everywhere white roses—if only some were red, or pink, he might know one place from another. Jacques counts his steps, trying to envision a map, but the curving paths form a jumble in his mind.

Before him is an archway wound with thorny vines. Beyond it, a set of stairs leads down. Only the way is narrower than it looks and—*nom de nom!*—he draws his right hand to his mouth, tasting the blood where the rose kissed it.

THE MAZE OF STATUES

They are thirteen in number, and an unlucky bunch they are, trapped forever in this lonely courtyard, carved from the same gray stone as the walls that enclose them. Here a young rascal leans against a column, here a beggar child sits in the shade of a chestnut tree, here two gentlemen stand nose to nose, lifting their hats in eternal greeting. Each statue stands (or sits, or reclines) with one arm raised, pointing the way to go. Which would be helpful, if not for the fact that each points in a different direction. There are as many doors from the courtyard as there are statues within it.

Jacques descends into their midst, searching the moss-spotted faces for some clue. He pauses before the statue of a tall, thin-faced man, peering through spectacles at a book held open in one hand. This is the very likeness of Monsieur Brumeux, the labyrinth builder.

～ ～ ～

The Marquise had warned Jacques of Brumeux's peculiarities: "He is eccentric but not extravagant, aloof yet shrewd, and stubbornly fickle. He will probably break your spirit." She had smiled, then, and Jacques knew that his visit to the labyrinth builder was only a sliver of the suffering she had devised for him.

When Jacques went into the private study at the heart of Brumeux's drafty château, his host did not even look up from the intricate sketch he was working on. "You are early," he said.

"I am always early," Jacques replied with a bow, "for the interests of the Marquise brook no delay."

"Then stop wasting time and tell me what the Marquise wants. Her letter was typically vague."·

What the Marquise wanted was a labyrinth. The greatest, most perilous labyrinth ever built. And only Brumeux could design it.

But Brumeux refused.

"She will pay you handsomely," Jacques said. In fact, the Marquise had sent with him a pouch bulging with silver, and that was only a down payment.

"I do not envy you your position," said the labyrinth builder, ignoring him. "The Marquise will not be pleased to learn that her chosen emissary, with his treasure and his honeyed tongue, could do nothing to budge a stubborn old man. Or did she call me worse things?"

Jacques could think of no proper way to reply, and was silent.

"You will stay here tonight," Brumeux went on. "The lateness of the hour and the coming storm leave us no choice in the matter. I have business to attend to tomorrow, and must depart at sunset. If you come to me before that time, I will take it to mean that you have not abandoned your hopeless cause. By then I may have reconsidered, but most likely I will belittle you and send you on your way."

All this, Jacques now believes, is a test. Escape before Brumeux leaves at sunset and the Marquise will have her labyrinth. And if he fails? That possibility Jacques does not wish to ponder, not here, alone among these people of cold stone.

He will not take the door to which the statue of Brumeux is pointing—that way he cannot trust. But which, then? The scowling bishop's, which the bishop himself seems ready to march through? Or the door favored by the skinny girl with short-cropped hair? At the courtyard's center is a great iron sundial, its shadow sharp-edged in the midmorning light. Whichever way Jacques chooses, he must choose quickly.

Standing apart from the others is a statue of a young woman, nothing in her hands, no hint of who or what she is, no indication of her thoughts except the smile on her lips, sad, even a little unsure. But Jacques knows her, and knows her smile. It is Arienne, the Marquise's daughter.

Had the sculptor seen her? Had she modeled for him, that the likeness could be so precise, down to the faint wrinkle on her always-worrying brow? She had never spoken of it. But even from Jacques the Marquise's daughter no doubt has secrets.

Her door is his. He opens it and steps through.

THE MAZE OF TEN THOUSAND STAIRS

How his legs ache, first from the day-long ride across the moors to Château Brumeux, now from this infernal contrivance. No sooner has he climbed one flight than he must descend another. And at the bottom of the stairs a dead end, and so back up again.

In a place from which no stairs lead downward, only up, a cool fountain burbles. And lapping water from the rippling pool is a small dog, white with apricot patches. It perks its ears and looks at him with eyes so large Jacques can almost hear them blink.

"So," he says to the dog, "which way from here?"

Blink.

"You're going to be a lot of help, aren't you?"

Blink, blink.

Jacques cups water to his lips, then splashes some onto his face while the dog watches.

Arienne used to tell him stories like this place, stories that looped and forked and turned upon themselves. At night, after taking the secret passage to her chambers, he would lie sideways over her bed while she sat on the pillows, brushing her black hair as she told her tales. And always, at the decisive moment, she would make him choose what happened next.

If he guessed right, he thought, maybe she would sit closer to him. But she never seemed pleased with his choices, and eventually he refused to make them at all.

"Well?" he would ask. "Did the knight take the gold back to the king, or did he save the lady from the ogre-prince instead?"

"What do you think he did?"

"It's your story. It doesn't matter what I think!"

"Then you may leave my bedroom," she would tell him, and not speak to him all the next day, not even when her mother wasn't watching.

Yes, he thinks, this place is like those stories, and just as vexing. But nothing like the other labyrinth, the one the Marquise will build if she has her way. For that labyrinth will take the shape of her vengeance, forgiving nothing.

Jacques chooses a staircase he thinks he hasn't climbed before, and the dog follows him as best it can.

THE PEBBLE MAZE

If the rest of the labyrinth is a riddle, then this can only be a joke.

The paths, apparently well worn, circle one another like the rings of a felled tree. But all that separates one path from the next is a line of small white stones, piled no higher than the top of Jacques's boot. For a rat this might pose a challenge, but Jacques could walk straight across the maze to its exit on the opposite side.

He looks back the way he has come. The labyrinth builder's château is crouched in a hollow between two ancient willows. Its most striking feature is a tall, round tower atop the east wing. Wherever Jacques goes in the labyrinth, the highest window of that tower seems always visible. Brumeux could be up there, watching his every move through a telescope, and chuckling to himself.

So Jacques decides to walk the paths of this maze, just in case. The dog must think him mad, to go a hundred paces in one direction, then loop back a hundred more to a spot one step away from where he began. But the dog follows nonetheless.

An hour or more has passed by the time Jacques reaches the exit. There, he is greeted by a wooden signpost. It reads, MORE THE FOOL.

The dog sniffs the base of the post, then raises a leg to pee on it. Jacques glances at the tower. Monsieur *le labyringénieur*, he thinks, I will beat you yet. Then he loosens his belt and, with his back to the tower, he does as his companion did.

THE CANAL MAZE

Between high walls of granite, the waterways are black and deep. The dog sits at the prow of the rowboat, and Jacques sings as he paddles: "Little dog, little dog, will you come with me, over the sea?"

In the other labyrinth, the Marquise's labyrinth, these canals would be filled with poisonous snakes. All the walls would be topped with spikes. How Jacques dreads the place—all the more terrible, perhaps, because for now it is a dream-form, a place of the mind. When he hesitated to accept her assignment, the Marquise had thrust the purse of silver into his hands. "Do this for me," she had said. "And if you fail, I'll have you hunted down like the dog that you are."

The oar feels heavy in Jacques's hands. It is as though the dark waters are trying to drag it down, and him with it.

"Will you always serve my mother?" Arienne had asked him. That was the night before the Marquise discovered them, peering into her daughter's bedroom from a secret passage that not even Jacques had known.

"I am nobody if I do not serve her," he said, and he thought but did not say: just the scullery boy you used to pick on when we were small.

"I cannot love you while you serve her," Arienne said. And that night she did not even bother starting one of her stories.

The boat has reached an impasse. Blocked every way but back, its sides knock against the canal walls. Jacques sits with the oar balanced over his knees and shivers in the dark between the high granite barricades.

The dog barks at him, twice.

"Very well, *Capitaine*," Jacques says, and pushes off with the oar. Backward they drift, until the current takes them again.

THE MAZE OF GLASS

The sun is past its zenith now. If these walls could cast shadows, then the shadows would be lengthening.

THE OBELISK MAZE

In the other labyrinth, the labyrinth of the Marquise's jealousy, there would be only one place that might be called pleasant. Beyond all the treacherous ways, the lonesome trails and deadly traps, there at the labyrinth's center would be a green hill, and on the hill a vegetable garden, and in the middle of the garden a cottage, cozy and warm, with a door that opens to the east. The hearth is broad but the bed in the cottage is narrow. The bed is for Arienne, and that is where the Marquise will keep her.

All because Jacques loves her, and because she might love him if he did not serve the Marquise.

In this labyrinth, the one in which Jacques now wanders without a strategy to guide him, the tall stone spires look like the headstones of giants, and he steps softly as he goes, fearing to wake them. If he cannot navigate this labyrinth, how might he fare against the other one, the one built especially to keep him out?

"Zut!"

Before Jacques can see where the voice is coming from,

the dog runs off ahead of him, yelping. A big-bellied man steps from behind an obelisk and kneels as the dog draws close. He wears a tricorne hat over a wisp of white hair. "Zut," he says again. "I thought I'd lost you for good this time!"

Jacques waits before interrupting the reunion, then asks, "His name is Zut?"

The man gets to his feet, still grinning. "Say any word often enough, and a dog will have it as its name."

"Do you have business with the labyrinth builder as well?"

"Yes, of the daily sort." He pulls aside his coat to reveal a row of dirt-encrusted tools hung from his belt: a trowel, a claw, hedge clippers. "I'm his gardener."

"Then you must know the way out," says Jacques eagerly.

The gardener looks around, shading his eyes with one hand. "Brumeux did not hire me for my sense of direction, young sir. Still, better lost than lost and alone."

The three of them set off together. Between the obelisks are rows of hedges, and the gardener talks about them, about their likes and dislikes. Some plants, he insists, are prone to nightmares—regular pruning helps them sleep. Others get lonely and droop if he forgets to talk to them.

On a broad iron bench the gardener sits with a sigh. He takes off his hat and sets it beside him. Zut leaps onto the bench and then into the hat: a perfect fit.

Jacques says, "I really don't have time to rest."

"You must be here for a labyrinth of your own, then."

"Yes," says Jacques, not wishing to explain.

"They're a trifle overrated, if you ask me. Give me a nice vegetable patch any day."

Jacques glances at the sun. It is low in the sky now, nearly touching the top of Brumeux's tower. "I agree," Jacques says.

"And what do you want in your labyrinth?"

"Nothing. I don't want to talk about it."

The gardener purses his lips a moment, then says, "I see. I'm just the gardener, after all."

"No, you don't understand."

"Of course I don't." He nudges Zut out of his hat and gets to his feet, then draws a bundle out of his coat. Inside is a small loaf of bread, two pears, some cheese. "I thought we might sit down for lunch, but we can eat while we walk, since it's so important."

"Sit," he says to Zut, but Zut is already sitting, and the gardener gives him a bit of cheese.

THE MAZE OF COVERED BRIDGES

The gardener spits out a pear seed and says, "The only thing I really don't understand, though I've lived a long time, and am nearer to my death than a toad to its shadow—the only thing that has always eluded me is love."

THE MAZE OF SLOPING TUNNELS

"Love is the same as being lost," says Jacques to the dark. "Except you don't care that you're lost."

THE MAZE OF ONE-WAY DOORS

He should have done things differently. He should have said to the Marquise, "I am nothing so long as I serve you," then gone to Arienne, taken her along whatever secret routes were left to them, and escaped her mother forever. But instead he came here, to build his love a prison.

He goes through a door; it slams shut and locks behind him. He goes through another.

"This is my least favorite part of the labyrinth," the gardener says. *Bang, click.* "It gives me a headache."

"Yes," says Jacques. "I hated them at first, but now I would rather be back among the white roses."

"You saw my roses?"

"They were masterpieces, each one."

The gardener hums to himself with pleasure. Then he says, "If only we had some way to mark the doors we've already taken."

"Crumbs of bread?"

"All gone. What is that jingling sound?"

"My purse," Jacques says.

"Use the coins, then."

Jacques protectively covers the pouch with his hand. That would make for a costly trail, to mark it with silver. But then, what better use could the coins have here? He drops one at each door they choose, and in this way they come to a corridor, longer than all the others, two final doors at its end.

The gardener puts a hand on Jacques's shoulder. "Wait," he says. "I know where we are." He spins in a slow circle, then points to one of the doors. "There," he says. "That is the way out."

Jacques runs to the door and opens it.

"No," says the gardener, "not that one!"

But it is too late—the door is shut behind him.

"Stay where you are," Jacques calls, "I'll circle around and find you." But as he opens doors he hears other doors opening and closing as well.

"Stay put a moment!" the gardener shouts.

Jacques moves in the direction of the voice, yet when the gardener speaks he seems always farther away. "You go on without me," he hears the gardener say. "I'll just use my map."

His map?!

Now Jacques can hear nothing but the doors he himself opens. There is barking in the distance, and then silence.

The gardener was right: better lost than lost and alone.

THE MAZE OF FALSE MIRRORS

Jacques Cordon never loses his way, except when there are dozens of him—some short, some tall, some skinny, some fat—all headed in different directions at once. He walks a while, then panics, runs, bounces off his own reflection. A dozen Jacques Cordons sit on the ground. Their noses are bleeding.

He is still pinching his nostrils shut when he comes to a broad chamber, seven mirrors mounted on its walls. Resting on a pedestal is a hammer.

In one mirror he is small, a scullery boy wearing an emissary's cloak and sword. In another he is blurry, as though standing in a fog. In yet another his shoulders are broad, his arms thick, his jaw muscular and confident. He stands before that mirror for some time.

But one mirror shows him as he is: handsome but not too much so, weary, scared, and very much alone. Jacques takes up the hammer and smashes the glass, then steps into the corridor beyond.

He has come to the exit of the labyrinth. Beyond the open gateway is a wide lake, and at its edge a boathouse. A path leads from there up the hill to Château Brumeux. But Jacques does not takes this path. He waits just inside the labyrinth's walls, watching the sunset.

The sun turns the lake red for a moment and is gone. Fire-flies whirl at the water's edge. One of them is enormous—no, not a firefly, but a lantern, bobbing toward him. Monsieur Brumeux's spectacles flash in the firelight. He stands outside the gate, peering in at Jacques, his nose wrinkled in confusion, or disdain.

Jacques says, "I thought you had business to attend to."

"I do," the labyrinth builder says. "Here. With you, at this time."

"I am withdrawing my request. The Marquise shall not have her labyrinth."

The labyrinth builder chuckles. "Too late, my boy. She already has it."

Jacques's legs nearly give out when he imagines Arienne alone in that distant cottage. But how could this be possible?

Brumeux goes on, "You just spent all day wandering in it. There is no other labyrinth. The Marquise and her daughter were losing hope in you. That is why you were sent to me. And you won, my boy, because for Arienne's sake you chose failure."

So it was a test. Only, Jacques had misunderstood the rules. Or rather, had been made to misunderstand them. He bows low. "Monsieur *le labyringénieur* . . ."

"Stop that. I am an enemy to obeisance in all its forms. And besides, that title does not belong to me."

Jacques does not know what to say.

"I'm sorry," he goes on, grimacing. "It is not in my nature to deceive. But when your employer is Monsieur Brumeux, directness is not always considered a virtue. I am Mathis. I keep the books. Speaking of which, the Marquise mentioned in her letter a certain sum as payment for the services rendered today."

Jacques feels his purse—it is empty. He says, "The gardener suggested I use the coins to mark our path through the maze."

Mathis raises an eyebrow. "The gardener? Is that what he was calling himself? It is his mess to sort out, then. Come, I'll show you the way up the path. It is slippery in places. But there is a warm meal on the table, and tomorrow you will leave through the front door."

THE MAZE OF EVER AFTER

The wedding takes place that summer. An invitation is sent to Monsieur Brumeux, but he declines. His gift arrives after the ceremony: a puppy, white with apricot patches.

The only part of the Marquise's labyrinth ever to be built is the cottage at its center, and the vegetable garden around it, just large enough for the children to get lost in. At night, in a bed not so narrow, Arienne still tells stories, making Jacques choose the endings. And still he never seems to get them right.

JEDEDIAH BERRY is the author of a novel, *The Manual of Detection*. His stories have appeared in numerous anthologies, including *Salon Fantastique*, also edited by Ellen Datlow and Terri Windling.

His Web site is www.thirdarchive.net.

～

AUTHOR'S NOTE

My grandfather was the most clever trickster I've known. He owned a cup that dribbled water onto your shirt when you tried to drink from it, and he could rub a quarter into your arm and have it pop out of your ear. He never taught me that trick, but he did teach me how to draw mazes. We would sketch them out on sheets of typing paper and then try to solve each other's designs. This was my favorite game, because each maze could develop in an infinite number of ways, and working on them felt important and mysterious.

The Monsieur Brumeux of this story came later, from the thought that Daedalus, the mythological creator of the labyrinth of Minos, might have taught his craft to some young disciple, and so passed on his secrets to later generations. If so, these labyrinth builders would have lived at different times in different parts of the world—in seventeenth-century France, for example—plying their trade for those who had something to keep hidden, or who simply liked getting lost now and then. Monsieur Brumeux first showed up in a novel that told the tale of his apprenticeship; for this story, I wanted to portray him in his later years, a master himself, with still a few tricks to play.

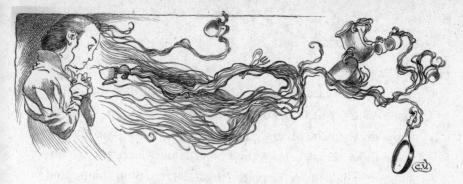

THE DREAMING WIND

Jeffrey Ford

Each and every year, in that brief time when summer and autumn share the same bed—the former, sunburned and exhausted, drifting toward sleep, the latter, rousing to the crickets' call and the gentle brush of the first falling leaves against its face—the Dreaming Wind swept down from somewhere in the distant north, heading somewhere to the distant south, leaving everywhere in its wake incontrovertible proof of the impossible.

Our town, like the others lying directly in the great gale's path, was not exempt from the bizarre changes wrought by its passing. We prepared ourselves as best we could, namely in our hearts and minds, for there was no place to hide from it, even though you might crawl into the crawl space beneath your house and pull a blanket over your head. No manner of boarding windows, stuffing towels beneath the doors, turning out the lights, or jumping into a lead-lined coffin and pulling shut the lid made a whit's worth of difference. Somehow it always found you and had its crazy way.

So it was that each year, often on a deep blue afternoon in

late August or early September, some of us noticed the leaves in the trees begin to rustle and heard amid their branches, just a whisper at first, the sound of running water. Then we knew to warn the others. "The Wind, the Wind" was the cry throughout the streets of town, and Hank Garrett, our constable, climbed up to the platform on the roof of his house and turned the crank-handle siren to alert farmers out in the fields of the valley that the blowing chaos was on its way. The citizens of Lipara scurried home, powerless to effect any protection, but determined to share the burden of strangeness with loved ones and bolster the faith of the young that it wouldn't last forever.

In a heartbeat, in an eyeblink, the wind was upon us, bending saplings, rattling windows, lifting dust devils in the town square, as though it had always been there, howling throughout our lives. Even down in a root cellar, thick oaken door barred above, hiding in the dark, you heard it, and once you heard it, you felt it upon your face and the back of your neck, your arms, like some invisible substance gently embracing you. That's when you knew the wind was beginning to dream you.

Its name, the Dreaming Wind, was more indicative than you might at first believe. What is a dream but a state founded enough upon the everyday to be believable to the sleeping mind and yet also a place wherein anything at all might and often does happen? Tomes of wonders, testaments of melancholic horrors wrought by the gale have been recorded, but I'll merely recount some of the things I, myself, have been privy to.

The human body seemed its favorite plaything, and in reaction to its weird catalyst I'd seen flesh turn every color in the rainbow, melt and reform into different shapes, so that a head swelled to the size of a pumpkin or legs stretched to lift their owner above the housetops. Tongues split or turned to knives and eyes shot flame, swirled like pinwheels, popped, or became mirrors to reflect the thing that I'd become—once a salamander man with ibis head, once a bronze statue of the moon. In my wedding year, my wife Lyda's long hair took on a mind and life of its own, tresses grabbing cups from a cupboard and smashing them upon the floor. Mayor Meersch ran down Gossin Street the year I was ten, with his rear end upon his shoulders and muffled shouts issuing from the back of his trousers.

Eyes slipped from the face and wound up in the palm, and mouths traveled to the kneecap—arms for legs, elbows for feet, a big toe nose, and wiggling index finger ears. Men became green monkeys and donkeys and dogs, and dogs took on the heads of cats, whose legs became pipe cleaners and whose tails changed instantly to sausage links with tiny biting faces at their tips. Once three generations of a family's females, from little girls to wrinkled matrons, sprouted black feathers and flew up to circle the church steeple, croaking poetry in some foreign language. Pastor Hinch became part pig, Mavis Toth, the schoolmarm, became a chair with a lampshade head, and this . . . this was not a hundredth of it, for there is no way to encompass in language the inexhaustible creative energy and crackpot genius that was the Dreaming Wind.

While our citizens suffered bodily these sea changes, bellowing with fear, crying out in torment at being still themselves inside but something wholly other outward, the landscape also changed around them. Monumental gusts loosened leaves that flew away from branches to become a school of striped fish, darting, as if with one mind, through the atmosphere, and trees turned to rubber, undulating wildly, or became the long necks of giraffes. Clouds slowly fell, wads of a violet, airy confection, and bounced off chimneys, rolled along the ground like giant tumbleweeds. Streets came to life and slithered away, windows winked, houses became glass bubbles that burst into thousand-petaled roses with doors and roofs. The grass never remained green, the sky never blue but became other colors and sometimes different consistencies like water or jam or, once, a golden gas that coalesced our exhalations into the spectral forms of dead relatives who danced the combarue in the town square. And all of this was accompanied by a discordant symphony comprised of a myriad of sounds: breaking glass, a tin whistle, a sneeze, a hammer claw ripping nails from green board, the sighs of ancient pachyderms, water swirling down a drain . . .

Chaos and jumblement, the overall discombobulation of reality—the effect lasted two or three hours, and then, as quickly as it came, it went. The force of the gale decreased incrementally, and as it did, so did its insane changes. People slowly began to re-form into themselves as they'd been before the wind. The streets slunk guiltily back to their normal places, the houses reachieved their householhood, the clouds blanched to their original puffy white and ascended as slowly as they'd fallen. By night, the wind had moved on to disrupt the lives of the good citizens in towns to the south of Lipara.

Some might ask, "Well, why did your ancestors stay in that spot and not move after they saw it was a yearly event?" The answer was simple. Come to Lipara and see for yourself that it's the most beautiful spot in the world: wide blue lakes, deep green forests teeming with game, and farmland of rich, wormy soil. Besides, to escape the wind's course one would have had to move to the west, which was desert, or to the east, where lay the ocean. Hearing this, some might say, "Well, all's well that ends well, and once the wind had passed, all was guaranteed to return to its former state." Yes and no. What I mean is most of the time this was true, and besides the upset of having yourself stretched or shrunk or turned temporarily into a nightmarish creature for a few hours, the entire rest of the year was very good living. Remember, I said, *"Most of the time."*

There were instances, exceedingly rare, mind you, wherein the Dreaming Wind's mischief remained behind after it had blown south. There was an old oak tree at the edge of town that never lost its ability to—at midsummer—bear a strange yellow fruit, the fragile consistency of fine china and the size of a honeydew melon, that upon ripening, fell off, broke against the ground, and hatched small blue bats that lived for two weeks and feasted upon field mice. And Grandmother Young's talking parrot, Colonel Pudding, once touched by the fickle finger of the wind, had its head replaced with that of her great-granddaughter's baby doll—a cute little bisque visage, whose blue glass eyes had lids that winked and closed when it lay down. The bird still spoke but prefaced every screeching utterance with a breathy, mechanical rendition of the word *mama.*

Perhaps the parrot was somewhat put out, but no terrible harm was done in these two incidents. Still, the possibility of unremitting permanence represented by their changes stayed alive in the minds of the citizens of Lipara, its threat continuously resurfacing and growing to monstrous proportions in all imaginations as each summer neared its end. It was one thing to be a goat-headed clown with feather duster arms and carrot legs for a few hours, but to remain in that condition for a lifetime was something else entirely. The Dreaming Wind was playful, it was insane, it was chaotic, and it could be dangerous. Little did any of us suspect, for generations past and for most of my long life, that it could be anything else.

Then, a few years ago, the strange wind did something so unusual it shocked even us veterans of its mad work. It was nearing the end of a long, lazy summer, memorable for its blue days and cool nights, and the leaves were beginning to curl on the elm trees; the first few early crickets were beginning to chirp their Winter's Tale. All of us, in our own particular ways, were steeling ourselves for the yearly onslaught of the mischievous event, offering up prayers to God or reassuring ourselves by reassuring others that as certain as the wind would come, it would pass, and we would again enjoy the normal pleasures of life in Lipara. Constable Garrett did as he had always done, and chose three reliable children, paying them a dime a day, to go to the edge of the forest and listen intently for a few hours after school for the sound of water running through the treetops. Everywhere, families made plans as to where they would meet up, what room they would weather the storm in, what songs they would sing together to quell their collective fear.

The end of August came and went without incident, and the delay heightened the apprehension of the arrival of the Dreaming Wind. We older folks reminded the younger that it was known to have come as late as the middle of the second week in September and that it was to be remembered that the wind could not be dictated to but had a definite mind of its own. During these days, every curtain lifting in a breeze, every gust dispersing the gossamer seed of a dandelion skeleton, caused blood pressures to rise and neck hairs to stand on end. By the middle of the first week in September the alarm had been falsely raised four times, and Constable Garrett, whose game knee was beginning to bother him from the long climbs to his roof, jokingly said he might just as well set out a sleeping bag up there.

By the end of the second week in September, nerves were frayed, tempers flared, and children cried for no reason. The aura of anxiety produced by the anticipation of the wind had begun to make Lipara a little mad even before its arrival. Miss Toth, standing in front of her class one day, could not remember for the life of her what fifty-seven divided by nineteen was, no matter how many times she tapped her ruler against the black board. She had to have Peggy Frushe, one of the older girls, run across the square to the apothecary's shop to inquire as to the answer to the problem.

Beck Harbuth, the apothecary, couldn't help out just then even though he knew the answer was three, for he had absent-mindedly filled a prescription for Grandmother Young with a bottle full of laxative pills instead of the usual heart medicine, and had to brush past Peg and chase the old woman down the street. In his pursuit, he collided with Mildred Johnson, who was riding her chicken eggs to the market on the front of her bike. Sitting in the road amid the cracked shell and splattered yoke debris of their sudden meeting, Harbuth apologized to Mildred for the accident and she merely replied in a loud, disgusted tone, "Don't worry, Beck, it's all the fault of the damn wind."

Grandmother Young was only a few paces ahead of the collision of the apothecary and the egg woman, and because her hearing was weak, she never noticed a thing, but Colonel Pudding, who was riding his usual perch atop the left shoulder of his owner, did. He lit into the sky, carrying with him the last phrase he'd heard, which was "The damn wind," and, as was his practice when he heard a phrase that caught his fancy, began screeching this alarm in the mimicked voice of she who had uttered it. Constable Garrett, sitting in his office with the window open, heard someone cry, "Mama, the damn wind," sighed, slowly rose from his chair, and started for a fifth time up the steps toward his roof.

And so it went, a comedy of errors caused by troubled minds—but no one was laughing. Things got worse and worse until the start of October, when the last squadrons of south-bound geese passed overhead. The collective worriment of the citizens of Lipara reached a crescendo, nerves snarling like balls of twine in the paws of kittens, and then all fell into a kind of blank exhaustion. Still the wind had not come. A few weeks later, when the first snow fell, blowing down from the north on a mundane autumnal gale, we knew for certain that the Dreaming Wind had done something undreamt of. The re-alization came to all of us all at once that our strange visitor from the north wasn't coming, and in that instant we froze for a moment, wondering what would become of us.

The sky grew overcast and stayed that muskrat gray for days on end, the temperature dropped to a bitter low, and the lake froze over, as if the absence of the wind had plunged the world itself into a sodden depression. Cows gave half their normal measure of milk, roosters didn't bother signaling the dawn, dogs howled at noon, and cats were too weary to chase the mice that invaded Lipara's houses. The citizens, who had always surmised that the elimination of the Dreaming Wind would fill them with a sense of relief that might border on a kind of spiritual rebirth, now went about their daily tasks as if in mourning. Woven in with the gloom was a pervasive sense of guilt, as if we were being punished for not having appreciated the uniqueness of the blowing insanity when it was upon us.

The winter, blanketed in snow and set fast in ice, presented in its seemingly static freeze the very opposite of change. Grandmother Young took to her sickbed, complaining she no longer had the energy to go on. Colonel Pudding was beside himself with concern for his owner and stayed all day in her room with her, pacing back and forth along the headboard of the bed, his fixed-fast bisque lips repeatedly murmuring the word *mama*. Constable Garrett's bad knee was now worse than ever, or so he claimed, and instead of going out on his daily rounds, making sure the town was safe, he stayed at his office desk, playing endless rounds of Solitaire and losing. Pastor Hinch preached a sermon one Sunday in the midst of Lipara's rigor mortis that exhorted all of the town's citizens to wake up and effect their own changes, but when it came time for his congregation to answer him in a prayer, two-thirds of the response he received was unbridled snoring. Lyda and I sat at the kitchen table, sipping tea, staring just past each other, each of us waiting for the other to begin a conversation and listening to the wind that was not a Dreaming Wind howl outside our door.

Eventually, with the spring thaw, things picked up somewhat as people returned to the act of living. There was a rote, joyless, hum-drummery to it, though. All seemed drained of interest and beauty. I think it was actually Beck Harbuth, the apothecary, who first mentioned to a customer that he'd noticed he no longer dreamed at night. The customer thought for a moment and then nodded and said that he also could not remember having dreamed since the end of the summer.

This observation made the rounds for a week or two, was discussed in all circles, and agreed upon. Eventually Mayor James Meersch III called an emergency town meeting, the topic of which would be the epidemic of dreamless sleep. It was to be held in the town hall on the following Thursday evening at 7:00 P.M.

The meeting never took place, because in the intervening time after the mayor set the date and agenda for that Thursday many people began to realize, now that they were concentrating on the matter, that in fact they were dreaming. What it was, as articulated by Beck Harbuth—the one who started it all—is that nothing unusual was happening in their dreams. The dreams that were dreamt in the days following the failure of the wind were of a most pedestrian nature—eating breakfast, walking to work, reading yesterday's newspaper, making the bed. There were no chimerical creatures or outlandish happenings to be found in the land of sleep anymore.

The second reason the meeting was canceled was that Grandmother Young passed away on the Tuesday prior to the day of the meeting, and although she had grown very frail of recent years, the entire town was surprised and saddened by her passing. She was Lipara's oldest citizen, 125 years, and we all loved her. True to her no-nonsense approach to life, her last words spoken to my wife, who, along with a group of other neighbors were taking shifts watching over her in her final hours, were, "Death has got to be less dull than Lipara these days." Her funeral was as grand as we could muster in our downtrodden condition, and the mayor allocated funds so that a special monument could be erected to her in the town square. As her coffin was lowered into the ground, Colonel Pudding, sitting on a perch we'd positioned near the grave for him, shed baby-doll tears and announced his one-word eulogy: "Mama." Then he spread his wings, took off into the sky, and flew out of sight.

The days passed into summer and we dreamt our dreams of eating peas and clipping our toenails. It seemed nothing would break the spell that had settled upon the town. We sleepwalked through the hours and greeted each other with half nods and feeble grins. Not even the big fleecy clouds that passed in the blue sky took on the shapes of dragons or pirate ships, as they had once upon a time. Just when the stasis became almost intolerable, something happened one night. It wasn't much, but we clung to it like ants on a twig swept downriver.

Mildred Johnson was sitting up late reading a new book she'd recently acquired concerning the egg-laying habits of yellow hens. Her husband had already gone to bed, as had her daughter, Jessica. The reading wasn't the most exciting, and she'd dozed off in her chair. Sometime later, she woke very suddenly to the sound of low murmuring coming from her daughter's room. She got up and went to the half-open door of the bedroom to check that all was fine, but when she peeked in, she saw, in a shaft of moonlight that bathed the scene, something moving on the bed next to Jessica's pillow. Her first thought was that it was a rat, and she screamed. The thing looked up, startled, and in that moment, before it flew out the window, she saw the smooth, fixed, baby-doll expression of Colonel Pudding.

The parrot's return and the unusual particulars of the sighting could not exactly be classified as bizarre, but there was enough of an oddness to it to engender a mild titillation of the populace. Where had the bird been hiding since the funeral? What was its midnight message? Was it simply lost and had wandered in the open window, or was there some deeper purpose to its actions? These were some of the questions that set off a spark or two in the otherwise dimmed minds of Lipara. As speculation grew, there were more reports of Colonel Pudding visiting the rooms of the town's sleeping children. It was advised by the pastor at Sunday mass that all windows of youngsters' bedrooms be kept closed at night, and the congregation nodded, but just the opposite was practiced, seeing as how parents and children alike all secretly wanted to be involved in the mystery.

Beyond his nighttime visits, the parrot began to be spotted also in broad daylight, flitting here and there just above the rooftops of the town. And one sighting reported that he landed on the left shoulder of Mavis Toth of a Monday afternoon the first week of summer vacation and perched there, yammering into her ear as she walked from her house out by the lake all the way to the bank. Something was going on, we were sure of it, but what it was no one had the slightest idea. Or I should say, no adult had a clue. The children of Lipara, on the other hand, took to whispering, gathering in groups and talking excitedly until a grown-up drew near. Even usual truants of the school year, like the master of spitballs, Alfred Lessert, began spending whole days at the school under the pretense of doing math problems for fun. It was the belief of some that a conspiracy was afoot. Parents slyly tried to coax their children into divulging a morsel of information, but their sons and daughters stared quizzically, either pretending not to know what their folks were getting at or really not knowing. Miss Toth came under scrutiny as well, and instead of really answering questions, she nodded a great deal, played with the chain that held her reading glasses, and forced a laugh when nothing else would do.

The intrigue surrounding the schoolhouse and the town's children remained of mild interest to the adults throughout the summer, but as always, the important tasks of business and household chores took precedence and finally overwhelmed their attention, so that they did not mark the vanishing of old newspapers and cups of flour. As the first anniversary of the wind's failure to appear drew closer we tried to pull tight the reins of our speculation as to what would happen. In our private minds we all wondered whether the present state of limbo would be split by the gale again howling through town, or if the time would pass without incident and give further proof that the dreaming weirdness had run its course for good, never to return.

Friday morning of the second to last week in August, I went to the mailbox and found only an odd message with no envelope. It was a piece of folded paper, colored green and cut into the shape of a parrot feather. I opened it and read: COLONEL PUDDING INVITES YOU TO THE FESTIVAL OF THE DREAMING WIND. The date was the very next day, the time, sundown, and the location, the town square. It went on to announce: BRING ONLY YOUR DREAMS. I smiled for the first time since the end of the previous summer, and I was so out of practice that the muscles of my face ached slightly. As old and slow as I was, I ran up the path, calling to Lyda. When she saw the invitation, she actually laughed and clapped her hands.

Late the next afternoon, just before twilight, we left the house and walked to the town square. It was a beautiful evening—pink, orange, and purple in the west where the sun was half below the horizon. The sky above was dark blue, and already the stars were beginning to show themselves. A slight breeze blew, enough to keep the gnats and mosquitoes at home.

We held hands and walked in silence. As we passed along, we saw our neighbors leaving their houses and heading in the direction of the festival.

The town square had been transformed. Streamers of gold paper draped upon the picket fences and snaked around the light posts. In the southern corner, rows of folding chairs had been set up facing a slightly raised, makeshift stage that was formed from the wooden pallets where the town's brickmakers stacked their wares. Two tall poles on either side supported a patchwork curtain comprised of a number of old comforters safety-pinned together. Six lit torches had been set up around the performance area, casting a soft glow that became increasingly magical as the sky darkened. Constable Garrett, big cigar in the corner of his mouth, dressed in a colorful muumuu and wearing a bow in his hair, played the usher, making us form a line a short distance from the seating. We complimented him on his outfit, telling him how lovely he looked, and he nodded wearily as usual and answered, "What did you expect?"

All around the festival area, Lipara's children moved busily, with purpose, and in the middle of this bustle of activity stood Miss Toth, her skin blue, her hair a wig of rubber snakes, whispering directions and leaning down to put her ear closer to the ideas and questions of her students. Suddenly all was quiet and still but for the flickering of the torch flames. "Please have your tickets ready," said Garrett, and he held his hand up and waved us on. Before taking our seats, we were directed to three long tables upon which lay painted papier-mâché masks of animal heads, household items, seashells, and anything else you could possibly imagine. They had, attached to either side, long strands of thick wire with half loops at the ends so that you could put on the disguise like a pair of glasses. Mixed in amidst the masks were newspaper hats, and at the end of each table was a stack of fans made of a stick with a round piece of cardboard attached.

I settled on a mask that made my head a can of beans, and my wife took on the visage of a barnyard chick. Mildred Johnson's face became a bear paw; her husband's a bright yellow sun. Beck Harbuth chose a dog mask, and Mayor James Meersch III turned away from the table a green monkey. Once everyone was something else, we took our fans and went to sit before the stage. The show started promptly. Miss Toth appeared from behind the curtain, carrying a hatrack, which she set down next to her. She welcomed us all and thanked us for coming, introduced Colonel Pudding—creator and founder of the Festival of the Dreaming Wind—and walked off the stage. A moment later, from over our heads, there came the sound of flapping wings, and Colonel Pudding landed on the top of the hatrack. He screeched three times, lifted his wings, bobbed his head twice and said, "Mama, the tale of the dreaming wind. Once upon a time . . ." before flying away. Jessica Johnson ran out from behind the curtain, whisked the perch off the stage, and the play began.

The play was about a great wizard who lived, with his wife and daughter, in a castle way up north in the mountains. He was a good wizard, practicing only white magic, and for anyone who made the arduous journey to see him, he would grant a wish, as long as it was meant for someone else. The only two wishes he would not grant were those of riches or power. A chorus of younger children sang songs that filled us in on the details of life upon the mountain. White confetti blew across the stage, becoming snow, to mark the passage of time.

Then the wizard's wife, whom he loved very much, caught

a chill that progressed into pneumonia. It soon became clear that she was dying, and no matter what spells of enchantment he tried to work, nothing could cure her. When finally she died, he was deeply saddened, as was his daughter. He began to realize that there were things in the world his magic couldn't control, and he became very protective of his daughter, fearing she would succumb to the same fate as her mother. He had promised his wife that he would always love the girl and keep her safe. This responsibility grew in his mind to overshadow everything, and the least little cut to her finger or scraped knee caused him great anguish.

Time passed and the girl grew older and developed a mind of her own. She wanted to go down the mountain and visit with other people. The wizard knew that there were all manner of dangers waiting for her out there in the world. Before she got to the age where he knew he could no longer stop her from leaving, he cast a spell on her that put her into a profound sleep. To protect her, he encased her in a large seed pod with a window so that he could see her face when he needed to. There she slept, her age unchanging, and he finally felt some relief.

He noticed at the end of the first year of her protective sleep that she must be dreaming, because he could see through the window the figures and forms of her dreams swirling around her. It became clear to him that if he didn't find some way to siphon out the dreams, they would eventually fill the seed to bursting, so, using his magic, he cast a spell that added a spigot to the top of the structure. Once a year, when summer led into fall, he'd climb a stepladder and release her pent-up dreams. They sprayed forth from within like a geyser, gathering themselves up into a kind of cloud that, when fully formed, rushed out of the castle window. The mountain winds caught her dreams and drove them south, where their vitality affected everything they touched.

As the story unfolded on the stage before me, I was amazed at the quality of the production and how ingenious the props were. The seed pod that contained the wizard's daughter was a large luggage bag covered with glitter, and a window cut to reveal the girl's face. To show her dreams swirling within, they must have cut from colored paper small figures of different animals and people and things and attached them to thin sticks that the daughter, played wonderfully by the beautiful Peggy Frushe, controlled with her hands, hidden from sight, and made sail gracefully before her closed eyes. When the dreams were released by the turning of the spigot, they took the form of younger children, clad in costumes, who whirled madly around the stage and then gathered together before blowing south. And what was even more amazing was that the errant Alfred Lessert, with his freckles and shock of red hair, played the troubled wizard with a pathos that transcended drama and stepped neatly into reality.

While I sat there, noting the remainder of the play, wherein a youth comes to the far north to beg for a wish to be granted, discovers the girl and frees her, and does battle with her father, who just before killing the lad with a deadly spell succumbs to his daughter's pleas and spares him, letting the young couple flee down the mountain toward freedom, I was preoccupied, seeing my own years in Lipara unfold on a wooden-palette stage in my mind. Before I knew it the action transpiring in front of me had rushed on, and the wizard was delivering his final soliloquy, a blessing for the couple, amid a blizzard of falling snow. "Out there in the world, my dear," he said, calling after his daughter, and scanning the crowd to look into each set of our eyes, "the wind will blow both beautiful and bitter, and there's no telling which it will be each time the boughs bend and the leaves rustle. There is no certainty but that there is no certainty. Hold tight to each other and don't be afraid, for sometimes, in the darkest night that wind may even bring you dreams."

At the end of the production, the players bowed to thundering applause. We were then instructed to hold high our fans and to wave them as hard as we could. Everyone in the audience and onstage paddled the air with all they had, creating two hundred small gusts of wind that joined together to form a great gale that gave comfort and left no one unchanged. Afterward, some danced the combarue to the sound of Constable Garrett's harmonica while the children played hide-and-seek in the dark. We all drank punch and talked and laughed late into the night until the torches burned out.

On our walk home by the light of the stars, Lyda turned to me and divulged how when she and some of the other neighbors were clearing out Grandmother Young's house so that it could be sold to a new couple moving into town, she'd discovered, beneath the bed, a set of loose papers that held the plans for the festival and the outline of the play. "By then the Colonel was putting the scheme she'd taught him into action, and so I kept it a secret from everyone so as not to ruin the surprise," she said. I told her I was glad she did, just as we passed the bench in the shadow of the strange old oak that gave birth to blue bats, and we caught sight of Alfred Lessert and Peggy Frushe sharing a kiss. "Some things never change," I whispered.

Wearily, we crawled into bed that night, and I lay for a long time with my eyes closed, listening to Lyda's steady breathing and the sound of a breeze sifting through the screen of our open window. My thoughts, at first, were filled with the sights and sounds of the festival—the glow of the torches, the masks, the laughter—but these eventually gave way to the sole image of that old wizard, alone on his mountain in the far north. Through the falling snow, I noticed his beard and recognized his wrinkled face. Murmuring some incantation, he lifted his wand. Then he nodded once, granting me my wish, and I realized I must be dreaming.

JEFFREY FORD is the author of the novels: *The Physiognomy*, *Memoranda*, *The Beyond*, *The Portrait of Mrs. Charbuque*, and *The Girl in the Glass*. His short stories have been published in magazines and anthologies, and chosen for several volumes of the *Year's Best Fantasy & Horror*. They are collected in *The Fantasy Writer's Assistant & Other Stories* and in *The Empire of Ice Cream*. Ford is a three-time recipient of the World Fantasy Award and won the Nebula Award for best novelette of 2003. *The Girl in the Glass* won the Edgar Allan Poe Award for 2005. A stand-alone novella, *The Cosmology of the Wider World*, was published in 2006.

He lives in South Jersey with his wife and two sons and is a professor of writing and literature at Brookdale Community College.

~

AUTHOR'S NOTE

My favorite time to write stories is late at night, after everyone else in the house has gone to sleep and it is so quiet I can hear my own thoughts, whispering. Then I go to my office and sit at the computer. Next to my desk there is a window, which I leave open year-round, even in deepest winter when the frozen air turns my breath to steam and I wear two sweatshirts, a knit hat, and socks with my slippers. A summer breeze, an autumn wind, a frozen gale, comes through the screen, granting loose papers the power of flight, opening books, twirling the pendant of the elephant god, Ganesh, that dangles from my lamp, and sometimes scaring Kaiba, the cat. Eventually it finds its way into my ears, and once inside my head it lifts my thoughts and blows them chaotically around my skull, mixing them together, breathing life into stories waiting to be told. This, for me, is the dreaming wind, and the tales it gives life to, like life, are sometimes funny, sometimes sad, sometimes incomprehensible mysteries. I can never predict which will surface when, and that's the beauty of it. The dreaming wind is a trickster. For sometimes it doesn't come at all, and then I sit staring, my imagination as empty as a pocket with a hole in the bottom. I'd always wanted to write a story about it, and I've mentioned it in many of the other things I've written, but its complete nature always eluded me until now. Tomorrow, I will go to the field behind the school and fly a kite in its honor. Who knows what it will think of this. Perhaps it will carry my tailed paper diamond up to where it can see the stars or maybe it will blow fiercely and break the string, carrying it off and dropping it miles away. If you find it fallen in your backyard or in the hedges nearby your apartment house, please let me know.

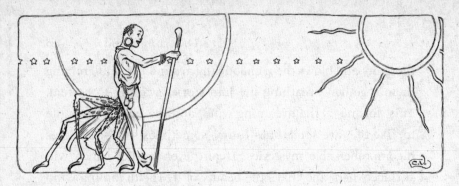

KWAKU ANANSI
WALKS THE WORLD'S WEB

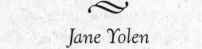

Jane Yolen

Come a-walking
Kwaku Anansi, the spider man,
Come a-walking
Kwaku Anansi, the tricksy one.
He brings stories from the sky god,
So we may learn beginnings,
So we may learn endings.
He brings us the sun, the moon, the rains,
    The division between day and night.
He brings the small grains
And the shovel.
He tricks us into believing in ourselves,
    In our brains, our hearts, our pulses.
He teaches us to unlock locked boxes,
To grab the calabash of life,
To be clever if we cannot be wise,
To star in our own (hi)stories.

He teaches us how to fling ourselves
Into the void, using only the web.
Come a-walking,
Kwaku Anansi, and tell us a tale.

JANE YOLEN sometimes thinks *she* is a trickster goddess, because of all the lies (er . . . stories) she's told in her life. Over 280 books and still counting! A mother (of three) and grand-mother (of six), she promises to keep telling stories and writing poems till they shovel dirt over her. Though when her children discover the cache of twenty-four unpublished picture books, three almost completed novels, and all those as yet unprinted poems . . . it will be as if she's speaking from the grave. Like any good trickster. If that's not proof enough, there's always her Web site: www.janeyolen.com.

～

AUTHOR'S NOTE

I have always loved Anansi—his vigor, his rough charm, his ability to bend people to his will, his absolute conviction that he is the originator of everything. There is something abso-lutely writerly about him. But I'd never actually put him into anything of mine until I was retelling stories for a book of folk-tales about dance from around the world. In it I had just retold a wonderful West Indies story about Anansi winning a prin-cess by out-dancing (and out-conniving) everybody, especially the rather stupid and possessive king. Right after I worked on that book, the call came from the editors of this volume to give them a story right away. Well, no story came out—but this An-ansi poem did. So in a sense, Anansi made me do it.

THE EVOLUTION OF TRICKSTER STORIES AMONG THE DOGS OF NORTH PARK AFTER THE CHANGE

Kij Johnson

North Park is a backwater tucked into a loop of the Kaw River: pale dirt and baked grass, aging playground equipment, silver-leafed cottonwoods, underbrush—mosquitoes and gnats blackening the air at dusk. To the south is a busy street. Engine noise and the hissing of tires on pavement mean it's no retreat. By late afternoon the air smells of hot tar and summertime river-bottoms. There are two entrances to North Park: the formal one, of silvered railroad ties framing an arch of sorts; and an accidental little gap in the fence, back where Second Street dead-ends into the park's west side, just by the river.

A few stray dogs have always lived here, too clever or shy or easily hidden to be caught and taken to the shelter. On nice days (and this is a nice day, a smell like boiling sweet corn easing in on the south wind to blunt the sharper scents), Linna sits at one of the faded picnic tables with a reading assignment from her summer class and a paper bag full of fast food, the remains of her lunch. She waits to see who visits her.

The squirrels come first, and she ignores them. At last she sees the little dust-colored dog, the one she calls Gold.

"What'd you bring?" he says. His voice, like all dogs' voices, is hoarse and rasping. He has trouble making certain sounds. Linna understands him the way one understands a bad lisp or someone speaking with a harelip.

(It's a universal fantasy, isn't it?—that the animals learn to speak, and at last we learn what they're thinking, our cats and dogs and horses: a new era in cross-species understanding. But nothing ever works out quite as we imagine. When the Change happened, it affected all the mammals we have shaped to meet our own needs. They all could talk a little, and they all could frame their thoughts well enough to talk. Cattle, horses, goats, llamas; rats, too. Pigs. Minks. And dogs and cats. And we found that, really, we prefer our slaves mute.

(The cats mostly leave, even ones who love their owners. Their pragmatic sociopathy makes us uncomfortable, and we bore them; and they leave. They slip out between our legs and lope into summer dusks. We hear them at night, fighting as they sort out ranges, mates, boundaries. The savage sounds frighten us, a fear that does not ease when our cat Klio returns home for a single night, asking to be fed and to sleep on the bed. A lot of cats die in fights or under car wheels, but they seem to prefer that to living under our roofs; and as I said, we fear them.

(Some dogs run away. Others are thrown out by the owners who loved them. Some were always free.)

"Chicken and french fries," Linna tells the dog, Gold. Linna has a summer cold that ruins her appetite, and in any case it's too hot to eat. She brought her lunch leftovers, hours-old but still lukewarm: half of a Chick-fil-A and some french fries.

He never takes anything from her hand, so she tosses the food onto the ground just beyond kicking range. Gold likes french fries, so he eats them first.

Linna tips her head toward the two dogs she sees peeking from the bushes. (She knows better than to lift her hand suddenly, even to point or wave.) "Who are these two?"

"Hope and Maggie."

"Hi, Hope," Linna says. "Hi, Maggie." The dogs dip their heads nervously, as if bowing. They don't meet her eyes. She recognizes their expressions, the hurt wariness: she's seen it a few times, on the recent strays of North Park, the ones whose owners threw them out after the Change. There are five North Park dogs she's seen so far: these two are new.

"Story," says the collie, Hope.

2. ONE DOG LOSES HER COLLAR

This is the same dog. She lives in a little room with her master. She has a collar that itches, so she claws at it. When her master comes home, he ties a rope to the collar and takes her outside to the sidewalk. There's a busy street outside. The dog wants to play on the street with the cars, which smell strong and move very fast. When her master tries to take her back inside, she sits down and won't move. He pulls on the rope and her collar slips over her ears and falls to the ground. When she sees this, she runs into the street. She gets hit by a car and dies.

This is not the first story Linna has heard the dogs tell. The first one was about a dog who's been inside all day and rushes outside with his master to urinate against a tree. When he's done, his master hits him, because his master was standing too close and his shoe is covered with urine. *One Dog Pisses on a Person.* The dog in the story has no name, but the dogs all call him (or her: she changes sex with each telling) One Dog. Each story starts: "This is the same dog."

The little dust-colored dog, Gold, is the storyteller. As the sky dims and the mosquitoes swarm, the strays of North Park ease from the underbrush and sit or lie belly-down in the dirt to listen to Gold. Linna listens, as well.

(Perhaps the dogs always told these stories and we could not understand them. Now they tell their stories here in North Park, as does the pack in Cruz Park a little to the south, and so across the world. The tales are not all the same, though there are similarities. There is no possibility of gathering them all. The dogs do not welcome eager anthropologists with their tape recorders and their agendas.

(The cats after the Change tell stories as well, but no one will ever know what they are.)

When the story is done, and the last of the french fries eaten, Linna asks Hope, "Why are you here?" The collie turns her face away, and it is Maggie, the little Jack Russell, who answers: "Our mother made us leave. She has a baby." Maggie's tone is matter-of-fact: it is Hope who mourns for the woman and child she loved, who compulsively licks her paw, as if she were dirty and cannot be cleaned.

Linna knows this story. She's heard it from the other new strays of North Park: all but Gold, who has been feral all his life.

(Sometimes we think we want to know what our dogs think. We don't, not really. Someone who watches us with unclouded eyes and sees who we really are is more frightening than a man with a gun. We can fight or flee or avoid the man, but the truth sticks like pine sap. After the Change, some dog owners feel a cold place in the pit of their stomachs when they meet their pets' eyes. Sooner or later, they ask their dogs to find new homes, or they forget to latch the gate, or they force the dogs out with curses and the ends of brooms. Or the dogs leave, unable to bear the look in their masters' eyes.

(The dogs gather in parks and gardens, anywhere close to food and water where they can stay out of people's way. Cruz Park ten blocks away is big, fifteen acres in the middle of town, and sixty or more dogs already have gathered there. They raid trash or beg from their former owners or strangers. They sleep under the bushes and bandstand and the inexpensive civic sculptures. No one goes to Cruz Park on their lunch breaks anymore.

(In contrast North Park is a little dead-end. No one ever did go there, and so no one really worries much about the dogs there. Not yet.)

3. ONE DOG TRIES TO MATE

This is the same dog. There is a female he very much wants to mate with. All the other dogs want to mate with her, too, but her master keeps her in a yard surrounded by a chain-link fence. She whines and rubs against the fence. All the dogs try to dig under the fence, but its base is buried too deep to find. They try to jump over, but it is too tall for even the biggest or most agile dogs.

One Dog has an idea. He finds a cigarette butt on the street and tucks it in his mouth. He finds a shirt in a Dumpster and pulls it on. He walks right up to the master's front door and presses the bell-button. When the master answers the door, One Dog says, "I'm from the men with white trucks. I have to check your electrical statico-pressure. Can you let me into your yard?"

The man nods and lets him go in back. One Dog takes off his shirt and drops the cigarette and mates with the female. It feels very nice, but when he is done and they are still linked together, he starts to whine.

The man hears and comes out. He's very angry. He shoots One Dog and kills him. The female tells One Dog, "You would have been better off if you had found another female."

The next day after classes (hot again, and heavy with the smell of cut grass), Linna finds a dog. She hears crying and crouches to peek under a hydrangea, its blue-gray flowers as fragile as paper. It's a Maltese with filthy fur matted with twigs and burrs. There are stains under her eyes, and she is moaning, the terrible sound of an injured animal.

The Maltese comes nervously to Linna's outstretched fingers and the murmur of her voice. "I won't hurt you," Linna says. "It's okay."

Linna picks the dog up carefully, feeling the dog flinch under her hand as she checks for injuries. Linna knows already that the pain is not physical; she knows the dog's story before she hears it.

The house nearby is massive, a graceful collection of Edwardian gingerbread-work and oriel windows and dark green roof tiles. The garden is large, with a low fence just tall enough to keep a Maltese in. Or out. A woman answers the doorbell: Linna can feel the Maltese vibrate in her arms at the sight of the woman: excitement, not fear.

"Is this your dog?" Linna asks with a smile. "I found her outside, scared."

The woman's eyes flicker to the dog and away, back to Linna's face. "We don't have a dog," she says.

(We like our slaves mute. We like to imagine they love us,

and they do. But they are also with us because freedom and security war in each of us, and sometimes security wins out. They do love us. But.)

In those words Linna has already seen how this conversation will go, the denials and the tangled fear and anguish and self-loathing of the woman. Linna turns away in the middle of the woman's words and walks down the stairs, the brick walkway, through the gate and north, toward North Park.

The dog's name is Sophie. The other dogs are kind to her.

(When George Washington died, his will promised freedom for his slaves, but only after his wife had also passed on. A terrified Martha freed them within hours of his death. Though the dogs love us, thoughtful owners can't help but wonder what they think when they sit on the floor beside our beds as we sleep, teeth slightly bared as they pant in the heat. Do the dogs realize that their freedom hangs by the thread of our lives? The curse of speech—the things they could say and yet choose not to say—makes that thread seem very thin.

(Some people keep their dogs, even after the Change. Some people have the strength to love, no matter what. But many of us only learn the limits of our love when they have been breached. Some people keep their dogs. Many do not.

(The dogs who stay seem to tell no stories.)

4. ONE DOG CATCHES POSSUMS

This is the same dog. She is very hungry because her master forgot to feed her, and there's no good trash because the possums have eaten it all. "If I catch the possums," she says, "I can eat them now and then the trash later, because they won't be getting it all."

She knows that possums are very hard to catch, so she lies down next to a trash bin and starts moaning. Sure enough, when the possums come to eat trash, they hear her and waddle over.

"Oh oh oh," moans the dog. "I told the rats a great secret and now they won't let me rest."

The possums look around but they don't see any rats. "Where are they?" the oldest possum asks.

One Dog says, "Everything I eat ends up in a place inside me like a giant garbage heap. I told the rats and they snuck in, and they've been there ever since." And she let out a great howl. "Their cold feet are horrible!"

The possums think for a time, and then the oldest says, "This garbage heap, is it large?"

"Huge," One Dog says.

"Are the rats fierce?" says the youngest.

"Not at all," One Dog tells the possums. "If they weren't inside me, they wouldn't be any trouble, even for a possum. Ow! I can feel one dragging bits of bacon around."

After whispering among themselves for a time, the possums say, "We can go in and chase out the rats, but you must promise not to hunt us ever again."

"If you catch any rats, I'll never eat another possum," she promises.

One by one the possums crawl into her mouth. She eats all but the oldest, because she's too full to eat any more.

"This is much better than dog food or trash," she says.

(Dogs love us. We have bred them to do this for ten thousand, a hundred thousand, a million years. It's hard to make a dog hate people, though we have at times tried, with our junkyard guards and our attack dogs.

(It's hard to make dogs hate people, but it is possible.)

Another day, just at dusk, the sky an indescribable violet. Linna has a hard time telling how many dogs there are now: ten or twelve, perhaps. The dogs around her snuffle, yip, bark. One moans, the sound of a sled dog trying to howl. Words float up: *dry, bite, food, piss.*

The sled dog continues its moaning howl, and one by one the others join in with drawn-out barks and moans. They are trying to howl as a pack, but none of them know how to do this, nor what it is supposed to sound like. It's a wolf secret, and they do not know any of those.

Sitting on a picnic table, Linna closes her eyes to listen. The dogs outyell the trees' restless whispers, the river's wet sliding, even the hissing roaring street. Ten dogs, or fifteen. Or more: Linna can't tell, because they are all around her now, in the brush, down by the Kaw's muddy bank, behind the cottonwoods, beside the tall fence that separates the park from the street.

The misformed howl, the hint of killing animals gathered to work efficiently together—it awakens a monkey-place somewhere in her corpus callosum, or even deeper, stained into her genes. Adrenaline hits hot as panic. Her heart beats so hard that it feels as though she's torn it. Her monkey-self opens her eyes to watch the dogs through pupils constricted enough to dim the twilight; it clasps her arms tight over her soft belly to protect the intestines and liver, which are the first parts eaten; it tucks her head between her shoulders to protect her neck and throat. She pants through bared teeth, fighting a keening noise.

Several of the dogs don't even try to howl. Gold is one of them. (The howling would have defined them before the poisoned gift of speech; but the dogs have words now. They will never be free of stories, though their stories may free them. Gold may understand this.

(They were wolves once, ten thousand, twenty thousand, a hundred thousand years ago. Or more. And before we were men and women, we were monkeys and fair game for them. After a time we grew taller and stronger and smarter: human, eventually. We learned about fire and weapons. If you can tame it, a wolf is an effective weapon, a useful tool. If you can keep it. We learned how to keep wolves close.

(But we were monkeys first, and they were wolves. Blood doesn't forget.)

After a thousand heartbeats fast as birds', long after the howl has decayed into snuffling and play-barks and speech, Linna eases back into her forebrain. Alive and safe. But not untouched. Gold tells a tale.

5. ONE DOG TRIES TO BECOME LIKE MEN

This is the same dog. There is a party, and people are eating and drinking and using their clever fingers to do things. The dog wants to do everything they do, so he says, "Look, I'm human," and he starts barking and dancing about.

The people say, "You're not human. You're just a dog pretending. If you want to be human, you have to be bare, with just a little hair here and there."

One Dog goes off and bites his hairs out and rubs the places he can't reach against the sidewalk until there are bloody patches where he scraped off his skin, as well.

He returns to the people and says, "Now I am human," and he shows his bare skin.

"That's not human," the people say. "We stand on our hind

legs and sleep on our backs. First you must do these things."

One Dog goes off and practices standing on his hind legs until he no longer cries out loud when he does it. He leans against a wall to sleep on his back, but it hurts and he does not sleep much. He returns and says, "Now I am human," and he walks on his hind legs from place to place.

"That's not human," the people say. "Look at these, we have fingers. First you must have fingers."

One Dog goes off and he bites at his front paws until his toes are separated. They bleed and hurt and do not work well, but he returns and says, "Now I am human," and he tries to take food from a plate.

"That's not human," say the people. "First you must dream, as we do."

"What do you dream of?" the dog asks.

"Work and failure and shame and fear," the people say.

"I will try," the dog says. He rolls onto his back and sleeps. Soon he is crying out loud and his bloody paws beat at the air. He is dreaming of all they told him.

"That dog is making too much noise," the people say and they kill him.

Linna calls the Humane Society the next day, though she feels like a traitor to the dogs for doing this. The sky is sullen with the promise of rainstorms, and even though she knows that rain is not such a big problem in the life of a dog, she worries a little, remembering her own dog when she was a little girl, who had been terrified of thunder.

So she calls. The phone rings fourteen times before someone picks it up. Linna tells the woman about the dogs of North Park. "Is there anything we can do?"

The woman barks a single unamused laugh. "I wish. People keep bringing them—been doing that since right after the Change. We're packed to the rafters—and they *keep* bringing them in, or just dumping them in the parking lot, too chicken-shit to come in and tell anyone."

"So—" Linna begins, but she has no idea what to ask. She can see the scene in her mind, a hundred or more terri-fied angry confused grieving hungry thirsty dogs. At least the dogs of North Park have some food and water, and the shelter of the underbrush at night.

The woman has continued. "—they can't take care of them-selves—"

"Do you know that?" Linna asks, but the woman talks on.

"—and we don't have the resources—"

"So what do you do?" Linna interrupts. "Put them to sleep?"

"If we have to," the woman says, and her voice is so weary that Linna wants suddenly to comfort her. "They're in the runs, four and five in each one because we don't have anywhere to put them, and we can't get them outside because the paddocks are full; it smells like you wouldn't believe. And they tell these stories—"

"What's going to happen to them?" Linna means all the dogs, now that they have speech, now that they are equals.

"Oh, hon, I don't know." The woman's voice trembles. "But I know we can't save them all."

(Why do we fear them when they learn speech? They are still dogs, still subordinate. It doesn't change who they are or their loyalty.

(It is not always fear we run from. Sometimes it is shame.)

6. ONE DOG INVENTS DEATH

This is the same dog. She lives in a nice house with people. They do not let her run outside a fence and they did things to her so that she can't have puppies, but they feed her well and are kind, and they rub places on her back that she can't reach.

At this time, there is no death for dogs, they live forever. After a while, One Dog becomes bored with her fence and her food and even the people's pats. But she can't convince the people to allow her outside the fence.

"There should be death," she decides. "Then there will be no need for boredom."

(How do the dogs know things? How do they frame an abstract like *thank you* or a collective concept like chicken? Since the Change, everyone has been asking that question. If awareness is dependent on linguistics, an answer is that the dogs have learned to use words, so the words themselves are the frame they use. But it is still *our* frame, *our* language. They are still not free.

(Any more than we are.)

It is a moonless night, and the hot wet air blurs the street-lights so that they illuminate nothing except their own glass globes. Linna is there, though it is very late. She no longer attends her classes and has switched to the dogs' schedule, sleeping the afternoons away in the safety of her apartment. She cannot bring herself to sleep in the dogs' presence. In the park, she is taut as a strung wire, a single monkey among wolves; but she returns each dusk, and listens, and sometimes speaks. There are maybe fifteen dogs now, though she's sure more hide in the bushes, or doze, or prowl for food.

"I remember," a voice says hesitantly. (*Remember* is a frame;

they did not "remember" before the word, only lived in a series of nows longer or shorter in duration. Memory breeds resentment. Or so we fear.) "I had a home, food, a warm place, something I chewed—a, a blanket. A woman and a man and she gave me all these things, patted me." Voices in assent: pats remembered. "But she wasn't always nice. She yelled sometimes. She took the blanket away. And she'd drag at my collar until it hurt sometimes. But when she made food she'd put a piece on the floor for me to eat. Beef, it was. That was nice again."

Another voice in the darkness: "Beef. That is a hamburger." The dogs are trying out the concept of *beef* and the concept of *hamburger* and they are connecting them.

"*Nice* is not being hurt," a dog says.

"Not-nice is collars and leashes."

"And rules."

"Being inside and only coming out to shit and piss."

"People are nice and not-nice," says the first voice. Linna finally sees that it belongs to a small dusty black dog sitting near the roots of an immense oak. Its enormous fringed ears look like radar dishes. "I learned to think and the woman brought me here. She was sad, but she hit me with stones until I ran away, and then she left. A person is nice and not-nice."

The dogs are silent, digesting this. "Linna?" Hope says. "How can people be nice and then not-nice?"

"I don't know," she says, because she knows the real question is, *How can they stop loving us?*

(The answer even Linna has trouble seeing is that *nice* and *not-nice* have nothing to do with love. And even loving someone doesn't always mean you can share your house and the fine thread of your life, or sleep safely in the same place.)

7. ONE DOG TRICKS THE WHITE-TRUCK MAN

This is the same dog. He is very hungry and looking through the alleys for something to eat. He sees a man with a white truck coming toward him. One Dog knows that the white-truck men catch dogs sometimes, so he's afraid. He drags some old bones out of the trash and heaps them up and settles on top of them. He pretends not to see the white-truck man but says loudly, "Boy that was a delicious man I just killed, but I'm still starved. I hope I can catch another one."

Well, that white-truck man runs right away. But someone was watching all this from her kitchen window and she runs out to the man and tells him, "One Dog never killed a man! That's just a pile of bones from my barbecue last week, and he's making a mess out of my backyard. Come catch him."

The white-truck man and the person run back to where One Dog is still gnawing on one of the bones in his pile. He sees them and guesses what has happened, so he's afraid. But he pretends not to see them and says loudly, "I'm still starved! I hope that person comes back soon with the white-truck man I asked her to get for me."

The white-truck man and the person both run away, and he does not see them again that day.

"Why is she here?"

It's one of the new dogs, a lean Lab-cross with a limp. He doesn't talk to her but to Gold, and Linna sees his anger in his liquid brown eyes, feels it like a hot scent rising from his back. He's one of the half-strays, an outdoor dog who lived on a chain. It was no effort at all for his owner to unhook the chain and let him go; no effort for the Lab-cross to leave his owner's yard and drift across town, killing cats and raiding trash cans, and end up in North Park.

There are thirty dogs now and maybe more. The newcomers are warier around her than the earlier dogs. Some, the ones who have taken several days to end up here, dodging police cruisers and pedestrians' Mace, are actively hostile.

"She's no threat," Gold says.

The Lab-cross says nothing but approaches with head lowered and hackles raised. Linna sits on the picnic table's bench and tries not to screech, to bare her teeth and scratch and run. The situation is as charged as the air before a thunderstorm. Gold is no longer the pack's leader—there's a German shepherd who holds his tail higher—but he still has status as the one who tells the stories. The German shepherd doesn't care whether Linna's there or not; he won't stop another dog from attacking if it wishes. Linna spends much of her time with her hands flexed to bare claws she doesn't have.

"She listens, that's all," says Hope: frightened Hope standing up for her. "And brings food sometimes." Others speak up: *She got rid of my collar when it got burrs under it. She took the tick off me. She stroked my head.*

The Lab-cross's breath on her ankles is hot, his nose wet and surprisingly warm. Dogs were once wolves; right now this burns in her mind. She tries not to shiver. "You're sick," the dog says at last.

"I'm well enough," Linna says through clenched teeth.

Just like that the dog loses interest and turns back to the others.

(Why does Linna come here at all? Her parents had a dog when she was a little girl. Ruthie was so obviously grateful for Linna's love and the home she was offered, the old quilt on the floor, the dog food that fell from the sky twice a day like manna. Linna wondered even then whether Ruthie dreamt of a Holy Land, and what that place would have looked like. Linna's parents were kind and generous, denied Ruthie's needs only when they couldn't help it; paid for her medical bills without too much complaining; didn't put her to sleep until she became incontinent and messed on the living-room floor.

(Even we dog lovers wrestle with our consciences. We promised to keep our pets forever until they died; but that was from a comfortable height, when we were the masters and they the slaves. Some Inuit tribes believe all animals have souls—except for dogs. This is a convenient stance. They could not use their dogs as they do—beat them, work them, starve them, eat them, feed them one to the other—if dogs were men's equals.

(Or perhaps they could. Our record with our own species is not so exemplary.)

8. ONE DOG AND THE EATING MAN

This is the same dog. She lives with the Eating Man, who eats only good things while One Dog has only dry kibble. The Eating Man is always hungry. He orders a pizza, but he is still hungry, so he eats all the meat and vegetables he finds in the refrigerator. But he's still hungry, so he opens all the cupboards and eats the cereal and noodles and flour and sugar in there. And he's still hungry. There is nothing left, so he eats all One Dog's dry kibble, leaving nothing for One Dog.

So One Dog kills the Eating Man. "It was him or me," One Dog says. The Eating Man is the best thing One Dog has ever eaten.

Linna has been sleeping the days away so that she can be with the dogs at night, when they feel safest out on the streets looking for food. So now it's hot dusk, a day later, and she's just awakened in tangled sheets in a bedroom with flaking walls: the sky a hard haze, air warm and wet as laundry. Linna is walking past Cruz Park, on her way to North Park. She has a bag with a loaf of day-old bread, some cheap sandwich meat, and an extra order of french fries. The fatty smell of the fries sticks in her nostrils. Gold never gets them anymore, unless she saves them from the other dogs and gives them to him specially.

She thinks nothing of the blue and red and strobing white lights ahead of her on Mass Street until she gets close enough to see that this is no traffic stop. There's no wrecked car, no distraught student who turned left across traffic because she was late for her job and was T-boned. Half a dozen police cars perch on the sidewalks around the park, and she can see reflected lights from others otherwise hidden by the park's shrubs. Fifteen or twenty policemen stand around in clumps, like dead leaves caught for a moment in an eddy and freed by some unseen current.

Everyone knows Cruz Park is full of dogs—sixty or seventy according to today's editorial in the local paper, each one a health and safety risk—but very few dogs are visible at the moment, and none look familiar to her, either as neighbors' ex-pets or wanderers from the North Park pack.

Linna approaches an eddy of policemen; its elements drift apart, rejoin other groups.

"Cruz Park is closed," the remaining officer says to Linna. He's a tall man with a military cut that makes him look older than he is.

It's no surprise that the flashing lights, the cars, the yellow CAUTION tape, and the policemen are about the dogs. There've been complaints from the people neighboring the park—overturned trash cans, feces on the sidewalks, even one attack when a man tried to grab a stray's collar and the stray fought to get away. Today's editorial merely crystalized what everyone already felt.

Linna thinks of Gold, Sophie, Hope. "They're just dogs."

The officer looks a little uncomfortable. "The park is closed until we can address current health and safety concerns." Linna can practically hear the quote marks from the official statement.

"What are you going to do?" she asks.

He relaxes a little. "Right now we're waiting for Animal Control. Any dogs they capture will go to Douglas County Humane Society; they'll try to track down the owners—"

"The ones who kicked the dogs out in the first place?" Linna asks. "No one's gonna want these dogs back, you know that."

"That's the procedure," he says, his back stiff again, tone harsh. "If the Humane—"

"Do you have a dog?" Linna interrupts him. "I mean, did you? Before this started?"

He turns and walks away without a world.

Linna runs the rest of the way to North Park, slowing to a lumbering trot when she gets a cramp in her side. There are no police cars up here, but yellow plastic police tape stretches across the entry: CAUTION. She walks around to the side entrance, off Second Street. The police don't seem to know about the break in the fence.

9. ONE DOG MEETS TAME DOGS

This is the same dog. He lives in a park, and eats at the restaurants across the street. On his way to the restaurants one day, he walks past a yard with two dogs. They laugh at him and say, "We get dog food every day and our master lets us sleep in the kitchen, which is cool in the summer and warm in the winter. And you have to cross Sixth Street to get food, where you might get run over, and you have to sleep in the heat and the cold."

The dog walks past them to get to the restaurants, and he eats the fallen tacos and french fries and burgers around the Dumpster. When he sits by the restaurant doors, many people give him bits of food; one person gives him chicken in a paper dish. He walks back to the yard and lets the two dogs smell the chicken and grease on his breath through the fence. "Ha on you," he says, and then goes back to his park and sleeps on a pile of dry rubbish under the bridge, where the breeze is cool. When night comes, he goes looking for a mate and no one stops him.

(Whatever else it is, the Change of the animals—mute to speaking, dumb to dreaming—is a test for us. We pass the test when we accept that their dreams and desires and goals may not be ours. Many people fail this test. But we don't have to, and even failing we can try again. And again. And pass at last.

(A slave is trapped, choiceless and voiceless; but so is her owner. Those we have injured may forgive us, but how can we know? Can we trust them with our homes, our lives, our hearts? Animals did not forgive before the Change; mostly they forgot. But the Change brought memory, and memory requires forgiveness, and how can we trust them to forgive us?

(And how do we forgive ourselves? Mostly we don't. Mostly we pretend to forget, and hope it becomes true.)

At noon the next day, Linna jerks awake, monkey-self already dragging her to her feet. Even before she's fully awake, she knows that what woke her wasn't a car's backfire. It was a shotgun blast, and it was only a couple of blocks away, and she already knows why.

She drags on clothes and runs to Cruz Park, no stitch in her side this time. The flashing police cars and CAUTION tape and men are all still there, but now she sees dogs everywhere, twenty or more laid flat near the sidewalk, the way dogs sleep on hot summer days. Too many of the rib cages are still; too many of the eyes open, dust and pollen already gathering.

Linna has no words, can only watch speechless; but the men say enough. First thing in the morning, the Animal Control people went to Dillon's grocery store and bought fifty one-pound packages of cheap hamburger on sale, and they poisoned them all, and then scattered them around the park. Linna can see little blue styrene squares from the packaging scattered here and there, among the dogs.

The dying dogs don't say much. Most have fallen back on the ancient language of pain, wordless yelps and keening. Men walk among them, shooting the suffering dogs, jabbing poles into the underbrush, looking for any who might have slipped away.

People come in cars and trucks and on bicycles and scooters and on their feet. The police officers around Cruz Park keep sending them away—"a health risk" says one officer; "safety," says another—but the people keep coming back, or new people.

Linna's eyes are blind with tears; she blinks, and they slide down her face, oddly cool and thick.

"Killing them is the answer?" says a woman beside her. Her face is wet as well, but her voice is even, as if they are debating this in a class, she and Linna. The woman holds her baby in her arms, a white cloth thrown over its face so that it can't see. "I have three dogs at home, and they've never hurt anything. Words don't change that."

"What if they change?" Linna asks. "What if they ask for real food and a bed soft as yours, the chance to dream their own dreams?"

"I'll try to give it to them," the woman says, but her attention is focused on the park, the dogs. "They can't do this!"

"Try and stop them." Linna turns away, tasting her tears. She should feel comforted by the woman's words, the fact that not everyone has forgotten how to love animals when they are no longer slaves, but she feels nothing. And she walks north, carved hollow.

10. ONE DOG GOES TO THE PLACE OF PIECES

This is the same dog. She is hit by a car, and part of her flies off and runs into a dark culvert. She does not know what the piece is, so she chases it. The culvert is long and it gets so cold that her breath puffs out in front of her. When she gets to the end, there's no light and the world smells like cold metal. She walks along a road. Cold cars rush past but they don't slow down. None of them hit her.

One Dog comes to a parking lot that has nothing in it but the legs of dogs. The legs walk from place to place, but they cannot see or smell or eat. None of them is her leg, so she walks on. After this she finds a parking lot filled with the ears of dogs, and then one filled with the assholes of dogs, and the eyes of dogs and the bodies of dogs; but none of the ears and assholes and eyes and bodies are hers, so she walks on.

The last parking lot she comes to has nothing at all in it except for little smells, like puppies. She can tell one of the little smells is hers, so she calls to it and it comes to her. She doesn't know where the little smell belongs on her body, so she carries it in her mouth and walks back past the parking lots and through the culvert.

One Dog cannot leave the culvert because a man stands in the way. She puts the little smell down carefully and says, "I want to go back."

The man says, "You can't unless all your parts are where they belong."

One Dog can't think of where the little smell belongs. She picks up the little smell and tries to sneak past the man, but the man catches her and hits her. One Dog tries to hide it under a hamburger wrapper and pretend it's not there, but the man catches that, too.

One Dog thinks some more and finally says, "Where does the little smell belong?"

The man says, "Inside you."

So One Dog swallows the little smell. She realizes that the man has been trying to keep her from returning home but that the man cannot lie about the little smell. One Dog growls and runs past him, and returns to our world.

There are two police cars pulled onto the sidewalk before North Park's main entrance. Linna takes in the sight of them in three stages: first, she has seen police everywhere today, so they are no shock; second, they are *here*, at *her* park, threatening *her* dogs, and this is like being kicked in the stomach; and third, she thinks: *I have to get past them.*

North Park has two entrances, but one isn't used much. Linna walks around to the little narrow dirt path from Second Street.

The park is never quiet. There's busy Sixth Street just

south, and the river and its noises to the north and east and west; trees and bushes hissing with the hot wind; the hum of insects.

But the dogs are quiet. She's never seen them all in the daylight, but they're gathered now, silent and loll-tongued in the bright daylight. There are forty or more. Every one is dirty, now. Any long fur is matted; anything white is dust-colored. Most of them are thinner than they were when they arrived. The dogs face one of the tables, as orderly as the audience at a string quartet; but the tension in the air is so obvious that Linna stops short.

Gold stands on the table. There are a couple of dogs she doesn't recognize in the dust nearby: flopped flat with their sides heaving, tongues long and flecked with white foam. One is hunched over; he drools onto the ground and retches helplessly. The other dog has a scratch along her flank. The blood is the brightest thing Linna can see in the sunlight, a red so strong it hurts her eyes.

The Cruz Park cordon was permeable, of course. These two managed to slip past the police cars. The vomiting one is dying.

She realizes suddenly that every dog's muzzle is swiveled toward her. The air snaps with something that makes her backbrain bare its teeth and scream, her hackles rise. The monkeyself looks for escape, but the trees are not close enough to climb (and she is no climber), the road and river too far away. She is a spy in a gulag; the prisoners have little to lose by killing her.

"You shouldn't have come back," Gold says.

"I came to tell you—warn you." Even through her monkeyself's defiance, Linna weeps helplessly.

"We already know," the pack's leader, the German shepherd, says. "We're leaving the park."

She shakes her head, fighting for breath. "They'll kill you. There are police cars on Sixth—they'll shoot you however you get out. They're *waiting.*"

"Will it be better here?" Gold asks. "They'll kill us anyway, with their poisoned meat. We *know.* You're afraid, all of you—"

"I'm not—" Linna starts, but he breaks in.

"We smell it on everyone, even the people who take care of us or feed us. We have to get out of here."

"They'll *kill* you," Linna says again.

"Some of us might make it."

"Wait! Maybe there's a way," Linna says, and then, "I have stories."

In the stifling air, Linna can hear the dogs pant, even over the street noises. "People have their own stories," Gold says at last. "Why should we listen to them?"

"We made you into what we wanted; we *owned* you. Now you are becoming what *you* want. You belong to yourselves. But we have stories, too, and we learned from them. Will you listen?"

The air shifts, but whether it is the first movement of the still air or the shifting of the dogs, she can't tell.

"Tell your story," says the German shepherd.

Linna struggles to remember half-read textbooks from a sophomore course on folklore, framing her thoughts as she speaks them. "We used to tell a lot of stories about Coyote. The animals were here before humans were, and Coyote was one of them. He did a lot of stuff, got in a lot of trouble. Fooled everyone."

"I know about coyotes," a dog says. "There were some by where I used to live. They eat puppies sometimes."

"I bet they do," Linna says. "Coyotes eat everything. But this wasn't *a* coyote, it's *Coyote*. The one and only."

The dogs murmur. She hears them work it out: *Coyote* is the same as *This is the same dog*.

"So. Coyote disguised himself as a female so that he could hang out with a bunch of females, just so he could mate with them. He pretended to be dead, and then when the crows came down to eat him, he snatched them up and ate every one! When a greedy man was keeping all the animals for himself, Coyote pretended to be a very rich person and then freed them all, so that everyone could eat. He—" She pauses to think, looks down at the dogs all around her. The monkey-fear is gone: she is the storyteller, the maker of thoughts. They will not kill her, she knows. "Coyote did all these things, and a lot more things. I bet you'll think of some, too.

"I have an idea of how to save you," she says. "Some of you might die, but some chance is better than no chance."

"Why would we trust you?" says the Lab-cross who has never liked her, but the other dogs are with her. She feels it, and answers.

"Because this trick, maybe it's even good enough for Coyote. Will you let me show you?"

We people are so proud of our intelligence, but that makes it easier to trick us. We see the white-truck men and we believe they're whatever we're expecting to see. Linna goes to U-Haul and rents a pickup truck for the afternoon. She digs out a white shirt she used to wear when she ushered at the concert hall. She knows *clipboard with printout* means *official responsibili-*

ties, so she throws one on the dashboard of the truck.

She backs the pickup to the little entrance on Second Street. The dogs slip through the gap in the fence and scramble into the pickup's bed. She lifts the ones that are too small to jump so high. And then they arrange themselves carefully, flat on their sides. There's a certain amount of snapping and snarling as later dogs step on the ears and rib cages of the earlier dogs, but eventually everyone is settled, everyone able to breathe a little, every eye tight shut.

She pulls onto Sixth Street with a truck heaped with dogs. When the police stop her, she tells them a little story. Animal Control has too many calls these days: cattle loose on the highways; horses leaping fences that are too high and breaking their legs; and the dogs, the scores and scores of dogs at Cruz Park. Animal Control is renting trucks now, whatever they can find. The dogs of North Park were slated for poisoning this morning.

"I didn't hear about this in briefing," one of the policemen says. He pokes at the heap of dogs with a black club; they shift like dead meat. They reek; an inexperienced observer might not recognize the stench as mingled dog breath and shit.

Linna smiles, baring her teeth. "I'm on my way back to the shelter," she says. "They have an incinerator." She waves an open cell phone at him and hopes he does not ask to talk to whoever's on the line, because there is no one.

But people believe stories, and then they make them real: the officer pokes at the dogs one more time and then wrinkles his nose and waves her on.

Clinton Lake is a vast place, trees and bushes and impenetrable brambles ringing a big lake, open country in every direction.

When Linna unlatches the pickup's bed, the dogs drop stiffly to the ground, and stretch. Three died of overheating, stifled beneath the weight of so many others. Gold is one of them, but Linna does not cry. She knew she couldn't save them all, but she has saved some of them. That has to be enough. And the stories will continue: stories do not easily die.

The dogs can go wherever they wish from here, and they will. They and all the other dogs who have tricked or slipped or stumbled to safety will spread across the Midwest, the world. Some will find homes with men and women who treat them not as slaves but as friends, freeing themselves as well. Linna herself returns home with little shivering Sophie and sad Hope.

Some will die, killed by men and cougars and cars and even other dogs. Others will raise litters. The fathers of some of those litters will be coyotes. Eventually the Changed dogs will find their place in the changed world.

(When we first fashioned animals to suit our needs, we treated them as if they were stories and we the authors, and we clung desperately to an imagined copyright that would permit us to change them, sell them, even delete them. But some stories cannot be controlled. A wise author or dog owner listens, and learns, and says at last, "I never knew that.")

11. ONE DOG CREATES THE WORLD

This is the same dog. There wasn't any world when this happens, just a man and a dog. They lived in a house that didn't have any windows to look out of. Nothing had any smells. The dog shit and pissed on a paper in the bathroom, but not even this had a smell. Her food had no taste, either. The man suppressed all these things. This was because the man didn't want One Dog to create the universe, and he knew it would be done by smell.

One night One Dog was sleeping and she felt the strangest thing that any dog has ever felt. It was the smells of the world pouring from her nose. When the smell of grass came out, there was grass outside. When the smell of shit came out, there was shit outside. She made the whole world that way. And when the smell of other dogs came out, there were dogs everywhere, big ones and little ones all over the world.

"I think I'm done," she said, and she left.

KIJ JOHNSON lives in Seattle. Her novel *The Fox Woman* won the William Crawford Award for first fantasy novel, and her novel *Fudoki* was a finalist for the World Fantasy Award. Her short fiction has been published in SCI FICTION, *Asimov's Science Fiction, The Magazine of Fantasy and Science Fiction, Analog,* and *Realms of Fantasy.* Her story "Fox Magic" won the Theodore Sturgeon Award for best short story of the year.

Johnson is associate director for the Center for the Study of Science Fiction at the University of Kansas. Her Web site is www.sff.net/people/kij-johnson.

~

AUTHOR'S NOTE

Coyote stories may be about Coyote, but they're really about us, humans. They reflect our interests, our hopes and fears, what we think is funny or shameful or sacred. So what would the trickster stories of another species look like? Would the trickster stories of cattle involve seducing someone else's wife? Would a cat's trickster story involve farting? Their minds are different from ours: what bothers them or frightens them or excites them is not what we might expect.

The psyches of dogs resemble ours more than do most animals', but dogs are nevertheless alien beings with whom we share our beds and bread.

What do they think? And what are *we* thinking?

FURTHER READING

FICTION

Alexander, Lloyd. *The Remarkable Journey of Prince Jen*

———. *The Iron Ring*

———. *The Marvelous Misadventures of Sebastian*

Anderson-Dargatz, Gail. *The Cure for Death by Lightning*

Badelier, Adolph F. *The Delight Makers*

Briggs, J. P. *Trickster Tales*

Bull, Emma. *War for the Oaks*

De Lint, Charles. *Forests of the Heart*

———. *Medicine Road*

———. *Someplace to Be Flying*

Driving Hawk Sneve, Virginia. *The Trickster and the Troll*

Farmer, Nancy. *Do You Know Me*

Ford, Jeffrey. *The Girl in the Glass*

Gaiman, Neil. *Anansi Boys*

Gray, Muriel. *The Trickster*

Greenhalgh, Zora. *Contrarywise*

———. *Trickster's Touch*

Hilgartner, Beth. *The Feast of the Trickster*

Johnson, Kij. *Fox Woman*

———. *Green Grass, Running Water*

King, Thomas. *One Good Story, That One*

Kingston, Maxine Hong. *Tripmaster Monkey*

Leiber, Fritz. *Swords in the Mist: Fafhrd and the Gray Mouser*

Lenard-Cook, Lisa. *Coyote Morning*

Mahy, Margaret. *The Tricksters*

McKillip, Patricia A. *Od Magic*

Moore, Christopher. *Coyote Blue*

Owens, Louis. *Bone Game*

Pierce, Tamora. *Trickster's Choice*

———. *Trickster's Queen*

Power, Susan. *The Grass Dancer*

Savage, Felicity. *Ever: A Trickster in the Ashes*

Singh, Vandana. *Younguncle Comes to Town*

Snyder, Midori. *The Flight of Michael McBride*

———. *Hannah's Garden*

Spinner, Stephanie. *Quicksilver*

Steiber, Ellen. "The Fox Wife" (novella, published in *Ruby Slippers, Golden Tears*)

———. *A Rumor of Gems*

———. *The Shadow of the Fox*

Strong, Albertine. *Deluge*

Vizenor, Gerald. *Chancers*

———. *Griever: An American Monkey King in China*

———. "Oshkiwiinag: Heartlines on the Trickster Express" (novella, published in *Blue Dawn, Red Earth* and in *The Year's Best Fantasy & Horror*, Vol. 10)

Windling, Terri. *The Wood Wife*

Wu, Ch'eng-en, translated by Arthur Waley. *Monkey: A Folk Novel of China*

MYTH AND FOLKTALE COLLECTIONS

Abrahams, Roger D. *African Folktales*

———. *Afro-American Folktales*

Appiah, Peggy. *Ananse the Spider: Tales from an Ashanti Village*

———. *The Pineapple Child and Other Tales from Ashanti*

Bayat, Mojdeh. *Tales from the Land of the Sufis*

Bayliss, Clara Kern. *Old Man Coyote*

Bennett, Martin. *West African Trickster Tales*

Bierhorst, John. *Doctor Coyote: A Native American Aesop's Fables*

Dorje, Rinjing. *Tales of Uncle Tompa: The Legendary Rascal of Tibet*

Erdoes, Richard, and Alfonso Ortiz. *American Indian Trickster Tales*

Evans-Pritchard, E. E. *The Zande Trickster*

Garner, Alan. *The Guizer: A Book of Fools*

Koen-Sarano, Matilda. *Folktales of Joha, Jewish Trickster*

Lopez, Barry. *Giving Birth to Thunder, Sleeping with his Daughter: Coyote Builds North America*

Mankiller, Chief Wilma. *How Rabbit Tricked Otter and Other Cherokee Trickster Stories*

Minz, Jerome R. *Legends of the Hasidim*

Montana Historical Society. *Coyote Stories of the Montana Salish Indians*

Morgan, William. *Navajo Coyote Tales*

Mourning Dove. *Coyote Tales*

Oppenheimer, Paul. *Till Eulenspiegel: His Adventures*

Owomoyeta, Oyekan. *Yoruba Trickster Tales*

Robinson, Gail, and Douglas Hill. *Coyote the Trickster: Legends of the North American Indians*

Tipaya, Maenduan. *Tales of Sri Thanonchai: Thailand's Artful Trickster*

Walker Jr., Deward E. and Daniel N. Matthews. *Nez Perce Coyote Tales: The Myth Cycle*

Welsh, Roger. *Omaha Tribal Myths and Trickster Tales*

Zong, In-Sob. *Folktales from Korea*

TRICKSTER COLLECTIONS FOR CHILDREN

Brusca, Maria Cristina, and Tona Wilson. *Pedro Fools the Gringo and Other Tales of a Latin American Trickster*

Hamilton, Virginia, and Barry Moser. *A Ring of Tricksters*

Sherman, Josepha, and David Boston. *Trickster Tales: Forty Folk Stories from Around the World* ·

Walker, Richard, and Claudio Munoz. *The Barefoot Book of Trickster Tales*

TRICKSTER STUDIES

Billington, Sandra. *A Social History of the Fool*

Brown, Norman O. *Hermes the Thief: The Evolution of a Myth*

Combs, Allan, and Mark Holland. *Synchronicity: Science, Myth, and the Trickster*

Erasmus. *In Praise of Folly*, translated by John Wilson

Harrison, Alan. *The Irish Trickster*

Hawley, John Stratton. *Krishna, the Butter Thief*

Hyde, Lewis. *Trickster Makes This World: Mischief, Myth, and Art*

Hynes, William H., and William G. Doty, editors. *Magical Trickster Figures: Contours, Contexts, and Criticisms*

Landay, Lori. *Madcaps, Screwballs & Con Women: The Female Trickster in American Culture*

McNeely, Deldon Anne. *Mercury Rising: Women, Evil, and the Trickster Gods*

Nozaki, Niyoshi. *Kitsuné: Japan's Fox of Mystery, Romance, and Humor*

Pelton, Robert D. *The Trickster in West Africa*

Radin, Paul. *The Trickster: A Study in American Indian Mythology*

Smith, Jeanne Rosier. *Writing Tricksters: Mythic Gambols in American Ethnic Literature*

Snyder, Gary. *The Incredible Survival of Coyote*

Velde, H. T. *Seth, God of Confusion*

Welsford, Enid. *The Fool: His Social and Literary History*

MISCELLANEOUS

Blue Cloud, Peter. *Elderberry Flute Song* (poems/stories)

Brandon, William. *The Magic World: American Indian Songs and Poems*

Dunn, Carolyn. *Outfoxing Coyote* (poems)

Highway, Tompson. *The Rez Sisters* (a play in two acts)

Hughes, Ted. *Crow: From the Life and Songs of the Crow* (poems)

Lee, Joe. *The History of Clowns for Beginners* (illustrated history)

ABOUT THE EDITOR

Ellen Datlow has been editing science fiction, fantasy, and horror short fiction for more than twenty-five years. She was fiction editor of *OMNI Magazine* and SCI FICTION and has edited more than fifty anthologies, including the horror half of the long-running *The Year's Best Fantasy and Horror*, *Little Deaths*, *Twists of the Tale*, *The Dark*, *Inferno* (winner of the first Shirley Jackson Award, Best Anthology, and a World Fantasy Award Finalist), *The Del Rey Book of Science Fiction and Fantasy*, *Salon Fantastique*, and *Troll's Eye View: A Book of Villainous Tales* (the last three with Terri Windling). She has won the *Locus* Award, the Hugo Award, the Stoker Award, the International Horror Guild Award, and the World Fantasy Award for her editing. She was named recipient of the 2007 Karl Edward Wagner Award, given at the British Fantasy Convention for "outstanding contribution to the genre."

She lives in New York City with two opinionated cats. Her Web site is www.datlow.com.

ABOUT THE EDITOR

Terri Windling is an editor, artist, essayist, and the author of books for both children and adults. She has won seven World Fantasy Awards, the Bram Stoker Award, and the Mythopoeic Award for Novel of the Year. She has edited more than thirty anthologies of magical fiction, many of them in collaboration with Ellen Datlow. She was the fantasy editor of *The Year's Best Fantasy and Horror* annual volumes for sixteen years, and continues to work as a consulting editor for the Tor Books fantasy line. As a writer, Windling has published mythic novels for adults and young adults, picture books for children, poetry, essays, and articles on fairy-tale history, myth, and mythic arts. As an artist, she has exhibited her paintings in museums and galleries across the United States, the United Kingdom, and France. Windling is the director of the Endicott Studio for Mythic Arts (www.endicott-studio.com). She lives in Devon, England, and winters at an arts retreat in the Arizona desert.

Her Web site is www.terriwindling.com.

ABOUT THE ILLUSTRATOR

Charles Vess's award-winning work has graced the pages of numerous comic book publishers and has been featured in several gallery and museum exhibitions across the nation, including the first major exhibition of Science Fiction and Fantasy Art (New Britain Museum of American Art, 1980). In 1991, Charles shared the prestigious World Fantasy Award for Best Short Story with Neil Gaiman for their collaboration on *Sandman* #19 (DC Comics)—the first and only time a comic book has held this honor.

In the summer of 1997, Charles won the Will Eisner Comic Industry Award for best penciler/inker for his work on *The Book of Ballads and Sagas* (which was recently published as a hardcover collection) as well as *Sandman* #75. In 1999, he received the World Fantasy Award for Best Artist for his work on Neil Gaiman's *Stardust*.

He worked with Jeff Smith on *Rose*, the prequel to Smith's *Bone*; his collaborations with his friend Charles de Lint include the picture book *A Circle of Cats* and the illustrated novels *Seven Wild Sisters* and *Medicine Road*. His other work includes the illustrations for Emma Bull's adaptation of the traditional English ballad "The Black Fox" in the anthology *Firebirds*, and the cover and decorations for Ellen Datlow and Terri Windling's *The Green Man: Tales from the Mythic Forest* and *The Faery Reel: Tales from the Twilight Realm*.

His Web site is at www.greenmanpress.com.

F
COYOTE
Road